"With toe curling swoons, witty banter, and enough true crime references to make Truman Capote proud, this is not one to be missed."

—Sonia Hartl, author of *Heartbreak for Hire*

"Fans of Christina Lauren and Rachel Lynn Solomon will adore this ode to true crime and its poignant message of opening your heart to love, even when that's the scariest thing of all."

—Amy Lea, author of *Set on You*

"The perfect blend of romantic comedy and true crime you didn't know you needed. A charming and darkly funny read, this book is a love letter to murderinos, romancerinos, and those of us still trying to figure out who the heck we are."

—Nicole Tersigni, author of *Men to Avoid in Art and Life*

"Thompson's clever premise is a trendy hook for a romance that explores family, grief, and the relationships that define us."

—*Washington Independent Review of Books*

"The fast-paced plot is alternately hilarious and touching, and readers won't be able to put it down. True crime is an incredibly popular genre, and this book is a must-read for crossover romance fans."

—*Library Journal* (starred review)

"Highly recommended for romance readers who enjoy flirty dialogue, pop-culture references, strong female characters, and, of course, true crime." 　　　　　　　　　　　　—*Booklist* (starred review)

Berkley Romance titles by Alicia Thompson

Love in the Time of Serial Killers

With Love, from Cold World

With Love, from COLD WORLD

ALICIA THOMPSON

Berkley Romance

NEW YORK

BERKLEY ROMANCE
Published by Berkley
An imprint of Penguin Random House LLC
penguinrandomhouse.com

Library of Congress Cataloging-in-Publication Data

Names: Thompson, Alicia, 1984– author.
Title: With love, from Cold World / Alicia Thompson.
Description: First edition. | New York : Berkley Romance, 2023.
Identifiers: LCCN 2022053215 (print) | LCCN 2022053216 (ebook) |
ISBN 9780593438671 (trade paperback) | ISBN 9780593438688 (ebook)
Subjects: LCGFT: Romance fiction. | Novels.
Classification: LCC PS3620.H64775 W58 2023 (print) |
LCC PS3620.H64775 (ebook) | DDC 813/.6—dc23/eng/20221104
LC record available at https://lccn.loc.gov/2022053215
LC ebook record available at https://lccn.loc.gov/2022053216

First Edition: August 2023

Printed in the United States of America
1st Printing

Book design by Shannon Nicole Plunkett
Illustrations on pages iii, iv, v, and xi by Jenifer Prince

For found families

AUTHOR'S NOTE

THIS BOOK CONTAINS BACKSTORIES INVOLVING FOSTER CARE, parental drug addiction, and death by overdose; religious intolerance to sexuality, and an involuntary outing as a teenager. It also contains an estranged relationship with parents in the present day, a scene of sexual harassment (unwelcome comments), and Christmas content.

With Love,
from **COLD WORLD**

Chapter

ONE

LAUREN FOX HAD THE MOST BORING JOB AT THE COOLEST
place. Literally, the coolest—it said it on the website and everything. If you felt the sudden urge to build a snowman or ice skate in Central Florida, Cold World was the place to do it. Lauren was Cold World's bookkeeper, meaning that she was mostly holed up in her office, which was kept just as frigid as the rest of the place, reconciling bank records and paying vendor invoices and making sure the Zamboni didn't get repossessed.

She loved her job, though. There was something so satisfying about entering numbers into spreadsheets, sorting the data into different permutations, and keeping her filing cabinet like a finely manicured garden of color-coded folders. And there was something just a little magic about stepping into a blast of winter every Monday through Friday, no matter how humid and gross the Florida air was outside.

Like today, the first day of December, clocking in at a muggy eighty-three degrees. Lauren had dressed in her usual uniform of skirt, tights, button-up, and cardigan, holding her arms slightly away from her body in hopes of staving off the sweat until she could reach the relief of a central air-conditioning system that set Cold World back four figures a month in the dead of summer.

It hit her in a wave as she walked through the front door, the air frigid with a slight whiff of cinnamon. They'd been decorating for Christmas since before Thanksgiving, because it was obviously their biggest holiday. The front ticket counter was draped with garlands, and giant ornaments hung from the ceiling. Life-sized reindeer statues, spray-painted with glittery silver and gold, stood watch in one corner, and the finishing touches had almost been put on the twelve-foot tree they put out in front of the gift shop every year.

The converted warehouse building opened up to the right of the ticket counter, holding the Snow Globe, an enclosed area kept even colder with real, actual snow on the ground. (It was a little icier than people expected, and not the *best* for snow angels, but hey, it felt miraculous when you could drive an hour away and be at the beach.) Then there was the small ice skating rink, and Wonderland Walk, a lane flanked by stands selling hot chocolate, warm cookies, and various artisanal goods.

Lauren didn't have much reason to go right. The administrative space was to the left—the Chalet, as they called it for the decorative faux ski-cottage front that hid the entrance to the offices, the break room, and the storage space. That was where she spent most of her day, and thank god, because it was at least moderately warmer than the rest of Cold World.

It could never get *too* warm, though, or it threw the whole balance of the building off, hence Lauren's ubiquitous cardigan. Even thinking about it made Lauren superstitious that the unit would fail, and as she entered the break room she kissed her fingers and pointed at the ceiling, a tribute to the air-conditioning gods.

"You find Jesus last night?"

Lauren startled in the act of reaching for coffee, dropping the K-cup on the floor. Normally, she had a couple hours to herself before most of her coworkers showed up to begin their shifts. But from the low, sardonic voice behind her, at least one person had decided to make an early morning of it.

"If Jesus is certified for commercial HVAC work," she said, bending to pick up the small container filled with life-saving coffee grounds. "Then yes."

She liked the people she worked with. She genuinely did. Except . . .

Asa Williamson just got under her skin for some reason. Like now, he was leaning casually against the supply closet door, his eyes crinkle-smiling at her over his coffee mug, and she knew, she just *knew* that he was laughing at her.

He was tall and lean, lanky in a way that should make him seem awkward. But instead he always seemed easy, effortless, and comfortable in his own skin. His arms were covered in tattoos, which she couldn't help but notice because he wore short-sleeved shirts even when everyone else on the floor layered long sleeves under their baby blue Cold World polos. He was always doing something different with his hair—it had been long when she'd started two years before, down to his shoulders, and now it was short and dyed a bright aqua blue.

He'd been there ten years, longer than anyone else who wasn't the owner, Dolores, or her son Daniel. Maybe that was why he always felt like the Cool Kid around the place, or maybe it was because he was genuinely friendly with every-one. He was even housemates with Kiki, one of Lauren's clos-est friends at Cold World. Not that Lauren had ever gone to their place, which they shared with another couple of people she'd only heard about. It was important to have boundaries at work, she thought.

Of course, that was probably one reason why Lauren had never been one of the Cool Kids. Not back in school, not anywhere she'd worked, and definitely not here.

She resented that about Asa, just like she resented that little pinch he got at the corner of his mouth, like he was always thinking about some inside joke. He didn't take anything seriously, and that was something Lauren couldn't stand. She took *everything* seriously.

"Why are you here?" she asked now, the question coming out more churlish than she'd intended as she slammed the top of the Keurig over the K-cup.

"The meeting?" he said. His eyebrows shot up at her confused frown. "The first of December. Holiday season. The planning meeting. Did you forget?"

She *had* actually forgotten. Which was totally unlike her. Lauren lived her life with lists and systems and plans. Three months ago, she'd Googled "best skincare routine" and clicked through the results until she found one that was numbered and affordable and easy to follow, and now she did it every morning and night. She updated her Goodreads page religiously, not to leave reviews but just to ensure that she had some kind of record of every book she'd ever read. It annoyed her to get the biannual postcards from the dentist's office about her next cleaning, because she'd already put a reminder on her Outlook calendar at work to follow up.

"Shit," Asa said, squinting at her. "Is there a problem with your programming? I knew we'd see the effects of Y2K eventually."

"I didn't *forget*," Lauren muttered, even though by now it was obvious she had. She'd already hit the button to brew a cup of coffee, but it wasn't lighting up, so she hit it again. She could hear the churn of the machine as it started to heat the water, but still no coffee. If she was actually a robot like Asa loved to tease her about being, shouldn't she have more proficiency with the stupid thing?

"And you saw all the extra cars in the parking lot and thought, what?" he continued, ignoring her denial. "Maybe it's overflow from the Waffle House?"

She hadn't even noticed the extra cars. She'd been on autopilot, lost in her own thoughts. Scarily, she only had vague impressions of the twenty minutes it took her to get from her apartment to Cold World. She had a volunteer engagement after work, and even though she'd been preparing for it for months, *planning* for it, now that it was here it still tied her stomach in knots.

"I have—" *A lot on my mind*, she almost finished, but she didn't have that kind of relationship with anyone at work. And if she was going to start confiding in someone, it certainly wouldn't be Asa Williamson. She stabbed the Keurig button again with her finger, mentally urging the machine to start already so she could extricate herself from the awkwardness of this moment.

He set down his own mug on the counter, reaching over her to fiddle with the machine. Not for the first time, Lauren couldn't help but notice that he smelled good. Like, *really* good. It was one of life's true mysteries, because she felt like she'd know his scent anywhere, but she couldn't quite place what it *was*. Some mixture of cedar and citrus, not overpowering, never burning her nose like some colognes did. But always *present* whenever he was nearby, and sometimes she'd catch the tail end of it when she entered a room he'd just been in. She lived in fear that one day he'd catch her inhaling a big whiff whenever he was close, and she'd have to quit her job and move to North Dakota.

"There," he said as the Keurig whirred to life, dispensing a steady stream of coffee into her mug. As far as she could tell, all he'd done was lift the top and place it back down again. Of course he'd make it look easy.

"Thanks," she said grudgingly.

He settled back with his coffee. "No problem."

This might be the longest Lauren had ever spent one-on-one with Asa. They hadn't exactly hit it off right away, despite his ability to charm his way into friendship with everyone else. Lauren wasn't even sure of his technical job title—he seemed to do a little bit of everything. She'd seen him working the gift shop with Kiki, serving hot chocolate wearing an apron the same color as his hair, even skating circuits around the rink, making sure everyone was traveling in the right direction and no newer skaters needed help.

And it was Florida, so they often needed help.

She'd started at Cold World only days before the staff holiday party two years ago, which was an awkward time to be the new person. She'd still been reeling from her job interview. It had been pretty standard until Dolores mentioned the need to get Cold World's books more organized. Somehow, that had set Lauren off into an impassioned speech that, embarrassingly, had brought actual tears to her eyes. When she'd finally come up for air, she thought she'd blown it. She must have seemed unhinged. Instead, to her surprise, Dolores had told her on the spot that the job was hers if she wanted it.

Since she hadn't been there long enough to *know* anyone at the holiday party, she'd spent most of it taking note of ways to cut costs at the next shindig. It was part of what Dolores had hired her to do, after all. Lauren thought they could dial back the sandwich platters since there were tons of leftovers, she figured a closed bar would be more money-saving and probably more responsible, and if there was already a Secret Santa she saw no reason for Dolores to separately give gift cards to each employee.

"Those come out of my own pocket, dear," Dolores had said when she brought it up, patting her hand kindly.

But one of Lauren's best—or worst, as in this case—qualities was her tenacity. For some reason, she had a hard time letting it go. She'd turned to the person next to her, who was piling his plate high with two each of the five different types of cookies. She hadn't learned his name, and normally someone with that many tattoos would've intimidated her, but there was something about his eyes that had seemed kind.

"It makes no sense," she said. "If you think about it, if everyone buys a twenty-dollar Secret Santa gift, and then they get a twenty-dollar gift card, doesn't it all come out a wash? If the gift cards are going to mean something, why not cancel Secret Santa?"

"Bold move," he said. "Running on a platform of *cancel Secret Santa*. How long have you worked here again?"

She'd felt her face heat. "Three days."

He'd pointed a cookie at her. "Love your initiative, though," he said. "Keep at it and by March we can get all the toilet paper down to one ply."

He held the cookie in his mouth and walked away, still facing her, one hand holding his plate and the other holding up crossed fingers as though he were actually hopeful. The most infuriating thing was that his tone hadn't even sounded sarcastic. It wasn't until a full minute after he'd walked away that it hit Lauren that there'd been a spark in his eyes as he'd left, and it hadn't been kindness. And a week later, she'd received her generous hundred-dollar gift card from Dolores along with everyone else, and a token coffee mug from Kiki as a belated Secret Santa present.

"This is a regift because my aunt gets me a new one every year," Kiki had said. "So don't feel bad that you didn't get anything for anyone."

"The holidays are kinda . . . intense around here, huh?"

Kiki shrugged. "Dolores thinks that we work so hard to make all our guests' holidays special, so we deserve something special, too. She's a little eccentric, but she's a sweet boss. You'll get used to it."

"Ah." Lauren ran one finger along the rim of the mug. It was white, printed with a rainbow and flowers and an aspirational quote that encouraged her to **BLOOM WHERE YOU ARE PLANTED!** "It's nice," she said hesitantly. "That she arranges the Secret Santa thing and goes out of her way to get everyone in on it."

"Oh, that's all Asa," Kiki had said. At Lauren's questioning expression, she gestured to her shoulders, as if telling a stylist where to cut her own bleached strands. "Long hair? Tall? Tattoos? When it comes to Christmas, he doesn't play. Secret Santa was totally his idea."

The guy she'd vented to at the party. Great.

From that moment on, Lauren had always felt on the wrong foot with Asa, especially during the holiday season. Especially during the holiday *parties*. She didn't even want to think about what had happened at last year's.

Now, he was still watching her as she took her first sip of coffee from that same **BLOOM WHERE YOU ARE PLANTED!** mug. There was a slight aftertaste to it that made her grimace, and she could've sworn she saw that corner of his mouth twitch. She'd been wondering why he seemed intent on hanging around, why he was paying her such close attention. As the aftertaste crystallized on her tongue—definitely something with vanilla—the pieces fell into place.

"You made your coffee before mine, didn't you."

He held up his mug in a cheers. "Not just a prop," he said.

She took another tentative sip, her mouth turning down with the full impact of the flavor. "French vanilla."

He'd done it on purpose. She didn't know how she knew, but she did—the flavor from the K-cup before always bled into the next one, and Lauren couldn't stand flavored coffee. This whole time he'd been helping her with the machine, he'd really just been setting her up.

She dumped the coffee down the drain, rinsing out her mug before grabbing another K-cup to try again.

"Whoa," Asa said, his eyebrows raised. "You better not let our accounts person see that kind of waste. She'll take the coffee machine away from us."

Lauren was about to say something immature and not even face-savingly clever, but luckily Kiki walked in at that moment and rescued her from herself.

"Hey," she said, looking from one to the other. "Dolores was asking about you guys. The meeting is starting in five minutes."

Lauren could vaguely make out noises in the front lobby now, the shuffling and footsteps that indicated more people were arriving. She'd been so wrapped up in this break room melodrama over the coffeemaker that she hadn't even noticed. Between that and her complete blanking on the meeting in the first place, what was *wrong* with her? Maybe it was more than just her worrying about her new volunteer role.

Maybe it was the grad school application she'd sent off to get her master's degree in accounting, which she'd told herself she wasn't sweating. Maybe it was just the holidays, which she'd never liked.

Asa gave her a final salute with his mug, then turned back to Kiki. "Where are we sitting?"

"Top bleacher, next to Saulo."

At least now the Keurig machine was working perfectly for her. Lauren filled up her mug, making a face at Kiki while she did so.

"Sorry," she said. "I'm running a little behind this morning. I guess I'm . . . distracted."

"Is it about the visit tonight?"

Kiki was the only person Lauren had told about finishing her guardian ad litem training and her appointment to meet the kid she'd been assigned to for the first time. She probably would've kept even that information to herself, except she'd had to take an afternoon off to get fingerprinted. Since Lauren never took time off work, Kiki had been worried and texted her. Lauren hadn't even thought Kiki was on shift that day, but it was kind of nice. To have someone notice, and care.

"I just don't even know what I'm doing," Lauren said. "I'm not good with kids. I mean, I haven't been around many. But I never know what to say. I'm like, *How's school?* and then that's it, I'm tapped out."

"I still don't fully know what a guardian whatever is, but you're responsible and kind. You're going to kill it." Kiki's eyes widened as her own words seemed to sink in. "*It* being the role, not the kid. Not that you'd call the kid an *it.* Pretty sure there's a whole book about that."

Lauren smiled. "I knew what you meant." They were walking together back to the ice skating rink, which was flanked by several sets of bleachers that accommodated everyone when they had these rare staff meetings.

Her gaze scanned the twenty or so faces she'd come to know over the last two years. There were more employees, mostly part-time or seasonal, but they weren't the core group that came to meetings like this one. Asa had taken his spot on the top bleacher, deep in conversation with Saulo, who worked the front ticket counter. Most people had grouped in their cliques—those who worked the stands on Wonderland Walk, those who did maintenance and back-of-house, the front office people who Lauren assumed she would end up sitting with. Including . . .

She stiffened, and next to her, Kiki sucked her teeth. "Right," Kiki said. "I was going to warn you . . ."

There, in the bottom row of the bleachers, was Daniel Alvarez. Dolores' son, vice president of Cold World, and the target of all Lauren's stupid, pointless infatuation feelings since the first day she'd set eyes on him.

He looked like he should play a sexy doctor on TV—all dark hair and smoldering eyes and perfect teeth. Although he didn't actually work on site at Cold World very often, when he did he always wore impeccable button-up shirts, stretched over his muscles and ironed within an inch of their life.

The vice president thing was little more than a title, Lauren knew. She wasn't even entirely sure what he did—something with investments? She'd never had the chance to ask him because she'd spoken approximately five words to him, and she could remember exactly what they were.

"Oh, I don't handle payroll."

He'd stopped by her office because he had some question on the last check he'd received, and after blinking up at him for several awkward moments—during which Lauren had the uncomfortable feeling he knew *exactly* why she was rendered so speechless—she'd come up with that brilliant rejoinder.

It was true, though. They contracted payroll to an outside company, which meant at least Lauren wasn't put in the uncomfortable position of knowing down to the penny what her coworkers made.

She wished she could say she was subtle in her crush, but Kiki at least had noticed. And once, Dolores had made a joke about wondering when her son was going to settle down, and then given Lauren a look of such pity that she'd literally tossed and turned in bed for nights afterward, prickling with the memory. God, she was pathetic.

"It's fine," she said now. "You don't have to *warn* me anytime he's on the premises. I can handle—"

In a completely unrelated, *not*-affected-by-Daniel move, Lauren tripped slightly on the transition to the carpet around the ice rink, sloshing hot coffee over her hand.

"*Ow*," she said, switching the mug to the other hand so she could survey the damage.

"Damn, you okay?" To her credit, Kiki immediately defaulted to concern rather than mocking.

Lauren sucked on the sensitive skin between her thumb and her index finger, trying to soothe the burn. It was probably the exact wrong thing to do, but maybe at least she'd get a trace amount of caffeine in her system from her coffee-drenched skin. She almost couldn't have blamed Kiki if she *had* laughed—it was hilarious, after all, how tied up in knots Lauren could get. If Asa knew about her crush—which, *god*, she would die—and he'd seen her make this kind of an ass of herself, he definitely would've laughed.

Her gaze lifted to the bleachers. Daniel was slouched slightly, typing furiously into his phone with both thumbs. With any luck, that meant he hadn't seen her clumsy moment. She glanced then at Asa—it was the blue hair, she couldn't *not* notice him—but he was rubbing the back of his neck, squinting intently at something in the distance. She turned, trying to figure out what he could be looking at, but the only thing she saw was the posted sign with all the ice rink rules.

"Everyone is here—good!" Dolores exclaimed, clapping her hands together. She was a thin, birdlike woman with long black hair streaked with a single, classy line of silver. She'd come over from Cuba when she was a teenager, and worked her way through various service jobs before a well-connected customer had offered to help her start a business. Cold World had been little more than a café with a higher-than-average air-conditioning bill when she started it at twenty-eight, the same age Lauren was now. Thirty years later, she'd built it into a true destination.

One of the best parts of Lauren's job—her boss was a total badass.

Kiki encouraged her to climb the bleachers and sit up with them, but after already tripping once, Lauren didn't trust herself to make the journey. She perched on the very edge of the front bleacher at the opposite end from Daniel, sneaking a glance at him. His mother had already launched into her usual speech—the holiday season is our most important, we need all hands on deck, let's make this a magical time—but he was still on his phone. She supposed he must have important investment-y stuff to stay on top of.

"There is approved overtime from now until Christmas," Dolores was saying, "but please remember that if you didn't place a specific vacation request already, we are unable to accommodate any last-minute changes. See if you can switch shifts with a coworker! Find someone to cover for you! I'm sorry, my babies, but that's how it has to be."

Dolores referring to a room full of adults as "babies" should've been infantilizing, but somehow she carried it off. Part of it was how dramatic her appearance always was—sparkly jumpsuits, dresses with cinched waists and full skirts and quirky patterns, bright red lipstick. If Lauren tried to pull off any of it—the endearments, the style—she'd look like an awkward try-hard. But Dolores made it all look fabulous.

There were changes to the closing schedule that only came about because *someone* (everyone looked at Marcus, a college kid who slumped in his seat under the scrutiny) had been starting to mop when there were still guests present. There was the usual reminder that the Cold World sweatshirts were their biggest seller, and if a guest looked underdressed and uncomfortable, staff could gently remind guests that the gift shop was always open.

"*Gently*," Dolores emphasized, pushing her hands down like they were all trying to rise up to shill branded merch and she had to physically restrain them.

"Annual passes," Daniel said, glancing up from his phone. Apparently that was all the reminder Dolores needed, because she went off on another speech about the need to push the annual passes, bonuses available if a staff member sold more than a threshold number. Lauren tuned out—since she wasn't customer-facing, none of those incentives applied to her. Dolores did this staff meeting each year before the holiday season, and each year Lauren thought that most of it was stuff that could've been put in an email.

But she guessed there was at least *one* thing that couldn't go in an email. With an indulgent smile, Dolores called Asa to come down and hold out the Santa hat they'd filled earlier with slips of paper with their names written on them. Asa tripped a little himself bounding down the bleachers—more a hitch in his step than a full-out face-plant, luckily, but still. He held up his arms in an *I'm okay!* gesture, and everyone laughed good-naturedly. Trust him to turn a clumsy moment into a reason for everyone to love him *more*.

"Okay, okay," he said. "You know how this works. Grab a name, if it's yours put it back, but otherwise you gotta keep it. Honor system! Presents can be handmade or bought, but try to keep them around twenty bucks. The exchange will happen at the holiday party, which is . . ."

He glanced back at Dolores for help.

"The eighteenth," she inserted. "Here at Cold World, after hours."

A Saturday night holiday party on-site, which meant that no matter how good a job the caterers did in breaking everything down, some poor suckers were going to have to come in the next morning to ensure that it was ready for the public. Lauren didn't normally work weekends, but last year she'd worked an hour or two just to help out.

"There you have it," Asa said. "Now, we're going to try to do this in some semblance of an orderly fashion . . . Let's start with the first row and work our way up. Daniel, do the honors?"

Asa's voice retained its usual cheerful tone, but there was a slight restraint to it that gave Lauren the impression he didn't think much of Daniel. She wondered if it was obvious to anyone else, then figured she must be imagining it. It wasn't like she had any special insight into Asa Williamson.

Daniel stood, sliding his phone into his pocket, and reached into the Santa hat with a charming smile toward the bleachers, like he was a contestant on a game show. Lauren's stomach tightened with anticipation. What if he pulled her name? What would he get her?

Probably something elegant, like a scented candle from a boutique, or a small, tasteful pin of something he'd associate with her. Like a bird, because he'd noticed she was shy, or an ant, because she was a hard worker.

Lauren frowned. That was the best she could do? Even in her imagination? Not, like, a butterfly because she was unique or a flower because she was beautiful? And the truth was that Lauren didn't particularly care for scented candles, and had only worn a watch and the same necklace for years.

She'd been so lost in her own thoughts that she missed the opportunity to watch Daniel's face after he selected his name, see if he gave anything away. Everyone in the first row had already gone, and people from the second were starting to make their way to the front, skipping over Lauren. She jumped up to take her place in line.

"I thought I'd have to jiggle your mouse," Asa said when she reached him. "Wake you up."

It took Lauren a minute to figure out what he meant. Maybe it was something about the rasp of his voice when he'd said it, that insider jokey tone, but it had almost sounded like he'd said something *dirty* to her.

But no. Just another computer/robot joke. She pulled a face and put her hand in the Santa hat, withdrawing a scrap of paper and putting it in the pocket of her cardigan.

"You have to look at it," he said.

"I will later."

"But if you pick yourself, you have to go again," he said patiently. "Come on. Take a peek."

She didn't know why it felt oddly vulnerable to unroll the paper while Asa watched. She knew her poker face was shit, that she'd probably look around for her gift recipient immediately, try to figure out what she might be able to get them that would feel personal but not *too* personal, useful but not *too* boring . . .

"Oh," Dolores said, stepping in. "You two, stay after the meeting. I have something specific I want to discuss with you."

Lauren's gaze shot to Asa's, but his expression was as confused as hers must have been.

Their boss wanted to speak to *them*? Together? Why?

They did snipe at each other sometimes. But Lauren thought they kept it professional when other people were around . . . at least she hoped they did. There was the time he'd gift-wrapped her desk chair. Then there'd been the *weeks* where these tiny little plastic penguins popped up around Cold World, hidden in the oddest places. Lauren had actually been kind of charmed by them—she'd even slipped one into her pocket to take home. And yet when it came out that he was behind the prank, all she'd been able to say was something about how it had been confusing to customers.

He'd also eaten her microwave burrito once—which, to be fair, had been unlabeled and in the freezer for months— and she'd threatened to take it out of his paycheck.

Like she had that power.

Anyway, they were all fairly harmless skirmishes. But thinking about them all together made Lauren squirm, because the fact was that they *were* unprofessional, and she never, *never* would've acted that way with anyone else.

Holy shit. Were they about to get fired?

Chapter

TWO

ASA KNEW THEY WEREN'T ABOUT TO BE FIRED. BUT HE could tell by Lauren's intense eyes that *her* mind had immediately gone to the worst-case scenario. It was fun to watch. In the couple of minutes it took to finish the Secret Santa, she'd have worked herself up into a real lather.

He gestured her aside with a flick of the Santa hat. "Gotta keep the line moving," he said.

She stepped away, still looking dazed, and he almost felt bad. He could've tried to say something reassuring, but the truth was that he didn't know what Dolores could want, either, or why she'd singled them out.

He smiled at people as they came to select their names out of the hat, but his mind was already racing with possibilities. It could be something related to preparations for the holiday party—that would make sense for him, since he'd been there so long and had done things in the past like arranging the Secret Santa or booking his housemate John's band to play the event. But Lauren was the biggest Scrooge he knew. Why would Dolores put *her* in charge of anything to do with holiday cheer?

Once everyone had chosen their gift recipients and cleared

out, Asa thrust his hand in the hat, reaching into the narrow point of the very tip to retrieve the last slip of paper. *Sonia*. That would be a relatively easy one. She loved romance novels, and he bet he could find ones with particularly salacious titles and package them together in a fun way.

He wondered who Lauren had gotten. Whoever it was, they probably could look forward to a new calculator. She wouldn't even buy it—just take one from her massive stockpile.

"Take a seat, my babies," Dolores said now that it was just him and Lauren. And Daniel. Asa hadn't noticed, but Dolores' son had stayed back, too, and she wasn't sending him away, so he must be part of whatever this announcement was. Daniel sat down right next to Lauren, and although he didn't even look up to acknowledge her, Lauren straightened her posture and self-consciously tucked her hair behind her ear. It was no secret that she had a thing for their boss' son— technically their boss, too, since he outranked both of them— but for some reason it felt particularly annoying to see her fawn over him now. If she seriously thought they might lose their jobs, shouldn't she be more focused on *that*?

"Let me ask you all a question," Dolores said, steepling her fingers in front of her. "When people think of Orlando destinations, what comes to mind?"

"Disney," Lauren said immediately.

"Universal," Daniel put in, flicking a glance at Lauren like he was almost impressed. Asa resisted the urge to roll his eyes. Low-hanging fruit.

"Sea World," Lauren said, visibly blushing under Daniel's attention.

"Ripley's Believe It or Not!," Asa said dryly.

Collectively, they all seemed to realize that they were only rubbing it in just how far down the list Cold World was, and they stopped naming more popular attractions. But instead of looking upset, Dolores seemed delighted by their answers.

"Exactly!" she said, pointing at them. "We never make those lists, what do you call them, Top Ten lists? We're never included. I think because Cold World is getting stale."

"It's an institution," Asa said defensively, although he could see her point. There had been maintenance and improvements since the nineties, obviously, but the main decor hadn't changed much. The carpet around the ice rink was basically a nondescript-colored pad; most of the design on Wonderland Walk had the green, red, and cream palette of a TV Christmas special from the Clinton years; and the Snow Globe produced more icy slush than a powdery snow that children would actually want to play in. They had guests come in just for the novelty of it all, but they didn't necessarily come back—and then they had locals who'd grown up coming to Cold World, who brought their kids now because it was part of a tradition they associated with the season. Working there as long as he had, Asa had seen plenty of those people . . . but not enough to sustain the business by themselves.

"Maybe it's the name?" Lauren asked tentatively. "Sometimes on the phone people think I'm saying *Cold War*."

Asa snorted, and she glared at him.

"It's time we do something," Dolores continued, as if she didn't hear the question. "We need a new exhibit, new decor, new promotion, *something* to get people excited about coming here again. I know we can't do much for this holiday season, but I'd like to have an idea by the new year so we can work on getting it implemented for next season. That's where you come in."

She looked at each of them in turn, like she was about to unveil the biggest, most exciting news. Asa loved his boss, but she had such a flair for the dramatic.

"I want you to come up with an idea—everything from the design to the budget to how you expect it to improve Cold World's ticket sales—and present it to me at a meeting after Christmas. I've selected you because, Daniel, you're leadership"—hilarious, because Daniel was rarely on-site to lead anybody—"Lauren, you know more than anyone here about the money side of things, and Asa, you've been here the longest of any employee and know this place backward and front."

That was true, at least. Asa had thought about quitting Cold World several times, mostly when his yearly rent increase hit and he thought about how maybe it was time to level up, find a job that came with a competitive benefits package. Or when he was on a first date and felt a sinking dread at the inevitable *So what do you do?* question, knowing that whatever was expected of a twenty-eight-year-old man, it wasn't . . . still working at a novelty winter attraction. The problem was that Cold World was so *comfortable*. He felt like it needed him. And weirder, he felt like he needed it.

"You can work together, or separately. It doesn't matter to me. One really good idea is better than three half-baked ones, but there's also something to be said for choice. Track any hours you spend on the project outside of work, and put it in for overtime."

Asa could feel Daniel perk up next to him. Lauren must've felt it, too, because she got a little frown line between her eyes. "Aren't you exempt?"

Asa had to hold his hand over his mouth, as if he were

deep in thought, to hide his smirk. He couldn't deny that—when it wasn't aimed at him—Lauren's processing chip of a brain could be pretty funny.

"I thought you didn't do payroll," Daniel muttered petulantly.

"We'll work it out," Dolores cut in, clearly losing interest now that she'd said her piece. "If you have any questions, find me."

And with that, she spun around, her full skirt printed with little teal flamingos swaying as she walked away. The three of them stayed on the bench for a moment, as though they were all too shell-shocked to move. Then, just as Asa was about to speak, Daniel turned to Lauren.

"I think we should work together," he said, giving her a smile that he probably practiced in the mirror when he was rehearsing *charming*. "I'm a big-ideas kind of guy, but you, you're—"

"Detail-oriented?" Lauren said.

He snapped, pointing at her. "Exactly."

She seemed pleased by the compliment, which was a joke because she'd essentially given it to herself. Asa thought about inserting himself into the conversation, to remind them that there was another person in this little game, but he could also think of nothing he wanted to do *less* than work side-by-side with Daniel Alvarez. Even working with Lauren would be better than that. Anyway, there was no way she was falling for this shit. Daniel clearly just wanted someone to shovel all the work onto.

But maybe Asa underestimated the situation, because suddenly Daniel was staring at Lauren like she was his phone. "You free tonight?" he asked. "We could discuss over dinner."

Had Daniel just *asked Lauren out*?

From her expression, yes. Suddenly, it was like she believed in Christmas after all. Her whole face lit up, her eyes shining even as her mouth started to lift in a smile . . .

And then dropped as she bit her lip. "I can't tonight," she said. "I have something. Maybe tomorrow?"

Daniel lifted one shoulder in a dismissive shrug. "I'll be thinking up a few ideas to pitch," he said. "If I need your help with the numbers on any of them, I'll let you know."

Daniel stood and, without a backward glance, started toward the door, pulling his phone out of his pocket and pressing it to his ear as he disappeared through the front lobby. Asa bet he was calling in a takeout order.

When he turned back to Lauren, she looked crestfallen. He couldn't blame her—Daniel could be a dick, and there was literally no reason why he should flip from hot to cold on Lauren just because she said she couldn't make dinner. She might have a cash register for a heart, but that should suit Daniel just fine, since he probably stuffed his pillowcases with stock sheets. And she wasn't bad to look at.

Okay, objectively, Lauren was beautiful. Maybe her glasses kept Daniel from seeing it, like she was a character in a teen rom-com. Her hair was dark and shiny, hanging just past her shoulders and sweeping across her forehead in bangs that Asa happened to know from overhearing her talk to Kiki that she regretted and was trying to grow out. It made her reach up to push them out of her eyes all the time, a gesture that Asa tried not to find endearing. Earlier, when he'd seen her put her hand in her mouth and suck, he'd felt a jolt of awareness so unexpected he'd almost fallen off the bleacher.

His gaze dropped to her hand now, and he frowned. "You should put some cool water on that," he said.

"What?"

"Your skin's all red." He let out a huff of a laugh at her confused expression. "When you were so stricken by Daniel's macho charisma that you spilled coffee on yourself?"

"I . . . wasn't."

"Hey," Asa said, holding up his hands. "No shame in that game. I mean, except that it shows you have incredibly shallow taste. I've dated some douchey dudes, but even I can tell you to watch out for the ones who only make eye contact when they want something."

It was a test. Asa didn't know if Lauren already knew he was bisexual, from talking to Kiki, or if now she'd assume he was gay. And he didn't know why it mattered, suddenly, but he'd dropped it into the conversation just to see how she would react.

"When I'm desperate enough to want dating advice from *you*," Lauren said acidly, "I'll be sure to let you know."

He had a retort about just how desperate she seemed every time she got around Daniel, but it died on his lips. Maybe it was because he'd basically just come out to her, and he wasn't sure why. Maybe it was because she'd taken it in stride, volleying back one of her usual insults without missing a beat.

Or maybe it was the memory of the way her face had brightened in that brief moment after Daniel had asked her out, that naked hope that had made her eyes spark. She didn't look like that very often. Asa hadn't even noticed, like living through years of gray skies, until one day the sun came out.

She stood up, still clutching her coffee mug in her clenched hand, and after a beat, Asa stood, too, and followed.

"We should work together," he said.

"No."

Two maintenance workers were crouched down in front of

the bank of vending machines in the back hallway from the ice rink to the lobby, and he cut in front of Lauren as they went down to single file to get through the narrow space.

"You heard Dolores," he said. "She doesn't want half-baked ideas."

"Mine won't be half-baked."

"But Dolores is right—I *know* this place." He'd turned to face her, and she almost ran right into him. He put a hand out, as if to steady her, then dropped it back to his side. "Like we sell more boiled peanuts on the weekends than we do hot pretzels, but more pretzels during the week. Seriously. It's a phenomenon."

"So publish in a peer-reviewed journal," Lauren said, moving impatiently to try to get past him. "I don't think that bit of trivia is going to revolutionize Cold World."

He mirrored her action, stepping back into her path.

"Can't hurt."

She put one hand on her hip, glaring up at him until he moved aside to let her through. "I know stuff, too," she said as she strode off ahead. For someone a head shorter than him, she walked fast. He picked up his pace to stay close enough where he could hear her supposed superior knowledge. This should be priceless.

"Oh yeah?"

"Do you know how much money we've made from switching from plastic bags to reusable totes people buy in the gift shop? And it's better for the environment."

"Ah," Asa said. "But do you know how many dads I see walking around, trying to juggle handfuls of stuff their families bought while getting the full Cold World experience? Bet they'd leave better reviews if they'd had a nice, free bag to put that stuff in."

He didn't even know what he was saying at this point. He had nothing against the reusable tote initiative, which had been one of Lauren's pet projects this year. They'd reached her office, which he hadn't been in since the day he messed with her chair. He couldn't even remember at this point what had inspired him to do it.

She was sitting in that chair now, pushing into her desk and already focused on her computer screen, as if she simply had too much important work to do to give him one more second of her time. "I know exactly why you want to work together," Lauren said, "and I've carried the weight of enough slackers doing group projects in school. No, thank you."

The word *slacker* blinked in the air between them like a neon sign, and she still wasn't looking at him. At this point, Asa was already regretting his impulsive decision to suggest partnering with Lauren. He wouldn't want to deal with this shit all month. At the same time, he was damned if he was going to retreat now.

"You didn't seem as opposed to working with Daniel."

"Maybe if you were as respectful in the way you asked . . ." She lifted a shoulder, as if it couldn't be helped. She lifted her coffee cup to take a sip, and he took a perverse delight when she made a face at the surprise of only getting cold dregs.

"Personally, if I were as respectful as Daniel, I wouldn't sit front and center at a staff meeting if I planned to be on my phone the whole time."

He'd landed one there. He could tell by the way her mouth pinched together. Finally, she gave up the pretense of getting back to work and leaned back in her chair, looking up at him. From this angle, he could see the slight shadow at her V-neck top, the delicate silver rose pendant she always wore resting against the pale skin of her throat. He glanced around the office instead, taking it in.

It was small and utilitarian. She'd been there two years, but she didn't appear to have personalized the space at all, unless you counted the colored Post-its at the bottom of her computer monitor with scribbled reminders or the yellow legal pad where she was keeping some kind of list. Otherwise, it was a filing cabinet, her desk, and a single fake plant in the corner that he knew had been there since before he'd been hired ten years ago. The only nod to any wall art was a framed poster of an almost offensively generic winter scene, and somehow Asa knew that she hadn't selected that, either.

"Why do you want to work together, anyway?" Lauren asked. "It's pretty obvious that there's no . . . I mean, that we don't . . ."

She didn't finish her thoughts, but she didn't have to. *There's no love lost between us* or *we don't get along*. Either was true.

"I'm a naturally collaborative person," he said.

She raised an eyebrow, as though she doubted that very much. "Well, I'm a naturally competitive person," she said. "And there has to be something in it for the winner of this little contest. A bonus, a promotion, a new title, *something*."

That caught his attention. "Why do you say that?"

"Think about it. Why not open this up to more people? Dolores could have even more ideas to choose from. She selected the three of us because we're basically her short list for whatever this thing is."

"But why ask Daniel, then?" Asa pointed out, bracing himself against her desk. "What title can the Crown Prince of Cold World get promoted to?"

She chewed on her lower lip, as if really considering this question. His gaze dropped of its own accord to her mouth—what was *wrong* with him?—before landing on the notepad with her scratchy handwriting on it. 3 call re Iscaping quote, 1 update vendor ss A-C, 4 cat pants . . .

Her hand came down on the notepad, dragging it back toward her where he could no longer read it. He had no idea what to even make of such a cryptic list. *Cat pants?*

"I really do have a lot to do," she said, one hand still covering the notepad, the other double-clicking something on her computer. He'd be willing to bet she was just opening and closing random folders until he left. Which he really should do—he'd come in early for the meeting but wasn't actually on shift for hours. He had time to run home and take a quick nap. The thought had seemed appealing when he woke up hours before his usual alarm, but now he was feeling wired and sleep was the last thing on his mind.

"What is it that you're doing tonight?"

She blinked up at him, as if trying to figure out why he was asking. If she had even half a guess, it was more than he had. It wasn't his business. He wasn't about to ask her out—if she'd shot down Daniel that fast, he could only imagine what she'd say if he tried. And he definitely didn't want to try.

But maybe that was the part that got him curious. Whatever it was, it was more important than the chance to have dinner with Daniel Alvarez. His impression of Lauren had always been that she had very little life outside of work, but maybe he was wrong.

"I'm—" She grabbed her coffee mug, standing so abruptly she sent her chair flying back against the wall. "I'm going to get more coffee, since this morning was such a disaster. I look forward to seeing what you come up with for your proposal."

The last part was delivered so stiffly that it was obviously more a formal send-off than a genuine expression of interest. And before Asa could come back with a retort, she was gone, leaving him standing alone in her own office.

Also leaving her notepad completely unguarded, sitting next to her keyboard. He slid it closer, his eyes scanning the rest of the entries after the cryptic *cat pants*. It was clearly a to-do list, mixed up and abbreviated in some trademark Lauren way. He was lucky it wasn't in binary.

Grinning, he grabbed a pen.

Chapter
THREE

IT HAD BEEN LAUREN'S EVERY INTENTION TO LEAVE WORK a few minutes early, but of course that meant she ended up stuck on a call at five minutes past five.

"Your payment *does* show on the ledger, Mr. Stockard," she said, trying to keep her voice patient. "If you look at it again, you'll see we applied three fifteen to the overdue balance on October's booth rental, and one eighty-five toward this month's bill. That's why the amount due is—"

"Yes," Mr. Stockard cut in, "but where is my *five-hundred-dollar* payment! I brought it in myself. And I don't see it on the ledger!"

Mr. Stockard was one of Cold World's vendors who rented space along Wonderland Walk to sell their wares. In his case, it was adorable hand-whittled woodland creatures that were surprisingly popular among hipsters. He also insisted on paying his rent via check, which he brought in person, always for a number that was *not* listed on the ledger that Lauren had to provide him to try to get him trued up . . . and then the cycle continued.

He was still ranting, and Lauren doodled little circles in the margins of her notepad, waiting for the moment when she might be able to cut back in. When she'd come back from getting coffee earlier that morning, Asa was gone. Which, of course, had been the entire point of her leaving. But afterward her office had *smelled* like him, and then it turned out he'd left behind something else, too—a new entry on her notepad, no number next to it. Just **INITIATE HOLIDAY SPIRIT SEQUENCE!** written in blocky capital letters, bold and surprisingly neat. Whatever that meant.

Messing with someone's to-do list should be illegal. Like opening someone's mail or stealing their identity. Or reading their diary—it felt as bad, to Lauren. Not even that he'd written something on it, but that he'd *seen* it at all. It made her read back over every entry, wondering if there was anything incriminating, how each one might look through his eyes.

Cat pants was a definite low point.

She realized Mr. Stockard had paused to take a breath, and she'd been tracing over Asa's letters with her pen, building them up with scratchy lines of ink. She set her pen down and tried to make her voice firm.

"I'll look into it first thing in the morning, Mr. Stockard," she said. "And have a new ledger ready when you open your booth this weekend. How does that sound?"

"Well, I suppose—" he started to grumble, and she cut him off before he could go into another rant.

"Great," she said. "You have a wonderful day, Mr. Stockard. Thank you for trusting Cold World with your business."

She hung up the phone, glancing at the digital clock on the display. If she left right now, she could still make it by five thirty, but it was going to be cutting it close . . .

"Oh, good," Kiki said, stopping in the doorway. "I was hoping to catch you. Listen, do you still have my red off-the-shoulder dress?"

"Yeah," Lauren said. "Sorry, I—"

She'd borrowed it from Kiki six months ago, for a date that had never ended up happening. Kiki had insisted she hang on to it until the date got rescheduled, but it got pushed back twice more and then eventually the guy had stopped responding to messages on the app, and somehow that stupid dress was still in her closet, a reminder of what a failure her romantic life was.

You could've been wearing it tonight, at dinner with Daniel, a voice in her head reminded her. She didn't know how long this visit was going to go, but she probably could've met up with him after. Why hadn't that occurred to her in the moment?

Kiki waved off her apology. "It's fine," she said. "But I'm going to have to go to Marj's holiday party this year and I promised her I'd show her all the options. I think she's seriously afraid I'll show up at a swanky law firm shindig wearing a negligee or something."

Kiki's girlfriend, Marj, was a brand-new associate at a law firm downtown and apparently had become a huge stressball over navigating the hierarchies and networking events. It was even harder given that they were in an openly gay relationship and Marj, who was Korean, was the only associate of color at her law firm. Lauren knew it had been causing tension in their relationship, which sucked because Kiki seemed to really care about Marj, from everything she'd heard.

"I can bring it to work tomorrow," Lauren said.

"I was hoping to get it tonight, if that's not too much trouble," Kiki said. "When does your thing end? Text me and I can come over."

Lauren hesitated. In theory, that sounded fine. Nice, even. She'd never had anyone from work over to her apartment. She'd barely had anyone *not* from work over to her apartment, unless you counted her landlord that time her faucet kept leaking.

Kiki must've read her reluctance, though, because she said, "Or you can stop by my place. Asa won't get home from his shift until after nine, if you're worried."

Lauren made an incredulous expression that she knew without a mirror just looked like bad acting. "Why would I be worried about *that*?"

"Um," Kiki said. "Okay. Maybe I misread into why you didn't come to our Thanksgiving, even though I totally invited you and I happen to know you spent yours watching that documentary about the McDonald's Monopoly scam again."

"The *again* seems unnecessary," Lauren muttered. "Anyway, I really have to get out of here—but text me your address and I'll drop by later."

She thought about Kiki's words all the way to her car, though, and kept thinking about them as she pulled onto the highway and let her phone's GPS guide her to the address where she would be meeting her guardian ad litem kid for the first time. Maybe knowing that Kiki and Asa were housemates *had* been partially behind her decision to skip Thanksgiving over there, although she hated the idea that her antipathy toward him was that obvious. Or that she might've hurt Kiki's feelings by turning down an invitation that had been made in friendship.

The truth was, Lauren never quite knew how to handle the holidays. Her memories of Christmas with her mother were that it was always a stressful time—cold, sleeping in the car, or hectic as they moved from one motel to another. There had never been enough money, or food, or *joy*, and then the state had removed Lauren from her mom's care. She understood why it had happened—the drugs in the car, the long nights nine-year-old Lauren had been left alone—but she still sometimes wondered if she'd really been better off. She'd been safer, for sure. But she'd never seen her mother again.

And she'd been one of the lucky ones, relatively speaking. She'd landed in a foster home with Miss Bianca, who'd provided structure and stability and if not quite love, then a type of care that seemed awfully close to it. Every Christmas, Miss Bianca would send Lauren a card, just a quick note to wish her a happy holiday. It made Lauren feel valued and remembered, reminded her of what Miss Bianca had done for her. It also reminded her that Miss Bianca had already moved on, and there wasn't a place for Lauren back there anymore.

Lauren's background was definitely the reason why, when she'd seen a flyer in her building's lobby about becoming a guardian ad litem, she decided to volunteer. She'd never had one, but other foster kids who'd lived in the home with her had. If she could help a kid out, be their advocate in court, monitor their placements and whether their parents were working their case plans, ensure that their schools were following any education plan needed . . . she wanted to do that.

Of course, when she'd signed up and completed the training, she hadn't focused on the part where she'd have to actually interact with a child. A child who might be defensive or closed off or jaded in ways that she'd have a hard time breaking through. She'd gotten a short blurb on the child she'd be working with—his name was Eddie, he was nine years old, he liked Avengers, and he'd already witnessed more abuse from his stepfather than anyone should have to, much less a child.

She pulled up ten minutes late to the suburban house where Eddie was staying, which wasn't ideal but wasn't as bad as she'd been fearing. She agonized over where to park before finding a spot halfway down the street, then slid her badge on its lanyard around her neck. She hadn't been expecting the flash when they took the picture, and it made her look wide-eyed and surprised.

Inside the house, dogs were barking at the sound of the doorbell. Lauren thought that was already good. They hadn't had pets at Miss Bianca's, but she could see how it would be a comfort, having animals around. When the door swung open, it revealed a woman much younger than Lauren had expected, around Lauren's own age.

"Yes?" she said, sounding a little harried. "Oh. Yes, I remember. You're here for Eddie. Come in."

"I'm Lauren Fox, with the guardian program." Now that she was actually there, she tried to remember all the procedures and protocols that had been drilled into her head during training. *Make sure you introduce yourself. Talk to the caregiver about the child, but also talk to the child separately. Ask to see the child's room.*

"He's in the bonus room," the woman said, before yelling up the stairs. "Eddie! Turn the video games off and come down! Your person is here."

"Oh, that's okay," Lauren said. "I was hoping to—"

"If he's not down in two minutes, come get me," the woman said, then disappeared into the kitchen.

It was a really nice house. New construction, with vaulted ceilings and an open plan. Lauren could see straight through the living room to a sliding glass door that led out to a pool. She made a mental note to ask if Eddie could swim.

On a side table, there was a picture of the woman in a white wedding dress, her hand resting possessively on a bearded man with a kind smile. Lauren stared at it for a minute, her eyes unfocusing, while she idly petted the dog who'd come to sniff her hand. Finally, she followed the woman into the kitchen.

"I'm sorry," she said. "I didn't catch your name?"

"Jolene," the woman said without looking up from the can of corn she was struggling to open with an opener that looked like it had seen better days.

"How long have you been fostering?" Lauren knew from Eddie's blurb that he'd been there for four weeks, but she wouldn't be surprised if Jolene had other kids living here, too. There was the padlock on the pantry, for one thing, which looked kind of scary. She knew sometimes kids who'd experienced food scarcity were prone to stealing or hoarding, but she made a mental note to bring it up with her supervisor to get her take. The house looked like it would have at least four bedrooms, if not more, and Lauren bet that Jolene and her husband had bought it with the express plan to operate a small group home.

Lauren had no issue with any of that. It had been essentially what Miss Bianca had done, after all. She'd treated caring for foster children as a job, a calling, with the goal of providing a safe environment for as many kids who might be passing through as possible. Sure, there might be people who wanted foster kids only for the state-issued paychecks they came with, but there were others who were making a true difference in these kids' lives. Lauren didn't want to be cynical, wanted to believe there were more of the latter than the former. Miss Bianca had driven them to every appointment, showed up for every teacher conference, allowed social workers and therapists and caseworkers full access to her home no matter the inconvenience.

"We finished the licensure six months ago," Jolene said, blowing her blond hair away from her face. "We're hoping to be licensed for therapeutic by next year."

Lauren asked how many other kids lived in the home right now (one, with another to arrive this upcoming weekend), and how Eddie was doing (fine). But it was clear that Jolene was distracted, trying to get dinner ready, and the child in question still hadn't come downstairs, so Lauren asked if it would be okay if she went up to him.

Staccato video game gunfire filled the stairwell as she made her way to the room at the top of the landing. A boy sat on an ottoman pulled close to the TV, leaning to one side as he frantically mashed a combination of buttons on his controller. He had a buzz cut and wore a red T-shirt that said THE STRUG-GLE IS REAL with some picture underneath that Lauren couldn't make out. He looked impossibly young, but Lauren supposed that was how nine-year-olds looked.

His gaze flickered to her, as if he couldn't help it, but then he went back to focusing on the game. She stood there by the stairs for several minutes, past the point where it would've felt natural to introduce herself, and just watched him play.

"What does the white circle mean?" she asked finally.

"Storm," he said.

She watched as it closed in. There were numbers and stats on the screen that she probably could've figured out if she studied them hard enough, but right now they were all nonsense to her.

"The storm is bad?"

He was busy in a shootout with another player who was leaping all over the place, so either he didn't hear her or deemed the question too clueless to bother with. The other player got a final shot that brought up an elimination screen, and Eddie threw the controller to the ground in disgust.

"I'm Lauren," she said, then realized she probably should have introduced herself as Miss Lauren, or Miss Fox. She was already messing this up. "I'm your guardian ad litem. Do you know what that means?"

He shrugged. They'd had to do a whole exercise in the training where they role-played how they would explain who they were to a child, varying it depending on the age and the circumstances. Lauren had felt pretty good about how she'd done. But now, faced with a kid who didn't really seem to care, she felt herself faltering. She remembered how it had been, talking to a revolving set of grown-ups who asked the same questions over and over. And now she was just another one of those grown-ups, earnest and well-intentioned and obviously the last person this kid wanted to talk to.

She explained anyway, and then asked to see his room. She'd hoped to segue into that more gradually—had had a fantasy that their bond would be so immediate, his eagerness to share his life with her so natural, that he'd pull her by the hand, chattering happily the whole time. Instead, he opened a door off the landing to a small room with a twin bed, plastic set of drawers, clothes spilling out, and a single lamp set on the floor.

It was hardly Pinterest-worthy, but it was clean, and a space that was all his. At least for now.

"You like Avengers?" she asked, pointing to his Marvel-themed sneakers on the floor. Of course she already knew the answer, but she was hoping to get him to open up a little.

"Yeah."

"Me, too," she said. Was it wrong to lie to a kid, if it was about something as innocuous as a superhero franchise? The truth was that Lauren seemed to be one of the only people in the modern world who'd never seen any of the movies, who still had trouble distinguishing which characters were in which universe. Asa had made a comment once, about how she was a *pop culture wasteland*. It had stung more than it probably should've.

She attempted more awkward small talk, about how school was going, how he liked living with Jolene, about the other foster kid who lived in the house, to mostly monosyllabic answers. When Jolene called up the stairs that dinner was ready, Lauren felt guilty when her first feeling was . . . relief. Relief that the visit could be over, and she could retreat back to her car, where she could finally breathe again.

Worst guardian ad litem in the world.

She said her goodbyes to Jolene, waved to the other kid who was already seated at the dinner table, and made arrangements to visit the next week. As she was on her way out, Eddie followed her into the front hallway.

"Miss Lauren?"

"Yeah?"

"When is my mom coming to get me?"

Lauren wished she'd had a chance to role-play this exact scenario. Not something like it, not a hypothetical, but this exact one. Where a tough-looking boy with shadowed eyes strung together the most words she'd heard so far, asking the one question she didn't have an answer for. She remembered asking that question over and over when she'd first arrived in care, and she never remembered getting a satisfactory answer, because there wasn't one. Lauren couldn't say *soon* because she didn't know that; she couldn't even say *she's working on her case plan* because she didn't know that, either.

"I don't know," she said finally.

She'd lied about the Avengers, but she couldn't lie about this.

AFTERWARD, LAUREN SWUNG BY HER APARTMENT TO EAT A quick dinner of leftover takeout and grab Kiki's dress, then headed over to her friend's house. It looked older than she'd expected, with a wraparound front porch with rocking chairs on it and a rainbow flag hanging from the railing. Lauren tried to rack her brain to remember the names of Kiki's other housemates other than Asa, in case any of them opened the door, but luckily it was Kiki who ushered her in.

"Turns out Marj is working late again," Kiki said, "so she's not even coming over tonight. Sorry. How was your visit?"

More emotionally exhausting than expected. Not only had it brought memories rushing back that Lauren would rather leave behind, of those early days when she'd been put in the system, but it was also surprisingly tiring having to navigate a conversation with a nine-year-old who didn't want to talk. But she didn't feel like getting into all of it, so she just waved the question away. "This place is really nice," she said instead.

"Thanks," Kiki said. "Asa already lived here with other housemates when he heard I was looking for somewhere to live relatively cheap and close to Cold World. I met with everyone and we just clicked. Elliot is a freelance writer, and they're home a lot but mostly holed up in their room under deadline. John is super quiet—like, even when he plays his guitar he plugs it in and wears headphones. It's a lot more chill than I worried it would be."

"Mmm," Lauren said, glancing around. Two strange houses in one night. This had to be a record.

The living room featured two overstuffed leather couches, arranged in an L around a large-screen TV, paused on some slick-looking show that wasn't familiar to Lauren. There was a bike propped against one wall. An IKEA shelf unit packed with records. And a Christmas tree, already decorated, a star on top and everything.

"It's been up since the day after Thanksgiving," Kiki said. "If you think Asa is only like that at work, you're wrong. The boy loves Christmas. By the way, what was that whole thing all about, where Dolores asked you guys to stay after the meeting?"

Lauren hesitated, not sure if it was supposed to be a secret or not. Eventually, she just decided to answer the question but keep it vague.

"She's looking for some suggestions on ways to improve for the holidays," she said. "Not a big deal."

"Huh." Kiki was clearly not convinced by the explanation, and Lauren pointed at some artwork hanging on the wall to change the subject.

"That's really cool," she said. "Where'd you get it?"

It was the size of a movie poster, the colors vibrant and saturated. Magenta background, stairs painted in gradients of purple leading diagonally up to nowhere. A boy leaned from the stairs on tiptoes, reaching out toward a hand of someone out of the composition. In his other hand, he clutched a tangle of lines and swirls that seemed to lead to balloons, or vines, or jellyfish—something abstract that Lauren couldn't quite make out. The picture made her feel happy, her spirits buoyed by the colors and the whimsy, but then the more she looked at it the more that she felt like there was something sad about the boy, painted in shades of light blue and reaching for someone he might not be able to grasp before falling off the stairs. She wished she could see the expression on his face, but it was turned away.

"It's Asa's," Kiki said. "You want to see the other outfits I'm considering for Marj's work party?"

Lauren gave the picture one last look before scooping the red dress off the back of the couch where she'd set it and following Kiki into her room. There were two other dresses laid out on Kiki's bed—one sparkly as a disco ball, the other a rather severe black—and a green jumpsuit. Lauren knew Kiki would look amazing in any of them. She was one of those people who had natural style, on whom everything looked intentional and cool and easy. In the end, Lauren hadn't even tried on the red dress. It had seemed like the kind of thing she could never pull off.

"Too much?" Kiki asked, pointing at the sparkly dress.

Lauren bit her lip, considering. "Maybe? For a conservative law firm party."

Kiki nodded, like the answer was pretty much what she'd been expecting. "This is probably the one," she said, picking up the black dress. It had a high collar and long sleeves, although the swingy skirt saved it from seeming totally puritanical.

"I kinda like the jumpsuit," Lauren said, reaching out to rub the silky green fabric between her fingers. "I bet it looks great on you."

"You don't think it's too . . . gay?"

Lauren grinned. "Considering you'll be at the party with your girlfriend, I say lean in."

She thought back to what Asa had said earlier, about having dated dudes before. She'd had a vague idea that his relationship history was more varied than hers, but she didn't know exactly what that meant for how he defined himself now, or who he was interested in. A part of her was dying just to ask Kiki, but she knew that it wasn't really any of her business, and it would be squirrelly to put Kiki on the spot just to satisfy her idle curiosity. Because that was all it was—his comment had made her curious.

Another comment from Kiki that afternoon also kept sticking in her brain. "What did you mean earlier, when you said you'd read into my reason for not coming to Thanksgiving?"

Kiki shrugged, still looking down at the jumpsuit, spreading it across the bed as if she needed to see the whole thing to better assess it. "Everyone knows you and Asa don't get along," she said. "You think he's a clown, and he thinks you're the ultimate wet blanket."

Something about the way she said it—*the ultimate wet blanket*—made Lauren positive that it was a direct quote from Asa himself. She could hear the way he'd say it. It would come out exasperated, both fists in his hair as he pulled it away from his head, as if she was driving him so crazy he almost couldn't contain it. Or it would come out snarky, a casual aside while he was busy doing something else, a flippant comment tossed over his shoulder.

The ultimate wet blanket. That was Lauren.

"I'm thirsty," she said, her throat feeling suddenly tight. "Would you mind if I—"

Kiki waved her hand vaguely toward the door. "Sure," she said. "Help yourself. Sorry, I should've offered."

Lauren found a glass in the cupboard and filled it from the filtered water dispenser in the fridge door. She took a long, cool gulp of water before holding the glass to her cheek. Her face was getting that hot feeling like it did before she was about to cry, which was ridiculous. She *knew* what Asa thought of her. And although she'd never used the exact word, *clown* was fairly accurate for the way she'd always thought of him. He seemed to treat everything like it was one big lark, from his job to his stupid hair.

There were various papers cluttering the surface of the fridge, held in place by quirky magnets from a bouffant-sporting psychic in Cassadaga, a local pizza place, and a quote from John Waters—*"True success is figuring out your life and career so you never have to be around jerks."* There was also a sticky pad grocery list with a pen clipped to it, and maybe it was the John Waters quote, or maybe it was *ultimate wet blanket* still rattling around in Lauren's head, but she set her water down on the counter. Ripping off a piece of the sticky pad, she drew a little word bubble and then wrote inside: I'm getting a strong "A" vibe . . . Asa? Ass?

She slapped the note on the fridge, making it look like the words were coming from the psychic, and replaced the pen where she'd gotten it. There.

It might be juvenile as hell, but it certainly wasn't *wet blanket*. And weirdly, it made her feel better. That would teach him to mess with her to-do list.

Chapter

FOUR

IT WAS ALMOST TEN BY THE TIME ASA GOT HOME FROM work. Somehow Marcus had convinced *him* to do the dirtiest parts of the closing checklist, including mopping the lobby, taking the trash out to the dumpster, and checking under the bleachers for gum. There was always gum.

He was tired, and what he definitely *wasn't* up for was a call with his older sister, who'd probably want to make the case again for why bygones should be bygones, family was family, and on and on. But Becca'd called three times in a row, and it was the rule of sisters—any summons made thrice had to be answered. Or maybe he was thinking of fairy-tale witches.

It might be too late to call by then, but Asa dialed her anyway, figuring that was what she got. Sure enough, she picked up almost right away, sounding annoyingly undisturbed.

"About time," she said. "What's the point of having a cell phone at all?"

"I was at work," he said, trying to keep the edge out of his voice. He had no direct issue with Becca. She'd been collateral damage when he'd moved out of their parents' house. Been kicked out. Whatever the current party line was.

"Did you get the baby shower invite?"

"Uh . . ."

"Shut up," she said. "I know you did. The United States Postal Service is extremely reliable, no matter what the check-is-in-the-mail people want you to think. I addressed it very carefully and mailed it out three weeks ago."

"Didn't realize you were part of the USPS lobby," Asa said, but she had him and she knew it. "I do live with house-mates, you know. And I'm not the one who usually gets the mail—that's Elliot."

He'd pulled into the driveway, holding the phone between his cheek and his shoulder as he climbed out of the car. He could picture the invitation—he'd sliced open the egg-yolk yellow envelope himself, turned it over to see the dancing brown sock monkeys with their red yarn bow ties. Becca had always had a thing for sock monkeys.

The lights were all on in the house. Asa really didn't feel like continuing this conversation with an audience, so he leaned against the hood of his car, sighing down into the phone.

"Becca," he said. "They'll be there."

"Well, it's a Sunday. But yeah, they might be—they're about to be grandparents. And *you're* about to be an uncle, and I'd just—" Her voice hitched with an unusual emotion coming from his no-nonsense big sister. "I'd really like you there. Please? It's the nineteenth, at ten in the morning. My house. I can send you the address if you don't have it."

"I have it."

She was quiet for a moment, and Asa could almost hear all the things they could say to fill that silence. He could ask if they'd considered names yet, if they were doing stuff like putting plastic covers over all the outlets, or he could apolo-gize for not coming to her wedding. And she'd talk about painting the nursery and how much she missed being able to drink and tell him it was fine, she understood.

But it wasn't fine. It killed him, but he also didn't see any way to change things. Not unless his parents were willing to change, and he doubted they ever would.

"I gotta go," he said. "You take care of yourself, all right? And the baby."

"Of course. And you'll—"

Asa hung up. It was a coward's move, but that was what he was. A big, fat coward.

When he walked through his front door, all three of his housemates were on the couches, watching a terrible dating reality show John was obsessed with and the rest of them tolerated. Well, secretly more than tolerated.

"Just in time," Elliot said, looking over their shoulder. "They haven't made the eliminations yet."

Elliot claimed to watch the show out of purely professional curiosity, based on the one article they'd written about the trans representation last season. As a health writer, Elliot's main beat wasn't usually entertainment, and they'd vowed to never write for that particular publication again after it took six months to chase down their fifty-dollar check. And yet here they were, still watching the show. For research.

Kiki never turned down anything she could make fun of, and she was Asa's main partner in watching Hallmark holiday movies until they couldn't stand another second of ex–sitcom stars in henleys. The trick was not to watch anything you actually *liked* with Kiki, as she showed no mercy in ripping any media to shreds.

Of all his housemates, John was the biggest mystery. He used to be the guitarist in some one-hit-wonder band, apparently. Asa had no idea how royalties worked, but he knew that John *still* made money off that song—enough that he didn't need to work aside from playing a few gigs here and there with various local bands. Despite any rock-star stereotype, though, John was a homebody and kept to himself. Most nights, Asa found him a lot like he was now—his wild black curls sticking out over the top of the couch as he watched this show, a bowl of cereal in his lap.

"It'll be that guy," Asa said after watching a few minutes of the episode. An earnest ginger was doing a talking head about how much he'd given up to be on the show, but how worth it the experience was for the chance to meet the love of his life. "He's talking sacrifices. That's a death knell."

"Yeah, but the other guy cried on his phone call home," John pointed out.

"Fuck," Asa said. "They're onto me."

So far, he'd been able to predict who was going home the last five episodes. He was very proud of his streak. He would've liked to settle in and hang out, see which unlucky bastard would have his dreams crushed on streaming television, but he'd told himself he would at least start thinking about his idea to revamp Cold World. He went into the kitchen to grab a drink from the fridge, planning to take it back to his room while he worked.

He almost missed the note, but his own name caught his eye. There was a word bubble suspended over one of their magnets: I'm getting a strong "A" vibe . . . Asa? Ass? It was a fairly regular occurrence at the house, them all riffing on one another, coming up with new and creative ways to call each other names. But he would know that scratchy, crowded handwriting anywhere, despite only really studying it for the first time that day.

He leaned out into the living room, grasping the kitchen doorframe with one hand. "When was Lauren here?"

"Oh, uh," Kiki said, not taking her eyes from the TV. "Earlier."

"*Why* was she here?"

That got Kiki to peel her attention away from the show. "She was returning my red dress," she said. "What's it to you?"

It was nothing. It was weird, that was all. The day that they both got an opportunity at work, the day that he'd offered to work together and she'd shut him down in no uncertain terms . . . *that* was the day she showed up at his house for the first time? And he wasn't even there.

Plus, he thought she'd had some big plans for tonight. He wondered if that meant they'd gotten canceled or pushed back. He wondered if she regretted saying no to Daniel's dinner invite.

He couldn't get her voice out of his head, the way she'd said there had to be something in it for the winner of Dolores' little contest. Whatever it was, she'd made it clear that she was in it to win it. Well, so was he.

He *did* know Cold World better than anyone. Maybe better than Dolores herself, at least in a boots-on-the-ground kind of way. When he'd gotten hired there, he'd been barely out of high school, staying at a friend's while he figured out where to go. Someone from the church had seen him making out with his then-boyfriend, and had sent pictures to his pastor father. He never did discover who it was, but it didn't really matter—the damage was done. He was out.

Officially, his first job at Cold World had been Snow Globe Guard. That wasn't a recognized title, but was essentially what the role had amounted to. He would stand just inside the doorway to the Snow Globe and make sure people were being responsible with the fake snow (mostly, that there weren't kids shoving it into their younger siblings' faces when their parents weren't watching). He'd ask people not to put it in their pockets, reminding them that it *would* melt. After ten minutes, he'd politely encourage them to move on to another feature, to give the next group of people a chance to play in the snow.

He definitely knew Cold World better than Lauren. She'd only worked there for two years, and in the front office. He doubted she'd even been *in* the Snow Globe.

Asa pulled out a sketchpad from his desk, settling onto his bed with the pad on his lap. Art had always been one way he could express himself, a place where he could tuck every emotion or memory or whim without needing to explain it. Just colors and lines and composition. He could draw a boy on the stairs, reaching for a hand he'd never grasp, and Elliot would say something like, "Cool, man."

He liked the idea that he could put so much into a piece and then let it speak for itself. But for whatever reason, he didn't like the idea of just anyone entering into that conversation. At one point, he'd thought maybe he'd try to make a career out of his art—selling stuff independently, or looking into graphic design school, or whatever that might entail. But then he thought of putting himself out there over and over, and he just couldn't do it. Big, fat coward.

Well, maybe this was his opportunity to do *something* with his art, even if it was just to design a new look for Cold World. The problem was that his mind was a total blank. He doodled a few snowflakes, wrote out the letters and traced over them several times, even drew a little snow globe with a wintry scene inside.

Lauren would *hate* playing Snow Globe Guard. She'd overly

police everyone's fun, and get flustered if people didn't seem like they were moving on fast enough. He might be struggling to think of an idea to revamp the place, but suddenly he had a hell of a good idea as to how to make the competition more fun.

HE SHOWED UP EARLY FOR HIS SHIFT THE NEXT DAY, HEADING into the Chalet to see if he could find Dolores. She had an office there, technically, but could be found just as often wandering around the place. There were some days when she didn't come in at all, taking off-site meetings with possible vendors or representatives from the city who were always changing some minor code or regulation that sent Dolores into a tailspin. No matter what, she always stayed hands-on with the business, and Asa respected that about her. It would've been easy for her to be an absentee owner, signing their paychecks but otherwise invisible to most of the staff.

Asa had no doubt that if Daniel ended up inheriting this place, that was the kind of owner he'd be. Not that Asa would be around long enough to know—a change in ownership from mother to son would be the one thing guaranteed to make him quit.

Luckily, Dolores was in her office, and he gave a perfunctory knock on her open door to get her attention. Today's outfit included a blouse printed with polka dots of all different colors, and she had her silver-streaked hair piled high on the top of her head. He had to marvel at how rare it was to see her in the same look twice.

"Asa!" she said with a huge smile. "Let me guess. You have a question about the presentations."

"More an idea than a question," he said. "You mentioned that we could work together, but it occurred to me that we all have such different roles here . . . I thought maybe we could learn from each other."

Dolores leaned back in her chair, her fingertips pressed together. "Interesting," she said. "Like job shadowing, is that what you're suggesting?"

"Nothing as intense as that. Just like, for example . . ." He looked around the office, as though he were searching for inspiration. As if he hadn't spent half his night dreaming up how delicious this would be. "Lauren could work the Snow Globe for an hour. Just to see what it's like. I bet it would give her some really good ideas."

She tapped her finger on her chin, considering. "We'd have to think of what you could do that's part of her job description."

He hadn't exactly thought that far, but he wasn't opposed to it. It would probably mean doing a bunch of filing. Reading numbers off an old-fashioned ticker tape ledger. He had no idea.

"Sure," he said. "Happy to."

"And I'll need to call Daniel, let him know about this new twist," Dolores continued. "He should have an opportunity to learn the ropes of different roles here. That would be good for him, actually."

Fuck, he *really* hadn't thought that far. Working with Lauren in the Snow Globe would be sweet torture—she might be irritating, but he knew he'd irritate her far more, and it would cause a minor malfunction in her programming to be thrown into a new situation like that.

Working with Daniel would just be torture.

"I'll make all the arrangements," Dolores said. She beamed up at him. "Thanks, Asa. Already you're coming up with some great suggestions. It makes me excited to see what you think up for your presentation."

He turned on his heel and almost ran smack into Lauren, who was lurking in the hallway.

"Listening at the door?" he said. "You know, eavesdroppers never hear anything good about themselves."

"What are you up to?" she asked.

"Just talking to my boss," he said. "Busy day ahead?"

Her eyes narrowed. From a distance, they looked almost black, but up close he could see that they were brown with flecks of gold around the irises. He didn't even realize he was making intense eye contact until her eyes widened again, then dropped to a spot over his shoulder.

"Every day is busy," she said.

"Really? *Every* day? There's never a lull on a Thursday afternoon? You never have time to deep-dive on an *Atlantic* article or do some online shopping at your desk?"

He'd been idly throwing that out there, but from the flush that crept over her cheeks, he could see he'd landed a hit. Her skin was so fair, her face so expressive, that he felt like he could read every emotion that crossed over it. He had a feeling she'd hate knowing that.

"What *are* cat pants, anyway?" he asked. "I've seen sweaters for dogs, but this is taking it to a whole new level."

She tugged his arm, pulling him away from Dolores' office. He guessed they were in a bad location to discuss all the ways they fucked off at work. Personally, he had no issue with her taking some time for herself during the day while she managed her workload. Everyone needed that, and god knows if he had a job where he was sitting at a computer all day he'd use at least some of his time looking up funny memes or reading interpretations of song lyrics. But somehow he knew that Lauren held herself to a stricter standard, and even if she carved out those times, she'd feel guilty and secretive about it.

"Instead of a houndstooth pattern," she said now, "they were tiny cats. They were cute, and they were on sale yesterday, so I wanted to remind myself to buy them. There. Are you happy?"

"Oh," Asa said. Those did sound cute. "Did you buy them?"

"No."

Why was he not surprised. "What do the numbers on your list mean? They're out of order."

The level of priority, he'd figured. He'd really spent way too much time thinking about Lauren Fox's to-do list. He also couldn't seem to shake the tingling feeling in his right forearm, from where she'd briefly touched him. He rubbed the pad of his left thumb against the spot, then turned the gesture into more of a massage, as though his muscle ached. The way her gaze dropped to track the movement, he didn't want her reading more into it than that.

"What were you talking to Dolores about?" she asked finally.

Ah, so it was going to be like that. He could play that game, but he liked seeing her sweat, so he just shrugged. "Let's just say I hope you brought something warmer than your usual cardigan to wear."

He could practically feel her vibrating with frustration as he walked away.

Chapter FIVE

LAUREN HATED LOSING, AND SHE FELT LIKE SHE'D LOST that particular round with Asa. Not that she was keeping score.

He'd essentially called her out for online shopping at work, which she didn't do a *lot* . . . but which she did do sometimes. Online browsing, at least. And somehow he'd gotten her to tell him about *cat houndstooth pants*, which she definitely could've gone to her grave without ever having to describe out loud to her work nemesis. It wasn't enough to write snarky notes on his refrigerator. She needed to find some way to dig in under his skin, to make him feel as uncomfortable and exposed as he made her feel.

She didn't know if that was possible.

And what had his last comment meant, anyway, about needing something warmer than a cardigan? Almost reflexively, she took hers off the back of her chair and put it on as she sat back down at her desk. It was a cream color that had looked soft and elegant when it was brand-new, but by now it just looked dingy and sad. She reached into the pockets and was surprised when she felt a crumpled slip of paper at the bottom of one.

Three letters, each one landing like a thud in her stomach.

They were written with a bold ink, the strokes strong and sure, a small flick at the tail of the second *A* the only sign that they'd been written by hand and not printed in some designer font.

Asa. Of *course* she would get Asa for Secret Santa. The poetic justice was so acute that she almost suspected him of sneaking into her office, switching out her paper for his name somehow. She wouldn't put that kind of stunt beneath him, except that he did seem disproportionately concerned with preserving the integrity of Secret Santa.

She was still looking at the slip of paper, wondering where one could actually get a lump of coal, when Dolores came in.

"Hello, darling," Dolores said. "How busy are you today?"

A quicksand trap of a question if Lauren ever heard one. It was also extremely suspicious that it was a variation on what Asa had said earlier. She knew he was cooking up something.

"Fairly busy," she said carefully. "The insurance reconciliations are due next week."

"Ah, that's right," Dolores said, but in a way that suggested she'd barely registered what Lauren said. "Well, how about a fun Freaky Friday kind of experiment?"

The lump of trepidation in Lauren's stomach grew. She could think of nothing *less* fun than Freaky Friday. She'd always had a thing about stories where people were trapped in another body, or time, or space.

Dolores seemed to get that she wasn't going to get any more active participation from Lauren on that score, so she plowed ahead. "How would you feel about spending an hour in the Snow Globe this afternoon?"

"Like as a punishment?"

Dolores laughed, even though Lauren hadn't been entirely

joking. Presumably, the Snow Globe would be even colder than her office. Which meant . . . Asa's comment earlier clicked into place.

"This was Asa's idea," she said flatly.

"Yes!" Dolores seemed pleased that Lauren had caught on. "I thought it was fabulous. Since you, Asa, and Daniel are all working to come up with ideas to give Cold World a makeover, it makes some sense for you to spend time in different departments, yes? I've asked Daniel to come in next week and you can put him to work."

That made Lauren sit up a little straighter. Was it because she was so desperate for Daniel, or because she was just desperate in general, that "put him to work" sounded vaguely suggestive? But this was his mother talking. Lauren tried to get her head out of the gutter.

Dolores already seemed committed to this idea, and to be honest it . . . wasn't the worst thing Lauren had ever heard. Considering the source. Maybe she *could* get inspired by spending more time in various roles at Cold World. The end of the year was always a busy time for her, but she also wasn't one to shy away from extra work.

So she said the only thing she could say. "Sounds good. I have a call at two, but could head to the Snow Globe when it wraps up."

"Perfect," Dolores said. "Make sure you report back. I want to hear all about how it goes."

THE CALL WASN'T FOR WORK, EXACTLY, BUT DOLORES DIDN'T have to know that. There was a last-minute staffing on Eddie's case, and so Lauren spent twenty minutes listening to the latest status of his schooling, his medications, how he was adjusting to his placement. Since she was new to the team, she mostly just listened, until the caseworker brought up possible visitation with the mom.

"She says she's not with stepdad anymore, but you know how those things go . . ." Several people on the call chuckled. Yeah, they knew.

And Lauren didn't want to seem naive. It was hard to leave an abusive relationship—often paradoxically *harder* because of the very abuse itself. She had far less experience than any of the professionals on the phone dealing with that, and didn't have personal experience to fall back on, either. As tough as things had been with her mom, it had always been just them. Lauren knew next to nothing about her father, or what role he'd played in her mom's life, if any.

"If the visits are supervised for now," Lauren put in tentatively, "there would be no harm in letting her see Eddie more regularly, right? It sounds like she's been engaging with the parenting class."

"So far," a woman with a Southern drawl broke in. From Lauren's recollection of the introductions at the start of the call, she was the caseworker's supervisor. "You'll find that a lot of them drop off."

"Okay," Lauren said, "but right now she's engaging, and I think more visits could only benefit Eddie."

"Until she bails and he's disappointed," the supervisor said. "It's better to manage expectations early."

That seemed like a really bleak approach, but Lauren didn't know how much authority she had to push back. She was relieved when the caseworker spoke up. "The department can supervise two visits a week instead of one," she said, and Lauren pumped her fist at her desk like she'd just won a huge victory. She spun in her chair, and was surprised to see Asa leaning against her doorway, quirking an eyebrow at her.

How long had he been standing there?

Dimly, she was aware that they were confirming the date for the next staffing, and she murmured her agreement into the phone, knowing she'd need to wait for the email invite to even know what date they'd chosen.

"Let me guess," Asa said once she'd hung up. "They've released a software update to extend your battery life."

He had his arms crossed over his chest, and Lauren couldn't help but notice one tattoo that she'd wondered about before—a tree, ripped out at its roots, which dangled down Asa's forearm as the rest of the tree stretched up and disappeared under the short sleeve of his shirt. She wanted to see the whole thing, wanted to know the story behind it.

She realized the longer she sat there, just blinking at him, the more she played into this running joke that she was some kind of cyborg. She scowled at him instead.

"Stay out of my office," she said. "Don't write stuff on my to-do list, don't lurk in my doorway. Just don't."

"Sorry. Guess I'm being a real ass."

Lauren was taken aback by his apology, until she saw that his eyes were glittering. The refrigerator note. She'd almost forgotten about that.

"Why are you here?"

"Dolores told me you agreed to work the Snow Globe this afternoon," he said. "I thought I'd come by to make sure you didn't forget."

"Well, I didn't."

"Okay," he said. "In that case, let's go."

He explained the rules of the Snow Globe as they headed

over, and she almost interrupted him twice, saying she *had* worked here for a couple years, thank you very much. But the truth was, as much as she hated to admit it, some of this information *was* new to her. Like how to tell if a snowball fight was escalating. That the limit was no more than twenty guests total inside at any given time. The time that someone had decided to test the whole "yellow snow" thing.

"Ew," Lauren said. "That's disgusting."

"You have no idea. And it was actually more like orange snow, which was very concerning from a hydration standpoint. Before I kicked him off the premises, I sold the guy a couple bottled waters from the gift shop."

Asa was walking ahead, which had to be the only reason why he held the door open for her to pass through into the Snow Globe. There was an unexpected chivalry to the gesture that surprised her, and she wasn't even someone who noticed that kind of thing. Just like she wasn't normally the type to obsess over the way a person *smelled*, but there she was, taking in such a big breath as she walked by Asa that she ended up coughing from the impact of the cold air hitting her sinuses.

"You good?"

She gave a thumbs-up, wishing the ground could open up and swallow her whole. Luckily, he seemed oblivious to her embarrassment, telling the kid on duty that he could take his break or see if help was needed in another section, that they had this for a bit. Lauren hadn't thought she'd be working directly *with* Asa. She'd assumed he'd drop her off and then head back to whatever else it was that he was doing today.

"What is it you *do* here exactly?"

"Jack-of-all-trades," he said, rubbing his hands together. It seemed to be more an affectation of cold than an actual expression of it. She didn't understand how he was still in only his shirtsleeves.

"Master of none?"

It came out sounding a lot nastier than she'd meant it. This was why she hated spending time with Asa—he brought out the worst in her. They'd be going along, conversing normally, maybe almost with something approaching friendliness, and then she'd take a jab, or he'd make one of his teasing comments and ruin it.

"Why aren't you in management by now?" she asked, suddenly curious. He'd been there so long. Clearly Dolores thought highly of him, or she wouldn't have included him as one of her chosen three to make a presentation about how to make over Cold World. And yet he still spent his days doing relatively entry-level tasks. Pumping frothed milk into spiced lattes. Helping a kid tie his skate laces tighter. Changing lightbulbs.

"Because I don't want to be in management."

"You'd make more money."

"Oh, man," he said. "My financial advisor really fucked me over on that one."

Lauren glanced around, automatically nervous about profanity when they were on the clock, working in a contained space with children around. But Asa's voice had been low, and no one seemed to be paying attention to them. The one family in the Snow Globe with young children were busy trying to all cram together to take a selfie in front of a drooping snowman they'd tried to build.

"It looks like they need help with their photo," Lauren said.

Asa followed her gaze, shaking his head. "It's a trap. They all want to do selfies now. If you offer to take the picture for them, they look at you like you're definitely, one hundred percent planning to steal their phone."

"But I work here."

"You're not wearing an official Cold World shirt or a name tag."

She could point out that this whole thing had been *his* idea, so if she wasn't dressed appropriately with her usual office attire, that was on him. She could also point out that he *was* wearing a Cold World T-shirt and a name tag, so he could go over himself and offer to help. The mom's arm was shaking from trying to hold up the phone for so long, and the kids' smiles were starting to look rictus and unnatural.

Throwing Asa an exasperated glance, Lauren crunched through the snow to approach the family. "Excuse me," she said. "Would you like me to take a picture for you?"

Sure enough, the expression on the mom's face was dismissive, bordering on distrustful. "It's okay," she said. "I got it!"

That was ridiculous. Clearly, she didn't have it. "Are you sure? I could frame it really nice. It'd make a great holiday card."

Lauren could tell from the way the mom's lips pinched together that she was about to refuse again, this time more forcefully, but then the dad reached into his pocket and withdrew his phone.

"Would you mind?" he asked.

"Of course," Lauren said, fighting the urge to look over her shoulder and make sure Asa was watching this moment of triumph. "Gather in close."

The family huddled together around their snowman, and Lauren snapped a couple quick vertical photos before she realized that the perspective was all wrong. They were already starting to come out of the pose, the dad reaching for his phone, but Lauren gestured them back together. "A few more," she said, kneeling down in the snow so she could get a horizontal shot of them with the snowman, their faces filling the frame better. Immediately, the cold wetness from the snow soaked into the knees of her tights.

"Everyone smile!" she said, snapping a few more pictures before, satisfied, she got back to her feet.

"Thank you so much!" the dad said as she handed him back his phone. She hoped his voice carried enough that Asa could hear it.

"See?" she said once she was back at his side. "Your laziness almost resigned that poor family to an off-center, blurry picture to remember their time here."

"I didn't know you took your photo shoots so seriously." He was looking at her legs, which had two damp patches on both knees and rivulets of melting snow running down into her ballet flats. There was nothing really to see, the bare skin covered by sheer black tights, and yet something about the way he was looking made her shiver all the same.

"Pictures are important," she said, wrapping her arms around herself in an attempt to warm up. "They're memories."

She watched the family as the kids packed the snowman with more and more snow, until eventually the lumpy head collapsed on one side and rolled off into the slush below. The younger kid's face screwed up for a minute, like he might cry, but then the mom bounced him up to her hip and murmured something that made him laugh instead. They were still laughing as they left the Snow Globe, and Lauren stared at the doorway, lost in thought.

Next to her, Asa cleared his throat. "You can let four more people in," he said. "Since they left."

"Oh." Lauren turned in the wrong direction before orienting herself to where a few people stood in line for entrance to the Snow Globe. She waved in a group of three but then after that was a couple, and Lauren glanced back at Asa. He waved his hand in a *go ahead* gesture, and she stepped back to allow the couple to enter, too.

"You're the one who told me no more than twenty," she said.

He shrugged. "One more won't be the end of the world."

"But then what's the point of having a limit?"

The entire time they'd been in the Snow Globe, he'd been standing with his hands clasped behind his back, surveying the guests with a slightly bored expression. She knew it was probably part of the job, mastering that *ignore me, I'm not even here* type of demeanor, but it was driving her crazy.

"You'd be one of those people who bring eleven items to the *ten items or fewer* line at the grocery store, wouldn't you?"

"No," Asa said. "But I also wouldn't be one of those people who count every single item of the person in front of them."

Lauren started to protest, but she could already see the corner of his mouth quirk. She'd tried to get a rise out of him, and instead he'd gotten one out of her. Once again, he was winning.

She kicked at the snow with the toe of her ballet flat. She did like the sound of it, that cold crunch. But just from watching people interact with it, she could see that it was a sorry replica of the real thing. She bent down, scooping some into her hand.

"They should call this place the Snow Cone," she said. "That's what this stuff reminds me of."

"There's an idea," Asa said. "Dribble a bunch of different-colored syrups all over the place, let in all the kids at once, lock the doors. Their parents can go shopping and pick them up half an hour later coming down from their sugar high. We could charge a fortune."

"Such a relief that you're already thinking of your presentation," Lauren said. "I was worried you were going to come sniffing around the night before, wanting one of my cast-offs."

The snow was making her hand numb, but she had to admit that there was something about holding it, about experiencing such a completely different texture and temperature from what she was used to. She closed her fingers around it, letting it squish between her fingers.

"So I take it you have an idea for yours."

As if she'd share it with him. And she definitely wasn't about to share that she'd spent hours brainstorming on her commute to work, in the shower, at her desk, with so far . . . nothing to show for it.

The hem of her cardigan sleeve was now cold and clammy from the melting snow, but still she scooped up another handful. She molded it into a round ball, suddenly understanding why people might be tempted to start snowball fights in here. She wished she could chuck this one right at Asa's face, just to see how he'd react.

His eyes were hooded as he watched her. It was almost as if he knew what she was thinking, was daring her to throw it.

"It must be good," he continued. "Was that what your phone call was about?"

She had to think for a minute before she made the connection—when he'd come into her office earlier and she'd been pumping her fist. At least this suggested he hadn't actually heard the content of her call, or figured out that it was technically not work-related.

"Wouldn't you like to know," she said. Great. What a classic comeback. What was next, *I'm rubber, you're glue*?

Asa broke off momentarily to gesture toward a young couple who'd started to make out in one corner. "Aren't you going to break that up?"

"Why—because I'm such a wet blanket?"

His brows drew together. "No . . ." he said, drawing the word out. "Because it's part of the job? We try to keep things PG here in the Snow Globe."

Right. Lauren glanced over at the couple. They were really going at it by now. The guy's hands were wandering dangerously close to a place that would definitely bump the rating to PG-13 at least.

She desperately wanted to ask Asa to take care of it. He'd know just what to say, with enough levity to make it seem like not a big deal but enough firmness to make them stop. In high school, there'd been a couple who would meet every single morning right in front of her locker, and Lauren had never bothered saying anything. She'd just started carrying all her books in her backpack.

But she knew that went against the whole point of this exercise, and she didn't want Dolores getting word that she hadn't been up to it. She *really* didn't want Asa to be able to hold it against her, that maybe she really was hopelessly out of touch with the day-to-day of Cold World. She dropped the snow she'd been holding to the ground, clenching her hand to get the feeling back in her fingers.

She marched over to the couple, reaching out to tap the guy on the shoulder before thinking better of it. Instead, she cleared her throat loudly, and then, when that had no result, said, "Excuse me?"

Their faces were still shoved together. She wouldn't have been able to identify either one in a lineup without the other one plastered on top of them. She glanced back at Asa, but he just gave her a little smirk, like *Well?* God, she hated him in that moment.

"Excuse me!" she said again. "We, uh, keep things PG in the Snow Globe."

She'd borrowed Asa's line because it had sounded so breezy, the way he'd said it. But of course coming from her it sounded prissy and uptight instead. Seriously. She was going to kill him. He *knew* she'd fail this test, and that was why he'd sent her out here on her own. The college kid they'd hired part time because he'd given Dolores a "good vibe" could do this job, but meanwhile Lauren was going to make a complete ass of herself.

Now a few other people had noticed Lauren trying to get the couple's attention and were watching with ill-concealed interest to see what would happen next. Great. Her chances of getting out of this without a scene had just taken a nosedive.

The guy did break contact long enough to give her a withering stare. "This ain't a library," he said. "Go shush someone else."

"Actually—" She was about to point out that she worked there, but the guy didn't let her get another word out.

"Unless you were trying to cut in?" He gave her an insulting once-over. "I'll pass."

His girlfriend tittered, but Lauren could tell it was more a nervous sound than one of genuine mirth. She bet the guy was a real laugh riot to spend time with. Now that they'd pulled apart, she also saw that he was wearing a Confederate flag T-shirt, which, yeah. That checked out.

"Hey," Asa said from behind her. "You need to move on."

She'd been wrong about his tone of voice. There was no levity in it at all—only a low authority that made her toes tingle.

The guy spat into the snow, narrowly missing her shoe. "Jesus," he said. "We were about to. Come on, babe. Let's go somewhere else that's not filled with geeks who can't get laid."

Lauren flushed, sure that comment was more directed at her. But Asa only gave the couple a sarcastic little smile.

"Try the Ripley's Believe It or Not!," he said.

The guy doubled back for a second, as though unsure whether to take that as a sincere recommendation, before he led his girlfriend out of the Snow Globe, muttering the whole time. Eventually, the people who'd been watching to see if things would escalate turned their attention back to playing with the snow, and Lauren glanced up to see Asa frowning at the door.

"Should we let more people in?" she asked.

"No," he said shortly.

"Okay." She didn't know how to read Asa's mood. Was he pissed at that guy, for being such a jerk? Was he pissed at *her* for some reason, because she couldn't handle it? "I could've dealt with that guy. I was about to—"

Asa cut her off. "This was a mistake. You should go back to your office, finish up your work there. I'll cover this shift until the next person comes to relieve me."

Earlier that morning, Lauren would've leapt at the chance to get out of this new Freaky Friday initiative. But now she resented Asa thinking he could make a unilateral decision to kick her out, the same way he'd made a unilateral decision to bring her in in the first place. And she really didn't like that word *mistake*.

"We said an hour, and I'm going to stay the hour," she said, glancing at her watch. It had been barely fifteen minutes.

"You have a busy job," Asa said. "So go do it. I can do this better without you."

He wasn't even looking at her. It was back to the detached-sentry look, except instead of standing with his hands behind his back, he reached down to pick up a candy wrapper that someone had dropped into the snow. And Lauren had no idea what got into her, but something made her bend down to grab another handful of snow. She didn't bother to mold it into a ball.

Instead, she dumped the whole cold, wet handful straight onto Asa's exposed neck.

Chapter

THIS TIME, WHEN ASA AND LAUREN WERE ASKED TO SPEAK to Dolores, they were definitely in trouble.

It felt a lot like being called into the principal's office. Asa had taken one chair in front of Dolores' desk, Lauren the other, and Dolores even closed her office door before standing next to it, her arms crossed over her chest like she was waiting for one of them to speak first.

He tried to sneak a look at Lauren, to see how she was handling all of this. Somehow she struck him as someone who'd never been in trouble a day in her life. He bet she freaked out if she got anything less than an A in school.

Her cheeks were pink, whether from the cold or embarrassment, he didn't know. Under her chair, she kept sliding her feet halfway out of her shoes before sliding them back in again. It was mesmerizing. He kept waiting to see her toes, still covered by the sheer fabric of her tights, but then she would push her feet back in her shoes and start the whole process over again. She still had a damp blotch at the hem of her cardigan from where he'd gotten her with some snow as a retaliation for that first hit.

It had taken him by complete surprise. Not only the shock

of the sudden icy pressure on his neck, but the fact that she'd done it at all. It seemed very un-Lauren.

But then, so had a lot of things lately. He was beginning to wonder if maybe he'd just had her pegged wrong from the start.

"I expected better from both of you," Dolores said finally, seemingly giving up on letting them sweat out the silence. "Asa, when you suggested this work exchange idea, I certainly never expected that it would be used as an excuse to play the goof. If you want to snowfight so badly, you can buy a ticket on your day off and fling snow to your heart's content."

Next to him, Lauren frowned. "Well, you're never supposed to fling the snow."

Asa leaned back in his chair, looking up at the ceiling. He swore, she made everything harder than it needed to be. "I'm sorry, Dolores," he said. "It was a lapse in judgment. It won't happen again."

The corners of Dolores' mouth pinched so tightly her smile lines deepened. If he didn't know any better, he would say she looked more amused than angry. "Well," she said. "See that it doesn't."

"In fact," Asa said, "I'm thinking it might be better to cancel the experiment altogether. Lauren should do her job, I should do mine, and—"

"That's not fair," Lauren cut in. "I did my time. He should have to do his."

Dolores lifted her perfectly arched brows. "And what did you have in mind?"

He could tell by the panicked look on Lauren's face that she hadn't thought this through. Just like he hadn't, either. He'd been so focused on trying to get one up on Lauren, trying to shake her out of her comfort zone, that he hadn't actually thought about what a bad idea it was. She didn't deserve to be thrown into a role she'd never done before, forced to deal with entitled, belligerent dudebros. And he doubted there was much he could do to help her with her job, anyway. Math had never been his best subject.

"It's fine," he said. "We should probably focus on coming up with our actual proposals for updating Cold World. That will take more than enough time without adding extra job duties on top of everything."

"And have you thought of anything?" Dolores asked, glancing at Lauren and then back at him. He could've sworn his boss looked almost . . . anxious. But that wasn't possible. In the decade he'd known her, he'd never seen Dolores as anything less than unflappable.

"The Snow Globe," Lauren said. "Is there any way to make it actually snow?"

"From the ceiling?" Dolores clarified, then shook her head. "We tried it. You remember."

That last part was directed at Asa, and he pulled a face. He *did* remember. They were lucky to get an hour out of the over-priced machine Dolores had gotten talked into at some trade show, although it turned out an hour was more than enough. They'd never quite gotten the formula right for some reason, and the faux "snow" would come out as cold rain, or tiny hard pellets that stung a little, like someone was throwing ice chips at you.

"It was a disaster," he said.

"That's too bad," Lauren said on a little sigh. "It would be really magical."

Not ten minutes before, he'd had a handful of snow dribbling down his back. His shirt collar was still wet. Maybe that was why he felt the back of his neck break out in goose bumps.

"Let's stick with our experiment for now," Dolores said. "Lauren, think of something Asa could do to help you with the bookkeeping, get an idea for that side of the business. I trust that you can manage to avoid snowball fights in such a situation?"

"*I* can," Asa said, and when Lauren rolled her eyes, he gave her his most beatific smile.

"Perfect," Dolores said. "And Daniel will be in on Monday, and we'll find things for him to do, too. Asa, do you think it would help for him to spend some time in the Snow Globe?"

Sure. By himself.

"Maybe," he said.

"I actually have a projected budget," Lauren said, "that I'd love to get his input on. And that would probably help as we think about ways to improve the business, too?"

Dolores beamed at Lauren like she'd just single-handedly solved world hunger. "Wonderful idea. Set that up for Monday."

They were finally dismissed from Dolores' office, and Lauren booked it out of there like she was afraid Dolores would decide there was some additional punishment if she stayed one second longer. Asa caught up to her in a few long strides, following her to her office.

"So now you have a budget meeting with *Daniel*?" he asked. "Don't you think that's something I should be invited to, if it's going to be so helpful to us as we come up with our proposals?"

"I don't see why," she said, tapping on her keyboard to wake up her computer. "If you have any specific questions as you start working on your presentation, let me know."

The implication was clear. She didn't expect him to do any work on his own. He flashed back to the comment she'd made when he tried to convince her to work together, how she'd carried the weight of enough slackers in school.

There'd been enough truth in that to sting a little. Asa had never been the most diligent student—in high school, he'd been way more interested in navigating the social side of things. He'd had his first girlfriend at thirteen, his first boyfriend at fifteen, and then there'd been the whirlwind of keeping any relationship secret from his hyper-religious parents, because the only thing worse than premarital sex was premarital queer sex.

And then he'd been on his own two weeks before graduation. He'd technically still gotten the credits to get his diploma in the mail, but he hadn't bothered to walk. There would've been nobody there to support him, anyway. It had never even occurred to him to go to college. With what money? And to do what?

Lauren had gone to college. He knew that because she had her diploma framed and leaning against a wall behind her desk. It was as if she meant to hang it but never got around to it, or maybe she was embarrassed to put it out front and center. The more he got to know Lauren, the more either explanation made a certain amount of sense.

"You *did* start it, you know," he said.

He expected a denial, or maybe defensiveness. What he didn't expect was for her to put her head in her hands and let out a low, guttural growl. A sound that shot immediately to his dick.

Well, *that* was unexpected.

"Ugh," she said, her fingers curling in her hair. "I do know. I am so sorry. I have no idea what came over me—"

"Hey," he said. "It's okay. I—"

I liked it. That was the sentence that was about to pop out of his mouth. But he couldn't say that.

"I think that guy got my hackles up," Lauren was saying.

"Got me feeling all aggressive. The snow was *there*, and I was frustrated, and . . . I took it out on you. I'm sorry."

"Yeah," Asa said. He didn't know why that explanation disappointed him a little bit, but it did. "That makes sense. I shouldn't have put you in that position."

She frowned. "I know to you I must seem really . . ." She blew her bangs out of her eyes, looking up like she was searching for the right word. "Timid. But I promise you, I can handle myself."

Weird, but *timid* wasn't a word Asa would've used to describe Lauren. *Careful*, maybe, or *reserved*. She was deliberate, and thoughtful. He had no doubt she'd been thinking her way through the confrontation with that guy, considering what would allow her to stay professional and courteous but also get out of the situation. She struck him as someone very concerned with doing the right thing, but definitely not timid.

He didn't know why he felt like he knew her well enough to say that, but he did.

He also didn't know what made him say what he did next, except that the more he saw Lauren outside of the rigid role she'd always occupied in his mind, the more she intrigued him.

"Kiki and I are both off this Sunday," he said. "We were all thinking of going up to New Smyrna Beach, if you wanted to come."

She blinked at him, as though the words coming out of his mouth were in a foreign language, and she was waiting for her translation software to catch up.

"Assuming you're free," he said. "And feel like making the drive."

This was such a mistake. She was looking at him now like he had two heads.

"The beach," she said. "In December."

He laughed, hoping it sounded more natural than it felt coming out of his chest. "I know it's hard to remember in this place, but it's seventy-five degrees outside. This is the best time of year to go. Not as crowded, you don't feel like you're melting . . ."

"I can't," she said. "I mean, I appreciate the invitation. I just have a lot to do before the holidays, and I should probably work on the proposal, and that's a pretty long drive. It would take up my whole day."

Asa held up his hand before she could keep going listing every reason she could think of not to go. It was fine if she didn't want to. But if it got to the point where she said she needed to stay home to wash her hair or wait for a delivery, he'd feel like a bigger chump than he already did. "No worries," he said. "If I don't see you around, I guess I'll see you at the budget meeting on Monday."

"You're not—" she started to say, but he never let her finish the sentence. He turned and left her office, rubbing at the back collar of his shirt, now completely dry.

ASA VOLUNTEERED AT AN LGBTQ YOUTH CRISIS LINE AS A TEXT counselor, which meant he spent three hours a week taking chats from teens who needed someone to talk to. Mostly they were dealing with coming out, or being bullied at school, or questioning their identity, but every once in a while one was in the middle of an active suicidal crisis, and those always required more time and care. On a call like tonight's, it was Asa's supervisor who did most of the work to call a consult, see if emergency services needed to be dispatched, and all of that. Asa's job was just to be present, check in with the person regularly, and try to offer some validation and empathy while gathering information about their safety.

Still, it had taken a lot out of him, and it had been a weird day in general. His housemates had promised to wait for him to finish his late shift at the crisis line, even after it ended up going longer than scheduled, but he almost hoped they'd started the show without him. He didn't know that he was up for a night of snarky guilty pleasure TV watching.

Since they *had* waited for him, he didn't want to say no, so he plopped down on the couch next to Kiki and made a few halfhearted comments about last episode's double elimination. When they had to pause it only ten minutes while Elliot left the room on a phone call, Asa leaned his head back against the couch and closed his eyes.

"Your shift okay?" Kiki asked.

"Fine," he said. "Just, you know. Long day."

"I don't know how you do it," she said. "Doing hours of that on top of working a ten-hour day at Cold World. All I did was show up for five hours of watching for shoplifters and ringing up magnets, and I'm beat."

Kiki looked at John, as if for support. He held up his hands and shook his head.

"Don't look at me," he said. "You know I haven't held a real job in . . . well, ever."

"Lucky bastard," Asa said.

Kiki snorted. "You of all people don't mean that. I swear I've never met anyone who finds more ways to have fun at their job than you. Is it true you got into a snowball fight today in the Snow Globe?"

Normally, Asa didn't mind the perception that he goofed off at work. He hadn't done much to disabuse people of that notion, and there was some truth to it, after all. Why was it such a bad thing, finding ways to have fun at work? If more people could do it, they might be happier.

But for some reason, he was getting tired of playing the role of the jester.

"Lauren started it," he said, which wasn't exactly a great beginning to his new mature persona.

"Lauren?" Kiki's eyes went wide. "Lauren *Fox*?"

"Yeah."

"Huh." Her face registered disbelief, then something more pensive. "I guess I can't blame her if she finally snapped. You can be pretty annoying."

"Gee, thanks." He was already regretting giving Kiki more information than was strictly necessary, but at the same time he couldn't seem to get off the subject. "I invited her out to the beach this weekend."

"Oh, that's awesome," Kiki said. "I would've invited her myself if I'd thought of it."

"Maybe then she would've said yes."

John was typing something on his phone, acting like he wasn't listening, but even his eyebrows rose at that. Asa didn't like this itchy feeling, like he was exposed in some way. He rushed to explain what he meant before Kiki could draw any wrong conclusions.

"Like you said, she finds me annoying," he said. "Or she thinks she's better than me, or both. I can't tell. The point is, she's not coming to the beach. I just wanted to give you a heads-up that I invited her, in case it came up, or she changed her mind."

Even to Asa's ears, that explanation sounded pretty flimsy. The truth was, he had no idea why he'd mentioned it at all. Kiki reached forward to grab her Coke off the coffee table and take a big gulp. John was off his phone now, watching him. For someone who didn't even know who they were talking about, Asa had the sneaking suspicion that John understood more of the undercurrents in the conversation than might be expected. He could be the very definition of *still waters run deep*.

"Why would she think she's better than you?" John asked.

Asa shrugged, resisting the urge to say *Because she is better than me?* He didn't believe that, deep down. But it was hard not to see all the ways that, if she believed that, she'd be right. She had a college degree, a job where she worked in an office, her own apartment (which she undoubtedly rented, but still—in this economy?). She was responsible and competent and professional.

Well, except for the snowball incident.

"She doesn't," Kiki said. "I know Lauren might seem stuck-up, but she's really not like that. Sometimes I think—"

Elliot came bounding into the room, plopping down on the second couch next to John. "Okay, sorry about that," they said. "I swear my mother feels the need to narrate every single second of any commercial that makes her cry. Which is practically all of them at this time of year. Have you seen the one with the old guy training to lift his granddaughter up to put the star on the tree?"

Kiki reached for the remote to restart the show. "Haven't seen it," she said. "But I know the type. You'll be internally rolling your eyes at how emotionally manipulative it is, and that's the moment when you'll get completely wrecked."

Asa forced a laugh. On the screen, the host was laying out this week's challenge, and the candidates were reacting with the appropriate level of excitement and trepidation. Asa found it hard to focus. He wished Kiki had been able to finish her sentence.

Chapter

SEVEN

LAUREN HAD BEEN MEANING TO CLEAN OUT HER CLOSET for a while, and now seemed as good a day as any. She'd taken out all of her clothes and piled them on the bed, putting on some upbeat music to try to trick her brain into finding the task fun.

Normally, this *was* the kind of thing Lauren found fun. She had an almost compulsive need to catalog things, to cull and curate them. The act of sorting her clothes into categories felt ritualistic and almost soothing—these to keep, these to be donated, these to be thrown away. Of the ones to keep, these were for work, these for casual gatherings, these for lounging around her apartment. Once, Lauren had read an article recommending a wardrobe of only thirty-three items, providing ways to mix and match for maximum efficiency. She'd been excited to try it herself, as a kind of experiment, only when she laid all of her clothes out she realized she didn't even have thirty-three items to begin with. She'd done too good a job keeping everything as minimalistic as possible.

That was one reason, at least, why she wasn't at the beach. The only bathing suit she owned was a green bikini she'd bought on one of those whims where you thought a new piece of clothing would turn you into a different person. Someone more confident and carefree, someone who didn't overthink everything and feel self-conscious every second of the day.

She lived in Florida, and that bathing suit still had its tags on it. It should really be one of the first items to go in the donate pile, but for some reason, Lauren couldn't bring herself to do it.

It wasn't just the bathing suit, either. Lauren didn't know why Asa had invited her, but she didn't trust it. Probably he hadn't meant anything by it at all, was just being polite. Or he knew what a hermit she generally was, and felt sorry for her. Or he had some dastardly revenge plot for the snowball fight, and planned to dump a handful of wet sand on her.

Besides, she hadn't been lying when she said she had a lot to do. There was the closet, but also she really *did* want to get some work done on her proposal for Dolores. It had been four days already, and she'd barely had a chance to even think about what might be done to update Cold World. Lauren's brain tended toward the practical, but she knew Dolores was looking for something more than just an efficiency hack like putting the lights on timers.

She wondered what Daniel would come up with. Maybe something that made Cold World classier, a destination for a wedding or a venue for corporate events. Briefly, Lauren thought about what that might look like, and she could almost picture it. It could be the type of place where Marj's law firm would host its next holiday party. She could picture Daniel standing at the end of a renovated Wonderland Walk, handsome in his tux with boutonniere, hands clasped behind his back, smiling down the aisle . . .

Lauren clenched the dress she'd been holding, bringing it

to her face to muffle her groan. The man spoke five sentences to her and suddenly she was envisioning him in full wedding cosplay. It was obscene.

And anyway, the more she thought about it, the more Cold World as a classy venue just didn't work. A large part of its charm was in its kitsch. There had to be a way to retain that but make it . . . better. Right?

Her phone buzzed, and she withdrew it from her pocket to see a picture on the screen. Kiki was front and center, clearly in charge of the selfie, sticking her tongue out of the side of her mouth and crossing her eyes. Next to her was a woman Lauren recognized from other pictures as Kiki's girlfriend Marj, smiling widely, leaning into a guy with dark curly hair who Lauren assumed to be one of the housemates she hadn't met. On his other side was presumably another housemate, one with a goatee and a look of being over it. And then there was Asa in the back, his blue hair mostly out of frame, his smile half-covered by the curly guy's head.

Weather's perfect. You should come out!! Park at the dunes if there's a spot—bit of a walk but ten bucks and you can stay all day.

Lauren bit her lip, considering. The drive didn't bother her. She liked spending long stretches of time in the car, just her and her thoughts. And it might be nice to get out.

She rotated her phone until the photo filled the whole screen. Everyone looked happy, and comfortable with each other. And why not? They hung out all the time. She'd feel silly, going all that way only to feel like a sixth wheel.

Another text message from Kiki appeared at the top of her screen. Please? We're going to be voting on lunch soon and I'm outnumbered by burger stans.

Lauren grinned. Personally, she had no issue with a good burger, but she knew that Kiki had some rant about how it was the most boring food choice in the world. Lauren didn't understand what made burgers persona non grata while chicken sandwiches appeared to be okay, but she knew better than to bring it up.

Maybe tacos? she typed back. I can be there in about an hour.

IN THE END, IT WASN'T HARD TO FIND THE GROUP AT ALL. LAUren parked where Kiki told her to, and she was going to text that she'd arrived, except that as soon as she stepped foot on the sand she saw them stretched out near the water. Kiki was on her stomach, talking to Marj, who was sitting cross-legged next to her on the same towel. The curly-haired guy was on a towel next to them, a book in his hand.

She didn't see the other housemate. Or Asa, for that matter. It was probably for the best, since the last thing she wanted to do was explain how she'd suddenly freed up her schedule after making such a big deal about how busy she was.

"Hey!" Kiki said, propping herself up on her elbows to smile up at Lauren. "So glad you made it. John, scooch over so Lauren can put her towel next to ours."

"Oh, that's—" Lauren started, not wanting to put anyone out. But John was already standing, sliding his towel over a few feet and plopping back down on it without looking up from his book.

"Thank you," she said awkwardly, and he did glance up at that, giving her a brief smile.

"You must be Lauren," Marj said, reaching over to offer her hand to shake. Only she was still holding her phone, and so she set it down in her lap with a little laugh before trying again. "Sorry. It's like an extension of my limb at this point."

"Makes our sex life very interesting," Kiki muttered, and Marj poked her in the side.

"It's the end of the year," Marj said. "And I'm still a little short of my billable-hour target."

Lauren didn't quite know what to say to that. "Well, good luck."

"If this conversation hits six minutes, she'll bill you for it," Kiki said. "Was the drive okay?"

"Not bad," Lauren said, shielding her eyes to look out at the water. Now that she was here, she wondered why she'd put off coming to the beach for so long. There really was something restful about it—the heat of the sun on the back of your neck, the slow roll of the waves as they hit the shore. She'd slathered some sunscreen on in the parking lot, and hoped it would last.

She'd ended up wearing a black tank top and jean shorts, her green bikini underneath just in case. She doubted she'd actually want to get in the water, but she supposed it was better to be prepared.

"I was saying before you got here that I might pick up some gimmicky handcrafted Florida ornament at one of the local shops. Normally, you'd think no one who lives here would want one, but you know Dolores eats that kind of shit up." Kiki seemed to register that Lauren needed to be brought more up to speed than that, and she gave a little laugh. "I got her for Secret Santa. Who'd you get?"

"I thought it was supposed to be secret," Lauren said.

Kiki rolled her eyes. "Sure, I guess. If you're a purist."

"Technically, I believe it's only the recipient who's not supposed to know," Marj said, still scrolling through her phone.

"See?" Kiki scooped up a handful of damp sand and started packing it into a wobbly, formless castle. "Adjudicated. John, what do you think?"

"Hmm," he said noncommittally.

"He abstains," Kiki said. "So who was yours?"

Lauren couldn't help but glance over her shoulder, paranoid that somehow he'd come up right as she was talking about him. "Asa," she admitted finally. "And I have no idea what to get him."

Kiki paused in the act of lining up tiny seashells neatly around the perimeter of her misshapen castle. "Really? Oh my god, that's too perfect. The gag gift potential is so high."

Except that in order to choose a truly on-point gag gift, you still had to know the person a little. Enough to know the kind of joke or prank they'd find funny, that would feel personal but not too mean. It was one of the reasons the holiday season stressed her out. There was so much pressure around gift-giving—did you choose something thoughtful enough? Did it show the person how you felt about them? On the flip side, maybe it showed the person *too* well how you felt about them, leaving you vulnerable. Even receiving a gift could be fraught with anxiety—did you react with the appropriate level of enthusiasm? Did you say the right thing, like *This is just what I wanted* or *This will be so useful* or even just *Thank you so much, I really appreciate it*? Lauren knew that she could come across as a little cold. Even when she was genuinely happy or excited about something, her natural reserve sometimes dampened her outer expression of those emotions. And if she *wasn't* happy? Forget about it. She was a terrible liar.

She knew she was overthinking it, putting way too much importance on something so small. But that was the part that carefree people like Asa and Kiki never seemed to understand.

For them, it was a simple Secret Santa—they'd buy a novelty ornament, wrap it up with a funny card, and call it a day. For Lauren, it felt like navigating a minefield.

She realized that getting assigned to Eddie right before Christmas meant she'd have to get him a gift, too. She didn't even know what kids that age were into. Something Avengers? An action figure or something? Was that too babyish?

Her first Christmas without her mom, she'd gotten a baby doll from a local charity organization. Her name must've been on some wish tree through the foster agency—to this day, she had no idea how that connection would've happened. She'd never asked for a baby doll. And it had been a nice one—clearly expensive, with a small quilted diaper bag and plastic bottles with white liquid inside to look like milk. It was a lovely thought, but even at nine years old she'd thought, *What am I supposed to do with* this? *Play mother when I can't even see my own?*

She was jostled momentarily as a warm, lanky body plopped down on the sand in front of her. Asa drew one leg up, linking his hands around his knee. "You came," he said.

Kiki was scowling, hovering protectively over her creation as their final roommate settled onto their own towel. "Watch your feet, Ell," she said. "You almost wrecked my castle."

"That was a castle? I thought it was just a pile of sand."

"The row of lovingly placed seashells didn't tip you off?" Kiki waved her hand in Elliot's general direction. "This is our last housemate, Elliot. Well, they moved in before me, but you get what I mean. The only one you haven't met yet."

Lauren was grateful for something to do, someone to look at who wasn't Asa. She was aware that he was sitting very close. He smelled more like sunscreen now, but still like *him*, and a quick glance had confirmed that he had at least one tattoo on his chest as well as his arms. That was as far as she'd gotten before she'd looked away.

The last housemate was the one from the picture with the goatee. Already, Lauren felt like she understood some of the dynamics of the house—Elliot would be the intense one, Kiki sarcastic, John more quiet. As for Asa . . .

Well, he'd be the goofball, probably. But it was a little hard to slot him into that role right now, when he was still watching her, his eyes squinted against the sun. She reached into her bag and slid her giant sunglasses over her regular glasses. She knew they looked ridiculous, but she hadn't felt like dealing with her contacts, when she wore them so rarely.

"I'm Lauren," she said, reaching up her hand to shake Elliot's. "I work at Cold World, too."

"She cooks the books," Asa said.

That got her head to whip back around. "I do not!" she said.

"I thought you kept the company's financial records? Isn't that what that means?" His face was completely straight except for a slight flick at the corner of his mouth that suggested he was holding back a smile. Ah. He was winding her up again, and she just kept falling for it.

"Don't worry," Elliot assured her. "We don't take anything Asa says seriously."

"It's a little hard to take Lauren that seriously with those humongous sunglasses," Asa said, leaning down to peer up at her. "Where did you *get* those? My grandmother's purse?"

She knew her skin was flushed, and not just from the sun. "A Circle K," she said defensively. "They were cheap. Do you have any idea how much prescription sunglasses cost?"

"For real," Marj agreed. "And they always look like regular glasses that have just been tinted."

That sent Kiki and Marj off in a discussion about ordering glasses online and whether they were comparable quality to the ones you could buy at a store—Marj was firmly in the camp that you had to go somewhere in person to try them on, whereas Kiki said the word *LensCrafters* with such a withering derision that Lauren didn't know that she'd ever be able to walk into one again. It was nice, just sitting there and letting the conversation wash around her. It was obvious this was a group of people who knew each other well, and cared about each other. The way Kiki talked right over Elliot, her voice rising in correlation to the faces they pulled in response, the way John's contributions were quieter but always seemed to weigh more, as though because he didn't speak as much they valued it more when he did. Asa was just like he was at work—laughing, easy, casual.

And yet somehow even he was a little different. She couldn't put her finger on it, but it was like the happy-go-lucky persona at work was an act, while this one was the more authentic version. The fake was so good you wouldn't notice the difference until you compared the two side-by-side, but it was there.

"What are you thinking about?" Asa said. His voice was low, and around them everyone else was still talking about whatever subject they'd moved on to. Lauren realized she'd been tuning it all out. And she'd also been staring directly at him the entire time. Whoops.

"Nothing," she said. But then that sounded vacuous, so she cast around for something to say instead, and landed on something that probably only made her seem like an even bigger creep. "What do your tattoos mean?"

He looked down at his arms. She could see the full tree on his right bicep that she'd noticed before, now stretching up to cover one shoulder. His other arm was more abstract, with a geometric pattern and some swirls of a foamy blue wave. There was a number in a bold slash of a font above his left nipple, but she *really* didn't want to be caught staring there. Even with her sunglasses on, it would be so obvious.

"Ah, come on," he said. "Nobody wants to hear about someone else's tattoos. It's like hearing someone describe a dream."

Lauren knitted her brows together. "You don't like hearing about people's dreams?"

"*I* do, actually. But you know what I mean. It's a thing."

"I love hearing about people's dreams."

Asa gave a little scoff of a laugh like he didn't believe her. "We're talking about nighttime dreams," he said. "Not just like, *hopes and dreams*. Not someone describing how they want to be a teacher or compete on a singing show or live in a tiny house one day. Even you wouldn't be so heartless as to say you hated hearing someone talk about *that* kind of dream."

His words made Lauren flinch a little. *Even you.* She knew that was how he saw her, maybe deservedly so after the *cancel Secret Santa* incident at that very first holiday party. So why did it feel like closing her fingers in a drawer each and every time he brought it up?

If that first holiday party had been bad, the second one was even more excruciating to remember. Lauren could only hope that, through some miracle, Asa had completely blocked it from his memory. He hadn't seemed drunk, but he'd had at least one beer. She knew because she'd tasted it on his lips.

In the most cliché moment ever, they'd gotten caught under the mistletoe. Why they even *had* mistletoe at a work function was beyond Lauren, but Dolores didn't cut any corners when it came to the holidays at Cold World. If they'd just kept moving, probably no one would've noticed. But Asa had stepped back, trying to let Lauren through the doorway, and she'd done the awkward *No, you go ahead* thing, and the next thing she knew, Saulo was calling out, "Lauren and Asa are under the mistletoe! You know what that means! Come on, man, lay one on her for Christmas!"

Saulo had definitely been drunk. Obviously, it was totally inappropriate to yell at your coworker to *lay one on* another coworker. It was also a little sexist, assuming that Asa had to be the one to make the move. Most of all, Lauren could think of nothing more mortifying than kissing someone for the first time in such a public spectacle.

By then, others were adding their encouragement. She'd looked up at Asa, trying to convey with her face something like *This is so weird* or *We totally don't have to do this.* But she also found herself looking at his mouth, and wondering what it would be like to kiss him . . . to be kissed by him. By the time she glanced back up at his eyes, he was making a face like *Sure, why not.*

And then he'd leaned in. That was the moment carved in Lauren's memory, because it was the split second when she could've made a different decision, and things would've ended so much better. His angle was a little odd, so instinctively she'd tilted her head to find his mouth, their lips connecting with an almost cartoonish *smooch* sound. It was only after she'd pulled back to find him blinking in surprise that she'd registered why he'd come in at the angle he had. He'd planned for a cheek kiss. An *air* cheek kiss, even. And she'd swooped her head under and gone for the kill.

Even thinking about it now made her wish the beach beneath her would suck her into a quicksand vortex and spit her back out at her apartment. She'd tried to make things right afterward—apologized, blamed peer pressure, apologized again for blaming peer pressure. And then after that, she'd tried to spend as little time around Asa Williamson as possible.

So she supposed she shouldn't be too bent out of shape by the robot jokes, or the *heartless* comments. At least it was better than the alternative, where he remembered the one time when she'd been all too human. When, just for a second, she'd thought, *You know what? A kiss under the mistletoe actually sounds kind of nice.*

"Tell me about one of your dreams, then," Lauren said now, staring out at the water.

He was sitting more behind her than next to her at this point, and on her one side Kiki, Marj, and Elliot were talking animatedly about what sounded like a dating show, based on the snippets Lauren could pick up. On her other side, John still sat reading his book, twisting a dark curl around his finger. He could be listening to every word of her conversation with Asa, for all she knew, but he did such a good job of fading into the background that it was easy to feel like she and Asa were in their own little bubble.

"I have one involving you," he said. She imagined she could feel the heat emanating off him, prickling her neck, but it was probably the sun.

"Me?"

"Uh-huh."

When her voice came out, it sounded strangled even to her ears. "Do I want to know?"

"It's December twenty-seventh," he said, "and we're in Dolores' office."

That was awfully specific. Did Lauren have any sense of exact dates and times in her dreams? She couldn't remember.

"You've just presented your proposal to revamp Cold

World. You put it on a trifold display, like you were gunning for first place in an elementary school science fair. Bubbly letters, cutesy border, that kind of thing. It looked nice—you worked hard on it. We won't even mention what Daniel's was like. He just rambled for a bit about turning Cold World into a rave club for his business-bro friends or something like that. It was embarrassing."

Lauren frowned. Daniel was in this dream, too?

"Thank god I'm there," Asa continued. "With my polished, professional proposal. It turns out you were right—there *was* a promotion in it for the winner. I'm modest about the new title, but I'll take the money. Dolores shoos us out of her office. She wants to put my plan into effect immediately, and needs to make several phone calls. You pack up your bulky cardboard presentation board, and the last thing you say to me before disappearing into your office to cry—do you want to know what it is?"

She didn't think she did, but he took her lack of response as a sign to keep going.

"You say, *I wish I had taken you up on that offer to work together when I had the chance.*"

Chapter

EIGHT

ASA WAITED FOR LAUREN'S REACTION, BUT THE BACK OF her neck gave nothing away. She scooped her hair in one hand, gathering it to one side. The green tie of her bathing suit top dangled down above her black tank, the bow crooked and double-knotted.

"I think I'm going to stand in the water," she said finally, and pushed herself to her feet. She brushed the sand off her hands onto her shorts and headed down toward the shore without looking back at him once.

He was still watching Lauren down by the water when John spoke up next to him. He'd almost forgotten his housemate was there.

"Why did you do that?"

"Do what?"

John closed his book with an air of *Fine, let's get into it.* "That was the most bullshit response to an honest question I've ever heard."

"It's a long story," Asa said. "Involving this project our boss wants us to work on, where we propose changes to Cold World. Lauren and I are each working on a separate presentation. It's a friendly rivalry kind of thing."

"Friendly." John snorted, letting Asa know what he thought of that. "Okay."

Did you have to be considered friends to call it a friendly rivalry? Asa didn't know the answer to that question. He wouldn't go so far as to call Lauren a *friend*, and he knew for a fact she wouldn't call him one. But they'd certainly talked more in the last week than they had in . . . pretty much since she started at Cold World two years ago.

"Lauren has this idea that there's some catch to the presentations," Asa said. "Like that the person who comes up with whatever Dolores goes with will get some kind of promotion, or bonus. So it makes sense that she would want to work by herself."

"What about you?" John asked.

Asa understood the question, because it was what he'd been asking himself the past few days. If there *was* a prize attached to the presentation, he should welcome the chance to throw his hat in the ring for it. Even if there wasn't, he *did* know Cold World better than anyone. Between him, Lauren, and Daniel, he should be the one best positioned to knock this out of the park.

Maybe that was what made him so nervous. Because what if he didn't? So far, all he had to show for his brainstorm sessions were a few doodles on a sketchpad. He felt like he could *see* what a new, improved Cold World could look like, but only in abstract terms. He might've teased Lauren about her potential science fair exhibit, but at this point he'd be walking into Dolores' office with nothing more than a few swatches of watercolors on paper.

Lauren was crouching down now, looking at something in the sand, and Asa stood up. He'd never answered John's question, but he knew his housemate wouldn't care—he was already cracking open his book again.

He reached Lauren before he actually knew what he planned to say to her. So instead he just knelt next to her, getting a closer look at whatever had grabbed her attention.

It was a swirled cone of a shell, pearlescent white on the outside. It was pretty enough, but nothing that special for the beach. But then he noticed four claws curled around the edge, looking almost like long, reddish-colored fingernails. They flicked out further, sending the shell scooting backward.

"It's a hermit crab," Lauren said. "This is what it's been doing—it'll stay really still and then all of a sudden, a burst of movement. It's—" The crab did another of its flick maneuvers, only this time part of its head poked out of the shell. Lauren gave a little laugh, glancing up at him. "See?"

"Pretty cool," he said. It really was. He could see how she'd gotten so mesmerized by watching the creature—there was something about waiting to see when it would move next, how much of a glimpse you'd get. At one point, its legs came out enough to actually carry it across the sand, traveling only a few inches before it settled its shell back over its body.

He glanced over at her. The wind had blown her hair over her face, a few strands stuck to her mouth, but she didn't seem to notice.

"Sorry for being a dick," he said.

The crab was in another motionless phase, easily mistaken for nothing more than an ordinary shell in the sand. The Atlantic didn't wash up as far as they were, but the sand was damp, as though the tides had recently been higher than they were now. Lauren's toenails were painted a coral pink.

"You weren't—" she started, but he cut her off.

"I was," he said. "Even John thought so."

She sat back in the sand, pulling her knees up to her chest and resting her chin on them, her gaze still trained down at the crab. "I wouldn't react like that, you know," she said. "If you *did* manage to come up with the best proposal—which I'm still skeptical about, for the record—I wouldn't go back to my office to cry."

He winced even remembering that part. He'd definitely taken the whole thing too far. He didn't want to make Lauren cry, even in some fake scenario he'd come up with to mess with her. "I might," he said. "Except I don't have an office, so I'd have to go break down in my car like a real winner."

"You would not," she said.

"Despite what the Cure might lead you to believe, boys *do* cry."

He was joking, trying to make her smile. But he realized he was cutting a little close to the bone, too. After what John had said, he didn't really want to do more of this dance with her, where he feinted around her questions or played things off. At the same time, he wasn't exactly in the mood to get into a heavy conversation about things like the last time he'd cried or why.

"Does this mean that much to you?"

Another Pandora's box of a question. He realized that it did, but he couldn't fully articulate the reason. He wasn't generally a competitive person—although Lauren seemed to bring it out in him—but that wasn't what was spurring him on. Something to do with giving back to Cold World, and to Dolores, and with proving something to himself.

"Nah," he said. "I won't break down if she chooses your idea. Don't worry. I'd just get back to work."

She was quiet for a minute. The crab had been still for so

long Asa wondered if it knew they were there and was playing dead. He didn't know the etiquette of finding a hermit crab on the beach. Did you just let it chill where it was, let nature take its course? Or should you move it to a safer spot, like a turtle in the middle of the road? He was about to bring it up to Lauren when she spoke again.

"I'd probably quit," she said.

"You'd *quit*?" The words sent a spike of some emotion through him that he didn't care to analyze. "That's a bit extreme."

"I don't mean it like that," she said. "Not like a rage quit or anything. It's more like . . . I have other goals, I guess. And if I had an opportunity to do something bigger at Cold World and it didn't work out, I'd take that as a sign that maybe it was time to move on."

He didn't know what to say. He could ask more about what those goals were, but something about the way Lauren drew her knees up tighter to her chest, the way her face got closed off and remote, made him think that she was done sharing. Knowing her, she probably regretted sharing that much with him already.

"I think we should move him," she said, tilting her chin toward the crab's shell. "Just put him by those rocks, where there are fewer people."

"I agree," he said. "You do the honors."

She picked up the shell delicately between two fingers, her face scrunching up in an almost-smile when the crab's legs flicked out for a second, brushing her hand. He followed her to the rocks, where she placed the crab down into the sand. It immediately came out to scuttle away from them, as if it were under attack. Couldn't blame the guy.

"Are you still thinking tacos?" he asked, glancing back up

at where the others were sunbathing on their towels. "Anything but crab."

She wrinkled her nose. "Definitely not crab. But you go ahead and eat without me. I really should get back and finish up some stuff."

She'd driven an hour to hang out for maybe thirty minutes. According to Kiki, tacos had been *her* lunch suggestion. She'd never even gotten down to her bathing suit, which Asa had to admit with a little zip of awareness was something he'd been looking forward to.

Not to ogle her or anything. Just because it would be interesting to see Lauren Fox in something that far removed from the cardigans and tights she wore for the over-refrigerated environment that was Cold World. Just because he couldn't seem to stop himself staring at her legs, that dip right behind her knee. Just because from the ties that hung down from around her neck, he couldn't tell if her bikini was more grass green or teal, if it had a pattern or was solid.

He hung back while she said goodbye to everyone. Kiki's gaze darted to him, like *What did you do?*, but he just shook his head.

"I'll walk you to your car," he said.

"You don't have to," Lauren said, gesturing toward the lot barely visible through the hill of beach grass behind them. "I'm just over there."

But he let Kiki know he'd catch up with them at the taco truck and fell into step next to Lauren. She was normally a fast walker, but now she was moving at a more leisurely pace. It was probably just the effect of walking on sand, but he was glad to have a little more time to think about what he wanted to say.

"So I guess tomorrow it's back on. Daniel is coming in for the budget meeting, right?"

"Yes," she said. "Which, again, your presence is *not* required at."

"We'll see."

She rounded on him. He wished he could see her eyes, but they were covered by those ridiculous sunglasses. "If you care so much about this opportunity, why aren't *you* at home working on your proposal? You can hang out at the beach all day with your friends, but it's not going to get you any closer to beating me, if that's what you want so bad."

A sharp, jagged sensation lodged in his chest, like a sand bur had found its way there. "It's not the worst thing in the world, to have friends. You should try it sometime."

She flinched back like he'd hit her. "I have a full and complete life, thank you very much. Maybe it doesn't look like anything to *you*, because it's not flashy or oriented around my own personal pleasure, but it's mine."

His own *pleasure*? Asa could argue with that characterization. What he did at Cold World was a job, after all, even if it didn't seem to be one she respected much. It paid his bills. It wasn't like he sat around doing nothing all day. And even if he did, what business was it of hers?

They'd reached her car. He recognized it from the number of times he'd seen it in the Cold World lot, there before his on weekdays, conspicuously absent from its usual spot on weekends.

"So you have a cushy office job," he said, "where you get to work regular hours and sneak in a little online shopping when you feel like it. That doesn't make your life more legitimate than mine. And what do you have against pleasure, anyway? If I'm going on this random, bizarre trip around the sun over and over, the least I can do is figure out a way to have fun while I do it. What's the problem with that?"

He really wanted to say *What's* your *problem with that?* Back at the beach, he'd thought they were . . . well, if not connecting, then at least sharing a small moment.

"No problem," she said, opening her car door. "I shouldn't have—just forget I said anything. I'll see you at work."

There was a stack of DVD rentals on her front passenger seat—*Captain America, Iron Man, The Incredible Hulk*. Normally, he would've teased her about the old-school discs, or about being such a deeply undercover Marvel fan. But whatever lightness he'd felt between them felt prickly and weird now. So instead he just shut her car door after her, raising his hand in a halfhearted wave as she started up her car and backed it out of the spot. Every time he thought he was getting closer to understanding Lauren, he realized he had no idea what made her tick at all.

Chapter
NINE

LAUREN NEVER DID FINISH HER CLOSET CLEAN-OUT PROJ-
ect. Instead, she just shifted the pile of clothes to the other
side of her bed and curled up next to it when it was time to go
to sleep. It had actually felt oddly comforting, sleeping next
to that pile. But the minute she had that thought, she had to
strike it from her brain. It was too sad and pathetic to con-
template.

She purposely gave very little care to what she wore to work
the next day, selecting a standard gray skirt and eggplant
purple cardigan. She'd thought extensively about dressing
up for Daniel, nervous at the prospect of spending a whole
block of time in a room with him one-on-one. But she also
didn't want to *look* like she cared.

It was weird, then, that when she gave herself one last look
in the mirror before leaving, it wasn't Daniel she thought of
but Asa. She knew she'd ended things badly at the beach,
snapping at him like that. She wasn't even sure why she'd
done it.

He *had* wound her up with the dream thing. The truth
was that Lauren could be quite gullible, and she'd always
hated pranks that preyed on that—ones where someone asked

you to believe something and then made the fact that you believed it the punch line. She'd never understood that kind of joke.

She had to acknowledge that, despite acting like the resident class clown of Cold World, Asa didn't usually resort to that kind of humor. She'd noticed that his jokes were generally not *mean*—he didn't seem to want to laugh at people so much as get them to laugh with him. And he could be just as self-deprecating as he was observant about other people's quirks and foibles, so it wasn't like he didn't play fair.

But she'd found herself curious about him, about the stories of his tattoos, the kinds of things he cared about or thought of. And so when he'd rebuffed that question, turned it around on her, it had felt like a bigger door slam in her face than it probably should have. She didn't have much in common with Asa Williamson, after all. She didn't need to unlock all his mysteries. She just needed to get through this stupid holiday season, and the presentation at the end of it.

By the time she got to work, she had half a mind to apologize to Asa when she next saw him. That ended up being sooner than she'd expected, though, as he was back in the break room, drinking his undoubtedly overly sweet coffee that would've contaminated the Keurig machine. There was no staff meeting today, and thus no reason for him to be there that early. Unless . . .

"You're not coming to this meeting with Daniel," she said flatly, lifting the machine's handle and starting the hot water to cleanse it of whatever today's flavor was.

"You seem to feel very strongly about that. You don't think you kids might need a chaperone?"

She tried to will her cheeks to stay cool and unflushed but didn't know if she was successful. Asa had twin stripes of pink on his own cheeks, probably from the beach yesterday. She wondered how long they'd stayed out. She wondered if they'd talked about her after she left—comparing notes on how weird she was, or why she hadn't bothered to hang around.

You should try it sometime. Of everything Asa had said, that had hurt the most. It hurt mostly because he wasn't wrong—she didn't really have friends. At work, she basically had Kiki, and even then it wasn't like they were besties telling each other all their secrets. At home, she had no one. Sometimes she was scared she'd signed up to be a guardian ad litem just to have people to see, something to *do*.

Again, she couldn't get the machine to actually brew the coffee once she'd put her K-cup in, and again Asa had to put down his own coffee to help her. This time she tried to hold her breath, to not even be tempted to take a deep inhale of that cedar-citrus scent of his. But she found herself staring at his arms instead, at the tree that she'd now seen in full on his bicep. The roots flexed now as he lowered the top of the machine until the whirring sound began. He finally leaned back against the wall with his coffee, and she let out her breath.

"Thanks," she said.

"I did have an idea last night," he said. "For a way to improve this place. *You* gave it to me, actually."

She had no clue if this was another trick, where he laid out some elaborate fake idea that was all for fun. She stayed silent, setting her coffee mug back down on the counter until it cooled a little.

"And?" she said finally, when he didn't appear inclined to go on. "What is it?"

He smiled at her over his coffee. "Oh, I have no intention of sharing it. I just wanted to let you know that yesterday, after a long day at the beach with my friends, I was in the shower washing off all that sand and salt and *bam*. It hit me. Don't you love when that happens?"

She knew her mind shouldn't catch on the word *shower*, but she couldn't help the image that immediately popped into her head. Now that she'd seen his bare chest, it wasn't hard to picture water sluicing down his arms, his hard, flat stomach, spiking his eyelashes as he looked down at her . . .

Lauren put the brakes on that train of thought. She had no idea how *she'd* ended up in this shower fantasy all of a sudden.

Or maybe she did. She was so lonely that sleeping next to a pile of clothing felt comforting, that she was having inappropriate thoughts about a coworker she didn't even know that she liked that much.

"You okay?" he asked.

She took a quick gulp of her coffee, wincing a little when it burned her tongue. "Of course," she said. "Fine. Great. I just have a lot of work to do, so I should probably . . ."

She didn't bother finishing that sentence before she turned and left. After the holiday season was over, she was going to figure out a way to try to meet more people. She'd try dating apps, she'd join a book club, she had no idea. She just clearly needed to get out of the house more.

It wasn't lost on her that it was the exact point Asa had been making at the beach.

LAUREN REALLY DID HAVE A LOT TO DO TO PREPARE FOR HER meeting with Daniel. She compiled all the annual numbers for income and expenses for Cold World, which was something she'd been working on as the end-of-year approached in general. But since this meeting was focused on Dolores' challenge, she wanted to specifically highlight opportunities to raise income or lower expenses in a few particular areas.

She couldn't help but wonder what idea Asa could've come up with—especially one supposedly inspired by *her*. She cast her mind on the various things they'd talked about in the past few days, trying to find a nugget of something he could've taken and run with. Had she unknowingly given away an idea that could've formed the basis for her own proposal?

But he wasn't going to have the benefit of information like what she was compiling right now. For example, he wouldn't have crunched the numbers on Wonderland Walk to know if they were making more on vendor rent than they might make if they just sold their own wares directly. He wouldn't know why they didn't work with Groupon yet and what it would take to make that profitable.

It *did* almost seem unfair, that she and Daniel would have this advantage. But it made sense for them to know the financial ins and outs of the company. Asa was . . . whatever he was. A jack-of-all-trades. He didn't necessarily need to add this arrow to his quiver.

There was a light rap on her door, and she looked up to see Daniel in her doorway. "Come on in," she said. "I was just printing out the last spreadsheet."

"Actually," he said, giving her his megawatt smile, "could we move this to my mother's office? She's out until after lunch."

It would make things a lot less convenient, because Lauren had wanted to stay near her computer in case she had to look anything up or make an adjustment. But she'd printed two copies of everything, so she supposed there was no reason why they couldn't meet in Dolores' office. "Sure," she said. "Let me just gather everything up."

Even a week ago, she would've had a much harder time staying chill this close to Daniel. Having his attention on her—*her!*—would've scrambled her brain. She was proud of herself for maintaining her cool. What had Asa accused her of, when he'd called her out for sloshing coffee on herself? Being stricken by Daniel's macho charisma?

Well, she was one hundred percent in control. If only he could see her now.

She reached the door to Dolores' office first, but she had her hands full with the folders of paperwork, and anyway, it felt weird to open someone else's office. She stepped to the side, but Daniel was busy typing something into his phone. He gave a nod down at the doorknob. "It's open," he said.

She shifted the folders to one arm so she could bend down to turn the knob, but she misjudged which side of the folder was the open side, and ended up sending a sheaf of papers floating to the ground. So much for being cool.

"You can put those on the desk," Daniel said, stepping around her. "I had something I wanted to run by you first."

She slid the last of the papers back in their folder, hoping they were still in the order she'd arranged them in. She wondered what he had to run by her—was it something work-related? Or was he maybe going to renew his invitation to dinner?

This time, she'd take him up on it.

He took Dolores' seat behind her desk, steepling his fingers together in a way that really did make him look like his mother's son. She took the same seat where she'd been sitting just a few days ago, getting in trouble with Asa for the snowball fight.

She kept one folder on her lap, sliding the other one across to Daniel. He didn't even glance down at it. Instead, he held up his hands, almost like he was quieting a crowd of adoring fans.

"Picture this," he said. "Snowboarding. Sledding. The Winter X Games right here in Orlando."

"Oh, cool," she said. She had only a vague idea of what the Winter X Games were, but from context she assumed winter sports. "When is that supposed to be?"

"Whenever we make it happen," Daniel said, leaning forward, his eyes bright. "Don't you see? If we build it, they will come. This is the future of Cold World."

"Snowboarding."

"In *Florida*." He smiled up at the ceiling, as if he was thanking the lord above for all the cash that was about to come pouring in. "The novelty alone will have people beating down our door. We'll need to completely revamp the place, obviously. If we build over the back parking lot, we can put the slopes there, and then—"

Lauren almost couldn't believe what she was hearing. "Where would people *park*?"

He waved his hand, as if it was no concern of his. "Where do they ever park in Orlando? At the Waffle House down the street and they can walk over. One of the garages downtown and then they can Uber. I don't care."

She pressed her fingertips to her temples. She felt a headache coming on, and she had a feeling it was the word *slopes* that had done it. He wanted to build actual snow slopes? Outside? In Florida? Was he absolutely off his rocker?

He picked up the folder in front of him, leafing through it quickly before closing it again. "So you're the numbers girl," he said. "You tell me how we can make this happen. I have a guy who says he'll put up three hundred thousand, but we'll probably need at least another one point two, something like that."

"Hundred thousand?"

A line of irritation marred his forehead, like he thought she was being dense on purpose. "Million."

"Million?" Lauren knew she'd reached the stage where she was just stupidly repeating words, but she couldn't think of what else to say.

"What's our overhead?" he asked. "There were a lot more people at that staff meeting than I expected. Do we employ too many people?"

She didn't think cutting a few entry-level jobs would get them to over a million dollars, but what did she know. She opened her mouth, about to point out that operating a full winter sports park would likely require *more* employees, when the door cracked open and Asa popped his head in.

"Sorry," he said. "Am I late?"

He didn't wait for a response before coming in and sitting in the same chair where he'd faced down Dolores a few days before, calling their snowball fight a "lapse in judgment." She hadn't fully appreciated it at the time, but it was pretty decent of him to take the fall for that. She *had* started it, but he hadn't even mentioned that in front of the boss.

Maybe it was that memory, but for some reason, she wasn't upset to have him crash the meeting—even despite the many, *many* times she'd told him he wasn't invited. Instead, she almost felt . . . relieved?

It was this new, harebrained idea from Daniel. Maybe Asa would be able to help him see sense.

But Daniel's face closed off, and it was clear he had no intention of meeting with Asa. "Not at all," he said, flashing him a fake smile. "In fact, we were just finishing up."

They'd talked for maybe five minutes. He'd barely even looked at the reports she'd prepared. "But we haven't—"

He picked up the folder of papers, giving her a little salute. "Thanks for these. If you can get me the numbers for what we talked about, that would be great."

She glanced over at Asa, but he only raised his eyebrows in an expression she couldn't quite read. It seemed to encompass his general feeling that Daniel was a douchebag, that Lauren was too mousy to stand up for herself, or all of the above. Whatever it meant, she shouldn't let it get under her skin, because it would only lead to doing something very ill-advised, something like . . .

"Dinner tonight?" she blurted, and immediately cringed. But the words were out. There was no shoving them back in her mouth, so the only option now was to commit. "I mean, maybe we can talk more about the budget over dinner tonight. I'd love to hear more about your idea."

Okay, that was laying it on too thick. She didn't know if she could sit through a whole meal of him throwing out exorbitant numbers and sketching out some pipe dream about a snowboarding renaissance in Orlando. At least, not with any semblance of an appetite.

She didn't want to look at Asa and see his expression of secondhand embarrassment, but she couldn't help a glance. But he was just looking down at his lap and frowning. He'd brought a yellow legal pad and a pen to the meeting, she noticed, like he actually expected to take notes.

"Can't tonight," Daniel said.

Of course. He wouldn't want to have dinner with *her*. Or maybe he would, but this was payback for the fact that she'd turned him down once before. She put a smile on her face and started to make the appropriate noises about how it was totally fine, she understood he was probably busy, when he cut her off.

"We have family coming in from Cuba for the holidays," he said. "My mother is hosting a huge dinner. That's where she is right now, in fact—last-minute shopping to make a bunch of ropa vieja and her guava cream cheese empanadas. She hasn't made those since I was a kid. Do you know how hard it is to get her to cook? Especially with how much time she spends here. But she's going all out for this."

"Oh," Lauren said. "Well, that sounds . . . nice."

It did. The idea of having not only a mother but extended family? Cousins and aunts and uncles and grandparents, this whole tree of people who cared about each other and were connected by something that ensured they'd be in each other's lives forever? It was more than nice.

"I guess you could come," he said. "It's not until late—ten o'clock. That's when their flight gets in. Dress is casual. You could wear that."

He swept his hand dismissively over her. Lauren kicked herself for not spending a *little* more time on her outfit today. She'd easily have time to go home and change first, but would that make her seem like she was putting too much energy into it? If he hadn't mentioned her outfit at all she would've changed before, no-brainer, but now she was paranoid.

She was surprised by how much she really, *really* wanted to go to this dinner. Not just because the idea of spending time with Daniel outside of work thrilled her. Not even because guava and cream cheese empanadas sounded amazing. Because the idea of being surrounded by this big, loving family seemed . . .

Well, it was the opposite of falling asleep next to a pile of clothes, for sure.

"Dolores wouldn't mind?"

"It'll be good," he said. "You can help me sell her on—" He stopped himself, his gaze cutting to Asa. So he really didn't want him to know about the whole Winter X Games idea. Interesting. "If you could put together that report and print three copies, that would be great."

What report exactly did he think she'd be able to put together? Was he looking for something on where the funding would come from? Because she was a bookkeeper, not a magician. Did he want projections on what a winter sports park might bring in above and beyond their current profits, a break-even analysis? She wouldn't even know where to start.

She was dying to ask him all these questions, but he was already making it clear the meeting was over. He spun in Dolores' chair toward her computer, and she thought she saw him pull up Shaun White's Wikipedia page.

And for the second time in a week, she found herself standing outside Dolores' office with Asa, unsure of what exactly had just happened.

"What report is he talking about?" Asa asked, tapping his legal pad against his thigh. "What's this idea he wants you to help him sell to Dolores?"

Lauren's head was still spinning. That meeting hadn't gone at all how she'd planned it, and she had a feeling it had taken a wrong turn the minute Daniel asked that it be moved from her office to Dolores'.

"If he wanted you to know," she said, "I'm sure he would've shared it with you directly."

Asa stared at her. "So you *are* working with him now."

"No, I'm not," she said. "I just . . ."

His lip curled. "You just want a date with him badly enough to sell out. Did he even look at any of the reports you'd already prepared, before asking you for another one?"

"These aren't what he needs." She didn't know why she was defending Daniel. She'd been annoyed herself at how little attention he'd given all her hard work. At the same time, she hated hearing Asa point that out. He hadn't been at the entire meeting. He hadn't even been *invited*. Any warm feeling she might've had toward him for that split second when he'd interrupted Daniel's pitch had long since faded.

"God forbid the Crown Prince of Cold World doesn't get what he *needs*," Asa said.

"Could you please—" She pulled him by the arm toward her office, afraid that Daniel might be able to hear them if they stayed outside Dolores' door.

"Could I what?" he prompted once they were in her office, the door shut almost all the way. He'd crossed his arms over his chest, and Lauren tried to ignore the way that made his T-shirt pull.

"Could you wear a long-sleeved shirt, like everyone else? We all know you have tattoos, you don't have to . . ." She gestured vaguely toward him. ". . . show them off all the time."

"You're the one fixated on my tattoos," he said, looking down at his arms in bemusement. "And that can't be what you were actually about to say."

"No, I was going to say could you please *shut up*." Lauren knew she was being rude, but she felt oddly unhinged by everything that had happened with Daniel, the whirlwind of hearing his bonkers proposal, then wangling an invite to his mother's big dinner. She couldn't decide if she was mortified or nervous or excited about the latter thing, and she felt like she couldn't *think* as long as Asa kept talking. "None of this is your business, okay? Whatever report Daniel wants or what I'd do for a date with him or why I want to go to this dinner. None of it has anything to do with you, and I don't understand why you keep coming around. So I'm saying could you please just . . . stop."

This whole time, she'd thought of his eyes as being blue. Maybe that was because of the hair, some effect where it made them appear blue from farther away. But now that they were standing so close to each other, face-to-face in her small office, she saw they were a smoky color closer to gray.

She also thought he'd always disliked her. Since the *cancel Secret Santa* incident, definitely after the horrible mistletoe kiss debacle, and maybe especially after their recent rivalry around this stupid contest or whatever it was. But she realized she'd never quite seen his eyes look that cold, his jaw that set in anger. Maybe he hadn't always disliked her, but he sure as hell did now.

"Consider me stopped," he said, setting the legal pad down on her desk next to her own where she kept her task list. "Have fun tonight."

Her throat felt tight, and she couldn't have replied even if she wanted to. But maybe that was for the best. She wished she could rewind and start the whole day over, apologize to Asa in the break room for snapping at him yesterday, find a way to avoid snapping at him again.

His notepad wasn't completely blank. There was an illustration up in the top corner, little circles of snow, a few larger snowflakes, and the start of a girl's profile turned up toward the falling snow. There wasn't much to it, but it still kicked her in the stomach.

She should go after Asa. She should get started on the report for Daniel. She was caught in between, so instead she just dropped her head to her desk and tried to take deep breaths. The worst of it was, she didn't even have a single clue how to make Cold World better. She just knew it seemed like, every day she showed up at work, she was making it incrementally worse.

WHEN KIKI KNOCKED ON HER OFFICE DOOR JUST AFTER SIX o'clock, it was clear from her tentative greeting that she must've been filled in on at least some of what happened from Asa.

"You're here late," she said.

"I'm trying to run this analysis," Lauren said, wiping her hand down her face. "But honestly, none of the numbers are making sense anymore."

The issue was that the underlying proposition made no sense. It was like trying to solve a word problem that had been written by someone with no knowledge of what concept they were trying to teach. She *had* spent an hour researching issues with fake snow production on such a mass scale, which had been quite informative but not particularly helpful for finalizing a report that Daniel would want to show Dolores.

"Asa mentioned something about a date?"

Lauren had to restrain herself from asking exactly *what* Asa had said, and how long ago, and in what tone. But she knew that if she and Asa were going to be in an all-out war, Kiki would have to take his side. She lived with him. She knew him way better. Lauren didn't think she had it in her to lose her only friend at work as the cherry on top of the sundae of this horrible day.

"Not a date exactly," she said. "But Daniel did invite me to have dinner with his family tonight."

"Still exciting!" Kiki said. "Want to come over, borrow that red dress? I decided to go with the jumpsuit for Marj's thing like you suggested. If I'm showing up on a woman's arm, I'm going to go full throttle."

He'd said *casual*. The red dress definitely said *date* more than it said *business meeting*.

"If it was fancy enough to be a contender for Marj's holiday party, it's definitely too much for this," she said. "I'd look ridiculous."

Kiki shook her head. "You'll look sexy, promise. Stop by your place first, and see if you have a strapless bra you could wear. Preferably not one of those scary bridesmaid ones. Even better if it's part of a matching set."

"I'm going to dinner at his *mother's* house," Lauren said. "Who just happens to be my *boss*. There is no need for special underwear."

Kiki waggled her eyebrows. "That's the beauty of special underwear," she said. "You never know when it will be called into service."

Maybe in Kiki's life—not in Lauren's. But she found herself considering it all the same. She already had at least a workup of a report for Daniel, projecting maintenance costs for a winter sports complex like the one he envisioned. She could run home, spend an hour or so at Kiki's house, then come back to Cold World in time to add any finishing touches and print it out. The offices were normally closed after five, but as long as the main building was open to the public, she'd be able to get back in. And she already knew that Asa was working the closing shift, so she wouldn't have to worry about running into him at his house.

She logged out of her computer and gathered up her stuff. "I'll be there in half an hour."

IT WAS CLOSER TO FORTY-FIVE MINUTES, WHICH SHE HOPED wasn't rude after Kiki had been kind enough to offer to help her get ready. But it had taken longer than she'd expected to locate her black lace strapless bra, and underwear that was at least also black, if not an exact match. She still thought it was a bit silly to put that much care into items of clothing that Daniel would never see, but Kiki also seemed much better at this kind of thing, so Lauren figured she'd trust whatever she said. Maybe sexy underwear beneath her clothes would give her more outer confidence. Worth a try.

Before she'd left Cold World, she'd seen Asa briefly. He'd been walking with Marcus, explaining something that involved a lot of hand gestures. His gaze had slid to hers, so quickly his head didn't even move, and then they'd walked right by. She wished she had slow-motion footage of the moment, just so she could see how he might feel toward her. Still angry? Disgusted? Or completely indifferent?

"Come in, come in," Kiki said now, ushering her inside their house. Elliot was seated at the dining room table, typing on a laptop, and they lifted a hand in greeting.

"Hi, Lauren," they said. If they felt any lingering weirdness over the way she'd left the beach outing, they didn't show it.

"Hey," she said. "What are you working on?"

"An analysis of every Carly Rae Jepsen song in order of worst to best," they said. "Worst being relative, of course."

"Hard-hitting journalism," Kiki said, and then held up her hand when Elliot seemed primed to launch into an argument. "You know I'll read it and enumerate every ranking you got wrong. But my girl's on a timetable right now, and we need to get down to business. Lauren, follow me."

The red dress was hanging up from the doorframe to Kiki's en suite bathroom, and Kiki pulled it down and shooed Lauren in to get changed.

Closed inside the bathroom, Lauren started unbuttoning

her sweater. "It must be really fun to live here," she called through the door. "Just because of all the conversations you get to have."

"I guess," Kiki said. "This Carly Rae thing started because Elliot said her version of 'Last Christmas' was the best one, which Asa took as sacrilege because he's a Wham! purist. John tried to make a case for Jimmy Eat World, but if he has to lean on phrases like *guitar tone* he has to know he's already lost."

"But that's what I mean," Lauren said, pulling her shirt over her head. "You have people you can debate that kind of stuff with. Which version did you vote for?"

"*I*," Kiki said, "do not care. Christmas music is annoying. It's bad enough we have to listen to it at work. But also, Arlo Parks' cover is the best and anyone who disagrees has no taste."

Lauren shimmied out of her skirt. Generally, she agreed with Kiki about the music selection being particularly annoying this time of year. The music didn't pipe into the office area, which was fortunate because she couldn't take having to listen to "Wonderful Christmastime" on an endless loop. But she had to admit, she did like the original Wham! version of "Last Christmas."

She switched out her underwear before sliding the red dress over her head. It was made out of a jersey knit, which did make it feel a *little* more casual at least. And because it was off-the-shoulder, it didn't actually show any cleavage—just a lot of her shoulders and collarbones, the rose pendant necklace she always wore. The dress ended in a swingy skater skirt around her thighs. She opened the door to show Kiki.

"I feel like I should wear my tights," Lauren said, glancing down.

"Absolutely the fuck not," Kiki said. "It's bad enough that you wear those to work every day. What is this, the 1950s?"

"It's not a modesty thing," Lauren said. Although maybe it was, a little. "I just get cold easily. Have you been in my office? I can't even use a space heater because of that time the one in Dolores' office caught fire."

"Daniel's gonna catch fire when he sees you in that," Kiki said. "Seriously. You look hot."

Lauren turned back to examine herself in the mirror. "I look overdressed."

"You see what Dolores wears to work," Kiki said. "Hell, you might be *under*dressed. But we'll keep your hair down and loose, you barely need any makeup, and you can wear your same flats. That will all keep the look more chill."

"Thank you so much for your help," Lauren said. "I really appreciate it. I'm hopeless at this kind of thing."

Kiki crossed behind her to reach for a few hair products on the counter. Lauren hadn't spent much time hanging out the last time she'd come over, so she hadn't fully clocked that Kiki had what was probably the main bedroom with the attached bathroom. She knew Kiki had moved in after Asa and Elliot, so maybe that was a nod to her being the only woman in the house. Lauren wondered where Asa's bedroom was—on the other side of the house? What would it even look like?

"Asa doesn't seem to like Daniel very much," Lauren said.

Kiki snorted. "Yeah, I kinda got that impression when he told me about your date."

"It's not a date exactly," Lauren felt compelled to remind her. Even if she'd been thinking of it that way in her head, she'd hate it getting back to Daniel somehow that she'd been going around calling it that. "What's Asa's problem with him? I thought Asa got along with most everyone."

That was part of what was really bothering her about the whole scene in her office, she realized. Asa might be maddening and mischievous and wisecracking, but he was friendly to everyone. The exceptions to that were Daniel, who he seemed to barely tolerate.

And, lately, her.

"Don't worry about Asa," Kiki said, spritzing some volumizing spray into the palm of her hand before running it through Lauren's hair. "He can't exactly judge you if you want to date someone hot, have a little fun."

Lauren frowned into the mirror. She hadn't even necessarily been thinking about Asa *judging* her for her choices, but now she was. What had he said to her back in her office? That she was willing to sell out for the chance to date Daniel? That wasn't true. She was helping him with his so far completely unrealistic idea only because it was part of her job, to analyze expenses and budgets for Cold World. And if she'd always found him attractive, and secretly crushed on him from afar, then why *not* use the opportunity to get to spend more time with him?

"Look," Kiki said, apparently reading Lauren's troubled expression in the mirror. "Asa is fickle. Not about his friends— he's loyal to a fault. But in relationships? I don't think I've known him to date someone for longer than two months. And it's not like he has sterling judgment. He hooked up with one chick who stole money right out of his wallet. And the guy he dated last year kept talking about how brilliant *American Psycho* was. Talk about a huge red flag. So if he gives you any shit for wanting to be with Daniel, ignore him. I doubt

Daniel's read a book in his life, but at least he's not an *American Psycho* stan."

Lauren gave a halfhearted laugh. Kiki's words should ease at least the worry that Asa had room to judge her for being shallow, or foolish, for treating this chance with Daniel as a real possibility. But they didn't. If anything, they only made her feel more unsettled. That word *fickle* had wormed its way into her stomach and flipped over. She didn't like the idea of Asa dating other people.

And Lauren found she really didn't like the idea of these other people potentially treating him badly, stealing from him or being . . . whatever kind of asshole Kiki seemed to believe would love *American Psycho*.

Lauren's longest relationship had ended just over two years ago, and he hadn't been terrible. He just hadn't been . . . *the one*, either. She honestly couldn't remember who'd broken up with who, because it had felt so inevitable by the time they'd had the big conversation about it. Lauren had moved into the apartment she had now, applied at Cold World, and only dated a few people here and there in the years since.

She tried to think of the last time she'd had sex. There'd been a guy she'd seen more than once, and they'd gone back to his place after their third date. In the end, she couldn't go through with it—it just hadn't felt right, sleeping with someone she didn't know that well yet. They'd made out a little and then she'd gone home. He'd never called her again, a fact which had piqued her on principle but not really broken her heart.

Not that she was going to *have sex* with Daniel tonight. God, the idea was absurd, Kiki's "special underwear" advice or no.

"Do *you* like Daniel?" Lauren asked.

Kiki's gaze slid away from hers. "I'm probably a bad person to ask," she said. "I don't like many men, my housemates excluded. But Daniel seems . . . fine. He owns his own condo, I think. That's pretty cool."

Lauren immediately thought of how much it was probably mortgaged, and how high the condo fees could be, but then shut down that train of thought. She didn't know why she was like this—always looking for the negative side, always nitpicking things. She knew in her heart that Daniel probably wouldn't give her the time of day if he didn't want the report from her. It still wasn't going to stop her from trying to just enjoy herself tonight.

Shit, the report. Lauren glanced at her watch and saw that it was close to Cold World's closing time. She'd probably lost the opportunity to make any adjustments to her report for Daniel, but at least she should have time to print it if she left now.

"Again," she said to Kiki. "Thank you so much for the makeover. I'm sorry I didn't bring my contacts so we could get the full movie experience."

Kiki waved her hand. "Laney Boggs looked hotter before, and I'll die on that hill. And you pull off the red way better."

That sounded like gibberish to Lauren, but she took it for the compliment it was. She folded up her old clothes, clutching them to her chest as she left, saying goodbye to Elliot and John, who was making cheese toast in the kitchen.

"If you hang out another fifteen minutes," John said, "Asa should be home."

"Oh, I'm not—" Lauren stopped in the act of explaining. It would be too much to get out, and would make it seem like she was protesting too much. She glanced at the refrigerator automatically, wondering if her juvenile little note would still be there. It wasn't.

Well, she hadn't expected Asa to want it up for long. There was something else in its place, an invitation with dancing sock monkeys on it, but she didn't have time to look closer. She made her apologies to John for having to run out and left.

She drove as fast as she could without breaking any traffic laws, but still when she got to Cold World the sign had been turned off, and the parking lot was empty.

"Shit," she muttered to herself. "Shit, shit, shit."

She was never there at closing time, but she'd hoped that it would take longer to finish up the cleaning and setting everything to rights. Maybe Marcus was on duty, and he was doing his early mop again. It would be just her luck.

Except Asa had also worked the closing shift, and she hadn't seen him arrive back at the house. So if they'd closed, it would have to be extremely recent. She parked her car and got out, circling around the back of the building to the fenced area where the dumpsters were. Sure enough, there was a single door propped open an inch. She slid through it, hesitating only a second before removing the brick that had held it open and letting it softly close shut. Even if the open door wasn't immediately visible to anyone passing by, it couldn't be a good idea to just leave it open like that.

She'd print three copies of the report and be out of there just in time to drive to the other side of town where Dolores lived.

Chapter
TEN

ASA LIFTED ONE EARBUD OUT OF HIS EAR, TILTING HIS HEAD to listen. He could've sworn he heard something, but maybe he was being paranoid. It wasn't every day that he stayed late at Cold World with a clandestine mission, after all.

Just to be safe, he carefully set down the faux snow machine he'd been carrying on the hallway floor, stepping over it to check on the back door.

Which was now closed. *Fuck.* He had no idea how that would've happened—he'd made sure the brick he wedged to keep it open was heavy enough.

He'd had a feeling that this plan wasn't the brightest idea he ever had. He should've listened to that instinct. But he'd been thinking about what Lauren had said a few days ago, about how much cooler the Snow Globe would be if it could snow from the ceiling, and he'd suddenly gotten an idea of how he might be able to get the machine to work.

He'd been thinking about Lauren.

God, she was frustrating. She treated *him* like he was a freeloader, while the whole time Daniel was asking her to run secret reports for whatever Drakkar Noir–drenched idea he'd come up with. She told *him* to stop, when the only thing he'd been trying to do was look out for her. She was so prickly.

If he managed to get this snow machine working, she'd have to admit *that* was impressive at least. While she and Daniel had been cooking up whatever pie-in-the-sky scheme they were going to present to Dolores, he would've actually found a way to make it snow better in the Snow Globe. It would be . . . what was the word she'd used?

Magical.

The look on her face would be priceless. He could almost picture it now.

But then Lauren herself came around the corner and scared the shit out of him. He wasn't proud of it, but he actually startled and gave a yelp that didn't sound fully human. Which caused her to look up and give a small shriek of her own. The sheaf of papers she'd been holding went flying.

"What are *you* doing here?" she asked.

"I closed tonight," he said, still clutching his chest like someone out of a gothic novel. "What are *you* doing here?"

"I had to print the—" She swallowed. "It doesn't matter. I'm about to leave."

Now that he'd calmed down a bit, he was able to take in the full picture. Lauren Fox, standing in front of him wearing a candy apple–red dress, her dark hair loose around her bare shoulders. She looked really . . . his mind blanked, unable to come up with a word other than *good*. But maybe it was less about the word and more about the emphasis, because she looked really, *really* fucking good.

She bent down to gather the papers, and he automatically started to crouch down to help her, but she waved him away. It was clear she didn't want him looking at whatever she'd printed.

The implications of it all hit him—why she was dressed

up, her plans with Daniel, the once-open door that was now closed. "Did you shut this when you came in?" he asked, gesturing toward the door.

"It wasn't safe," she said. "Anyone could come in off the street."

A calculated risk he'd taken, hoping that no one would bother entering the fenced-in dumpster area in the hour he thought it might take him to tinker with the snow machine. It wasn't *that* late at night, after all, and many surrounding businesses were still open. But none of that mattered, because his plan to keep everything secret was now about to blow up in his face.

"That was the only door not connected to the alarm system," he said. "So congratulations, now we're locked in."

From the line that appeared in between her eyebrows, it was clear she didn't believe him. If she thought he'd invent this elaborate a setup just to watch her freak out . . . well, okay, that did sound like him. But in this instance, the only thing he was guilty of was some light workplace breaking and entering. Kind of.

"That makes no sense," she said. "The doors can't lock from the inside. It's against fire code. And if that door's not connected to the alarm system, then we should just be able to open it."

She moved toward the door, and he had to slide over to block her path. She looked up at him uncertainly, the tiny pendant she always wore flexing in the hollow of her throat as she swallowed.

"Okay," he said, but the word came out as a rasp, and he had to clear his throat and try again. "Technically, we're not locked in. Any door will open from the inside. For whatever reason, the system doesn't register this particular door if it's open when the alarm is set . . . but once it's closed, it will absolutely register that someone opened it again. Which will trigger the alarm system and send an alert to the police and to Dolores that someone is trying to break in."

"You don't know the code?" she asked. "I thought you were the Cold World expert."

He shook his head. "The security guy does that."

She brightened at the mention of another person. "He must patrol the place," she said. "We'll just explain the situation, then. Maybe he won't even have to report anything to Dolores, if it was all a misunderstanding."

"He drives around outside," Asa said. "I purposely parked around the corner, but maybe he'll see your car and investigate. And there are cameras in the main guest areas. I don't know if they're actively monitored, though."

She chewed on her lower lip, obviously thinking through their options. "I could call Daniel," she said. "Tell him what happened. He could drive up here to disarm the system, and then we could head back to Dolores' for dinner."

Asa doubted that would happen. For one thing, he would be very surprised if even Daniel knew the security code, vice president or no. He wasn't exactly hands-on. But presumably he could ask Dolores, so that wasn't even the real issue—Asa just doubted that he would drive all the way out to help.

"So call him," Asa said.

"I can't bother Dolores," Lauren said. "This dinner tonight sounded important."

Asa shrugged. "It's up to Daniel what he does. He doesn't have to involve her if he doesn't want to."

Lauren dug in her purse and pulled out her phone, stepping away to make the call. He was surprised by just how much he missed the nearness of her. He knew she was distracted by the logistics of this situation, and she'd be back to hating him any minute, but for now he was relieved she was at least talking to him again.

He should be irritated with her. It was her fault the door was closed, after all, and he had definitely *not* planned to spend his night at Cold World after working a long day. But somehow he couldn't manage it. He found himself courting a *fuck it, whatever happens happens* attitude, which almost never boded well.

She was at the other end of the hall now, the phone pressed to her ear. He could make out bits and pieces of her conversation, but not enough to know if she was making any progress. Already the call with Daniel was lasting longer than he'd expected, he'd give the bastard that. He inched a little closer. It wasn't eavesdropping if they were both in a shared space, right?

"I totally understand," she was saying. "It was a long shot. I—" She broke off, and he couldn't help but notice how tense her body language was—her shoulders curved inward, her fingers tight around the phone. It was completely at odds with the light, breezy tone she was obviously striving for on the call. "No, no, of course. It sounds like Dolores really needs you there."

Lauren paused, listening. "Oh," she said finally. "Sure. I guess I could—but I'm not sure that you'd understand what the—"

She turned, giving Asa a little frown. Busted. He tried to raise his eyebrows in a *Well? Is Daniel coming?* expression, even though it was clear by now that he wasn't.

"Yes," she said finally, sounding more decisive. "I'll email them to you. Okay. You—"

She held the phone away from her ear, looking down at it

as if to verify that the call had dropped. When she looked up, she gave Asa a brittle smile. "Well," she said. "Maybe it's time to break out the flashlights. Do you know Morse code?"

"With all due respect," Asa said, "that seems like something *you* would know."

She furrowed her brow, like she was trying to figure that one out, before shoving her phone back in her purse. She folded the papers she'd been holding into a crooked, messy square, obviously not caring how crinkled they got.

"What *are* you doing here after hours? Why did you prop the door open?"

"I told you," he said. "I had an idea. I wanted to see if I could make it work."

He could tell she was dying to ask what the idea was. And in the mood he was in, he just might tell her. But he could also tell that it was the same moment she remembered their conversation in her office earlier, the way it had ended.

She glanced at her watch. She was the only person he knew who still wore one, but it fit her. He had a feeling she liked to know exactly what time it was no matter what she was doing, was the kind of person who would check a movie's runtime to know what she was getting into before agreeing to see it.

"They should be done with dinner around eleven," she said. "So maybe Daniel will be able to come then. If not, we'll figure something else out. We definitely can't stay *here* all night."

She looked at him, as if for confirmation, but it took him a second to catch up. "No," he said after a beat. "Definitely not."

She was still staring at him, as if expecting something more. He wasn't sure what that might be, so he just stared back.

"I'll be in my office," she said finally, turning on her heel.

He figured he might as well go back to trying to get the snow machine to work. If they were trapped in the building for the next couple of hours, there was nothing to be done about it now—until they heard whether Daniel was going to drive out or not. Asa wasn't holding his breath. But he understood Lauren's point about not wanting to interrupt Dolores' dinner. He didn't particularly relish having to explain to his boss why he'd been here in the first place.

The machine they'd bought years ago looked almost like a movie projector, connected to a reservoir of water. It was supposed to shoot very cold, atomized water into the air, which would then freeze into something resembling an actual snowflake. The problem was that, no matter how cold they kept the Snow Globe, it wasn't quite *that* cold, and the water couldn't freeze fast enough to keep up. This, apparently, was a common issue with the machine according to the online reviews, which Asa found out only after Dolores had already brought it back from the trade show.

He did find one video, though, where a guy filming a web series in California figured out how to re-jig the machine with a fabric filter and a special dry bubble mixture. The "snow" was essentially tiny bubbles, but it might work. They already had the colder stuff on the ground, after all, and only needed a little bit of falling snow to create an effect.

Of course, they sold other equipment that was built specifically for that purpose. But he knew that Dolores wouldn't be impressed if his proposal was simply *Buy new stuff*, so he was determined to make this conversion work. He'd made the bubble mixture at home based on the video's instructions, and now all that was left was to put it all together and see what happened.

He carried a ladder from the utility closet into the Snow Globe, crushing its legs down into the snow to try to stabilize it before climbing up and carefully setting the snow machine on top. He didn't love the way the extension cord was stretched across to the back wall, but it would have to do for now until he saw if this could be rigged up more permanently.

Holding his breath, he clicked the *on* switch.

Nothing. Not even a reluctant churn to suggest the machine had turned on and was trying to work.

He clicked the switch back to the *off* position, counting to five in his head before flicking it back *on*. As though that would make any difference. The machine still didn't even make a sound.

"Fuck!" He clenched his fists, but he stopped just short of shaking the ladder in frustration. Breaking the machine further wouldn't do anything, even if it was already busted to begin with.

He just wanted something to go *right* for once.

"What are you doing?"

Lauren's voice from behind him almost made him fall off the ladder. He squared his shoulders and steadied himself before he climbed down and faced her.

"Nothing," he said. "Any word from Daniel?"

"It's only been fifteen minutes."

"Oh. Right." He ran his hand through his hair, and she tracked the motion. There was an odd, tense beat where she just stood there, hugging her arms around herself against the cold. She'd put on her usual cardigan over the red dress, a drab shroud over the vibrant color, and he found himself wishing she'd take it off. Not just because he wanted to see her bare shoulders again—although he had to admit that was part of it—but because he liked the idea that she might not always have to be buttoned up and hidden away around him.

Of course, that was ridiculous. She was cold. She'd put on her sweater. They were barely friends, not much more than colleagues. There was no reason to read anything more into it than that.

"So why are you here?" he asked. It came out harsher than he'd intended, but then, he couldn't help but flash back to her words earlier that day. She'd told him to *stop*, and that was what he'd vowed to do. No more mentioning working together, either as a joke or in seriousness, no more pestering her for information, no more teasing her, no more trying to spend time with her outside of work.

Being trapped inside Cold World with her was really going to complicate matters.

"You're trying to get it to snow."

Not an answer to his question, but clearly as close as he was going to get. He gestured futilely toward the ladder. "I thought I'd found a way to rig something up, but if the machine wasn't a dud before, it definitely is now that I've tinkered with it. It wouldn't even turn on."

Her gaze followed the extension cord stretched across the space. He expected a lecture on safety, but eventually she just said, "Maybe it's the outlet."

"Ha," he said, giving the word a sarcastic bite. "Yeah. I found the one outlet in Cold World that doesn't actually have any electricity running through it."

"The wiring is old," she said. "An electrician is supposed to come out in January. Dolores is worried some of it won't pass next year's inspection."

"Well, the more likely explanation is that I'm just a fuckup. That's what you think anyway, right?"

This type of reaction wasn't like him. He tried to let things roll off his back, tried to take life as one big joke. There was no point in getting worked up about what people thought of you, or petty bullshit drama. It was what allowed him to have an easy relationship with everyone he knew—his coworkers, his housemates. Everyone but his parents, and *that* wasn't something he gave much thought to. Letting those thoughts intrude was a surefire way to get him *out* of whatever flow state he tried to achieve with his life.

"Have you eaten?" he asked suddenly. A stupid question, probably, given that she'd been expecting to eat dinner with Daniel and Dolores and their family. But he didn't want to give her time to respond to his last comment, didn't want to risk getting into an actual conversation about all the ways he'd let people down.

She paused, and for a minute he didn't think she'd let him off the hook that easily. She still seemed unsettled, small in her giant cardigan, framed by the slushy snow beneath her feet and the blue door to the Snow Globe at her back. But eventually she shrugged and said, "I was going to grab something from the vending machines."

"Nah," he said. "We can do better than that. Follow me."

SINCE COLD WORLD WAS HOUSED IN A CONVERTED WARE-house, there weren't any windows except for the glass doors that provided the main entrance. It would've almost been easy to forget that they were there so late at night, except that it was eerie to walk around the dimly lit space, the only sound the hum of the air conditioning and the dull thud of their own footsteps. Asa led Lauren to the hot chocolate stand near the entrance of Wonderland Walk, ducking under the counter to see what was available in the mini refrigerators stored below.

"We can't eat that stuff," Lauren said. "It's inventory."

"I'm not completely lawless," Asa said, rummaging through the wrapped sandwiches until he found two of the best one—

a basic ham and cheese that was nonetheless way better than the caprese, which tasted like vomit even when warmed up. "I'm planning to pay for them."

"The register's already been cashed out."

Asa pulled his phone out of his pocket, unlocking it before opening a new note to type in. "Two sandwiches, seven ninety-eight apiece. Do you want me to pop yours in the microwave?"

"Closer to eight fifty after sales tax," Lauren said, eyeing the sandwich he'd placed on the counter with a dubious expression. "For ham and cheese? That's an expensive sandwich."

"Cold World knows if you're desperate enough to need real food at a place like this, you're going to pay a hefty premium." He set two bottled waters next to the sandwiches on the counter, and made a show of typing the totals for both into his phone. "And here's us, the most desperate of all."

There was a small seating area just inside the entrance to Wonderland Walk, with a few white-painted wrought iron tables and chairs, barely big enough to fit two people each. On a normal, semibusy day, it was impossible to get seating there, since families would push tables together and hang out for a while. But now, with no one around, Asa pulled out a chair to one of the tables, gesturing for Lauren to take a seat.

She hesitated a minute before accepting the proffered chair. "Thank you—" she started, then did a double take when he took a seat at the next table over. "Wait, aren't you going to—"

"You made it very clear earlier today that you wanted me to stop coming around," he said, unwrapping his sandwich from its plastic. "Unless you're willing to set off the alarm and summon Dolores, I can't control our current predicament. But I figured your direction to *stop* did not include me sitting across a dollhouse tea table from you."

Besides which, sitting at the same table would make this feel an awful lot like a date. He'd offered to pay for the food. She was all dressed up, a detail he was too conscious of, even as he reminded himself of the person she'd actually dressed up for in the first place. Daniel. Who might be arriving at any minute to rescue Lauren from this situation, if she had anything to do with it.

She frowned down at her own sandwich but made no move to open it yet. "These tables *are* ridiculously small," she said. "Maybe Cold World needs a bigger eating area."

Asa had his mouth full by that point but tilted his head in what he hoped was the universal expression of *Yeah, probably, but where would we find the room?*

They ate in silence for a few minutes, until eventually Lauren took a big gulp of her water, screwing the cap back on with such deliberate determination that Asa knew she was gearing up to say something else. He found himself tensing, waiting for whatever it might be.

"I'm sorry," she said finally, still looking at her bottled water instead of at him. "I shouldn't have said all of that stuff about you needing to mind your own business and . . . everything else. The truth is that I was frustrated. You said you had an idea for your proposal, and Daniel had just finished telling me *his* idea, which was—" She shook her head, but he couldn't tell if the gesture meant that Daniel's idea was bad, or just that she wasn't going to reveal it. He hoped the former.

"Honestly I have zero idea what I'm going to propose to Dolores," Lauren said, lifting her gaze to his. "Not a clue. I thought something might occur to me while I was running the report for Daniel, but I'm still drawing a complete blank. Then I thought maybe I'd get inspiration from talking to Dolores tonight, but . . ."

She didn't need to finish that sentence. Obviously, that ship had sailed.

"If anything, I'm more stumped than I was before," she said. "I was looking back through past years' financials, before I even started at Cold World, hoping I could spot some trends that would tell me the right direction to go in. But the only trend I saw was that our profits are down. Like, way down."

This wasn't exactly a surprise. Just from looking around, Asa could see evidence that things weren't quite as they used to be. Minor signs of wear and tear that weren't rushed to be fixed, understaffing during their off season, employee perks that had been gradually phased out. Nothing huge. And the business was old—Dolores had been running it a long time, and things had stagnated. It was presumably the reason she'd come up with her request for proposals to give the place a makeover.

But the way Lauren said those words—*way down*—made it sound more serious. He couldn't tell if that was due to her propensity to worry, or if the situation really looked that dire.

He was working up the nerve to ask when his phone rang. "Hey, Kiki," he said into the phone.

"Where are you? You were supposed to be home an hour ago."

"Yeah, sorry, I'm still here. I'm actually—"

When he glanced over at Lauren, she was shaking her head emphatically, her eyes wide and stricken. It wasn't hard to read her body language, and he pivoted quickly to avoid telling Kiki she was there. "It's going to take longer than I thought," he said. "Don't bother waiting for me. And *don't* tell John, but I saw a spoiler online so I already know the elimination and it's—"

"La la la," Kiki sang childishly into the phone. "I'm not listening."

He grinned. "I was *going* to say it's totally unexpected. You won't see it coming."

"Well, now I will! Because you told me not to expect it! That's basically the same thing as a full-out spoiler."

"Oh, then you won't mind if I—"

She hung up on him. That didn't bother him—he knew he'd deserved it. He typed a quick message into the group chat just to confirm that no one should wait up for him because he didn't know how late he'd be. When he glanced back up, Lauren was watching him.

"Don't want anyone to know you're here with me, huh?" he asked.

She tugged the sleeve of her cardigan down over her hand, fiddling with a loose piece of yarn around the frayed edge. "Kiki helped me get ready for tonight. I just didn't want her knowing it didn't work out."

Of course. Now Asa remembered the reference Kiki had made to Lauren borrowing and returning her dress, and she must've loaned it out again to Lauren for this date with Daniel. The idea of Lauren at his house, doing her makeup and fixing her hair, giddy with excitement about spending time with Daniel, assessing herself in the mirror and wondering what *he* would think . . .

Under the table, Asa curled his hands into fists, then released them. "What is it about Daniel, anyway?"

He hadn't meant to ask the question. It had just popped out. For one thing, he adamantly didn't care to hear her extol his virtues. For another, he already had a fair idea of what they were—Daniel was conventionally handsome and had all the outward markers of success. He was a businessman. He'd probably never had a single job that restricted when he could use the bathroom, for christ's sake, whereas Asa had spent the last ten years counting out his federally mandated fifteen-minute breaks.

She'd finished her sandwich, the cling wrap folded into a neat square on the table in front of her. "He's close with his mom, for one thing," she said. "And I love Dolores."

Daniel *worked for* his mom—that didn't necessarily mean he was close with her. Asa got the impression that Daniel's main connection in life was to himself. But maybe he was being unnecessarily harsh, given that if one of Lauren's key attributes in a potential partner was *close with family*, that would eliminate Asa from the running.

Not that he wanted to be in the running.

"That's it?" Asa prompted. "He has a good relationship with his mother?"

She shot him a glare. *"No,"* she said. "He also happens to be extremely . . ."

She appeared to be struggling to come up with the word, so he tried to help her out. "Boring? Arrogant? Dismissive? Rude?"

"You don't even know him!"

"And *you* do?"

She opened her mouth but shut it again, and he couldn't hide his satisfied smirk.

"He also happens to be extremely sexy!" she burst out. "I'm not oblivious, okay? I know a guy like that would never look at someone like me. I know we're not going to get married and have kids and live in a big house with a mother-in-law apartment for Dolores. But he's an attractive guy who was *finally* paying me some attention, so sue me if I wanted to just see where it could go."

Her eyes were bright, and he had the uncomfortable feeling she was close to tears. When he'd started down this line of questioning, he hadn't thought she'd take it as an attack. He'd thought it was clear that his issues were with Daniel, and nothing to do with *her*. But then, maybe that was the problem—he hadn't really thought this through at all.

"Lauren—" he said.

She stood up, pushing her chair back, and gathered the remnants of her dinner. "Thanks for the sandwich," she said. "I'll pay you back tomorrow."

She chucked her folded cling wrap and crumpled napkin into the nearest garbage can and headed in the direction of the front office.

If he'd needed a reminder that what they were doing was *not* a date, he guessed he'd gotten it.

Chapter

ELEVEN

NORMALLY SPREADSHEETS WERE LAUREN'S HAPPY PLACE.
She loved formatting the columns to right-align all the numbers, loved dragging the cursor down to copy a formula to each cell, loved sorting the data in different permutations and seeing how it looked. She wouldn't have necessarily *chosen* to be at work at eleven o'clock at night playing with Excel, but it was far from the worst time she could come up with.

Now, she wasn't even finding comfort in work routines. She was tired, and saying all the wrong things, and forced to confront what had to be obvious to everyone else. It was definitely obvious to Asa.

Daniel wasn't coming. Tonight hadn't been a date—it had barely been a dinner between colleagues. He'd wanted her to bring him some paperwork like she was his secretary, and then she would've sat awkwardly around a table with a bunch of strangers who were eager to catch up with each other, not her.

Ugh. And she'd called Daniel *sexy* in front of Asa. She felt like she could burst into flames of embarrassment.

She wondered how she was going to sleep tonight. Maybe

if she folded her arms on her desk and laid her head down on top of them . . .

She was trying it out when a soft knock came at the door, and she jerked up straight so fast she sent her chair rolling backward.

"You look like me in high school," Asa said, the corner of his mouth quirking up. "Always sleeping in class."

He set a lidded paper cup on her desk. "Truce hot chocolate," he said. "I didn't know if you drank caffeine this late, or I would've made you your usual black battery acid."

She reached for the cup. It was warm under her fingertips, and that alone was surprisingly comforting. She took a tentative sip, trying not to grimace. She didn't normally like hot chocolate, but it was such a surprisingly sweet gesture, she didn't want to ruin the moment.

"Thanks," she said. "I'm sorry I overreacted. Again."

"Not an overreaction," he said, leaning against her desk. "You feel how you feel. And I was pushing your buttons on purpose. It's one of my least attractive qualities, as you've no doubt noticed."

"Well." Lauren felt a little disarmed by the fact that he'd so easily capitulated. By now, she expected the teasing, the jokes, the way he got under her skin. She was more surprised when he backed off, or apologized, or seemed to actually notice and care about the effect his teasing might have on her. She waved to her computer monitor, the list next to her keyboard. "I'm overly rigid and don't like not being in control. Some of *my* least attractive qualities, as you've no doubt noticed."

"Quite a pair, aren't we?" He smiled at her, but it didn't quite reach his eyes. But then he slid her list closer to him, and she thought she must've imagined that brief sadness that had passed over his face.

"What's with the numbering, by the way?" he asked, running his finger down the margin of the page. "They're not in order."

She grabbed for the notepad, but he'd already lifted it to hold it in his lap, and she wasn't going there. It was bad enough that his thigh was less than a foot away from where she usually placed her hands on the home keys. He was wearing jeans, the denim soft and worn, and she felt like she could feel the heat emanating from him sitting this close. She tried to look up at him but felt vulnerable from that angle; she couldn't stare straight ahead or she'd risk looking right at his crotch. Eventually she settled for watching her own hands, knotting and unknotting in her lap.

"I use a random number generator," she said. "To pick what task I do next."

"A random number generator."

She knew telling him would only open up more *Lauren is a robot* comparisons, but the cat was out of the bag now. "Yeah, like if I have to go through all the bank account transactions and reconcile them with our QuickBooks," she said. "It's not hard, but it's one of those tedious tasks that you just never *want* to do. Especially when something's off by like twelve cents, and you have to go pull up both screens and compare back and forth, trying to figure out where you input something wrong . . . but if I made it number three on my list, and the random number generator comes up with three, then I have to do it. No excuses."

"No excuses for yourself," he clarified. "This is you, cracking the whip on . . . yourself."

"It works!" she said. "Haven't you ever had a task you're scared of? Like, you don't even want to *open* that can of worms. So you write step one down on your list, put a number next to it, and boom. When that number comes up, you have to do it. You don't give yourself the chance to be scared of it."

He shifted back on her desk, bringing his ankle up to cross over his knee. She should care that he'd just pushed back a whole stack of papers that were now fanned precariously close to the edge. She should care that he was making himself so at home in here when they'd been arguing off and on all day. But she didn't. She was too focused on his face, which had lit from something within as he grabbed a pen off her desk and turned to the next page in the notepad.

"I like this idea," he said, starting to jot something down. "Random numbers to help you get over the stuff you're scared of."

"Or just don't want to do," she pointed out. "I use it for all kinds of trivial daily tasks. Anything urgent I bump to the top of the list, but everything else gets assigned a number one to ten, and then when I cross one off I assign the next thing on the list that number."

"Got it," he said. "We're going to play a little differently."

Lauren felt a frisson of . . . was it anxiety, or anticipation? "What do you mean *play*?"

"Shhh, hang on," he said, still writing. "Sorry, didn't mean to shush you. Just give me a second. I'm trying to think of two more."

"Two more *what*?"

"Okay," he said, finishing his writing and sliding the notepad back toward her. "What do you think?"

She turned it so she could better read the ten items he'd listed. His handwriting, which she'd already noticed before was almost unnaturally neat, was a little messier now, the letters joined in a half-print, half-cursive hybrid.

1. Ask me anything
2. My favorite_____ is . . .
3. I dare you to . . .
4. Tell me a secret
5. Would you rather . . .
6. Compliment me!
7. I can't stand _____
8. Contest
9. Take a break!
10. Freestyle

"What is this?"

"The Random Number Generator Game," Asa said, waggling his eyebrows. "I just invented it. Well, based one hundred percent on your original idea. So I guess you were right that you'd end up doing all the work if we ever paired up together."

She looked over the list again. *Tell me a secret* made her stomach flutter; the notion that she'd ever compliment Asa to his face or ask him for a compliment turned that flutter into a pit. She understood the concept now—a list of conversation starters that you'd have to answer without giving yourself the chance to be scared of them first.

"Contest?" she asked.

"Arm-wrestle, who can create the longest paper clip chain in twenty seconds, it doesn't matter," he said. "And before you ask, freestyle just means come up with something on your own. Really it's because I couldn't think of anything else."

She took another sip of her drink automatically, but she'd already forgotten that it was hot chocolate and not coffee. This time she couldn't stop herself from making a face. "It's late," she said. "I'm expecting Daniel to call back any minute."

"So we use this to pass the time." He pulled out his phone. "Is there an app for the random number thing?"

She sighed, giving in. "Try random dot org. It uses atmospheric noise to generate its numbers, instead of a pseudo-random algorithm."

He raised his eyebrows at her. "Okay, but you're not allowed to make *I'm a huge nerd* your secret, because that one's out."

She couldn't help but laugh. It was funny, how much she didn't mind his teasing when she knew that the spirit behind it was friendly. It actually made her feel oddly warm and fuzzy inside, the way he called her a nerd as if he liked it.

"I'll go first," he said, tapping his phone before turning it to her so she could see the number seven on his screen. "I can't stand . . . hmm. I can't stand hot chocolate."

"Oh my god," she said. "Me, either! I mean, it was very nice of you to bring me this, but yeah. It's not my favorite."

"Whoops," he said. "Slip of the tongue. I meant to say I can't stand raw onions. But I guessed you didn't like it, from the way your nose crinkled after that first sip. Why didn't you say anything?"

Lauren couldn't believe he'd set her up like that. She couldn't believe she'd *fallen* for it. "*Chocolate* is not a valid slip of the tongue for *onions*," she said. "And we're only on the first question and you're already cheating! That can't bode well."

"I should've warned you," he said. "I play dirty. May I?"

He reached for her hot chocolate, and she shrugged, letting him take it. Only one question in, and she could already see how this game could be dangerous. His words were ringing in her head—*I play dirty*—and she couldn't help but watch as he lifted her cup to his lips, putting his mouth where hers had been, and took a sip. Right now, if he asked her to tell him a secret she had no idea what filthy fantasy she'd blurt out. She wouldn't be able to think of a compliment that wasn't rated R, wouldn't be able to dare him to do anything without her pulse racing. When he handed his phone to her, she almost dropped it.

"Number five," she said, consulting the list. "Would you rather . . . live in the mountains or near the ocean?"

It sounded like a bland influencer poll on social media, but it was all she could come up with off the top of her head until she got herself back under control. From Asa's expression, he clocked that she was playing it safe, but he didn't call her on it.

"Well, I've done the ocean thing, so I guess the mountains," he said. "But it's not like I live right next to the ocean, so that might be nice. I don't know. They both sound cool."

She rolled her eyes. "You're terrible at this game."

"Mountains."

"Okay," she said, handing him back his phone. "It's—"

"No, ocean. I've always lived at least within an hour of a beach. I think I'd miss it if I didn't."

"So you must be from Florida originally, then."

"Born and raised," he said. "My dad's a pastor in Hernando County. My sister lives here in Orlando, though."

Lauren wanted to ask him more about his family, but something in his face had closed off, like he'd already said more than he meant to. She didn't know the rules of the game. Were follow-up questions allowed? But then she thought about her own past and decided, no. Better not to set *that* precedent.

They went back and forth a few times, clearly taking it easy on each other. Lauren got *Ask me anything* and Asa only asked her if she'd ever ended up ordering those cat-print pants; Asa got *I can't stand* again and revealed that he hated reading *The Scarlet Letter* in high school.

"The story itself sounds so good," he said. "So much drama with Hester and Dim-dude or whatever that guy's name was. And the symbols! Everything's a symbol and I'm sure it's brilliant, but I felt like I couldn't understand an actual god-damn word of it."

Lauren laughed, even though she felt like she was already starting to understand something about Asa. He often played down his intelligence, pretended stuff was over his head when she knew full well he was just as smart as anyone else. If she'd ever thought him a slacker, it was due at least in some part to the fact that he seemed to *want* people to see him that way.

Her next turn yielded a six, and she turned the phone to show him so he wouldn't think she was making it up just to fish for a compliment. "You don't have to," she said.

"I want to." His gaze raked over her slowly, from the top of her head to the toes of her shoes. She resisted the urge to check to make sure her hair wasn't all messed up, that she didn't have a mustache of hot chocolate on her face. She'd been sitting back in her office chair with her legs crossed, and only now did she realize the position made the swingy red skirt of her dress ride up a little on her thigh—not enough to be close to indecent, but definitely showing more skin than she'd realized. She shifted in her seat, pulling down the hem in a way that she hoped wasn't obvious.

Gray eyes were supposed to look cool. But when Asa's gaze returned to hers, his looked anything but.

Eventually, he cleared his throat. "I really admire that you took such care with that family's picture, in the Snow Globe."

Lauren blinked at him, unsure at first what he was even talking about. Already that felt like a lifetime ago. She had no idea what she'd expected him to say—had been holding her breath, waiting to see what it might be—but she never thought he'd go back to such a random event from last week. She felt oddly disappointed.

"It was just a photo," she said.

"Yeah, maybe. But like you said—it's a memory. And you wanted to make sure they had a good one."

She shrugged. "I don't have many pictures of myself, especially from when I was a kid. That's probably why I put more stock in them than I should."

"What about school photos? Those horrible ones where you can pay extra to have a jewel-toned background."

No one had been around to spend money on wallet-sized mementos throughout the years, much less shell out extra funds to change the color of the backdrop. She'd known that so well she hadn't even bothered bringing the envelopes of photos home, scared that if she forgot to bring them back they'd try to charge her anyway.

"Nope," she said. "Not even those."

He was quiet for a moment, and she was about to hand him his phone, just to keep the game moving and change the subject. But then he said, "I would always do the same goofy face in mine. Drove my mom crazy. I swear I wasn't doing it on purpose, but it was like every time a camera was pointed on me from ages five to sixteen, my facial muscles automatically twitched into this weird dopey smile."

"Let's see it."

"It feels like you should have to random-number-generate your way to this kind of gold," Asa said. "But I'll give this one to you for free, just because. The face went something like this . . ."

His eyes widened, his mouth stretching in what looked like half shock-surprise, half manic grin. It was so unexpected that Lauren actually choked on her own spit and ended up coughing through her laughter. Then, just when she'd started to recover, he did it again and she was back to a fit of giggles. It was several minutes before she was able to settle down.

"There's no way you weren't doing that on purpose," she said. "Nobody's face does that naturally."

"Maybe it's like the old urban legend, and my face got stuck that way."

"But only when a camera came out."

"Defense mechanism."

She giggled again, glancing down when she felt a buzz against her ankle. Her first thought, inexplicably, was that it was coming from Asa's phone that she still held in her hand. But that device had been idle so long his lock screen was already back up—a group selfie of him with his three housemates, clearly taken at the same time as the one Kiki had sent her of all of them at the beach. She set his phone down on her desk and reached into her purse to check hers.

There was a text from Kiki from over an hour ago—how's it going?!? with a string of fire and eggplant emojis. Then there was a text from Daniel that had just come in—You ok?

Well. That was kind of nice. She hadn't told him the complete story about being stuck inside Cold World—she hadn't wanted to look silly, or risk him telling Dolores and their dinner getting ruined anyway. So despite her bravado to Asa, she hadn't really expected Daniel to follow up in any way and come to their rescue. But here he was, texting to make sure she was okay after she'd told him she wasn't able to come to the dinner. She could easily reply with something like Not okay, actually—stuck inside Cold World! She could ask him to come. She could ask him to call with the alarm code.

Instead, she swiped to answer the text message, hesitating slightly before typing All good! Thanks! She added a smiley face at the last second, and sent it off.

"What's up?" Asa asked.

"Nothing," she said, feeling a little guilty as she slid her phone back in her purse. "It's your turn."

Chapter

TWELVE

NOT FOR A MINUTE DID ASA BUY THAT THE TEXT LAUREN had received had been about "nothing." It was almost midnight, for one thing, and the only person he knew she was expecting any communication from was Daniel. But if he'd texted to say he couldn't make it out, Asa wasn't going to complain. He found that he didn't want this party to break up. Not when it was just getting fun.

"Contest," Asa said, after the random number generator showed him an eight. The arm-wrestling idea wasn't half-bad—the prospect of holding hands with Lauren and sitting in such close proximity definitely had its appeal. But he had a pretty big advantage, and something told him Lauren didn't like participating in competitions where she didn't have a high chance of winning.

He glanced around her office, suddenly seizing on another idea. "Do you know where the storage space is?"

"In the scary back room?" Lauren asked. "It's not like I have any reason to go there."

"There's a bin of leftover Christmas decorations . . ." He stopped himself short, getting to his feet. "Just follow me."

He led her through the narrow hallway to the rear of the warehouse space, turning on his phone's flashlight when they got to the back area. Even he had to admit it was a *little* scary to be there when the building was so dark and silent. When they got to the storage space, he flicked the wall switch on to fill the room with light.

"See those?" He gestured toward the bin he'd been referencing, which had been left open, decorations draped carelessly over the sides when employees had rooted through it. He'd been one of those employees, tasked with helping to decorate the lobby area, so he couldn't judge anyone too harshly for the way it had been left. "I'm going to set a timer on my phone for three minutes. That's how long we have to gather materials and decorate your office. Whoever has the better display wins."

"Who judges *better*?"

"Me. You've gotta admit, I'm the expert here."

"That seems biased. And what's the prize?"

He grinned. "Bragging rights."

"That's hardly—"

He hit the *start* button on his phone. "Go!"

She may have been about to protest, but that didn't stop her from practically elbowing him out of the way to get to the bin. She scooped items into her arms with little care for what they were or how they might fit together, and when her arms were so full she couldn't possibly grab anything else, she made a beeline for the door, dropping bits of tinsel and red velvet bows in her wake.

Asa was laughing too hard to be quite as effective in gathering his materials, but he managed to snag a string of lights, some ornaments, and a stuffed polar bear. By the time he got to her office, she was already lining the top of her filing cabinet with a garland, adding more of the red velvet bows every few inches.

He got to work on the fake plant in the corner, stringing it with the lights and adding ornaments with big enough loops of string to fit around the plastic leaves. Just as the alarm went off, he nestled the polar bear into her garland display, and she threw a bunch of tinsel into the air. Pieces of it were still floating to the ground as he reached in his pocket to turn off the radar tone blaring from his phone.

"Jesus," he said. "Haven't you ever heard *less is more?*"

"I told you. I'm competitive."

There was tinsel in her hair. He reached over to pluck it out, letting his fingers rest in the soft strands a few seconds longer than the action called for. "Apparently."

She was still breathing harder than usual from all the energetic activity of their contest. Maybe that was why her lips were parted as she watched him twist the silver tinsel between his fingers, but all he could think was that he really, *really* wanted to kiss her.

"So?" she prompted.

"Hmm?"

"Who won?"

He placed the tinsel delicately on the polar bear's lap, like it was holding on to its own decoration to participate in the next contest. "I'm the clear winner, showing tasteful restraint with a nod to tradition in my decoration of a plastic Christmas ficus. But ultimately *you're* the winner for every day you work inside such a festive office."

"I knew it was rigged."

He switched off the harsh fluorescent overhead light, so the office was lit instead by the Christmas lights on the fake plant in the corner. He dropped down to sit on the carpet next to it, and after a moment Lauren sank down next to him, tucking her legs under her.

He unlocked his phone and handed it to her. "Your turn."

"Number four," she said, biting her lip. "Tell me a secret."

He leaned his head back on the wall, closing his eyes. "My passcode is just my house number, with the first two digits repeated. So one-six-eight-two-one-six. Now you can get into my phone without me."

"That's not a secret."

He cracked one eye open to look at her. "Do you go around telling people your personal security information?"

"Well, no," she admitted. "But you know what I mean. It's not like that number *means* anything. It's not the number of stuffed animals you slept with as a kid or the number of times you got blackout drunk and tried to jump off a roof."

"*One* stuffed animal," he said, "for the record. A dalmatian named Sparky my sister got me for Christmas when I was four. Unfortunately, I left Sparky at an Olive Garden when I was nine. And I've never gotten blackout drunk and jumped off the roof, but presumably it would only take one time?"

"Okay," she said. "Point taken."

Unconsciously, he rubbed his chest, the area above his heart where he saw the same four-digit number every morning when he looked in the mirror. "You asked me about my tattoos once," he said. "The truth is that most of them don't really mean anything—they're just stuff I thought looked cool. Some of them I even got on a whim, or a dare." He pointed to a small illustration of a flying saucer on his forearm, done in a solid black outline with some simple shading. "Like this one. Elliot had to go to this convention to cover a story, and there was an artist doing some flash work on the main floor. Elliot wanted to know who would get something as permanent as a tattoo that way, I said why not, they dared me to do it, and half an hour later I had this on my arm."

Lauren was looking at his arms with such focused attention now that he felt goose bumps prickle across his skin. And he generally ran warm—it was the reason why he rarely bothered with long-sleeved shirts even with the air conditioning running so cold inside. It wasn't just so he could show off his arms, whatever Lauren might think. Although with the way she was looking at him now, it gave him further reason not to cover up.

"You never have any regrets?" she asked.

"Nah."

"I guess by now you have so many, it probably doesn't feel like such a big deal. Was it hard to choose your first one?"

He rubbed at his chest again, thinking back to the tattoo parlor he'd walked into on his eighteenth birthday, the less than ten minutes it had taken to mark his body with the only tattoo he did regret. "I got the numbers six-five-four-three tattooed right here," he said, poking a finger so hard into the muscle around his heart that it almost hurt. "That was the number of days I lived in my parents' house. When I figured that out, it seemed significant somehow, that the number so perfectly descended like that. I don't know."

She was watching his face now, instead of looking at his arms, and it felt like she could see right through him down to his broken, shitty inside. "Was that a homesick kind of tribute, or more of a newfound independence kind of thing?"

"Neither?" He gave a bitter laugh. "Both? When I was seventeen, one of my dad's parishioners saw me making out with my boyfriend. Like I told you, my dad is a pastor, and while I know there are churches that are LGBTQ-friendly, let's just say that my dad's church was . . . definitely not. Long story short, we had a big fight, stuff was said, and he told me to pack my bags and get out of his house."

It had been a while since Asa had allowed himself to think about that last day. He'd come home from school to find his dad waiting for him at the kitchen table. His dad would often sit there with his books and papers, when he was preparing a sermon or working on church business, but it was never a great sign when he sat there with nothing in front of him but his hands, clenched together on the table. Those hands had never been raised against Asa, but he feared his father in other ways—the way his booming voice could rattle the windows, the way his disapproval could swallow you up like a sinkhole.

His father had given him the chance to deny it, even with the photographic evidence. Sometimes, late at night if Asa couldn't sleep, he still wondered how things might have gone differently if he'd just done that. Said that he didn't know what the parishioner was talking about, he hadn't even been *near* that Burger King, much less sucking face with some random dude. He had a feeling his father would've accepted it—not because he believed the explanation, deep down, but because it was easier to sweep the truth under the rug and move on as if nothing had happened.

Instead, he'd owned up to it. The worst part—the part he *never* let himself think about, no matter how late it was—had been the rush of exhilaration and power he'd felt at finally getting the words out. He'd told his dad to his face that he was bi, that his boyfriend's name was Mark, and that he'd love to bring Mark home for dinner to introduce him to the family.

Any confidence had been woefully naive, and short-lived.

Asa's father had said a lot of ugly things that Asa tried not to let take up space in his head anymore, although the general refrain of *no son of mine* was always there, pulsing like a heartbeat. Asa's mother had been there, lingering in the kitchen. He'd cried, she'd cried, but she hadn't intervened. An hour later, Asa had two bags packed and was on Mark's doorstep. That relationship hadn't lasted long—he and Mark were never destined to be anything more than a fun couple of months, and he could tell Mark's parents were sick of having him in the house—but luckily by then Asa had landed the job at Cold World and could rent his own place.

"I'm sorry," Lauren said now, her soft voice pulling him back up from the memories. "That must've been really hard, to hear that from your own father. You deserved to be treated with love and support, not kicked out."

"It's funny," he said, "because I say the same thing all the time to these teens I counsel through a crisis text line once a week. They're twelve, thirteen, sixteen years old, and wondering how to come out or how to ask their parents about transitioning or what to do about bullying at school. And I try to listen to their problems, validate their experiences, remind them that they're worthy. But sometimes I wish I could get on a direct line with their parents or their peers or whoever, and just say, do you have any idea how much this kid *cares*? How much they internalize your words, how much they want to please you, how much thought they've given to trying to figure out who they are and how they fit into the world? Can't you just for one fucking second *listen* to them, and tell them that they're worthy, so that they hear it from *you*?"

His eyes were burning, and he scrubbed his hand over his face, trying to unclench his jaw. "Obviously, there are also lots of people out there who have beautiful stories of support and acceptance. We don't tend to see as many of them through the crisis line, so my data set is a little skewed here. Elliot's parents have a cake delivered to the house every year on the anniversary of when Elliot came out to them. And it's Publix buttercream, so you know that shit's real love."

Lauren smiled. "You're really fortunate to have found Elliot, and Kiki, and John. They seem like great friends."

"The best," Asa said. "Whose turn is it? I've lost track."

"Yours," she said. "But we can stop, if you want. It's late."

He'd already tapped the button for a new randomly generated number, and he held up his phone to show her the six on the screen. "And miss a chance to get a compliment? No way. Tell me something good about myself."

She compressed her bottom lip with her teeth, as if thinking. He didn't know if she even realized how close she was sitting to him by now. If he turned at all they'd be practically nose to nose.

"Don't be so quick with it," he said dryly. "I'll get a big head."

"You smell really good," she blurted, then covered her face with her hands, like she needed to physically retreat from the words. But he wasn't about to let her off that easily. He lifted his arm, giving it a sniff.

"Do I?"

"It's your soap or something," she said. "It's not even really a compliment to *you*. More like a compliment to the products you use. Tell me what kind of soap it is and I'll leave the company a really nice online review."

"I know that trick. You want the name so you can buy it for yourself and smell me all the time."

"I'm not going to *buy* it—"

"You want to carve a little soap doll of me. It's sick. I refuse to feed this obsession."

"More like a voodoo doll, and I know right where I'd stick the first pin."

Her eyes widened, her mouth in an O, like she only just heard what she'd said and was shocked by her own words. He mirrored the expression right back at her, although he was laughing.

"Damn," he said. "Okay. I'll behave my good-smelling self."

She rolled her eyes, although a smile tugged at her own mouth. "I knew I should've just told you I admired your ice skating skills."

"Whoa." He turned toward her, holding his hands up in a gesture of *wait just a minute there*. "Is that a slam on *my* earlier compliment? Because that was genuine, I'll have you know. I thought it was really cool that you took the time to give that family a perfect memory. Very un-robot-like."

"It was quite a nice compliment," she said with a tilt of her chin. "I appreciated it."

But he thought he understood. Her compliment to him had left her feeling vulnerable. It wasn't just about *him* but about her *reaction* to him. He had plenty of those kinds of compliments, too. He just hadn't known if she would welcome one.

Well, here went nothing.

"You look incredibly hot in that dress," he said.

"Really?" Her voice pitched up in a squeak.

He'd been aiming for a matter-of-fact tone but didn't quite know if he'd achieved it. If he were talking about a painting in a museum, or a sunset over the beach, he'd be able to talk about it without getting weird, right? He should be able to tell Lauren how the vibrant red of the dress looked against her pale skin, how sexy her delicate ankle bone was where she'd crossed her bare feet, how her mouth . . . her perfect mouth . . .

Was saying something. He mentally shook himself and tried to tune back in.

"I feel stupid for even wearing it," she said, smoothing down the red skirt. "I know tonight was never going to be a date. Not really."

"Lauren." At this point it wasn't even about playing a game, it was about helping her see the facts that should've been in neon lights right in front of her face. "You're beautiful. You're always beautiful. Yesterday I would've said your best bet to get Daniel's head out of his ass long enough to notice it would've been to glue his phone to your forehead. But tonight . . ." He let his gaze drop to the small swell of her breasts under the red fabric, the slight gap that opened up between the neckline and her skin when she took a shallow breath. When he looked up again, her eyes were two bright, black sparks.

"Tonight I would say that your best bet is definitely that dress."

Chapter

THIRTEEN

YOU'RE ALWAYS BEAUTIFUL. ASA HAD DEFINITELY OUT-
done himself with the compliments, and it hadn't even been
his turn to give any. But it was the throwaway tone to his
voice when he'd said that particular one that made her actually believe it.

And there was that flare in his eyes as he'd looked her
over. It was hard not to believe that, too.

She was attracted to Asa Williamson. She didn't know exactly when it had happened—probably sometime around
when she was sniffing him in the break room—but there it
was. And for the first time, she thought maybe there was a
chance that he reciprocated the feeling.

Then again, she'd misjudged this kind of thing before.

"Why didn't you kiss me?" she asked.

Immediately, she wished there were a randomly generated
number that would allow her to shove the words back down
her throat. Especially when his eyes searched her face, a line
creasing his forehead. He had no idea what she was talking
about. He probably didn't even remember. He'd blocked it
from his memory . . .

"I didn't think you'd want me to," he said.

She swallowed. Now that she'd gone this far out on this limb, she supposed she might as well inch out a little more. "There was mistletoe," she said. "It's like . . . a rule."

"You never struck me as a stickler for Christmas tradition."

He was right, of course. The year before, she'd railed against Secret Santa, of all things. She couldn't be surprised when he then assumed she'd want nothing to do with something as silly and inappropriate as kissing under the mistletoe. She was sorry she'd brought it up.

"I'm a stickler for most things," she said, trying to keep her voice light. "In case you hadn't noticed. Like I just realized I broke the rules of our game by asking that question, so please. Disregard it."

"What if I *want* to regard it?"

Lauren's gaze met his before skittering away. She had no idea what he meant by that, was scared to even consider the possibilities. Time to climb down from this tree.

"It's seriously late," she said. "And we both have work tomorrow . . . which is a little ironic, since we're currently *at* work."

He rubbed his hands on his jean-clad thighs. They were sitting close enough that the motion ruffled the hem of her skirt a little, caused it to flip up and reveal the barest extra millimeter of skin. It was such a micro movement, and yet Lauren noticed it. Somehow, she knew Asa had, too.

"You got an unauthorized question," he said, his voice rough. "It's only fair if I get one."

She lifted her chin. "Fine. In the interest of fairness."

"Did you want me to kiss you?"

Don't look at his mouth. Don't look at his mouth. She was trying to keep her cool during this conversation, and it wouldn't work if she saw his lips forming those words. She knew it was useless to deny it outright—why would she have even brought it up in the first place? At the same time, this conversation felt like a minefield, and she was scared to take the next step.

"I thought it would be nice," she said finally, smoothing the crinkled hem of her skirt back down. "It's kind of a nice tradition."

"No," he said, tilting his head, like he was trying to get her attention, or searching her face for an answer to some question. It was impossible not to look up, not to stare at his mouth. There was a small scar on his lower lip, a perfect circle that must've been from a piercing at some point. She watched the corner of his mouth, waiting for it to quirk up, for a sign that he was laughing at her. But for once, he looked completely serious.

"I meant, did you want *me* to kiss you?"

The emphasis on that one word said it all. He wasn't asking if she wanted a generic mistletoe kiss at a holiday party. He was asking if she cared that the kiss came specifically from *him*.

Even a few weeks ago, Lauren would've said of course not. She barely knew Asa Williamson, and what she knew of him made it clear a friendship between them would be unlikely. Anything more than friendship even *more* unlikely. He was well-liked, easygoing, and confident. She was uptight and nervous and shy. He'd probably kissed a dozen people for no reason other than he felt like it, whereas she was always holding back, scared to put herself out there for fear of rejection.

That same instinct told her now that this would all be over if she simply said no, not *you*. It *could've been anyone*, she could say. *You just happened to be there*.

Instead she said one word, which came out more like a sigh. "Yes."

His hand clenched on his knee. She could feel him humming with a low frequency beside her—although maybe that was a projection, an echo of the unbearable tension she felt in her own body. She pressed her thighs together, taking a deep breath to slow her heart rate.

She glanced at him, trying to give him a look like *Well, this is awkward*, but he didn't look capable of cracking his usual joke.

"Let me make it up to you," he said. And then his fingers were at her jaw, tilting her face toward his, and his mouth was on hers.

It started off almost sweet, almost like the kiss they would've had under the mistletoe a year ago in front of all their coworkers. He pressed his lips to hers for the second that would've been appropriate for that kiss, but just when she expected him to pull away, he urged her mouth open with his tongue. He tasted of hot chocolate and courage, and she opened up for him, kissing him back like she wanted both for herself.

His hand was splayed full across her cheek by now, a warm imprint on her skin, and she felt suddenly dizzy at the idea that he was touching her, that she could touch him back. His ink-covered arms, his broad shoulders, the strip of skin where his T-shirt rode up . . . she was greedy for all of it.

But she was too shy to assert herself like that, so she settled for resting her hands lightly on his thighs. The denim was rough beneath her fingertips, and she tried not to press hard enough to feel the heat of him through the fabric. Already her stomach was a swirling flame, licking up into her chest as he deepened the kiss.

"Touch me," he said.

Her hands tightened reflexively. So much for not feeling the heat. "Where?"

He smiled against her mouth. "Anywhere."

She skimmed up his arms, pressing her thumb into the branches of the tree tattoo, letting her fingertips slide under his shirt sleeve to reveal the rest of it. He watched her with a hooded expression, giving a slight shudder when she scraped her nails against the dimple in his shoulder.

"I've never really cared for tattoos," she said, and could've kicked herself. Why would she say something like *that* now?

"Oh yeah?"

She swallowed, giving him a sheepish smile. "I seem to be kind of fixated on yours."

"'S all right," he said. "I don't mind being objectified."

He reached up, lifted the glasses off her face. He folded them gently before placing them on top of the fake moss in the potted ficus. "I've never seen you without your glasses," he said, smoothing her temples with his fingertips.

She let out a small huff of a laugh. "That's because I need them to see."

It was scarier, when they slowed down like this. It gave her time to think about what they were doing, to wonder if they were making a huge mistake. Even if Asa was determined to have a do-over of the mistletoe kiss, surely they were long past that now. She'd have to see him at work tomorrow—later today, technically. She'd have to look him in the eye knowing all the things they'd revealed to each other, all the places their hands had been.

At the same time, she didn't want to stop. They'd only *kissed* and she was aching down to her core, crying out for more of his hands, his mouth . . .

None of this was like Lauren. She wasn't the type to get carried away with passion, and she wasn't the type to make out with a coworker after hours on the floor of her own office.

She *definitely* wasn't the type to straddle that coworker until she was sitting on his lap, but somehow his hands were on her hips and she found herself so close she could see that his eyes were a thin rim of gray around large, black pupils.

He pulled her in for another long, deep kiss. She tugged on the hem of his shirt, and he broke off only long enough to whip it over his head, before returning his mouth to hers. She slid her hands over the bunched muscles in his shoulders, the flat plane of his chest, letting her fingers brush lightly over his nipple. It was an experimental touch, tentative even, but for a minute he leaned his head back against the wall, breathing hard.

"God, Lauren," he said. "You have no idea."

He didn't finish that thought, but she could finish it for him. *You have no idea how good this feels. You have no idea how long I've wanted this.*

He pushed the cardigan down off her shoulders, and for a minute she was trapped like that, her arms at her sides, his hands holding the bunched fabric around her wrists. Then he had her lower lip between his teeth, was sucking at the sensitive skin where her neck curved into her shoulder, was kissing along the swell of her breasts at the neckline of the dangerous red dress.

He pulled her closer, and the motion made her rub along the hard ridge of his erection. He swallowed her gasp with a kiss, but it turned into a moan as she felt the friction of him through the thin cotton of her underwear.

"Asa—" She didn't know what she was asking for, but he released her wrists, his fingers biting into her bare thighs under her dress as he dragged her across him again. This time, the sound she made wasn't like any other she'd made before—halfway between a grunt and a cry.

"Say my name again," he said into her ear. "Please, Lauren."

She'd say whatever he wanted as long as he kept doing *that*. She said it over and over, until the hitch in her breath made the word virtually meaningless. Her hands were on his cheeks, her shoulder in his mouth, and their frantic grinding through clothes was already the most earth-shattering sexual experience she'd ever had.

She arched her hips, pressing into him, and he squeezed his eyes closed like he was in pain. His hands were warm and strong on her hips as he shifted her back a bit.

"That's getting me close," he said. "Sorry. Give me a second."

"Oh." Lauren chewed on her lower lip. "I, uh, don't have anything."

"What?" His eyes hadn't totally lost their glazed look, and he pulled her back on top of him.

"Like a condom," she said, embarrassed that the word could still make her blush when she was here, doing *this*.

"Neither do I," he said, grinning at her as he pressed a hard, hot kiss to her mouth. "Not exactly how I thought I'd spend my night. But we can still do a lot without one."

"Yeah, but," she said, trying to get the words out between his kisses. "You said you were getting close. But since we can't, you know . . ."

He pulled back, his brow lowered as his gaze searched hers. "This isn't just about me wanting to get off," he said. "You know that, right?"

"No, I know—" She wasn't even aware of what she was saying at this point, she just wanted to go back to when they were kissing and he wasn't looking at her like she was defective.

"For that, I would've just jerked off in a bathroom stall

like I'd planned." From the quirk of his mouth, she could tell that he was deliberately trying to shock her. But it was also like he was trying to make her laugh, trying to make her relax.

And damned if it didn't work. "Gross," she said, biting back a smile. "At work?"

"It's not like I'd do it *on the clock*," he said, pressing a kiss to just below her ear. "But when I was staring down a night of being trapped in a building with a very beautiful . . ." He kissed her cheek, and she let her eyes flutter closed. ". . . very stubborn . . ." He kissed the corner of her bottom lip. ". . . very *unattainable* woman . . ."

She hummed against his mouth. "Mm-hmm?"

"Extenuating circumstances," he said. "I think I can be forgiven for the impulse."

"Well," she said, her voice a little unsteady as he burrowed his face into the curve of her neck. "I'm glad it didn't come to that."

She buried her fingers in his blue hair, inhaling the scent of him. He lowered her gently until she was lying on the floor, using her discarded cardigan as a makeshift pillow for her head. He ran his hand over her breasts, her ribs, her stomach. There was something erotic about still being fully clothed, about seeing his bare chest next to the siren red of her dress.

"What about you?" he asked, bunching up the material of her skirt around her thighs—not lifting it all the way, but enough that her breath caught.

"I wasn't planning on masturbating in the bathroom," she managed to choke out, and he gave a little laugh.

"No," he said. He brushed his knuckles over the pulsing core of her, the sensation through her underwear making her hips buck. "I meant, what gets you off?"

She licked her lips. She couldn't focus enough to answer the question when he was touching her like that. "It's okay," she said. "I usually take a long time . . ."

"What about this?" He pressed the pad of his thumb against the damp fabric of her underwear, rubbing in a hard circle. "Or this?" He scraped his nails lightly over her slit, which sent a spasm through her body like she'd been electrocuted.

"All of it," she managed to gasp out.

By the time his hand finally ventured under her panties, she was already wet and halfway there. He rubbed her clit in agonizingly patient circles, until the pressure building inside her was almost too much to stand. She reached down to grasp his wrist, looking down at her fingers wrapped around the lean muscle of his forearm, his hand inside her underwear. Then she looked back up at him.

He was watching her, a serious expression on his face. "Do you want me to stop?"

She felt like she was about to come apart. The idea of doing that in front of Asa . . . doing that *because* of Asa . . . it scared her. But she also couldn't imagine a world where she told him to stop. She shook her head.

"What do you want?" He slid one finger in her hot, tight center, and she clenched around him, still holding on to his wrist. "This?"

"Oh god," she said. "Yes."

It was the last word she was capable of speaking as he stroked her with one finger, then two, harder and faster until all the building pressure inside her crested and broke over her like a wave. Her whole body shuddered and Asa's fingers were still inside her, as if waiting out her body's response, which felt like it would last forever. She knew it wouldn't, knew eventually he'd have to withdraw, but she found herself wanting to delay that moment as long as possible.

It *did* normally take her longer to reach orgasm, even when masturbating. And yet it had immediately felt different with Asa. Like she was more in the moment, like there was no room in her mind for overthinking when there was so much to *feel*.

Aftershocks were still tingling through her when Asa lay down next to her, propping himself up on one elbow. He traced her collarbone, causing her to shiver. Her rose pendant must've gotten flipped around, and he fixed it, smoothing it until it laid flat.

"What's the story with the necklace?"

She reached up for it reflexively. She was still trying to catch her breath. "My necklace?"

"You always wear it."

The ridges of the rose petals were comforting against her thumb. It had been a long time since she'd given in to the nervous habit of rubbing the pendant like a talisman, but the old comfort was there. "My mom gave it to me," she said. "For my first day of first grade. We had a thing where we'd pick a flower for the year, and called it good luck if we spotted it out in the wild. Rose was for first grade, lotus for second, then violet, then iris . . ."

He smiled, his hand brushing hers as he reached to admire the pendant. "Then what?"

Iris had been for fourth grade. By the middle of that school year, she'd been pulled away from her mother and placed in another school on the other side of the county. They should've stacked the luck decks better. Chosen a common wildflower, a hibiscus, an azalea.

Asa could roll right back into conversation, as though those same fingers currently twisting the pendant hadn't been inside her only a few minutes before. She'd thought it was kind of hot, the way they'd never even gotten all the way undressed, the scratch of the carpet on her shoulder blades as he'd brought her to orgasm.

But now she was realizing that *he'd* never even finished. Maybe this had been part of his plan all along, to loosen her up and show her a good time. Wasn't he always mentioning that? How she needed to learn how to unwind and have more fun?

She didn't really think it had been planned. Or she didn't *want* to think so. It was hard to know the difference. All she knew was that *she'd* definitely never intended for any of it to happen.

She sat up, pushing back against the wall. Her legs still felt a little wobbly, a delicious soreness between her thighs reminding her of what they'd just done. In her *office*.

God, what had she been thinking?

"Where are my glasses?" she asked, feeling naked and empty without them on her face.

He reached over and retrieved them from the potted plant, handing them to her. That's right. She remembered him putting them there now. She'd been touched by how much care he'd taken with them, and the way he'd folded her sweater to make her a pillow. There'd been a tenderness to those gestures that had to mean he cared about her at least a little, right?

Asa is fickle. Wasn't that what Kiki had warned her just earlier that night? Maybe what had happened between them wasn't about pity, maybe it wasn't even about some stupid random number generator game, but whatever it was, it had a shelf life of a couple months, tops. And what then?

"I'm going to freshen up," she said, getting to her feet and trying to avoid eye contact with Asa without making it look like she was trying to avoid eye contact.

He stood, too, still wearing only his jeans, which sat low enough on his hips that she could see a strip of his hunter green underwear, the light dusting of hair that led down to his . . . well. Now she needed to avoid looking at his face or anywhere else on his body, so she directed her next comment to somewhere in the vicinity of the stuffed polar bear on the filing cabinet.

"And then we should try to figure out a way to get some sleep?" she said. "I may just try putting my head down at my desk . . . Dolores' office is probably open if you wanted to do the same."

"Lauren," he said.

She gathered her purse, making sure her phone was inside. "I'll be right back," she said. She knew the phrase was relative. She'd be gone however long it took her to regain control, and at that moment, it didn't feel like there were enough minutes in the world.

Chapter

FOURTEEN

SOMEWHERE, HE'D FUCKED UP. HE JUST COULDN'T TELL where.

He'd thought Lauren was with him every step of the way. She'd been shy at first, tentative about touching him, but he'd had no doubts that she wanted him just as much as he wanted her.

He'd been shocked when she brought up the kiss. He'd be lying if he said he hadn't thought about it, since it happened. But she'd seemed so mortified at the time that it had been clear to him that the only way forward was to pretend like it never happened, put it in a box somewhere under the bed and only bring it out during the occasional night when he couldn't sleep and wondered if she'd meant anything by it. He'd never imagined she might have a box of her own, that the memory of that kiss was more accessible than he thought.

And then tonight, when she'd said his *name*. He didn't know if she realized it, but Lauren had never called him by his name to his face. Not once. Until she'd written that note on his fridge, he'd sometimes wondered if there was a chance she didn't even *know* it.

Hearing her say it, and like *that*, her voice all breathy and low . . . well, he couldn't think about it too much, or he'd have to take care of himself in the bathroom after all.

It had made his blood start to boil, the way she'd rushed to worrying about his satisfaction while writing off her own. It made him wonder if that was what she'd been taught to expect from sex, if previous boyfriends had gotten what they wanted and then left her to do the rest herself. It made him want to take his time with her.

He'd thought time was one thing that they had. He wasn't oblivious—he knew that they were in a strange bubble tonight, that whatever was building here might not survive the light of day. But he'd had this vision of getting blankets from the gift shop and hunkering down in her office, finding more ways to get to know each other. He wouldn't have minded just snuggling together under the blankets, making a corny joke about doing it for body heat in Cold World or some shit like that.

Now, something told him she was *not* in the mood to cuddle. She wouldn't even look at him when she'd left.

Still, they *would* need to sleep. He decided to head to the bathroom to wash up and get ready for bed, and then maybe he'd grab those blankets from the gift shop after all. He might need double if they were going to make two beds. Add them to the tab.

BY THE TIME LAUREN CAME BACK, HE'D SET UP TWO MAKESHIFT sleeping areas—one behind her desk for her, with a folded blanket for a mattress and another one on top, a larger stuffed animal from the gift shop serving as a pillow. He'd made up his own similar arrangement just inside the doorway to the office. Not that he expected any nocturnal visitor—security or otherwise—but he figured it was better for him to be the first point of contact.

"I hope you don't mind," he said. "But I really don't want to sleep in Dolores' office. That would feel a little weird."

"Oh," she said, glancing around. "No, that's fine. This looks really . . . Thanks for setting it up."

"I'm also going to sleep in just my T-shirt and boxers," he said. "If you wanted to strip down, I could give you some privacy . . . or we could get something from the gift shop."

"I'm okay," she said. She had a handful of silky black fabric balled up in her hand, and he realized it must be her bra. Catching his gaze on it, she flushed and crossed her arms over her chest, where her nipples had pebbled against the red fabric of her dress in the cold office.

He cleared his throat, rubbing the back of his neck while he tried to look anywhere but at her. "I set my phone alarm for six," he said. "I think security comes by around seven to do a morning sweep and disable the alarm, so that should give us time."

She pulled her own phone out and tapped it a few times, cutting off the loud trill of her own alarm when it started to sound. "I set mine, too," she said. "Just in case. We don't want to be . . ."

She didn't finish that sentence, but he could imagine what she was going to say. They didn't want to be found sleeping together on the floor of her office. Even if they wouldn't be *together*, per se. He didn't particularly relish the idea of explaining all of this to their boss, either, but the dismissal in her voice still made something in his chest ache.

They both climbed into their makeshift beds, and he reached over to unplug the Christmas lights wrapped around the fake plant, leaving them with only the ambient glow from the lobby outside.

Her voice cut through the dark. "Asa?"

He closed his eyes. Eventually, he'd get used to hearing her say his name. But not yet. "Yeah?"

"Thank you for tonight," she said in a rush, like she had to get the words out before she swallowed them back up. "Not just, you know, but . . . I really enjoyed playing the random number generator game with you."

"Me, too." He hesitated, wanting to address the elephant in the room, which she apparently wouldn't even refer to directly. It would kill him if she regretted it.

But she swooped in before he could figure out what to say. "Do you think we could keep it all between us? Like *What happens at Cold World stays at Cold World?*"

He hadn't exactly planned on kissing and telling. Although he probably would've run it by Kiki at some point—not all the details, but enough to try to find out what she might've heard from Lauren. But he also knew that what Lauren was really asking was whether they could leave this whole night behind in its bubble, and move forward like it had never happened.

"If that's what you want," he said.

"Thank you," she said around a yawn. "God, I'm going to be wrecked tomorrow."

"Yeah," he said. "Me, too."

Eventually, he heard her breathing even out, and he knew she must've fallen asleep. It was a while before he joined her.

WRECKED WAS THE UNDERSTATEMENT OF THE YEAR. HE'D CON-vinced Lauren that he should stay and explain everything to the security guard, and later to Dolores, after Lauren had the chance to slip out the front door. It would be foolish—and practically impossible—to try to pretend like there hadn't been anyone there that night. But there was no need for both of them to get in trouble, and the explanation was a lot cleaner if Asa just talked about his plan to hook up the faux snow machine and how it had gone awry.

They had a narrow window to pull it off. The security guard would need to open the building and disable the alarm, doing a quick walkthrough before locking it back up and leaving it for when Dolores arrived soon after. Asa and Lauren hid behind the front counter, waiting for the series of beeps that indicated the alarm had been turned off before she'd dart outside.

"You should just take the day off," he said. At least his shift didn't start until two, so he was planning on going home first and taking a big nap. Lauren only had enough time to go home to shower and change, and then was planning on turning right back around and coming into work.

"You heard Dolores at that meeting. No last-minute vacation requests until after the holidays."

He frowned. "You can still call out sick. You need sleep."

"I'll be fine," she said, then raised her eyebrows at him when the chirp of the alarm sounded from the office area where they'd spent the night. "That's my cue. I'll see you later?"

She said it like a question, but of course they would see each other. At work, if nowhere else. He thought again of how much he wanted to see her somewhere else, how decadent it would feel just to sit across from her in a coffee shop.

She started to rise, but he pulled her back down, pressing a quick, hard kiss to her mouth. She blinked at him, a little dazed, and he hoped the expression on his face was the wolfish grin he was going for.

"What happens at Cold World, right?"

She gave him a shaky smile. "Right."

He stood, his hands in his pockets, to watch her as she sprinted through the doors and out to the parking lot, her red skirt swinging. There was probably no need for her to worry about getting out of there *that* fast—the security guard was still somewhere back in the offices. Asa's lips twitched as Lauren started her ignition and peeled out like she was driving the getaway car in a bank heist. He would definitely tease her about that later.

If he was allowed to. He didn't quite know the rules.

"Sir?" The security guard's voice came from behind him, firm and authoritative but a little confused. Asa supposed it was one benefit to his distinctive blue hair—the chances were good that the security guard would at least vaguely recognize him as an employee. "You're not supposed to be in here."

Asa turned around, holding his hands up in mock surrender. "I can explain," he said.

"OKAY, OKAY," KIKI SAID LATER, WHEN HE'D FINISHED DE-scribing the chew-out he'd gotten from Dolores for the third time. Their boss had been understandably upset that he'd stayed late without permission, that he'd exposed the building to possible security risks, and that he'd bought out their inventory of Cold World blankets. At least he'd also stayed to put the Snow Globe back to rights, feeling sheepish when Dolores mentioned that the problem with the faux snow machine probably had to do with the fact that he'd plugged it into a nonworking outlet, and the next time he did a *sanctioned* test of the equipment, he should use the outlet below.

Asa had thought about staying long enough to meet up with Lauren in the break room when she got in. He would've let her make her plain, boring coffee first, before he tainted the machine with his. He might even have been tempted to tell her she'd been right about the outlet.

But he could tell Dolores wasn't *too* upset with him, because she'd summarily kicked him out and told him to get some rest. She'd also switched his first duty to working the gift shop with Kiki, which was a much less strenuous gig than supervising the ice skating rink like he'd been originally assigned.

He'd filled Kiki in on his overnighter in the building, followed by his lectures from both the security guard and Dolores once she'd come in. He'd conveniently excised Lauren from all of it, which made the story about half as long and nowhere near as interesting.

"So what did you *do* all night?" Kiki asked, leaning against the counter.

Images flashed through his brain. Lauren, laughing at his goofy school picture face. Lauren, with tinsel in her hair. The flushed, wild-eyed look on Lauren's face when she'd grabbed him by the wrist and urged him to keep going.

He took a deep breath, trying to focus on what he'd been doing. Pens. The novelty pens by the cash register had been rifled through and placed back in all the wrong places, and he'd been going to sort them back into their neat cubbies.

"Just hung around," he said.

"Don't quote *Home Alone* at me, you little shit," Kiki said. "Why didn't you *tell* me you were stuck at Cold World when we talked last night?"

He shrugged. "There was nothing you could've done about it. And like I said, I didn't want to disrupt Dolores' dinner. It all worked—"

He broke off as Lauren came into the gift shop. He'd seen her a couple of times out in the lobby, heading back and forth from her office to the break room, only a flash of her navy cardigan, the bounce of her dark hair. But now here she was, walking right into the gift shop, heading straight toward him . . .

. . . with Daniel right behind her. What the fuck was *he* doing there?

Daniel rested his forearms against the counter, giving Kiki a practiced smile while completely ignoring Asa next to him. "We're on complimentary gift-wrap duty this afternoon," he said. "I've never wrapped a present in my life, so you'll have to show me the ropes."

Asa's gaze slid to Lauren's, and she gave a defensive shake of her head. "Part of the initiative for us to work in other departments," she said. "Learn more about Cold World."

Ah. So what she was really saying was that, in a roundabout way, Asa had no one but himself to blame for the teeth-gritting presence of Daniel Alvarez in the shop. It had been his original idea, after all, when he'd wanted to get Lauren to have to work the Snow Globe.

"We're not busy right now," Asa said. They weren't busy at *all*. It was only three thirty, a relatively dead hour before the after-work crowd started trickling in. He hadn't seen a customer in at least twenty minutes. "We could get by with one person on wrapping duty. Lauren, if you have more experience, maybe you'd . . ."

Daniel cut him off. "My mother was very specific. She wanted both of us to work together. Just show us where to set up and we'll be good to go."

What was Dolores up to? It hadn't made much sense to Asa to have him work the gift shop with Kiki in the first place, although he'd been grateful for the change. But it really didn't make any sense to have *two* people on gift-wrap duty, especially two people who presumably had much higher-level tasks to work on.

He glanced at Lauren, hoping for a clue, but she was fiddling with the pen display. Trust her to find the one powder blue pen he'd accidentally left behind with the silver ones.

Kiki reached under the counter, pulling out two rolls of metallic wrapping paper, two rolls of tape, and some scissors. "You'll have to share," she said. "We only have the one pair of scissors. Asa, you're the expert—want to show them how to do it?"

"It's wrapping a present," he said. "Not brain surgery."

But he grabbed an empty box meant for one of their display snow globes, flipping it facedown onto an unfurled sheet of candy-cane-striped paper. He grabbed a Sharpie from under the counter but didn't bother to uncap it. "On a real present, you'll black out or remove any price first," he said. "Put the best side of the box on the flat of the paper so the uglier taped underside ends up on the bottom of the gift. Cut the paper—" He sliced the scissors through the metallic wrapping, a sensation that always gave him a shoot of satisfaction whenever they slid right through. "Fold it under at the edges to create a clean seam, leave enough paper at the ends to fold into neat triangles but not so much that it gets crumpled, and if you've done it right you should only need three pieces of tape, one here—" He pressed a long piece down the center seam before adding two shorter pieces to each of the triangles folded into the sides. "And one each here. Voilà, the present is wrapped."

Lauren was staring at him like he'd just demonstrated advanced necromancy.

"Why do you black out the price?" Daniel asked.

Asa shifted his attention to him with some difficulty. "Because it's the class move, Daniel."

"And why do we wrap at all? Gift bags would be easier and more efficient."

"Wrapping is more cost-effective," Lauren pointed out. "A roll of that paper probably costs as much as a single bag, and we can get several gifts out of it."

A couple days ago, the human cash register joke would've written itself. But now he didn't know where he stood with Lauren, didn't know if humor would move him forward or set him back. "More importantly," he said, directing his words more to her than to Daniel, "gift-wrapping shows a certain amount of care. It shows that you took time and effort with your present, that you thought of the recipient. That you wanted them to have that moment when their pulse quickens, right before they tear off the paper. Or maybe they open it carefully, undoing each piece of tape, savoring the anticipation of revealing what's underneath."

Lauren's dark eyes looked big and luminous behind her glasses. He wouldn't have known she was up half the night except for the slight purple shadows there. And under that cardigan and button-up shirt, he knew she probably still had a small rosy circle on the curve of her neck, where he'd sucked at her skin.

"Are we still talking about wrapping up *snow globes*?" Daniel asked derisively. "I doubt there's anything in this shop worth being that precious about."

Kiki gestured over at a table in the corner, which they'd intended to be a gift-wrapping station once it got a little closer to Christmas. "You can set up over there," she said. "Just don't be surprised if no one comes."

Lauren gathered up the supplies and headed over to the table, but Asa called Daniel back, holding up the Sharpie. "You forgot this," he said. The way the other man snatched it from Asa's fingers, he seemed to understand that there was some kind of implied insult in the gesture, even if he couldn't figure out what it was.

"What do you think *that's* about?" Kiki whispered once Daniel and Lauren were settled in at the table on the other side of the gift shop.

"You know how Dolores gets around the holidays," Asa said gruffly. "She's obviously in the middle of some frenzied game of workplace musical chairs."

"The dinner date last night must've gone really well," Kiki said, ignoring him. "I tried to ask her about it this morning, but she was her usual Lauren self about it."

Daniel said something that made Lauren laugh, and for the life of him Asa could not think what that walking *GQ* background model could've said that would be remotely funny. Lauren glanced up, the smile fading from her face as their eyes caught, and he studied the sales tax guide slid under the glass top of the counter like he'd be quizzed on it later.

"What does that mean," he asked, "her *usual Lauren self*?"

"You know how she is," Kiki said. "Getting her to talk about anything personal can be like pulling teeth."

He thought back to things she'd revealed the night before. He got the impression she didn't have a lot of family, but he couldn't pinpoint anything beyond that. She'd mentioned not having a lot of pictures. The only time she'd mentioned any kind of family had been when she was talking about her mother, and the ritual they'd had around good-luck flowers.

That had been around when she'd gotten weird, come to think of it. He'd assumed she'd been freaking out because they'd fooled around, but now he wondered if there wasn't more to it than just that.

"Why are you pushing Daniel so hard? You know that guy is the worst."

Kiki shrugged. "Eh. It's like that *Love, Actually* plotline, the one with Laura Linney? He's the hot guy at work who she's had a crush on forever, and she deserves a chance for wish fulfillment. It doesn't have to be a relationship—just a chance to fuck her brains out. You know. If she wants. And if she doesn't get a call from her mentally ill brother in the middle of it."

As if Asa needed another reason to hate that movie. "First of all," he said. "Kiss your mother with that mouth?"

"Oh, like you—"

He held up his hand to stop her. He really, *really* didn't want to hear her say anything else about Lauren in that vein. Already those words were rattling around his head, pounding behind his temples.

"Second of all, if you see Daniel as *any* man in that movie— and yes, before you protest, including bumbling Hugh Grant the sexual harassment nightmare, including the dude with the cheesy boundary-crossing signs, including even that self-centered little kid—"

"Colin Firth," Kiki cut in. "You can't say anything against Colin Firth."

"I don't even remember his plotline," Asa said. "That's how forgettable it was. The point is, if you're comparing Daniel to any dude in that movie you're only proving me right."

Kiki straightened a stack of Cold World brochures so the edges were even. "I'm going to laugh my ass off when Lauren gets you coal for Secret Santa."

"Wait." He leaned against the counter so his back was to

Lauren and Daniel on the other side of the gift shop. "Lauren has me?"

Kiki put her hand over her mouth, looking genuinely stricken. "Shit," she said. "I just broke the first rule of Secret Santa, didn't I? And I had to do it to the chief of Christmas police himself. This was entrapment. You tricked me into saying it—"

"Don't worry about it," he said. "And don't call me the Christmas police. If anything, I prefer to think of myself as leading a holiday community support team."

He glanced over at the table again. Now Lauren was earnestly explaining something to Daniel, and wonder of wonders, he appeared to be actually listening. She was gesturing with her hands, forming some kind of slope, almost like a mountaintop, and Daniel reached over to adjust her wrists so that the angle was different. Asa waited for her to look annoyed, or irritated, or even just dismissive. But instead she got a dreamy look on her face for a moment, like she couldn't believe he was deigning to pay attention to her.

Asa pushed back against the counter. "Shouldn't they be wrapping presents?"

Kiki looked around. "There are no customers."

"They should wrap practice ones," Asa said. "I'm getting some boxes from the back."

When he dropped the empty boxes on the table a few minutes later, Lauren startled, like she'd had no idea he was even there.

"For you to practice your technique," he said. "Each of you can wrap a present, and I'll give you feedback. Once you've mastered that, I'll introduce you to ribbon curling."

"Come on," Daniel said. "That's completely unnecessary. That chick said it herself—nobody is even going to come."

"That *chick's* name is Kiki, and it sounds like this is what Dolores sent you here to do," Asa said. "You might as well do it."

"I'd like to practice," Lauren said, clearly wanting to defuse the tension. She reached for the blue metallic paper printed with tiny silver snowflakes, sliding it under one of the empty boxes.

Daniel grabbed the other roll of paper but made no move to unfurl it yet. "What do you say we make this interesting?" he said. "Have a contest to see who's the best wrapper."

Asa's gaze slid to Lauren. She wasn't one to turn down any competition. But already he didn't like this. Daniel was angling for something, and he didn't know what.

Clearly, Lauren was having her own doubts about the proposition. She flicked her thumb against the edge of the tape dispenser, wincing a little as she seemed to realize it was sharp. "What did you have in mind?"

"If I win, you help me with my PowerPoint for the presentations," Daniel said.

Asa resisted the urge to roll his eyes. If Daniel ever had a job in his life that required an actual résumé, he'd be the type to put "proficient in Microsoft Office" under the skills section and then spend the whole time at his new job demanding other people show him how to do the things he'd said he already knew how to do.

"And if you win," Daniel continued. "I'll take you on a date."

Making it sound like a prize for *her*, and a sacrifice for him. What a jackass.

Lauren glanced up at Asa, almost like she was waiting for him to intervene. But what could he say? *No, you can't do this because either way you lose? You can't do it because I hate the idea that you might want to win?*

"Go for it," he said. "Kiki can judge."

There was no way he could be impartial.

Asa called Kiki over, and they established the rules—the test boxes were chosen to be relatively equal in size and shape, and the task was to do the best wrapping job they could in a single try, with time factoring in only in the case of a tie.

Daniel actually put more effort into the competition than Asa might've expected. Such was the power of having someone else do your work for you as a potential prize. But Lauren went for the pro move of finishing off the sides of her present with the elegant double triangle approach, sealing the points in the middle with a single piece of tape. She had a crinkle in one corner, but Asa would've picked hers, hands down.

Kiki made a big show of picking up both presents, examining them from all sides like she was a judge on one of those cupcake shows they'd watched at the house.

Finally she set them down, stepping away from the table with an officious air. "And the winner is . . ."

There was no anticipation to it. Asa knew who it would have to be. He just found himself watching Lauren's face, wondering how she'd react once her name was called.

Lauren fingered the rose pendant around her neck, rubbing her thumb against it. She didn't look at Asa, but somehow that *not* looking felt more pointed than any direct attention could've been. He knew she wanted to. He could feel it, pulling taut between them like an invisible string.

"Lauren!"

Chapter

FIFTEEN

BY THE TIME LAUREN CAME HOME TO HER APARTMENT, tossing her keys on the counter and sorting through her mail, it felt like a lifetime had passed since that morning when she'd woken up on the floor of her office with Asa.

He'd gotten up first, which meant there was a good chance he'd seen her with drool on her face or in some other compromising position. But by the time she sat up, turning off her phone alarm, he was already folding up his blankets and setting her office back to rights. The potted ficus was still strung up with Christmas lights and ornaments, there were pieces of tinsel on the floor, and probably somewhere on her desk was the crumpled list from where they'd been playing their game, although she hadn't been able to find it.

She didn't know what to say or how to act around him, so she'd settled for not saying much at all. But then he'd kissed her.

That quick, emphatic kiss had put her in a daze all day. What did it mean? Was it an ending . . . or a beginning? And which did Lauren want it to be?

She was overthinking it. Asa had probably forgotten about the whole thing by now. He'd even facilitated the contest that had led to her winning a date with Daniel—a feat that only a few days ago she would've been over the moon about. But she'd had trouble concentrating on it at all, had struggled all day to focus on much of anything.

It had been a late night, and a long day. She was exhausted.

She looked first for whether there was anything from the accounting program where she'd applied for grad school, even though she was pretty sure they did all notifications by email now. Most of the mail was the usual coupon packs and glossy flyers, but there was an envelope from Miss Bianca. She sliced it open with her finger, smiling down at the picture of a llama wearing a festive scarf, FA-LA-LA-LLAMA! printed across the top in block letters.

She opened it, although she already knew what it would say. Miss Bianca's annual Christmas card often said a variant of the same thing, and even though it was a relatively short message, it always meant a lot to Lauren.

Thinking of you, and hope you're happy and healthy
xo MB

Miss Bianca probably bought the cards in a hundred-pack and sent one to each of the many kids who'd passed through her home over the years, even the angry twelve-year-old who'd lived there for a few months, who'd been removed after threatening Lauren with a knife. Eddie reminded her of that boy a little bit, although as far as she knew he was adjusting much better to his placement. It was something around the eyes, a toughness barely masking an almost desperate fear.

After advocating for Eddie to have more visits with his mom, she was supposed to meet the woman for the first time next week. Eddie's caregiver was dropping him off at Cold

World, and then his mom and the caseworker would arrive for one of the biweekly visits. It had seemed like a good idea when Lauren had set it all up—she was able to get them all in for free after using the complimentary employee guest passes she'd never taken Dolores up on before. She'd get to see Eddie and his mom interact, would hopefully get to strengthen her relationships with both Eddie and his caseworker.

But now, when all she wanted to do was sleep, the prospect seemed daunting.

Lauren placed Miss Bianca's card on the bookshelf in her bedroom, the only nod to any Christmas decor in her entire apartment.

She'd just collapsed back on her bed, trying to find the energy to do anything, when her phone buzzed from her purse. She thought about letting it go, but it wasn't like she got that many texts—for all she knew, it could be important.

It was Kiki. Is the date tonight?

Asa had filled Kiki in on the stakes for the gift-wrapping contest after she'd declared Lauren the winner. It was clear that Kiki was psyched to have had a role in helping Lauren along whatever burgeoning thing was happening with Daniel, and if she was a little confused because she'd thought they already had a date, at least she didn't say anything that would make it awkward.

But Lauren had left work with no definitive plans, which was fine. She didn't have it in her to even think about getting all dressed up, having to smile and try not to be her usual awkward self all night at some nice restaurant with Daniel. A date with him had been her fantasy for so long, but tonight she'd rather have a date with her bed.

No, Lauren typed back to Kiki, but the single word looked plain all by itself, so she added a crying emoji afterward. A little overdramatic, but oh well. There wasn't really an emoji that properly conveyed ambivalence.

Kiki's message popped up a few seconds later. We're about to watch the best Christmas movie ever made. Wanna come over?

It's been a long—Lauren started to type, then deleted it. What movie? she typed, but then deleted before sending that one, too. Finally she just typed Sounds fun. See you soon!

THE ISSUE, LAUREN LEARNED ONCE SHE GOT THERE, WAS that they hadn't actually decided *which* Christmas movie was the best ever made. Elliot was making a passionate case for *It's a Wonderful Life*, John was a surprisingly large fan of *Elf*, and Kiki had *Love, Actually* already up on the screen, pressing play before Elliot grabbed the PlayStation controller and turned it off again.

"You're trying to get away with it because Asa's not here to stop you," Elliot said. "But we are *not* watching that movie again."

"I didn't know you hated true love," Kiki said. "You've seen it, right, Lauren? Especially the Sarah-Karl storyline?" She waggled her eyebrows like those names were supposed to mean anything to Lauren.

"It's over two hours long," Lauren said, glancing up at the frozen still from the movie on the TV, the runtime information paused at the bottom. "Where is Asa, anyway?"

She hoped her voice sounded casual. She'd specifically checked his schedule before leaving work, just out of curiosity, and he wasn't supposed to close. Then something about the way Kiki had asked her over, the *we* in her text, had made Lauren assume she was referring to both her and Asa. But of course, Kiki had meant her other housemates. Which was fine.

"Crisis line shift," John said. "He does it on his laptop from his room."

"Ah." Lauren already knew from her previous visits to the house that Kiki's room was through the door leading off the dining room. She'd never gone to the other side of the house, through the kitchen, so she assumed Asa's room would be somewhere over there. Either way, it didn't matter. It was probably for the best that she didn't have to worry about facing him again.

"Which is perfect," Kiki said, "because he'd make us watch *A Christmas Story* again."

"I like that one," John said.

Elliot made a disgusted sound, scrolling through the recommended movies on Netflix, each of which looked cheesier than the last. "Manufactured nostalgia," Elliot said. "Hear me out, but are we sure the live-action *Grinch* isn't so bad it's good? Or maybe it's just good? I haven't seen it in years."

That really set off the bickering, with overlapping opinions coming in from each side, somehow degenerating to a heated debate about whether *The Nightmare Before Christmas* was a Halloween movie or a Christmas one ("Which of those holidays is in the fucking *title*?" Kiki said, while Elliot started listing all of the creepy features and characters in "Halloweentown, you know, the actual *setting*").

John stayed out of that one, until he turned to Lauren. "What's your favorite Christmas movie?"

Lauren was tempted to just pick one of theirs, provide a majority vote so they could move on to actually watching it. She knew Kiki the best, so it would make sense to choose *Love, Actually*, although the idea of a two-hour-long ensemble romance made her think wistfully of her bed. John had always been nice to her, and looked like he actually cared about her answer, so she could say *Elf* and align herself with him. But then again, Elliot seemed like someone who took their media very seriously, and everyone knew *It's a Wonderful Life* was a classic.

"I don't know," she said instead, a total cop-out. "They're all good, I guess."

"*Miracle on 34th Street* it is," Kiki said, taking the controller from Elliot to bring it up on the screen.

"The sad consequence of groupthink," Elliot said. "Everyone compromises and no one is happy."

"Whatever," Kiki said. "I'm making pizza rolls."

Lauren followed Kiki to help, even though there wasn't much to do other than lay the aluminum foil out on a cookie sheet for Kiki to dump the frozen rolls onto.

"So," Kiki said. "You have to at least tell me. Did the special underwear come into play at all last night, yes or no?"

The oven was preheating, which had to be the reason why Lauren suddenly felt warm all over. "He never even saw it," Lauren said. Not technically a lie. Asa had touched her through it, he'd touched her under it, but he'd barely gotten a glimpse. She slid her finger under the collar of her button-up shirt, wishing she'd changed out of her work clothes before coming over. "I think it's ready. The oven, I mean. It seems hot enough by now."

Kiki slid the sheet of pizza rolls in, frowning down at the bag before setting the timer. "Can you tell I don't cook?" she asked. "Even this is stretching my limits. Elliot does most of it, although Asa makes this amazing potato soup. John will just eat whatever. If left to his own devices he'd make a sandwich for every single meal."

Lauren thought again how nice that sounded, having people to come home to, to cook for, who'd cook for you. She'd always said she loved living alone, and she did—there was something to having her own space. She played whatever music she wanted on the Bluetooth speaker in her living room, she could read in peace without anyone interrupting her, she didn't have to share food or toothpaste or covers.

But it could get lonely. And lately, it was starting to feel lonelier and lonelier.

"You'll have to excuse me for being so focused on this thing with Daniel," Kiki said. "Even Asa thinks I should lay off. It's just that I know how long you've been into him, and I think it's great that he's finally paying attention. Also, I need *some* excitement in my life."

There was so much to unpack, starting with that comment about Asa thinking she should lay off. When would they have discussed that? After what happened last night?

He'd agreed to keep it between them, and Lauren found that she trusted him completely. Somehow she knew that he wouldn't even tell Kiki.

Which was almost a shame, because Lauren would've loved to get Kiki's perspective on what he *had* said, what she thought about the situation, whether she saw any future there . . .

Silly, really. Of course there was no future.

"How are things going with Marj?" Lauren asked. "Is she still stressed about her work party?"

Kiki frowned. "It's coming up—the night before ours, actually. I get the feeling that she'd almost be happier if I didn't go, because then she wouldn't have to deal with introducing me around to everyone and hearing me say 'I work in a fake winter attraction gift shop' the eight hundred times someone asks me what I do."

"I'm sure that's not true," Lauren said, then realized that

it very well *could* be true, and Kiki would be in a better position to judge that than she was. "I'm sorry. That sucks."

"Whatever." Kiki opened the oven door to check on the pizza rolls. "It's a minute early, but I think once they start oozing everywhere you can take them out. Wouldn't you agree?"

Lauren had no idea, but she grabbed the oven mitt from the counter and reached in to pull out the rolls anyway. Kiki warned her that they'd have to sit for a few minutes, and grabbed her phone, starting to text. Lauren took that as a good time to check her own phone, not that she would've missed any messages.

To her surprise, there was one from Daniel. Thinking for date I can take you to party next Saturday, it said. How does that sound?

It didn't sound much like a date. She would be going to the party anyway, and the whole idea had been to get Daniel *alone*, in a one-on-one situation where hopefully she could open up and show him she was more than just the mousy girl who could print him out five different charts analyzing the same data.

She was starting to type her reply when she heard a door open, and Asa walked into the kitchen, carrying his laptop, his earbuds still in. He did an actual double take when he saw her, stopping momentarily in the middle of the black-and-white checkered floor.

She didn't know if the crisis line involved any kind of audio or if it was all text, if she would disrupt him if she spoke. So she just lifted her hand in a small wave, and his mouth quirked in a smile even as his gaze drifted down her face to her throat.

Lauren had chosen her button-up very carefully that morning, because its starched collar hid the small love bite Asa had left on the dip of her neck into her shoulder. Or at least, she'd thought it did. She reached up to ensure that all the buttons were still done up, tugging at the bottom of the shirt in case it had started to gape over her chest.

"Careful," Kiki said in an exaggerated whisper, handing Asa a small plate of pizza rolls. "They'll burn your taste buds off."

"All part of the experience," he said. "Thanks."

He balanced the plate expertly in one hand, his laptop in the other, before disappearing back into his room. At least Lauren knew where it was now.

"How long has he done that?" she asked. "The crisis line thing?"

Kiki shrugged, dividing the rest of the pizza rolls onto four separate plates. "As long as I've known him," she said. "A couple years at least."

"Because of what happened with his dad?"

Kiki paused midbite, setting the roll back down on the plate. "Wait, how do you know about his dad?"

Lauren felt her face heat. It hadn't even occurred to her that maybe that might've been a secret, or at least something she shouldn't go mouthing off about. "He told me . . ."

Kiki looked like she was going to say something else, but luckily Elliot came in the kitchen just then, grabbing a flavored seltzer water from the fridge. "Are we going to start the movie, or not?" they asked. "Some of us have to work in the morning."

"Technically, my shift starts at eleven, which *is* the morning," Kiki said. "And I can't just roll out of bed and pound out words on my laptop. I have to actually get dressed and look presentable."

"Oh, *presentable*," Elliot said. "Sounds like you'll need

to be up at the crack of dawn, then, to give yourself enough time."

"You don't deserve these," Kiki said, handing them a plate of pizza rolls.

Lauren had settled into a spot on the couch, the movie already started, when her phone buzzed next to her. She realized she'd never bothered answering Daniel, and figured it was him again, but it turned out to be from a local number she didn't recognize.

Miracle on 34th Street—that your pick?

She knew who it had to be, but she couldn't help but glance around, verifying that everyone else was concentrated on the movie.

Group consensus. Couldn't decide which Christmas movie was the best.

His reply, when it came in, was a gif of Catherine O'Hara from *Home Alone*, shouting "Kevin!" Lauren couldn't stop the small snort-laugh that came from her nose, and she gave John an apologetic look when he glanced up. She even tried to put her phone away after that, so as not to be rude, but then another message buzzed in.

I didn't know you were coming over tonight.

Well, why would he? *She* hadn't even known she'd be coming over. And she didn't see how it would've made any difference. It wasn't like she'd come over specifically to see him.

Oh god. Was that what he thought? That she'd somehow engineered this as a way to spend more time with him after last night?

She hated this sudden awareness of him, of wondering what he thought or how he felt. Earlier, she'd felt a stirring from watching him *wrap a present*, for crying out loud, which she told herself was only because she found extreme competence a turn-on.

Before, she'd known where she and Asa stood—they were coworkers, not overly friendly ones, and rivals in a competition to figure out ways to improve Cold World. At various points last night, she'd thought they were becoming something more like friends. But then they'd messed around, which was a more polite way of saying that he'd fingered her until she saw stars.

And ever since, she'd felt . . . dreamy. Untethered. Like a balloon, released into the sky.

She was still trying to figure out how to reply to Asa's last text when another one came in. gtg—a chat is coming in. My shift ends at 10 if you'll still be around?

It was hard to focus on the movie after that. Lauren kept turning that question over and over in her head, trying to figure out if it meant anything. Did he *want* her to still be around? Or had it just been a throwaway comment, and she could leave or she could stay and it would make no difference to him either way?

Maybe what they really needed was to talk it all out, clear the air. Lauren would reiterate that she'd had a good time, but let him know that she knew it hadn't *meant* anything. He'd be relieved, and would say something about how he thought she was a nice person, but they'd gotten caught up in the moment . . . then they could return to having the occasional run-in in the break room, face off in front of Dolores for the presentations, and otherwise forget the other one even existed.

Lauren wiped her hands on her skirt, her palms suddenly feeling sweaty. Okay. She could do that. She could be mature and get it all out, so they didn't have to feel awkward around each other at work, so that she could come over to hang out with Kiki and not have it be weird.

"Are you going to eat those?" Kiki asked, gesturing to Lauren's untouched plate of pizza rolls.

Lauren had grabbed a chicken wrap on her way home from work hours ago, but somehow she just didn't have an appetite now. "No," she said. "You can have them."

"We'll *split* them," Elliot said, reaching over to grab a few off the plate as Kiki pulled it closer to her. "That's only fair."

Only fair. The words stuck in Lauren's brain, tugged something loose. Maybe what she needed was for things between her and Asa to feel more *even*. He'd brought her to climax, seen her fall apart in front of him, but he'd been more in control the whole time. There had been moments—Lauren could still remember that sharp intake of breath when she'd first rubbed against him, the look in his eyes when he'd said he was close.

Being with Asa had switched something on inside her, and she didn't know if it was going to go away unless she saw it through. Maybe the problem was that this was an open circuit, and she needed to close it.

Chapter

SIXTEEN

THE MINUTE ASA HAD SUBMITTED HIS LAST REPORT AND logged off the crisis chat software, he checked his phone. Lauren had never replied to his question, although he could still hear the movie coming from the living room.

He'd tried to gauge her reaction when he'd walked into the kitchen. Had she been happy to see him? Or disappointed, upset that her plan to hang out with Kiki without him around might be compromised?

He wished he could find a way to *talk* to her without scaring her off. The only thing he could think to do was revert back to his usual joking ways, hoping that keeping it light would at least lift the unbearable pressure off the situation.

Has the case against Santa been dismissed yet?

The three dots appeared that indicated she was typing, before disappearing again. Finally, she sent two words. Spoiler alert.

He grinned, settling back on his bed to type a response. Like they were ever going to let Santa go down for assault in a Christmas movie. What IS your favorite Christmas movie, anyway?

Why does everyone want to know that?

He assumed she'd already gotten grilled by his other housemates. *It's a very important question in this house.*

You already know I don't care about Christmas.

He thought about the energy she'd put into decorating her office with him, how closely she'd paid attention when he'd demonstrated proper gift-wrapping technique earlier that day. *You care a little.*

She didn't respond for so long that he thought he'd lost her. He could always go out to the living room, join everyone for the tail end of the movie. That was probably what he would've done if it were a normal night, if Lauren weren't out there.

But then another text came in, and he just stared down at it, unsure how to answer.

What are you up to?

This was Lauren Fox, texting him that question. She probably had no idea how suggestive those five words seemed just sitting at the bottom of the message screen. She'd be appalled if she knew that was where his mind went from such an innocent stimulus.

If he told her the truth—that he was just lying back in his bed, texting her—one hundred percent it would sound like he was coming on to her. Unless maybe he added the right emoji afterward. He typed it out, trying a winking face (*way* too flirty), the upside-down face (too sarcastic?) . . . the fake disguise–looking face with the glasses and mustache was his best bet, but then he just deleted the whole thing.

Working on my Cold World proposal.

It was a little true. He'd drawn out some ideas, and his sketchbook was still sitting on his desk where he'd left it, waiting for him to get more done.

He'd actually taken a break to sketch out an idea he'd had for Lauren's Secret Santa present. Once he'd learned she had him, he'd made it his mission to figure out who had *her*, and offer to trade. It was explicitly against the rules of Secret Santa that he himself laid out every year, but he wanted an excuse to give her something. Turned out, Marcus had drawn her name and was only too relieved not to worry about finding the right gift for someone he didn't know that well. Asa had shoved the romance novels he'd already bought for Sonia in Marcus' hands, ignoring the dubious expression on the dude's face and just clapping him on the shoulder in thanks.

Can I see?

He jerked up to a sitting position. She wanted to check it out *now*? In his room? He didn't know if it was because he'd sat up so abruptly, or because all the blood was rushing to the lower half of his body, but suddenly he felt light-headed. His desk was a mess of papers, colored pencil shavings, open reference books, and he did his best to straighten it up, flipping the sketchbook back to the Cold World drawings.

Sure, he texted back, and kicked a dirty T-shirt under his bed. At least his room was *mostly* neat.

Her soft knock came only a minute later, and he sat back in his desk chair, trying to look like he'd been there the whole time. "Come in."

She glanced around, taking in everything from the artwork on the walls to the bookshelf in the corner to his rumpled dark teal bedspread, his laptop and earbuds still discarded on his bed where he'd left them.

"Elliot got me that," he said when her gaze landed on a cactus-shaped lamp on his dresser. "From a trip to New Mexico with their boyfriend at the time. It stopped working about a month later—just longer than the relationship, actually—but I still like it, so."

He was rambling. Why would Lauren give a fuck about a *lamp*?

"It's nice," she said. She came up to the desk, so close he could reach out and pull her onto his lap if he wanted. Which, obviously, he wouldn't do. She touched the sketchbook page, tapping an illustration of swirling snowflakes he'd made in one corner.

"I should've known you were an artist," she said. "Your handwriting alone."

He forced himself to swallow the usual protest—that he wasn't *really* an artist. He'd never gone to school for it, never made money from it. He barely showed anyone the stuff he worked on. But if that was how Lauren saw him, he wasn't about to disabuse her of the notion.

"I'm thinking what Cold World needs is a total revamp of the Snow Globe," he said. "Not just to include a snow effect from the ceiling—not in the whole place, just in one corner—but also more color and visual interest. We need to make it more selfie-worthy. Social media–worthy. A place where families go to take their Christmas card photos and couples go to get engaged and influencers go to . . . whatever they do. Tell people to come visit Orlando. We're never going to have Cinderella's Castle, but we need *something* that feels iconic. Where you see a flash of a picture in a brochure and think, oh, that's the place with the snow!"

He took a breath, trying to gauge her reaction from her profile. Her lashes lowered as she turned the page to reveal more drawings, then flicked up to the paintings on his wall.

"You did those," she said.

They were from a while ago, when his style had been a

little looser, more abstract. But they shared a sense of color in common—Asa liked vibrant, saturated hues in his art.

"Yeah."

"You did the one in the living room," she said. "The boy on the stairs."

"That one, too."

She glanced back down at the sketchbook, running her fingers over the glossy imprint of a colored-pencil penguin wearing a blue-and-white-striped scarf. "These are amazing," she said. "I can see a whole mural of this kind of thing in the Snow Globe, and then you could design magnets, tote bags . . . all kinds of merch featuring the same art. That might bring more people in *and* move product in the gift shop all in one go. It's brilliant."

"Well," Asa said, rubbing the back of his neck. "Except that I've never painted a mural in my life. It's a lot different, doodling a few things in a sketchbook."

She started flipping more pages, and he reached out to grasp her wrist, stopping her mid-action.

"Sorry," he said. "Some of the rest are, uh . . ."

For you. He thought of the idea he'd had for her Christmas present, the general sketches he'd done already. *Of you.* He thought of a loose pencil sketch of her profile he'd worked on idly weeks ago, back when they'd been called into Dolores' office and Lauren had said having falling snow in the Snow Globe would be *magical.* He drew people all the time. If she went through the whole sketchbook, she'd see pictures he'd done of his housemates, of random customers at a local coffee shop, of celebrities. But the one of her had been different, and he worried she'd know it right away just by looking at it.

"Pornographic?" she asked, and he almost choked.

"*Private.*"

"Ah," she said, flushing a little. "Right. Sorry."

He still hadn't released her wrist. Her pulse jumped beneath his fingertips. "You really think I'd put all my pornographic drawings in the same notebook as that little penguin guy? There's gotta be a separation of church and state."

"So in this scenario, pornography is . . . church? Or state?"

"Okay," he said. "Bad example."

He stroked his thumb along the back of her hand, half because he wanted to and half to see if she'd pull away. When she didn't, he cleared his throat. "Lauren . . ."

Clearly, they were on a similar wavelength, because she cut him off before he could get another word out. "About last night," she said. "I can't stop thinking about it."

He didn't know what she'd meant to say, but he could tell from the way she clenched her eyes shut for a moment that it hadn't been that. He didn't even bother trying to hide the grin that cracked over his face. "Same here."

"I think some of that is because it feels . . . unfinished."

He drew his brows together in mock confusion. "I thought you finished?"

She rolled her eyes, smacking him playfully on the arm. "You know what I mean," she said. "Unless you don't, in which case welcome to the most embarrassing moment of my life."

Truthfully, Asa wasn't completely sure he *did* understand where Lauren was going with all this. But he didn't want to say the wrong thing and spook her. He caught her by the hips to draw her closer, until she was standing between his knees.

"If you're asking if I'd like to do it again," he said. "The answer is emphatically *yes*."

She pushed at his shoulders, her fingers digging into his T-shirt. "Not like we have to do *exactly* the same stuff . . ."

"Oh, we can change it up," he said, sliding his hands around the warm, bare skin of her waist under her shirt. "Like this time I'd really, *really* like to see you naked."

He pressed his lips to the hollow of her throat, tugging gently at the collar of her shirt with his teeth.

"Um," she said. "What are you doing?"

"Trying to undo your buttons with my mouth," he said. "It's a very sexy move if you'd stop ruining the moment and let me do it."

She threaded her hands in his hair, pulling slightly so his head tilted back to look up at her. "You're going to ruin my shirt. Or choke on a button."

"Well, I see which one of those you prioritized." He smiled, realizing he was also perfectly happy just doing this. Teasing Lauren, making her laugh, enjoying the rare privilege it felt like just to be able to touch her.

But then Lauren was reaching up to undo her top button, and he was more than happy to do *this*. She unbuttoned the second, then the third, all the way to the bottom until her shirt gaped open, revealing pale, smooth skin.

He parted the two sides of the shirt, his hands running up the dip of her waist to her rib cage to just under her breasts. Her bra was blush pink and simple, two cotton triangles that did nothing to hide the hard points of her nipples underneath. She shuddered when he brushed his thumbs across, her fingers tightening in his hair.

"I bet you have three of this exact bra," he said, pushing one of the triangles of fabric aside to reveal the swell of her breast, the tight pink bud of her nipple. God, she was beautiful. He wished he were enough of an artist to do justice to this image of her, half undone. He knew it was an image that would live in his head forever.

"I bet," he said, leaning in to take her gently between his teeth, swirling his tongue around her nipple. "You wear them under all your white shirts, because they don't show through."

"I have two," she said, sounding breathless as he continued ministering to her breast with his mouth. "Not three. And how do you know that, anyway?"

He pushed the bra up, pressing warm, openmouthed kisses to every inch of skin he revealed. "I'm starting to know you, Lauren," he said. "You're very practical. But not always. Like, when I do this . . ."

He flicked her nipple with his tongue, and she arched into him, her knee digging in his crotch. He was so hard it was almost painful, but a good kind of pain. He'd just cupped her ass to bring her closer, wanting to kiss and lick and suck her perfect breasts, when there was a knock at the door.

"Have you seen—" Kiki said, swinging the door open before hurriedly shutting it again with a gleeful *"Whoops."*

Lauren sprang back from him like she'd been administered an electric shock, drawing her shirt protectively around her body. "Oh my god," she said. "Oh my *god*."

He ran his hand through his hair, still feeling hot and flushed. "Sorry. I would've locked the door, only I didn't know . . ." *I didn't know we were going to pick up where we left off last night.* "I think she might've been looking for you. Did you tell them you were coming to talk to me?"

Lauren's eyes were wide and panicked. "I told them I was going to the bathroom."

Asa knew it wouldn't help the situation to point out that she'd been gone for almost twenty minutes, that the ending credits had probably started to roll and his housemates would've rightly started to wonder if she was okay. It definitely wouldn't help the situation to tell her how cute it was, that she'd thought to slip away on such a flimsy pretense to come see him in his room. How *hot* it was, that she'd apparently come with the express intention of seducing him. Not that he needed much seduction.

"I'm the rudest person on the planet," Lauren said. "Kiki invited me over to watch a movie, and I just *bailed* on it."

"Hey." He tried to reach for her hand, but she'd moved too far away. "Kiki doesn't care."

Lauren had already adjusted her bra and was starting to button up her shirt.

"And," he added, "for what it's worth, your back was to the door. I don't think she saw anything."

"She saw us together," Lauren said, "doing . . . *that.*"

Cold washed over him. He couldn't tell if Lauren was just freaking out because she was embarrassed to be caught in the act—which, fine, having housemates had inoculated him some to that kind of embarrassment, but he could understand if that was where she was coming from. Or was she specifically freaking out that Kiki had caught her with *him*? He'd thought that the change in venue meant they were no longer operating under a *what happens at Cold World* rubric. But what did he know?

He shifted in his chair, wishing his body would catch up to the change in circumstances a little faster. "We should talk about what *this* is," he said. "Because I don't know about you, Lauren, but I—"

"That was my first instinct," she said. "To come in here and talk to you about it. I should've listened to that voice, instead of the one that said this was an open loop that needed to be closed, that I would be able to move on once things were *even*, at least . . ."

He stood up, not caring when the chair banged against his desk and sent several pencils rolling to the floor. "What are you talking about? What do you mean by *even*?"

Her cheeks were pink as she struggled to get the last button in its hole. The entire shirt was misbuttoned, the hem hanging lower on one side, but if she didn't notice he wasn't about to point it out now.

"Wait," he said, her earlier words clicking into place. "Is this back to the fact that you came and I didn't? Because sex doesn't have to work that way. Give-and-take doesn't mean it has to be a transaction."

She gave a little growl, but whether it was at him or at her shirt, he couldn't tell. She'd clearly just realized her mistake and was starting to redo each button to make them straight again. "I know that. But I also don't want you to see me as some kind of charity case."

Charity case? The very phrase made him irrationally angry, and he didn't even know at who. Anyone in the past who'd made Lauren feel that way, himself if he'd contributed to it in some way without knowing . . . Lauren, for not giving herself or him more credit than that.

"You're going to have to make up your mind about me," he said, his voice low. "Because you used to think I was some hedonistic slacker who only cared about a good time, and now suddenly I'm this altruistic philanthropist giving out orgasms like UNICEF went into sex work. I can't be both of those guys, and if you actually paid attention you might see that I'm neither of them."

She'd finally stopped messing with her shirt, every button in its rightful place. When she spoke, she directed her words more toward the cactus lamp than him. "I'm sorry," she said. "I'm really not good at this kind of thing."

She shrugged, but he wouldn't let her off the hook that easily.

"What kind of thing?"

"And I'm sorry if I made you share your ideas for Cold World," she said, ignoring his question. "I won't steal them or use them against you or whatever. I play fair."

He ran his hand through his hair, exasperated by her even mentioning the presentations. Did she think he gave a fuck about *Cold World* right then? "You seem fixated on fairness," he said. "But honestly, it doesn't feel like you're treating me all that fairly right now."

"I'm sorry—"

"Stop *saying* that," he burst out. "You said your first instinct was to come talk to me, so do that. *Tell* me. What do you want?"

Ever since Kiki had interrupted them, Lauren had been retreating further and further away. Not just in distance, although that, too. He could tell by the way her face shuttered, by the fact that she was barely looking him in the eye. He'd wanted to jolt her back, somehow get through to her, and that question seemed to break through whatever barrier she'd put up. She turned on him, her eyes blazing.

"I *want* to be more like you," she said. "Okay? I really do. I wish I could hang out with people and not constantly worry that I'll say or do the wrong thing and mess it all up. I wish I could be brave enough to dye my hair or get a tattoo. I wish I could have casual sex and enjoy it for what it is. I wish I could be carefree, and easy, and not a giant *wet blanket* all the time, but that's just not how I'm built."

A sucker punch to the gut would've been easier to brace

against. At least the impact would've been concentrated, and over quickly. "Well," he said. "If it's not fun, don't do it, right? That's always been my motto."

If she caught his sarcasm, her expression didn't flicker. She stared at him wordlessly as he opened the door, glancing out to make sure the coast was fairly clear. The last thing he needed right now was a run-in with any of his housemates, especially Kiki.

"I'll walk you out to your car," he said.

She stood in the middle of his room for a moment, her fingers playing with the hem of her shirt, and he wondered what he would do if she wouldn't leave. He wouldn't have the heart not to hear her out if she had more to say, didn't trust himself to resist anything physical. The truth was that he didn't want her to go. But he also couldn't have her stay if that was how she saw him, how she saw whatever burgeoning thing had been growing between them.

Finally she moved, passing him carefully in the doorway to avoid even the slightest touch. "You don't have to," she said. "I'm just parked by the mailbox."

He ignored her, opening the front door to step out into the slight chill of the night. A cold front was coming through, which normally would've made Asa happy, excited at the prospect of a possible *cold* Christmas, if not the white one they never got in Florida. But it was hard for him to enjoy it as he watched Lauren climb into her car and drive away.

Chapter

SEVENTEEN

IT WAS FIVE O'CLOCK ON A FRIDAY NIGHT, WHICH MEANT all the little tables near the hot chocolate stand were taken. Lauren shouldn't have been surprised—especially this close to Christmas—but it still complicated her plans a bit. Eddie's caregiver, Jolene, was supposed to be bringing him by in the next few minutes, and Lauren had told her and the caseworker to meet up by the tables. It had seemed like a logical place at the time, but now that Lauren saw how impossible it would be to find a table to sit together, she was seeing the issues with the plan.

She spotted Marcus, sitting by himself nursing a hot chocolate, and decided to see when he might be leaving.

"Sorry to bother you," she said, approaching the table a little hesitantly. She didn't know Marcus very well, although he'd always seemed nice enough. "But are you going to be using this table for a while? It's fine if you are, but I wondered—"

"Oh," he said, getting up and jostling his drink in the process. He set down a few books he'd been holding, adjusting the crooked lid back on his cup. "No, no, take it. I was about to head home."

Lauren smiled, trying to make a conscious effort to be

friendly. She and Marcus had technically worked together for a year, although their jobs had no overlap. But the last week especially had made Lauren reflect on how isolated she was at work—she'd been avoiding Kiki since the incident in Asa's room, and she couldn't tell if she'd been avoiding Asa, too, or if that was coming from him. Either way, she'd barely seen him around Cold World since it had happened.

"I didn't know you read romance," she said, pointing at the books. The top one was called *Big Duke Energy* and had an illustration of a muscular man tossing his head back as if in the throes of passion, his long hair streaming behind him.

Immediately, Lauren could tell it had been the wrong thing to say. Marcus looked beyond mortified, his face turning a shade of red that rivaled the poinsettias lined up in the lobby.

"These aren't mine," he said. "I mean, they're a gift. For Sonia. For Secret Santa."

"She'll love them," Lauren said. She didn't know Sonia that well, either—god, she was sensing a really depressing pattern here—but she knew that the woman almost always had a book with a similarly salacious cover whenever she was on her lunch break. "That's really thoughtful."

"I can't do it," Marcus said. "I mean, she's old enough to be my *mom*."

If she'd been a mother in middle school, but Lauren didn't bother pointing that out. She wondered why Marcus would've gone to the trouble to choose the books, buy them, and carry them around Cold World, only to get cold feet about actually giving them as a present. But she supposed it wasn't her problem.

An assessing look came over Marcus' face, and suddenly Lauren knew he was about to *make* it her problem. "We could trade," he said. "You give Sonia the books—look, they're already picked out. Who do you have?"

Lauren paused. "Asa Williamson. But I—"

"That's ironic." Marcus gave a little snort-laugh. "But he's easy to buy for. Come on, trade with me."

Lauren's first thought was how *disappointed* Asa would be if he knew she was even considering it. Not because she fooled herself to think he'd care that much about whether she got him a present, but because "no trading" was pretty much the second rule of Secret Santa, after "don't tell the person you got them."

There was that. It wasn't like Asa would *know* that she had traded, since he didn't know she'd had him in the first place. And despite what Marcus was saying, Lauren found Asa incredibly difficult to buy for. She'd already considered and discounted flavored coffee (since he made it for free at work), art supplies (he probably had everything he needed, and had specific preferences as to what he used), and color-saving shampoo (weirdly intimate . . . and if she was completely honest, she didn't want to risk messing with whatever alchemy made up that distinctive smell that drove her crazy).

She couldn't think of anything to buy for Asa that didn't feel either way too impersonal or way too vulnerable, especially after everything that had happened between them.

Over Marcus' shoulder, she saw Eddie come through the front door with Jolene, and she gathered up the books on the table. "Okay," she said, sliding them into her tote bag. "Fine. You take Asa, and I'll take Sonia."

"Sweet," Marcus said. "Thanks. See you at the party."

As soon as the swap was done, Lauren wanted to call it

back, to change her mind. But he was already walking away, and Eddie had spotted Lauren and pointed her out to Jolene. Lauren plopped down in the chair at the table, not wanting to risk losing it.

"Sorry we're late," Jolene said. Eddie lingered behind her, the surly expression on his face barely changing when Lauren tried to smile at him. "We had a little incident with the PlayStation, didn't we, Eddie? Tell Miss Lauren about how you were a bad boy today."

Jolene hadn't said the words with any particular malice, but they were like nails on a chalkboard to Lauren. She had a feeling Eddie had already internalized what a *bad boy* he supposedly was, and regardless, her role in his life wasn't as another enforcer.

"I almost texted to say we wouldn't come," Jolene said, "since it seems wrong to reward behavior like that. But I actually really need to get my hair done . . . You said he'd be here until seven?"

Lauren confirmed that was the amount of time she'd discussed with Eddie's caseworker, and after Jolene gave Eddie another warning that he was to *behave*, she left.

Being alone with Eddie hadn't necessarily been the plan, but his caseworker and mother were apparently running even later. Lauren fired off a quick text under the table, inquiring as to their estimated time of arrival, before turning her attention to Eddie.

"When's my mom going to be here?" he asked.

She checked her phone, but of course it was too soon for a response. "Uh, any minute now. Do you want a hot chocolate or anything while we wait?"

"No," he said, and then, after a long beat, "thank you."

"How's school been going?"

"Yeah." He was staring around the place, as if taking in his surroundings for the first time. "How cold is it here?"

"The main areas are kept around sixty-eight degrees," Lauren said. "The Snow Globe is colder. I'll take you there once your mom comes."

"How cold does it have to be to snow?"

Lauren realized she didn't know exactly—the effects of growing up in a state where she'd never seen it happen. "Like thirty-two degrees, I think? There are a lot of factors that go into it."

"Like what?"

His questions were almost aggressive, as if he was challenging her rather than just curious. "The altitude," she said. "Water vapor in the atmosphere. That kind of thing."

She was actually impressed at how semiscientific her answers sounded, but Eddie didn't let up. "How cold does it have to be for someone to die?"

Well, that was a morbid question. Lauren glanced helplessly at the door, then at her phone. Still no text. "I don't know," she said. "It would depend on a few factors . . ."

On the ice skating rink, people were laughing and gliding around in circles—happy couples, families with young children, several teenage friend groups. Asa was working the rink that night, and she could see him skating in slow, deliberate laps, his hands clasped behind his back as he watched everyone on the ice.

She missed him. She'd hated the way they'd left things. She also didn't know what else there was to say.

"You're sure you don't want a hot chocolate?" Lauren asked Eddie.

"My mom will get me one," he said. "She knows how many marshmallows to put in."

"She's probably stuck in traffic," Lauren said. "This is a busy time of year."

Eddie was staring at the ice rink, too, and for a second his sullen expression split into something else. Next to her, Lauren's phone buzzed, and there was a text message from the caseworker: Mom can't find a ride. We'll have to reschedule.

Lauren started typing a response before giving up. If the caseworker were willing to drive Eddie's mother there, she would've said so. Lauren wasn't allowed to transport anyone, and she didn't know enough about Orlando's not-great public transportation system to be much help there.

One imperative Lauren had given herself before taking on this volunteer position was that she'd always be as honest as possible with Eddie. It had been one of the parts she'd struggled with the most when growing up in the foster care system—this idea that there was a big machine in charge of your care and sometimes you didn't even know the most important details of your own life. It was tempting now to keep making excuses for his mother, to delay the point when she'd have to tell him that the woman wasn't showing up. But she knew it would be better to get it over with.

"Eddie," she said. "I'm really sorry, but it looks like your mom's not going to make it tonight. She's having trouble finding a ride."

"We can go get her," he said. "You have a car, right?"

Lauren shook her head. "I'm not allowed to do that. I'm sorry, Eddie."

"This sucks," Eddie said, slumping down in his seat. "This place sucks. You don't even know any cool facts about cold stuff."

Lauren couldn't argue with him there. She hated this feeling of helplessness, of inadequacy. She'd advocated for Eddie to have more visits with his mother, and then his mother hadn't shown up, leaving Lauren to wonder whether she'd done the right thing or just set up Eddie for more disappointment. She'd thought meeting up at Cold World would give them something fun to do together, but she couldn't seem to find a way to make the outing enjoyable—from her lack of knowledge about how he liked his hot chocolate to her lack of knowledge about "cold stuff." Eddie kept looking toward the ice skaters, but she couldn't even offer to take him skating, because she'd never learned how.

Unless . . . Lauren stood up, holding out her hand to Eddie before dropping it again, figuring it was a babyish gesture he wouldn't want any part of. "Let's go see about ice skating," she said. "Have you ever been?"

"No," he said, still sullen even though he stood and seemed willing to follow her at least. "I went to a roller skating birthday party once. I was pretty good. My mom said I learned fast."

"Well, I'm sure they're the same," Lauren said, not sure about that at all. "Come on, let's try it out."

She got Eddie outfitted with a pair of rental skates, and rented some for herself, too, even though she knew she'd end up clinging to the wall the whole time. Once she'd made sure Eddie's were laced on tight, they walked gingerly together toward the entrance to the rink, trying to avoid getting jostled by the other, more confident skaters who pushed by to get onto the ice.

Asa was in the middle of one of his laps, but out of the corner of her eye she saw his blue hair as he broke away, glancing to see that the coast was clear before skating over to her and Eddie. "Hey," he said.

There was so much weight to that one word, Lauren almost wished she could pause the moment and analyze every nook and cranny of it. Was he angry with her? Indifferent?

But there wasn't time for that now, so Lauren gestured to Eddie at her side. "Asa, this is my friend Eddie," she said. "He was hoping to ice skate, but I don't really know how."

"You don't know anything," Eddie said, but without any real bite.

Lauren pulled a face at Asa. "Last week I blanked and called Thor 'the hammer guy,' and this week I don't know how cold it has to be to kill someone."

"And they let you have a driver's license?" Asa said, giving her a wink. "Give me a sec—I'll get Saulo out here to take over so I can skate with you."

"That's not—" Lauren started to call after him, to let him know that wasn't necessary. She hadn't intended for him to focus his full attention on them, had only hoped that maybe he could give them a couple tips and keep his eyes open to make sure nothing happened to Eddie.

Apparently, Eddie wasn't who she needed to worry about. He stepped out onto the ice with his skates and, although at first he was tentative and holding on to the wall, it was only a few moments before he was shuffling slowly in something that approximated ice skating. "I told you I could do it!"

Meanwhile, Lauren set one foot on the ice, and immediately her leg slid out from beneath her, landing her flat on her ass on the cold, wet surface.

Eddie turned his head but clearly had no idea how to change his current forward trajectory, drifting aimlessly away from her. "You okay, Miss Lauren?"

"Yeah," she said. "Just my . . ."

A pair of skates came toward her so fast she flinched, but

Asa came to an expert stop a foot away, sending little chips of ice flying into the air. He reached down a hand to pull her up, and she grasped his forearm, embarrassed when she had to cling to avoid falling again.

"Just your what?" Eddie prompted. "Your butt?"

"Ah, no," Lauren said, although there was a dull ache in that region already. "My pride."

"You got this," Asa said. "Bend your knees a little. Stay low while you're still starting out—it'll help a lot with balance."

"Like this?" Eddie crouched down slightly, gliding forward on the ice.

"Exactly," Asa said. "This kid's a ringer. Where'd you get him, a Russian hockey camp? His accent's impeccable."

"Miss Lauren is my guardian something," Eddie said. "Not the one I live with. The one who's supposed to help me get my mom back."

"Well, that's . . ." Lauren started, but Eddie was already shuffling farther ahead, and her voice trailed off. ". . . an oversimplification." She gave Asa a rueful smile. "Sorry about this. You can let go."

He lifted his hand from her elbow, and she instantly felt her arms start to windmill, her balance tilt. Asa reached for her again, keeping her so close she could feel his body heat. "I don't know that you're ready for the big leagues yet," he said. "You sure you don't want me to get you one of those skate helpers?"

So she could look like she was pushing a plastic high chair around the ice? No, thank you. "I know I dented my pride with that spill back there," she said. "But I do still have *some* left."

Asa cleared his throat. "Right."

The way that one word came out, it was like they weren't

talking about ice skating at all. Lauren wished she could apologize for what had happened in his room, but she didn't quite know what she would be apologizing for. For going in there and trying to seduce him in the first place? Because that was totally what she'd been doing, as terrible at it as she'd been. Or for freaking out afterward?

She'd tossed and turned all week, trying to make sense of the way she was feeling. All she knew was that somehow Asa had gone from someone she found vaguely irritating to the person she most looked forward to seeing. And then he went and did nice things like this, skating at a snail's pace with her, and it got her all confused and messed up inside.

Somehow they managed to catch up to Eddie—Lauren suspected he'd stopped to wait for them. "You really do learn fast," she said. "What's the secret?"

"You gotta do your skates like this," Eddie said, demonstrating slicing each of his skates out to the side, one and then the other, in a choppy motion that was nonetheless much better than any of her attempts. She'd *seen* ice skating before. Just for some reason, when she tried to mimic the movements, she got only a few inches on her own before she felt like she'd fall again.

"Maybe I should sit on the sidelines and watch," she said. "I'm slowing you down."

Asa raised his eyebrows at Eddie. "She doesn't like to do something unless she's good at it."

"What? That's not true."

"It's okay," Eddie said. "I get it. When I missed my no-scope headshot today, I threw the controller. That's why I was bad."

It occurred to Lauren that this conversation, ever since

they'd started skating, was the longest she'd heard Eddie ever speak. She didn't know if it was having something to *do* to distract him, or if it was Asa's neutral presence, but she was grateful for it.

"Well, it sounds like you made a bad *choice*," Lauren said, deciding to table any shock she felt over the violent description from the game itself. "Not that you were bad."

Eddie shrugged. "Same thing. I can't play video games for a week."

"That's a *consequence*," Lauren said. "If you'd broken the controller, think how much longer it might've been."

"Yeah, but—" Eddie clenched his little hands into fists, and for a minute she saw the storm overtake his face, like he could revisit his rage right here in the middle of the ice rink. Before she could think about what she was doing, she let go of Asa and gave Eddie's shoulder a quick, fierce squeeze.

"I know you're angry," she said, getting low not just to keep her balance, but also to better look Eddie in the eyes. "You're allowed to be angry. You're allowed to be sad. You're allowed to not even know *what* you feel. I was in foster care, too, you know, when I was your age. And I was fortunate, in so many ways. But it didn't stop me from feeling all the feelings."

She thought she'd gone too far, pushed too hard. She hadn't intended on getting into a conversation like this. The outing to Cold World was supposed to be fun, a little lighthearted romp before Christmas, but now here she was giving lectures. She braced herself against the wall, planning to stand back up, when Eddie's voice came so low she had to bend down again to hear him.

"What did you do with all of them?" he asked. "The feelings."

The most honest answer was that she'd pretended they didn't exist. She'd shoved them down, focused on being as *good* as she possibly could. She'd done her homework, helped around the house, kept to herself. And every once in a while, she'd taken a long, hot shower, staying in until Miss Bianca pounded on the door and yelled that she was wasting water, so she could have a place to cry.

For some reason, it was Asa she looked to, like he might have the answer. He was frowning down at her, his hands in his pockets, his gray eyes steady when they met hers. "I draw," he said finally, when the silence had stretched for longer than was comfortable. "When I need an outlet for my feelings, I draw."

"I used to cry in the shower, so no one would see," Lauren said. "Sometimes I still do. Sometimes I sing instead, as loud as I can, the goofiest or happiest songs I can think of. Sometimes it just helps to have someone to talk to."

From what Lauren could remember of Eddie's file, he had a referral to a local counseling agency but hadn't yet started any therapy services. He'd probably say he didn't need them. That was what Lauren had said, after having a couple sessions with a woman she could barely remember, who'd made her role-play fake conversations with her mother on an unplugged telephone. She made a mental note to bring it up with the caseworker, see what other support systems could be built around this kid.

"I bet I can get to the other wall before you," Eddie said, already gearing up in a competitor's stance, waiting for a starting gun.

Lauren gave him a wry smile. "Asa wasn't wrong," she said. "I don't like to take bets I know I'll lose."

"Ready," Eddie said, as if he hadn't heard her, "set . . . go!"

And he was off, looking a little wobbly, reaching out for the wall once but otherwise skating away on his own two feet. Lauren gave a little laugh, watching him. "No way I could even come close."

"Technically he never said you had to do it alone," Asa said, coming behind her to grasp the sides of her waist. His hands were firm, his proximity instantly warming her body by at least ten degrees. "What do you say?"

She had the sudden urge to just lean back against him, let him take all her weight. "I'm not going to beat a *child*."

"We gotta give him some competition, though. How else is he supposed to feel the sweet rush of victory?"

"I guess," Lauren said, "if you—"

But Asa had already started skating, building up speed as he pushed her ahead. She gave a gurgle of shocked laughter, her hands flying to cover his at her waist, exhilarated by the feeling of the air stinging her face even as she was nervous that he'd let go and she'd fall. But his grip stayed strong and sure, and he got her to the wall only a split second after Eddie had already touched.

"I win!" he said. "And hey, that's cheating."

Asa had braced himself against the wall, his hands moving from her waist to grasp the boards so that he wouldn't slam into her body as the momentum carried them forward. But still she felt the whole length of him against her, and it made her shiver even as she felt the color rising in her cheeks. *What do you want?* That was what he'd asked her that night in his room, and she was starting to see how wrong her answer had been, when what she should've just said was *you*.

His gaze was searching her face now, as though looking

for any sign that the ride had frightened her, or upset her. But all she felt was a bubbly, giddy feeling that felt something like . . . happiness. She wanted to do it again.

"Not cheating," Asa said now to Eddie. "Exploiting a loophole in the rules. Want to have a go?"

"I can skate by myself," he said stubbornly.

"You should try it," Lauren said. "It feels like flying."

Asa held up his hands, palms out. "I'll hold on to your shoulders. That okay? I promise I won't let you get hurt."

Eddie looked dubiously at Asa, but then he shrugged. "All right," he said. "I'll try."

Over Eddie's head, Asa shot a smile to Lauren that was so sweet she felt it somewhere deep in her stomach. He crouched down to grasp Eddie by the shoulders, starting up a little slower than he had with Lauren, then building up speed until they were sailing up the side of the rink. Lauren wished she could see Eddie's face.

She tried to venture out on her own, shuffling her feet back and forth in tiny, timid movements. She had a feeling skating was one of those ubiquitous situations where confidence was key to success, and those had never come easily for her. But she managed to travel at least three feet before she had to grasp the wall for support, and another six before her skate slid too far back and she fell down to her knee.

Any delusion she'd had that she'd be skating smoothly by the time Asa and Eddie made a lap around the rink was quickly dashed, but at least she was trying. She was picking herself up off the ice for the third time when they arrived back next to her.

"How about that hot chocolate now?" she said, examining her scraped palms. "I don't think I can take much more."

"Okay," Eddie said. "Then can we see the snow place?"

"Sure," Lauren said, glancing up at Asa. "Would you want to join us? I owe you a hot chocolate."

Maybe that was the wrong thing to say. It referenced back to that night at Cold World, and made it sound like she was getting all transactional on him again.

Or maybe he really just did need to get back to work, because he made a circle gesture with his finger in the air, as if indicating the rink. "Can't," he said. "But thanks. Eddie, good to meet you."

He stuck out his hand to shake, and Eddie took it, giving a few solemn pumps.

"See you tomorrow night," Asa said, then, at her confused expression: "The party?"

"Oh," she said. "Right. Of course. See you then."

It seemed like a billion years ago and just yesterday that they'd been in that staff meeting, discussing the holiday party coming up later in the month. Now that it was upon them, Lauren's anxiety was a tangled knot in her gut. She'd made an ass of herself in front of Asa at the first holiday party, and then again at the second. All she could hope for was that the third time really was the charm.

If it's not fun, don't do it. She could be fun. She just had to show him.

Chapter

EIGHTEEN

ASA BROKE HIS OWN RULE WHEN WRAPPING LAUREN'S present, but to be fair, it was hard to wrap a large, flat picture frame without using more than three pieces of tape. He'd just finished it earlier that day, vacillating between fear that it was too little and fear that it was too much.

Learning that Lauren had spent at least some of her childhood in foster care had made something click into place. He thought he understood better why she needed to feel in control, why she reacted so strongly to any risk of losing it. He hated that she apparently thought of him as some fuckboy, but he also couldn't deny that he hadn't done as much as he could to prove otherwise.

Hopefully she would see the gift as what it was, a gesture of how serious he was when it came to her.

There was a knock at his bedroom door, and a performatively long pause after he said *come in*, which meant he knew it was Kiki before she even poked her head in.

"Am I . . . *interrupting* anything?" she asked.

He flipped the wrapped gift over, using a Sharpie to write the *To* and *From* directly on the paper. "Ha ha," he said sarcastically, "but you *should* wait after knocking, it's kind of the whole purpose, so if this comedy bit means you respect people's private spaces more, I'm all for it."

"I'm just mad you didn't tell me you and Lauren were a thing," she said. "Obviously I wouldn't have kept droning on about *Daniel* if I knew you were in play."

"I'm not."

"You're wrecking my pretense of being the soul of discretion here, but from what I saw you are *definitely* in play."

"It's—" Asa started to explain that it was more complicated than that, before realizing that it was probably better he didn't go into all of it. "Can you give the soul-of-discretion thing another shot? For the party, at least? I really don't want it to be weird."

"Of course." Kiki mimed zipping her lips and putting the key in her pocket before having second thoughts, digging the key out, and tossing it over her shoulder. "Are you ready to go, by the way? John's the designated driver since he has to work the event."

As in past years, Asa'd convinced Dolores to book John's band to play at the party. They were used to playing lots of covers at weddings and other events, and they did a great job performing a medley of holiday songs for the first half of the evening and providing the backing music and lyric books for the karaoke portion of the evening after people had gotten enough liquid courage in them. Last year, Dolores and Daniel had done a version of "Happy Xmas (War Is Over)" where Dolores did John Lennon's part and Daniel took Yoko Ono's with the most beleaguered look on his face the whole time. Asa really hoped they reprised it again this year.

The only one of them who didn't have a reason to be at the Cold World party was Elliot, but they'd never missed it. Asa put the wrapped present in the trunk of John's beat-up Camry and piled into the back seat with Elliot and John's guitar case. He had that tingling, almost sick feeling he remembered from Christmas Eve when he was a kid, like you knew you were only hours away from finding out if all your dreams would come true. It had been melodramatic to feel that way about digging into his stocking when he was ten, and it was melodramatic to feel that way now. But he couldn't help it.

"*Don't* let the guitar fall," John said, glancing in the rear-view mirror.

"Don't drive like a maniac and it won't," Elliot said, but they also put a protective hand against the case in the event it tipped. Asa did the same on his side, but he hoped he wasn't called into service, because his mind was already at the party.

NOT FOR THE FIRST TIME, ASA THANKED HIS FORETHOUGHT in requesting the next day off. Since they had to wait until after hours to even get the party going, it often ran till two or three in the morning, with an open bar and punch that was so dangerous he hadn't touched it since his first holiday party after turning twenty-one. He swore that it was nine tenths straight rum.

He looked around for Lauren, but she must not have arrived yet. He busied himself by helping John and his bandmates carry in amps and drums from their van, then answered a few last-minute questions about Secret Santa (Yes, if you got yourself you were supposed to put the name back and draw again . . . Well, it was too late to do anything about it now, wasn't it?).

He was scanning the crowd again, looking for Lauren, when Dolores came up behind him. "Another year," she said, surveying the tall decorated tree in the lobby, real presents now added to the silver-and-blue fake-wrapped presents that were usually under there. "I always remind myself to enjoy it, because you never know if it will be your last."

Well, *that* was more intense than he'd expected. "Do you have reason to think this will be the last?"

She waved her hand, which glittered with a large ruby ring. She was in all red, from the feathered fascinator on her head to her stiff taffeta dress to her pointy-toed shoes. A small candy cane pin on her hat was the only formal nod to Christmas, but she was fully festive.

"I try to be realistic," she said. "As long as people enjoy coming to Cold World, I want it to be here for them. But I know that there are a lot of things that pull people's attention these days, ticking tock videos and whatnot. It can be hard to keep up."

"That's actually part of what I was thinking for my proposal," he said. "There are so many ways we could build up our social media presence. Like—"

"Oh, I don't want to talk *shop*," Dolores said, before waving to someone at the front door. "Over here!"

Asa glanced up to see Lauren walk through the front door. She must've put in contacts, because she wasn't wearing her glasses, and he could see even from a distance that she had some shimmer around her eyes and cheeks. She wore jeans and a simple fitted black shirt, long-sleeved and scoop-necked. She looked pretty and young and happy and . . .

From behind her, Daniel put his hand at the small of her back, in an almost possessive gesture. He must've seen his mother's wildly waving arm—not like he could miss it—and led Lauren over in their direction.

"Daniel!" Dolores leaned in to give her son kisses on each of his cheeks. "And I see you brought Lauren. How wonderful."

Lauren's eyes were bright, and not just from the clear

sparkle she'd applied on her eyelids. Just his luck, it appeared that she was finally getting that date with Daniel she'd wanted for so long, and it happened to be . . . tonight.

But as he watched, she stepped awkwardly to the side to get out from under Daniel's touch. He didn't know if she did it because she didn't want to be with him at all, or if it was just because she wasn't comfortable with the public display in front of her boss.

"You look nice," he said, leaning in so only she could hear.

"Thanks," she said, her gaze traveling down his face to his shirt, the slide so slow it was like she was counting every button. She jerked her eyes up before the survey went any lower, glancing away. "So do you."

Asa bit back a grin. He was dressed up for him, which meant a real collared shirt with the sleeves rolled up to just under his elbows. He was trying to figure out what to say next when Kiki came up, frowning down at her phone.

"Marj isn't coming," she said. "Of fucking course. After I made so much pointless small talk with every Stetson grad in a clearance suit at *her* party. She barely acknowledged me."

Kiki glanced up, seeming to notice her boss for the first time. "Oh, hello," she said, waving her phone. "Sorry about that. Girlfriend troubles."

"Are there any other kind," Daniel said. Asa supposed it was the guy's way of trying to show some sympathy, but the comment rankled nonetheless. Of course there were an infinite number of problems, including the inherent misogyny in Daniel's own statement.

Or maybe what really rankled was the way Daniel had stepped closer to Lauren when he said that, putting his arm casually around her shoulders. As if *she* were his girlfriend. As if *she* were trouble.

"Uh," Kiki said, voicing his thoughts aloud, "a ton of other kinds, actually." She turned to Asa, deliberately cutting Daniel out of the conversation. "You want to go grab a drink at the bar? I could use one."

"Sure," Asa said, raising his eyebrow at Lauren. "Want to join?"

Next to them, Dolores and Daniel had started speaking in rapid Spanish, the conversation appearing to escalate quickly. Daniel had dropped his arm from around Lauren's shoulders, or she'd sidestepped him again, but she was watching the exchange with a line between her brows.

Asa waited for her response, feeling more and more like a fool when it didn't come. Even Kiki seemed to take pity on him, throwing out her own "Do you want us to get you anything?"

Lauren dragged her gaze away from Daniel long enough to give Kiki a distracted smile. "No, thanks." Then she glanced at Asa, as if suddenly remembering something. "Actually, punch sounds good."

Under different circumstances, Asa might've warned Lauren about just how strong the punch was. He couldn't remember if he'd seen her drinking any in the previous years, but since he'd never seen her even close to tipsy, he doubted it. But she was already turning back to the conversation between Daniel and his mother, despite the fact that they were making no effort to even try to include Lauren. Asa would've expected that kind of rudeness from Daniel, but he was surprised at Dolores. It wasn't like her, especially at a holiday party where she normally went overboard trying to ensure that the employees enjoyed themselves.

He and Kiki headed to the makeshift bar that had been set up in the corner that inevitably attracted a bunch of discarded jackets, piled up while people were skating and forgotten more often than you might think. Their lost and found looked like a Burlington Coat Factory had exploded. But for tonight, the caterers had set up a counter with a limited selection of beverages, and Asa ordered a beer and a cup of punch before turning to Kiki.

"I'll have punch, too," she said, and he added another cup to the order.

"I'm sorry," the bartender said, giving him a polite smile, "but I'm only allowed to give one drink per person with valid ID."

"Just two punches, then," Asa said, sliding his driver's license across the counter with a five-dollar bill as a tip. "Thanks."

Kiki put her ID on the counter, too, and the bartender glanced at both before pouring the drinks.

"Can't believe we're getting carded!" Kiki said, sipping hers as they walked away. "What a time to be alive."

"I'm sure they have to for liability reasons." It was such a thing that Lauren would've said, had she been standing there, that Asa glanced back over in her direction. She was still standing with Dolores and Daniel, one arm at her side, the other crossed over her body to grasp her elbow. They still were deep in whatever debate they were having, and she looked uncomfortable but made no motion to leave.

"Okay," Kiki said, "as your housemate and friend and a person with sight I demand to know. *What* is going on?"

Asa didn't pretend to misunderstand the question. "Lauren won that date with Daniel," he said. "It looks like they're on it."

"Then why are *you* getting her a drink," Kiki said. "And why did I catch *you* with your hands all over—"

Asa shot her a glare, and she mimed a sarcastic zipping of her lips, which he could've pointed out she'd already pretended to do earlier and thrown out the key. Obviously he should've shaken her down for any spares.

"We're friends," he said. "I think."

"I didn't even know you *liked* each other. I thought you found each other annoying."

Asa supposed that must've been true at some point, although it was so hard to remember. It had only been a few weeks, and already he had a hard time not thinking of Lauren the way he did now—someone who'd start a snowball fight at work, who used random number generator lists to get through her day, who'd listened to his most painful memories with so much compassion that he felt like he could tell her anything.

But of course he couldn't. Because at this point, his biggest secret was probably just how much he *did* like her. The problem was that he couldn't quite figure out how she felt. She was attracted to him—that part couldn't just be in his head. But then there'd been her whole rant about not being capable of casual sex. Was that all she thought it was?

Asa took an automatic sip of the punch in his hand, making a face when he realized that yes, it was as strong as he remembered. It also wasn't his. "Fuck," he said. "I didn't mean to do that."

Kiki rolled her eyes. "I assume you and Lauren have swapped spit before, so it's not like—" She broke off as Lauren came up to join them. "Hey! We were just talking about you. About your drink. Asa accidentally had some."

"Oh," Lauren said, her fingers brushing his as she accepted the plastic cup from him. "That's okay."

She took a tentative sip, then immediately started coughing. "Wow. It's so . . . sweet."

"It's deadly," Kiki said, tapping her cup against Lauren's in a quick *cheers*. "Someone take my phone away, because after one of these I can't be held responsible for anything I text Marj."

Kiki started explaining to Lauren what she'd already told Asa, about how Marj had bailed on the holiday party at the last minute. Lauren made sympathetic noises in the right places, and it wasn't long before they were huddled together and giggling over something on Kiki's phone. Asa left to grab the beer he'd wanted, and by the time he got back, Lauren had somehow gotten monopolized by Daniel again, who was leading her away from Kiki and back over to Dolores.

After that, it was hard to keep track of where Lauren was at the party, because she seemed to move every five minutes. She was sitting on the bleachers next to Elliot, intent in conversation. She was laughing, trying to land a jingle bell in a cup for a chance to win a gift card. She was getting another drink. The band started playing "Last Christmas," and she was dancing with Kiki.

There was something so endearing about the way Lauren danced. She seemed self-conscious at first, unsure of what to do with her arms. All her moves were in her shoulders, which she shimmied to the beat, doing a cute little head bang when the drums kicked in louder. He found himself smiling, raising his beer to John when his housemate looked up from his guitar solo. It was obvious he was playing the Jimmy Eat World version, but that was okay. Asa could be magnanimous.

By the time Dolores gathered everyone around the bleachers for the gift exchange, Asa was all keyed up. When she handed him his Santa hat, he almost didn't know what to do with it.

"You're still handing out, yes?" she asked.

Of course. As he'd done every year. Almost everyone

ended up announcing themself when their gift was opened, but in the true spirit of the "secret" part, Asa distributed all the presents to their marked recipients to preserve anonymity. He grabbed one at random, reading Saulo's name before tossing it to him.

"Hey," Saulo said, catching the wrapped present. "This could've been that crystal snowman I had my eye on in the gift shop."

But the package was clearly something soft, and Saulo made an exaggerated face of surprise when he opened up a pair of socks with pug faces all over them. "Just like my Chappie!" he said. "Okay, who got this?"

Sonia raised her hand. "I saw them and couldn't resist."

Most gifts were pretty spot-on, although Asa couldn't help but notice that Marcus looked confused when he opened up his shrink-wrapped square of a gift.

"You can load your ten favorite songs on it," Dolores said, beaming. "And keep it in your pocket to listen to them whenever you want. And it comes with a lanyard in case you want to wear it around your neck."

"Cool," Marcus said, instead of *So like a minuscule fraction of what my phone already does.* It was a Christmas miracle of maturity, coming from him.

Asa grabbed the next present, sloppily wrapped in Charlie Brown wrapping paper, his name written on the tag. "Oh," he said, grinning. "Looks like it's mine."

He slid his finger along the taped seam, and he was just thinking that Lauren hadn't taken as much of his wrapping tutorial to heart when he flipped it over to see what it was.

"Well?" Kiki demanded, trying to crane her neck to see.

The packaging advertised: **WILL MAKE FIVE DIFFERENT**

FART NOISES! The button next to *Squeezed Fart* could be pushed through an opening in the plastic, next to a sticker that said *Try Me!* Asa pushed it and actually recoiled from the deep, wet sound that emanated from the gadget.

Well. He didn't know what he had expected.

"It's a Fart Maker!" Marcus called out. "They're hilarious. You can prank all your friends with it. I figured you could get Kiki and, uh, all the other people who are . . . at this party . . . so now know about it. Okay, I didn't think that part through, but the possibilities are endless."

Asa glanced up, his gaze connecting immediately with Lauren's. If he'd thought there'd been some kind of mistake, that Kiki had misunderstood Lauren having him for Secret Santa, the truth was written all over her face. She swallowed, looking down at her drink in her hand, then away.

"Thanks, man," Asa said, pressing the button one more time for effect before sliding the gadget into his pocket. "And the next one goes to . . . Kiki!"

Saulo had gotten Kiki a gift card to a local coffee shop, always a safe choice. Dolores opened Kiki's vintage-y flamingo ornament and seemed genuinely thrilled. Sonia gushed over a stack of romance novels from Lauren, which meant that Lauren must've traded names with Marcus sometime after Asa had done the same thing. He wondered about the exact timeline—whether Lauren had made the decision after the moment in his room, or after they'd gone ice skating with Eddie. Not that it mattered. The end result was the same.

And now they had reached the last present, and people were already starting to disperse while Lauren looked around, obviously trying to figure out where hers was. He had no idea what to do. The thought of giving her the gift he'd made, watching her open it in front of him, made his insides twist.

It was too much, especially for someone who'd actively arranged it so she *didn't* have to exchange gifts with him. At the same time, he couldn't stand to see that look on her face, the disappointment behind the smile she gave to Kiki.

He could tell her he just forgot, and then find something little to give her next week at work. It'd be relatively easy to get her a gift card for a takeout place near work, or a pound of ground coffee. Something impersonal that he knew she'd like.

But then Kiki was pointing down at him, waving her cup until pink punch sloshed over the side. "Asa, you idiot, you didn't bring Lauren's present in! It's still in John's trunk!"

The next time he added anyone to a lease, he was adding provisions like *Knock and actually wait for an invitation before entering a room* and *Keep your mouth shut about presents if the gift giver himself hasn't mentioned them first.*

"Yeah," he said, trying to figure a way out of this one. "The only—"

Lauren set her cup down on the bleachers, skipping down them so fast she ran right into Asa. He caught her by the shoulders, the loose waves of her hair tickling his fingertips as she angled her head back to look up at him.

"I'll come with you," she said, breathless. "I could use some fresh air."

He dropped his hands, shoving them into his pockets, where he immediately set off the Fart Maker.

"Not that kind of air," she laughed, nudging him with her elbow.

The first chance he got, he was throwing the stupid thing away. "All right," he said gruffly. "Give me a second to get John's keys from him."

Once Asa had the keys and no more excuses, he led Lauren

out into the cold night air. The afternoon had been deceptively nice when the sun was out, but now that it was dark with nothing but a sliver of moon in the sky, the temperature had dropped considerably. Lauren hugged her arms around herself, and he wished he had a jacket to offer her.

"John's such a good guitar player," she said. "Guitarist? What's the right word? Are they both right?"

He wouldn't say Lauren was drunk yet, but from the flush on her cheeks and the fast, slightly louder than normal way she was talking, she was definitely a little past tipsy. "He used to be in another band," he said. "They had that song, 'If Only'? It was a while ago, but it still plays on the radio sometimes."

"Oh my god," Lauren said, stopping in her tracks. "I *thought* there was something familiar about him. I loved that song! And the singer—what was her name, it started with an M . . ."

"Micah," Asa said. He hadn't followed the band, but he'd looked them up after John had moved in. Once, he'd even mentioned Micah to John, but that was all it had taken to teach him not to do it again. The internet had several theories about why the band had broken up, but whatever the reason, it was clearly something John hadn't wanted to get into. Now he played in a glorified bar band and kept to himself, and Asa respected those boundaries.

"Yes!" She shook her head, shivering a little. "God, that's really cool. Imagine doing something like that. My biggest dream is to be an accountant."

"Well, that's cool, too. And you're doing it."

She kicked a bottle cap on the ground. "Not really. I'm a bookkeeper. Which is fine, but I want to go into business for myself. Get my CPA license, do the big-picture stuff for a bunch of different companies and people, not just the smaller-picture stuff for one." She bent down to pick up the bottle cap, sticking it in her pocket. "I hate litter. And I'm rambling. And I'm boring myself, and probably you. Sorry!"

They'd reached John's Camry, and it was only getting colder, but Asa was putting off the moment when he had to open the trunk for as long as possible. He jangled the keys in his hand. "You're not boring me."

"That's right, you like to hear about people's dreams."

The wind blew her hair across her mouth, and she tossed her head, giving a little laugh. He wondered what she would do if he cradled her face in his hands and kissed her. Soft, hard, every which way he could get his mouth on hers.

He wished he could ask her why she'd traded his name away for Secret Santa. But he wasn't even supposed to know she'd had him in the first place, and he didn't really want to get into how *he'd* traded, too.

"You said once that you'd quit," Asa said, "if nothing happened with your proposal to improve Cold World. Do you still feel that way?"

"Probably." She laughed again, but this time there was a manic edge to it. "I guess I should pack up my desk, huh? Considering it's almost Christmas and I don't even have an idea yet. Not one! Zip! A not-so-randomly-generated big fat zero."

She brought her hand up to her face in a circle that he supposed was meant to convey the big fat zero in question, but soon she was pressing her fingertips to the area around her eyes. "My glasses," she said. "Where are my glasses?"

He circled her wrists with his hands, gently dragging her hands away from her face before she poked herself in the eye. "I think you left them at home," he said. "You must be wearing contacts."

"Well?" she demanded. "Am I?"

The parking lot was well lit, between the streetlights and the neon glow from neighboring businesses. Asa leaned in, studying the slim ring around Lauren's dark irises. "Yes," he said. "Definitely."

"That's right," she said, nodding like he'd just passed a test. "Lauren Fox wears glasses. Lauren Fox would never even *joke* about leaving a job until she had another one all lined up."

"Lauren Fox talks about herself in the third person?"

"She would never try the punch, or dance. If you'd told Lauren Fox a month ago she'd have a date with *Daniel Alvarez*, she would've snuck into the bathroom to dry-heave over the toilet."

He wanted to say that an inclination to vomit seemed about right around Daniel, but he didn't trust himself to get the words out in a way that didn't sound petty or jealous or both.

"You said it yourself," she continued. "*If it's not fun, don't do it.* That's my new motto, too! Being that Lauren Fox was exhausting. This way is so much better. Look, I'm not even wearing my necklace anymore."

She tapped her bare collarbone, goose bumps visible on her skin from the crisp bite of the air. He'd noticed she wasn't wearing it, but he hadn't put any particular significance behind the choice, any more than he'd thought she'd just been in a contacts mood instead of a glasses one.

"Time to let go of the past," she said. "And stop worrying about the future."

Something about Lauren's words didn't sit right with him, or maybe it was the desperate undertone to her voice. It came off less like she was running toward something and more like she was running away. If she truly felt empowered, he'd cheer her on, but none of it sounded like her. "There's nothing wrong with wearing a necklace that means something to you," he said. "Or taking your future seriously, for that matter. There's nothing wrong with being Lauren Fox."

"Well," she said, rubbing her upper arms. "I'm having a perfectly good time at the party without her, just living in the here and now. And speaking of, the here and now is freezing, so . . ."

He looked down at the keys in his hand. He'd almost forgotten why they'd come out in the first place, and their conversation had only made it that much more clear that there was no way he could give Lauren the present he'd made. It had definitely *not* been designed with an eye to forget the past, or ignore the future.

Reluctantly, he opened the trunk, reaching toward the back . . .

Where, at the last minute, he grabbed a bottle of coolant, peeling off the stick-on bow from the wrapped present and sticking it on the side of the plastic bottle with such sleight of hand he hoped Lauren wouldn't clock it.

"Here you go," he said, handing it to her and closing the trunk behind him. "If your car ever overheats, you know. You'll be covered."

She stared down at the bottle as if he'd just handed her a jar with a human brain inside. "It's . . . antifreeze."

"Yeah."

"It's half-empty."

"Or half-full, depending on your perspective," he said. God, this was painful. Maybe even worse than if he'd just given her the damn present. He suddenly felt like the whole party had been the worst idea he'd ever had, that he should've just stayed home and watched Netflix and gone to bed early.

And then she seemed to realize that her reaction might be rude, and that was even worse. Because he could see when the mask came down over her face, when she decided to smile and be polite the way Marcus had with the ten-song pocket gadget from Dolores.

"Thanks," she said. "I guess I'll just . . . drop this off at my car before we head back in."

She didn't bother unlocking her car, just set the bottle on top of her trunk like she knew it would be sitting right there waiting for her when she came back out. Dolores was always good about calling rideshares for anyone who needed one, and Lauren didn't strike him as someone who'd even try to drive home after drinking, so she probably intended to leave the coolant there until she could collect her car the next day. Maybe it was less that she didn't think it'd be taken and more like she didn't care if it was.

When they came back through the front door, Asa was taken aback by the sudden cheers and applause, like they were walking into a surprise party. It took him only a few seconds to realize that someone had hung mistletoe over the door, and once again he and Lauren had gotten caught under it.

Chapter
NINETEEN

IT TURNED OUT THAT LAUREN'S STRATEGY AT THE BEGIN-
ning of the night of looking at herself in the mirror and repeating *you are fun you will have fun* wasn't as effective as
she'd thought it would be. She'd tried. Her time talking with
Elliot and Kiki and other coworkers she normally didn't interact with had been genuinely enjoyable, and after the first
punch at least she'd felt loose and buzzy. She'd barely gotten
a chance to talk with Asa, but she'd figured the night was
young.

But Secret Santa had been a disaster, and she couldn't even
put her finger on why. She had a guilty pit in her stomach
about not keeping Asa's name, and then had been surprised
he'd apparently drawn her name, too. It wasn't like she'd expected anything big or super personal, but used coolant? After his speech about how wrapped gifts were more special,
he'd only stuck a sloppy bow on it. That had to be a message.

And now they were under the mistletoe *again*, and Lauren had no idea what to do. Fun Lauren would definitely kiss
him. Every version of Lauren *wanted* to kiss him. But apparently an entire personality change wasn't possible just from
the removal of glasses and a necklace, and the addition of

some glittery eye shadow and some lethal punch. She wasn't brave enough to make a move.

Asa reached up, the stretch lifting his shirt to reveal the tiniest sliver of bare skin at his stomach, and snatched the mistletoe off the top of the door. "This is a *work* party," he said to the crowd. He shoved the mistletoe in his pocket, setting off the Fart Maker again. "Jesus," he muttered under his breath, and somehow Lauren didn't think he was reminding himself of the reason for the season.

The only thing that saved her from total mortification was Kiki, who immediately came up and dragged her away by the arm. "I *told* you to take my phone," Kiki said, a slight slur on the last word, suggesting that she'd kept drinking while Lauren had been outside with Asa. "I just texted Marj that she could break my heart on Boxing Day, but she was *not* under any circumstances, to break up with me on Christmas."

Out of the corner of her eye, Lauren could see that Asa was no longer by the front door, although she couldn't see where he'd gone. Daniel was standing near his mother—he didn't seem inclined to spend time with anyone else at the party—and he waved her over when he saw her attention turn to him.

"But I don't want to break up *at all*," Kiki went on, "and now I've put the idea in her head! And I did it by paraphrasing the lyrics to a fucking *Christmas song*. As long as I have this phone in my hand I am a menace to society, I swear to god. Let's grab another drink and dance and forget that cell phone technology exists."

It sounded like a plan to Lauren, who decided to pretend she hadn't seen Daniel's gesture. She could be Fun Lauren without needing it to be about a guy at all.

The rest of the party passed in a blur. She danced with

Kiki, Sonia, even Marcus. At one point, someone came behind her and put his hands on her waist, but she knew without turning it wasn't Asa. He hadn't come out to dance at all, and she tried to remember if he'd danced in past years. She could've sworn he had.

"I've never seen this side of you before," Daniel breathed into her ear. He smelled like an overturned wine bottle in a brand-new Porsche—something stale and musty over the scent of expensive leather.

"Me neither," Lauren said, dancing out of his grip until she was next to Kiki again. "I think I need water."

Kiki fanned her face with the collar of her shirt. "Good idea. Would you bring me one?"

Lauren made her way to the cooler of bottled water and sodas that had been set up near the bar. When she'd retrieved two sweating bottles, she spun around and bumped right into Daniel.

She gave him a small, polite smile. "Excuse me."

"I have a confession," he said, taking one of the bottles from her hand, uncapping it, and taking a giant swig before she could stop him. "The wrapping contest was a setup. Even if you won, my plan was to take you on a date just so I could pick your brain more about the snow slopes idea."

It wasn't much of a confession, in that Lauren could've guessed that even *without* the conversation she'd eavesdropped on between Daniel and his mother earlier that night. Dolores must've forgotten that Lauren's résumé had included her working knowledge of conversational Spanish, because she hadn't held back when admonishing her son for stringing Lauren along. There'd been even more to that discussion that Lauren knew she'd have to unpack later, but for now her head was swimming and she didn't feel up to it.

"That was my water," she said, but then shook her head when he tried to hand it back. "Never mind. Keep it."

"My point is," Daniel said, leaning in, "I find myself thinking about another kind of snowy slopes. If you get my drift."

His gaze dropped to her cleavage, what little there was of it, just in case she didn't. Suddenly that third cup of punch didn't seem like such a great idea. She could feel it sloshing in her stomach.

Daniel looked back up at her face and smiled, like she was supposed to be flattered by his honesty. *Watch out for the ones who only make eye contact when they want something.* Asa had warned her away from Daniel back when they'd barely known each other, but she'd been too fixated on Daniel as some sort of symbol. It hadn't even been about him, but about wanting to be the kind of woman who got noticed by someone like him. And now that she was, it felt . . . gross. Wrong.

There's nothing wrong with being Lauren Fox. Even when their interactions had been limited to minor scuffles in the break room over the coffee machine, Asa had always made her feel *seen* in a way Daniel never could.

"This is not a date," Lauren said, drawing herself up as tall as she could. "I have no interest in dating you, or in helping you to bankrupt Cold World with your ludicrous proposal to pump manufactured snow into the parking lot. And not that it should need to be stated, but I definitely have no interest in being on the receiving end of any further disgusting commentary on my body or other sexual harassment."

She thought it was a pretty good speech, and she'd over-enunciated each word, trying to make sure she didn't trip over one.

"Whoa." Daniel put up his hands in a gesture of mock surrender. "How much have you had to drink? In no way was I"—he stuttered on the word, as if he couldn't believe she'd even used it—"*harassing* you. You're the one who's been panting over me for years. Everyone knows it."

There was enough truth in that statement to make Lauren burn with embarrassment. She really didn't want to cry—not at a work party, and *definitely* not in front of Daniel—but she could already feel the adrenaline from her earlier buzz sliding into something much more melancholy. And then she finally spotted Asa, standing over by the band, where they were already bringing up Kiki as the first person who'd signed up for karaoke. John was crouched down with his guitar, adjusting a pedal at his feet while he listened to something Asa was telling him.

She didn't want him to see her with Daniel and get the wrong idea. She wanted him to look up and see right through her, down to the part of her that just wanted to go home and cry. But then Asa was running his hand through his hair, turning as if to leave, and it hit her all at once. John's car. He was probably arranging to head home early at that very moment.

"I don't have time for this," she said to Daniel without bothering to look at him.

She headed over to Kiki, handing her the water. "Can I take your spot in karaoke?" she asked.

Kiki looked surprised, but shrugged. "Sure—everyone will probably thank you for it. What's the song?"

John had looked up from tuning his guitar, taking an interest in the last-minute change. "Normally Vance over there is staunchly anti-Bieber, but I'm sure we could convince him to play 'Mistletoe' if you wanted."

His smile was kind, letting her know that he was trying to make light of the incident earlier.

The guy who must be Vance handed her a microphone,

which she took, and a lyric book, which she refused with a shake of her head. "'Blue Christmas'?" she said. "Do you guys know that one?"

John's eyes sparked with something like amusement. "Elvis? Of course."

He leaned back to tell the bassist and drummer the song, then played the first jangling notes of the melody. He looped them one more time, giving her a nod, and she realized she'd completely missed her cue.

When she finally started singing, the first couple lines came out shaky, the wobble in her voice horrifyingly loud through the microphone even though she knew she was barely above a whisper. This had been a terrible idea. She'd never done karaoke in her life, so what would make her decide to start now, with a live band behind her, all her coworkers in the audience?

From the sidelines, Kiki gave her a big, cheesy thumbs-up, tilting back another sip of punch. Well, that was certainly one answer. How much rum had Lauren consumed tonight? At least two hundred percent more than she normally would've.

The other answer was moving through the crowd, and the way her head was spinning, she couldn't tell if he was headed toward her or away. Asa. She'd seen him about to leave, and she'd wanted to stop him. Lauren gripped the microphone tighter and closed her eyes, willing her voice to come out stronger.

She swayed side to side with the music, her eyes still squeezed shut. She knew she sang a couple too many *blues* at the end of the second part of the song, punctuating each one by hitting her clenched fist against her thigh. Then it was the instrumental part, and her eyes flew open, blinking against the sudden light and all the people staring at her.

Including Asa, right there in the front row.

He had an expression on his face she wasn't sure she'd seen before, or knew how to read. The word that flashed through her mind was *sad*, but surely her singing wasn't *that* terrible. Was it?

This was her issue with most Christmas movies, books, songs, whatever. Either they were depressing as hell—"Have Yourself a Merry Little Christmas," for example, made her feel nostalgic and tender from the first line. Or they were ostensibly happy, about the importance of family and togetherness during the season, and that only made her feel more alone than ever.

"Blue Christmas," in retrospect, had been a real mistake in this fragile mood she was in, and now she was supposed to sing the third verse. But instead she wanted to hug Asa so bad it was a physical ache. To hold him, and be held by him.

She started toward him before a burst of feedback from the microphone sent her stumbling back. John leaned over to her, still playing his guitar. "You okay?" he asked.

She tried to nod but had no idea if her head made the right movement. Suddenly, she felt so tired. She sat down cross-legged on the ground, bringing the microphone back up to her mouth. "Nobody drink the punch," she said. "It is very, very strong. You'd be better off drinking antifreeze."

Asa was above her from this vantage point, backlit by the overhead fluorescent lights, so she couldn't see his expression anymore. Probably for the best, considering that last time she'd checked he'd been looking at her like she was the most tragic person he'd ever seen.

She gestured in his general direction, fumbling the microphone to her other hand. "Which I have now! Thanks, Asa. You never know when your car might overheat."

John moved toward her again, and she waved him away, not wanting him to cut her off just yet. "This place is so special," she said. "It really is. Let's give it up for Dolores, everybody!"

At first, the applause was faint and uncertain, but eventually people were clapping in earnest, a few whoops and cheers coming from the back. Lauren felt oddly powerful, that she'd been able to summon a reaction like that all by herself. She joined in the clapping, the sound a dull thud reverberating through the microphone.

"And you're all like a family," she continued. "Like a big, caring family . . . that's how it looks from down here, anyway. I'm not really good with families, so I wouldn't know. There's one of those things—what are they called, the *I'm not a robot* tests—and I keep clicking all the wrong pictures. What's a traffic light? I can't get in until I select every last one."

A smattering of awkward laughter from the crowd, like they thought she was doing some kind of stand-up bit. She didn't know what she was doing. She shielded her eyes against the lights, looking up at John.

"Sorry," she said. "I'm done. I mean, I'll finish the song."

To her relief, he didn't make a big deal about her weird spoken-word interlude. Instead, he just played the vocal melody as a lead line on his guitar, giving her a nod to let her know to jump in. She sang the last two lines of the song still from her seated position on the floor, barely registering when someone took the microphone from her to pass it along to the next singer.

"Please drink responsibly," Vance said into it. "And this should go without saying, but just in case—don't drink antifreeze."

The band started up the next tune, a much more upbeat version of "Santa Baby" that Sonia was attacking with off-key gusto. A hand reached down to Lauren, and she glanced up to see Asa, looking down at her with a grave expression.

"Come on," he said. "I want to show you something."

Chapter

TWENTY

FOR A SECOND, ASA THOUGHT LAUREN INTENDED TO STAY on the floor for the rest of the night. But then she put her small, cold hand in his and let him pull her up, swaying slightly against his body as she found her balance. Even that incidental contact crackled up his spine, and he knew he had to be careful. His instincts wanted to gather her to him, to wrap his arms around her and not let go. But she was clearly in a vulnerable state, between the effects of that punch and whatever else was going on in her head.

He'd been surprised by what a good singing voice she had, low and husky and intimate. It had hit him right in the solar plexus, the raw yearning she'd given to a song he'd barely paid much attention to before. It felt like she'd ripped his heart out of his chest and shown it to him.

Or maybe it was her own heart. He'd been even more surprised by the things she'd said up there, in front of everyone. How Cold World was a family she felt left out of. How she would always fail the *I'm not a robot* tests. He hated that she felt that way, and he knew it was at least partly his fault, the way he'd always teased her.

"Why are we going to the Snow Globe?" she asked once

he'd led her inside. He realized he hadn't let go of her hand the entire time they'd been making their way to the enclosed space, but now that they were there, he had to drop it in order to hook up the machine. He'd been working on it all week, finding a way to attach it to the ceiling, a safer (and actually effective) way to plug it in. He'd tested it only briefly, but this would be the first time he'd see if it all worked the way it was supposed to.

"Close your eyes," he said.

She shot him a dubious look, but then her eyelids fluttered closed. He switched on the machine, holding his breath until the first clusters of bubble snowflakes started falling from the ceiling.

Her face was upturned, her lashes dark on her pale cheeks, and he could see the moment she felt the first bubble hit her skin. She flinched a little, then opened her eyes, letting out a surprised laugh at the snow falling down on her.

"Oh my god," she said. "Asa, you did it."

He rubbed the back of his neck. "You were right about the outlet," he said. "That was why it didn't work that night."

"It's so . . ." Her lashes were spiked with something that sparkled in the light, and at first he thought it was bits of the mixture that made up the snowflakes. He stepped closer to her, about to try to brush it away, to protect her against the sting of soap in her eyes. But then it tracked down her cheek, and he saw that they were tears.

"Lauren . . ." he said, and her face crumpled.

"I'm sorry," she said, backing up when he stepped toward her. "I don't know what's wrong with me. Well, I have a few ideas. Nothing about tonight has gone the way I planned it, and I just—"

She shook her head, brushing her hand across her cheeks

almost angrily, looking down as if any evidence of the tears on her skin would be a betrayal.

Asa wanted to reach for her, but he wasn't sure if she'd welcome it, so he shoved his hands in his pockets instead. He didn't know if she was referring to her date with Daniel, or something else. He'd noticed Daniel slip out of the party somewhere in the middle of Lauren's song, and as much as it annoyed him to think of Daniel bailing on Lauren halfway through the night, he couldn't deny that it had been a relief to see him go.

"I'm just tired," she said, and something told Asa that hadn't been her original idea for finishing that sentence. The fake snow was falling on her hair, glinting under the light for a second before dissolving into the dark strands. "Will you take me home?"

He switched off the snow machine, stalling long enough before answering that Lauren rushed to fill the silence.

"You can drive my car," she said. "Unless you've also had too much to drink, but I thought . . ."

His hesitation had nothing to do with his level of inebriation—he'd had a single beer and hadn't bothered to finish it, so he had no worries on that score. It hadn't even been about the car situation. He was just trying to figure out where Lauren's head was at.

"Sure," he said. "Of course I'll drive you."

She started digging around for her keys before giving up and handing him the whole purse. It was surprisingly messy inside, given what he'd seen of Lauren otherwise and her penchant for things being organized and minimal. Under her wallet was a crush of receipts, pens, tampons, breath mints, and finally, all the way at the bottom, her keys.

On the way out, Asa said a quick goodbye to Elliot, the

least occupied of his housemates, and told them he was leaving with Lauren.

He opened the passenger door for her and made sure she was settled inside before crossing behind the car, grabbing the antifreeze on his way and putting it on the floorboard in the back. He had to adjust the seat for his height, and it took a second to find the button for the headlights on the dashboard instead of off the steering column where it was in his car. It felt weirdly intimate to be driving her car, to have looked through her purse. He realized he was about to see where she lived. It felt . . . boyfriend-y.

He switched the radio on, partly to fill the silence and push thoughts like that out of his head, and partly to see what she listened to. He wasn't expecting the Spanish new wave that came from the speakers, but he wasn't mad about it.

"I think it's the Latin alternative hour on public radio tonight. They play this band a lot." She leaned her forehead briefly against the glovebox before tilting her head back against the seat and looking at him. *"Honestly, it would be so good to touch you."*

Her eyes were so dark, and he felt himself falling into them.

"But it's useless, your body's made of latex," she continued, and he blinked at her.

"What?"

"The song," she said, gesturing vaguely toward the radio. "That's what it's saying. Or something close. My Spanish is rusty."

He put the car in reverse, bracing his hand on her headrest while he backed out of the parking space. He asked for her address and she described her apartment building, which he recognized as being one he passed on the way to work every morning. "I didn't know you spoke Spanish."

"I understand more than I speak," she said. "Miss Bianca and her telenovelas . . . I could understand enough to get the gist of Dolores and Daniel's argument earlier. I think Cold World is in some serious trouble. This contest or whatever it is, it's more than just a fun game to see what we come up with. It's a last-ditch attempt to save the place."

Her words didn't surprise him, necessarily. He knew Cold World was struggling. And there had been Dolores' cryptic comment earlier that night, about never knowing when it might be the last holiday party. But still, he couldn't stop the lump of panic that rose to his throat at the idea of the place no longer being there.

"Who's Miss Bianca?" he asked.

She rolled her head from side to side, like she was half shaking her head *no* and half working out a kink in her neck. "I shouldn't have said all that stuff during karaoke. About families and traffic lights and who knows what else. I ruined everything tonight."

He'd long given up on following her train of thought. His impression so far of Lauren when impaired was that she rambled and was on her own internal emotional roller coaster. He just wanted to make sure she got home safely and was taken care of.

"You didn't ruin anything."

"Oh yeah? I had you for Secret Santa, you know. But I couldn't do it. I couldn't figure out what to get you. So instead I traded with Marcus . . ."

They'd reached her apartment complex, and he pulled into an empty space in front of the building she pointed out as the one she lived in. He switched off the headlights and engine, the silence in the car feeling heavy without the music on in the background.

Asa cleared his throat. "I knew," he said. "That you'd traded with Marcus. It's okay."

She sat back in her seat, tucking her hair behind her ears like she was bracing for something. Then she went to undo her seat belt, before seeming to realize that she'd already unbuckled. "Sorry, I— Thanks for driving me home. I'm just going to—"

She'd opened the door and exited the car before he could stop her. He still had her keys, a fact that she must've realized by the time she reached the front door of her second-floor apartment. He climbed the stairs after her, taking them two at a time.

"I think you're going to need these," he said, handing the keys to her. He stood back, watching as it took a few tries for her to get the right key inserted in the lock in the right direction. She gave him a sheepish look over her shoulder, then hesitated in the open doorway.

"Do you want to come in?"

He followed her into the apartment, glancing around as she switched on a couple lights. It appeared to be fairly standard, with a small common area, a narrow galley kitchen, and a hallway where he could see into the bathroom. He knew that she kept her office at Cold World neat and nondescript—at least until their decorating contest had spruced it up a little—but he was still surprised to find her apartment much the same way. There was a blue sofa, small enough to be more of a loveseat, with a scuffed coffee table in front of it. No TV, but the open laptop on the coffee table suggested that maybe Lauren watched on that instead. The tiny offshoot of the common area next to the kitchen was just large enough to house a table and two chairs.

"How long have you lived here?" he asked.

The place had evidence of being lived in—mail on the kitchen counter, flip-flops by the door, an empty bowl in the sink—but there were no pictures on the walls or any other personal touches. He was surprised when Lauren said she'd moved in two years before, and his face must've shown it because she glanced around as if seeing the place with new eyes.

"I never saw any point in decorating," she said, dropping her keys on the counter but missing by a few inches. She frowned at them down on the floor, as though she didn't understand how they'd gotten there. "I'd have to fill in any holes in the walls when I moved out, anyway. This place isn't permanent."

He was fortunate to have a pretty decent landlord, all things considered, but he knew that property management for larger complexes like this one weren't always as lenient. He couldn't blame her for not wanting to leave any marks. On the other hand, tonight had been her third holiday party at Cold World, and still she'd talked about moving on depending on how things went with the proposals to Dolores. She'd referred to whatever they were doing as *casual sex*. He wondered what it took to get Lauren to see something as permanent.

"So what's your plan, then?" he asked.

"For the apartment?"

He shrugged, trying not to look like her answers mattered as much as they did. "For the future. Go back to school to be an accountant? Buy a house you can decorate? Get married, have a family?"

She shook her head slowly. "It's better not to make plans. Things never go the way you want them to."

She was the one with the color-coordinated file folders, the organized task lists. If anyone had a solid five-year plan, he would've bet that it would be her. But he remembered what she'd said earlier, about how nothing that night had gone the way she'd hoped it would. He'd assumed she meant her date with Daniel and hadn't wanted to push for any more details. But now she looked so dejected, all he cared about was finding a way to get the light back into her eyes.

"Sometimes that's half the fun," he said, and she snorted her disbelief. "No, hear me out. I'd planned to get that snow machine rigged up the night I stayed at Cold World, right? If I'd been able to do it fast enough, maybe we never would've gotten locked in. Or if I'd listened to you about the outlet, maybe it would've worked and I would've been tinkering with it instead of having dinner with you or playing our random number generator game."

"So what, it's like fate or something?"

"Not fate," he said. "Just proof that sometimes it's not the way you plan it, it's how you make it happen."

Her lips parted, like she was going to say something, but then in two steps she was in front of him, her hand at the back of his neck, her fingers curling in his hair as she pulled him to her for a kiss. Her lips tasted sweet, and maybe it was the slight hint of rum punch that made him feel immediately dizzy. Or maybe it was just the intoxication of touching her, of feeling the slide of her tongue against his mouth. For a second he kissed her back—he couldn't help himself—but he pulled away before it could go any deeper.

"Lauren," he said, "we shouldn't—"

"I'm doing what you said." She stood on her tiptoes to nuzzle against his jaw, her arms clinging around his neck like she was drowning and depending on him for rescue. "No more plans. Just trying to make it happen."

He wanted her so much, it was actually painful. But he

didn't want their first time to be a quickie on her office floor, or a stolen moment while the credits rolled on a movie in the living room. And he really didn't want it to be when she'd been drinking, and might not be clearheaded enough to know what she was doing. He didn't want her to have any regrets afterward.

"I'm sorry I freaked out on you in your room," she said. "But I'm not that girl anymore. I can just hook up, have some fun. I even bought condoms."

Whoa. He didn't know if he was more surprised that she'd taken that step, or that she'd been able to admit it without blushing.

"Tomorrow, I will be *very* interested in hearing more about those," he said, "but tonight—"

She dropped her arms, his words seeming to deflate something inside her. "Right," she said. "Tonight I'm just making a complete fool out of myself. Again."

"No, that's not—"

"I'm going to get ready for bed," she said.

And with that, she shut herself inside the bathroom. Asa didn't know what to do. He could leave—she might be tipsy, but she didn't appear to be a danger to herself. But he also didn't feel right leaving on this note, with her seeming to think he'd rejected her.

He'd just taken a seat on the couch when a crash from the bathroom had him jumping back up to his feet. He lifted a hand to knock on the bathroom door before dropping it back down to his side. "Everything okay?" he called instead.

Silence. Then, the door opened a crack.

"I can't get my bra off," she said. "This is not another come-on, I promise, just—would you help me?"

She was still wearing her shirt, which he understood was

probably for his benefit, to preserve modesty. It couldn't have made it easier to get the bra off, though. He slid his hands up the slim curve of her spine, trying to feel for the clasp with his fingers. The straps were silky smooth, the fabric of the band more textured—lace, maybe? But he couldn't seem to locate the hook-and-eye closure.

"Ah," he said. "This is embarrassing, but I can't—"

She reached around, her fingers brushing his while she searched for the clasp herself. He swallowed, stepping back as he let her take over.

"Are you sure it's not one of those ones that fastens in the front?" he asked.

He saw her hands, still under her shirt, go to the bottom of her sternum, the *click* of a clasp being undone letting him know he was right.

"Oh," she said. "Well, this bra was the worst idea I've ever had. It makes it practically impossible to pull a—what was that movie, the eighties one about the dancer welder woman? She takes her bra off under her shirt and it's iconic."

"*Flashdance*," Asa supplied. She'd closed the door behind her to finish getting undressed but had left it ajar enough that he could hear her perfectly. He leaned back against the wall, not wanting her to think he was trying to sneak a peek, as well.

"She wasn't wearing one of these front-clasp ones," Lauren said. "I'll tell you that much. And see, I do know *some* movies, even if they're from decades ago. I'm not a complete pop culture wasteland."

The way she said that phrase, it was definitely something he'd said to her at one point. He thought about the comment she'd made during karaoke, too, the one about needing to do a reCAPTCHA to prove she wasn't a robot. All the times he'd teased her, he'd never meant to really hurt her feelings. Now he looked back on all those moments and cringed, wondering what he'd said and how it might've sounded to her.

The faucet ran for a minute, and he heard her brushing her teeth. Once she'd turned the water back off, he said, "I barely knew any pop culture until I went to high school. My parents wouldn't even let me read Harry Potter."

She opened the door, still wiping at her mouth with a paper towel. "Really?"

"Oh yeah. Too much devil's magic." He touched the delicate skin of her cheekbone with one finger. "You still have . . . do you mind?"

"Mind what?"

He reached behind her to grab another paper towel, getting it wet with some warm water and a tiny drop of soap. "Close your eyes."

"That's the second time tonight you've told me to do that," she said, but she followed his direction. He wiped gently at the shimmery makeup around her eyes, doubling over the paper towel and using the other side when he saw the streaks of glitter left behind.

"Did you feel left out?" she asked. "When you were a kid, I mean, and couldn't read what the other kids were reading."

"Sure," he said. "Although maybe I should be grateful, when it comes to that particular example. I have a feeling I would've been a hardcore Potter fan, and then when the author showed her TERF colors it would've broken my heart."

He swiped at the wetness left under her eyes, letting his thumbs linger on her skin before he crumpled the paper towel and tossed it in the trash. "All done," he said.

Her eyes fluttered open, and for a moment she looked dazed,

like she was emerging from a deep sleep. "Thank you," she said.

A lock of her hair had fallen over her face, and he reached out to tuck it behind her ear. "I think that's why I love Christmas so much," he said. "My mom went all out—it was the only 'magic' really allowed in my house. My dad would've much rather been a 'reason for the season' kind of family, but my mom wouldn't have it. Santa always left elaborate scavenger hunts for our big presents, we put out cookies and carrots for the reindeer every year, the works. I believed in Santa until I was twelve years old."

"Really?"

He smiled. "I almost got into a fistfight with a kid in seventh grade over it. My older sister Becca sat me down and told me the truth for my own protection."

He'd missed several texts that day from Becca, asking him again if he was coming to her baby shower tomorrow. But he didn't want to think about that now, any more than he wanted to connect the bossy, overprotective sister she'd been then with the woman she would be by now, grown-up and about to bring his niece into the world. It was too painful.

"Would you want to—" she started, and then broke off.

"What?"

She rolled her eyes in a self-deprecating gesture. "I just realized, since it's late and you don't have your car here . . . would you want to stay? We'd just be sleeping, and we've slept together before. Kind of. You know what I mean."

Asa was sure there were several reasons why that was a bad idea, but at that moment, he couldn't think of them. She pushed open the door to her bedroom, and he followed her inside, his hands in his pockets as he looked around.

There was more of Lauren in this room. The bed was covered in a lavender comforter, a couple fluffy decorative pillows pushed to one side. He crossed over to her bookshelf, tilting his head slightly to read the spines. Mostly fiction, books that looked like they'd been shortlisted for awards or featured on some culture podcast. But she also had a whole shelf of cozy mysteries with titles about a cat who talked to ghosts or sang for the birds, and he pulled one from its place to flip to read the back.

When he returned the book to its place, he accidentally knocked over a Christmas card that had been propped on the shelf. He picked it up, and couldn't help but notice that it was signed from *MB*. He didn't want to be nosy, but he also did want to know more about Lauren, and something told him this was an important part.

"Miss Bianca, with the telenovelas," he said. "She was your . . . foster mom?"

"Yeah."

He turned, trying to gauge her expression. She looked wary, but not necessarily closed off.

"I'd like to hear about it," he said. "If you wanted to tell me."

She shrugged. "Are you staying? Either way, I'm really tired. I think I'm going to lie down."

Before he could respond, she'd already switched off the light and climbed under the covers. There was still a glow coming from the kitchen through the doorway, so he could see the way she watched him as he stood by the bookshelf, trying to keep up with her constant changes in direction.

"I can sleep on the couch," he said.

"You're too tall," she pointed out. "Seriously, I know

you're trying to be a gentleman or whatever, but just take your clothes off and come to bed. It's not a big deal."

"Take my—" he choked on a laugh.

"Not *all* of them," she said, and even in the dim light he felt like he could see her blush. "But I doubt you want to sleep in a button-up and jeans."

He really didn't. If he were at home, he would've slept in nothing but his boxer briefs, but now he left his undershirt on as well in a slight concession toward propriety. He slid under the covers next to her, pushing the decorative pillows up against the headboard so he could rest his head on the normal pillow underneath.

She was quiet for so long he thought maybe she really had fallen asleep that fast. But then he heard an intake of breath, like she was about to speak, and eventually her voice, low and husky in the dark.

"I don't like to talk about it," she said. "Not because my experiences were all that bad . . . I mean, I know a lot of kids have it so much worse. I was never abused in foster care, or anything like that."

He folded the pillow under his head, propping himself up so he could face her. "Your experiences are your own," he said. "They don't have to be better or worse relative to anyone else's."

"I know," she said. "But somehow . . . never mind. It'll sound really stupid if I say it out loud."

"Try me."

He could practically feel her gathering her courage in the silence that followed. Finally, she took a deep breath and started talking.

"I always thought that people would reject me, if they

knew. Like my own mother abandoned me, you know? I don't know much about my dad—not a name or a job or anything real. So if people knew about that part of my past, they would see how easy it was to abandon me. And then they'd do it, too."

He reached between them for her hand, giving it a squeeze. "You're not easy to abandon," he said. "What happened to you . . . it says more about the adults in your life than it does about you."

"I know that," she said. "On some level. Most days, I don't even blame my mom. She didn't leave me on purpose. She had a drug problem, and she never got help. I know she loved me, but she couldn't take care of me. And at the end of the day, I think losing me made her give up. She died of an overdose less than a year later."

"How old were you?"

"Ten."

His heart ached for the kid she must've been then. He felt like he could see her with her glasses and her books, a quiet kid who tried to pretend that everything was going along fine.

"I do know what you mean," he said, "about worrying about rejection. I never thought about it that way, but it's probably one reason I don't tell just anyone about my parents kicking me out, either."

She made a face that he couldn't read in the dark. "I'm sorry if the random number generator game made you tell me anything before you were ready."

"No," he said. "I trust you."

"I trust you, too," she said, her voice a whisper.

Why did those words hit him in the gut so hard? Maybe it was because he knew how difficult it was to earn Lauren's trust, what an honor it was to have it.

She made a little snort of laughter, and it was so far from his own contemplative mood that he couldn't help but smile. "What?"

"This is what I meant, about plans," she said. "Tonight I was going to show you how *fun* I could be. I put on my glittery eye makeup and drank that awful punch and danced and it was all supposed to be for *you*, but instead . . . here we are talking about childhood traumas. The wet blanket strikes again."

Asa couldn't deny the possessive surge that went through him, at her confession that she'd made all that effort for him—not for Daniel, not because of any stupid contest or date, but for *him*. "Lauren," he said, "I don't know where you got the idea that you need to be someone different for me, or at all. I happen to like you exactly as you are."

She wouldn't know how close he'd come to saying something else, a bigger word than *like*. But he realized it was true. Somewhere along the way, he'd fallen in love with Lauren Fox. He couldn't pinpoint exactly when—it was more like a series of moments, going all the way back to the first time she'd ever spoken to him at the holiday party about wanting to cancel Secret Santa. It was hard to remember how he would've even described Lauren to himself then. But it was impossible not to imagine each interaction making some deposit, no matter how minuscule, another entry on the ledger of all the reasons he loved her now.

He would have to remember that language, for whenever he got up the courage to tell her how he felt. Something told him she'd like any comparison to spreadsheets.

But not tonight. He gave her hand another squeeze, leaning forward to kiss her forehead.

"I promise you're the *most* fun," he said.

"For a robot."

"Nah," he said. "You're clicking your way through all those traffic lights, baby."

He'd meant it to come out breezy, a lighthearted callback to the speech she'd made during karaoke that had made her so self-conscious. But the endearment came out sounding tender instead, and when she rolled to her other side, she snuggled into him. He wrapped his arm around her, pulling her closer, and it didn't take long before they both fell off to sleep.

Chapter

TWENTY-ONE

WHEN LAUREN WOKE UP, IT TOOK A MOMENT FOR THE night before to come flooding back. It all hit her in a highlight reel of bad decisions, from the karaoke to crying under fake snow to trying to kiss Asa and then asking him to help her take her bra off.

She curled into herself, as if making herself smaller would protect her against the worst of the mortification. But behind her, Asa shifted, his body warm and hard pressed against her.

So the night hadn't been all bad. She remembered the way Asa had gently cleaned her makeup off for her, the story he'd told about believing in Santa until he was twelve. She remembered the slight rasp in his voice when he'd said *I happen to like you exactly as you are.* And then she'd fallen asleep with him holding her, and woken up the same way. It was nice. She could get used to the feeling.

His arm was draped loosely over her hip, his bare leg wedged between her knees. He really did give off an insane amount of body heat.

"Asa?" she whispered, trying to gauge if he was awake.

She cleared her throat and said his name louder, but he didn't budge.

She thought about waking him up, or even just staying in the safe, cozy warmth of his embrace, but she really had to pee. It also wouldn't hurt to have the chance to brush her teeth, freshen up a bit.

She slid out from under his arm and edged herself off the bed, turning to see if the movements had disturbed his sleep at all. He burrowed a little more into her pillow, the blue of his hair extra bright against the white sheets, his mouth slightly open as he breathed the slow, steady breathing of someone still in the deepest non-REM stage. She adjusted her lavender comforter until it was covering him more completely, less because she thought he'd get cold and more because it was just something she wanted to do.

By the time he finally emerged an hour later, she'd showered and dressed and was sitting at the table, nursing a cup of coffee and jotting plans for Cold World down in a notebook. Something had happened overnight and suddenly she was bursting with thoughts and ideas. She couldn't wait to talk to Asa about them, but she figured if he was anything like her he'd need coffee first.

"Do you want me to pour you some?" she asked, holding up her mug.

He ran his hand through his hair, which was adorably flattened on one side and sticking up on the other. He was still wearing only boxer briefs and an undershirt, and even though he was more covered up than he'd been that day at the beach, her heart sped up a little at the sight of him. "That depends. Do you have cream and sugar, or do you keep your kitchen on some Soviet food rationing system?"

"Ha ha," she said sarcastically. "I have milk and sugar, if that'll suit your refined palate."

"I'm good, actually," he said. "I did use an extra toothbrush I found still in its packaging under your sink. I hope that was okay."

"It was probably a BOGO deal. It's fine."

He crossed over to where she was sitting, squeezing her shoulder as he came behind her. She liked that casual touch more than she probably should, liked the way he left his hand there as he looked down at the notebook.

"What are you working on?"

"Did you know that in 1977, it snowed as far south as Miami?" She tapped her pen against the bulleted list in front of her. "Places near Orlando reported as much as two inches. The coldest recorded temperature in Florida was negative two degrees, in Tallahassee back in 1899."

He pulled out the other chair to sit down, pulling the notebook closer so he could read what she'd written. "I see you still don't have an answer for how cold it has to be to kill someone."

"Because there are too many factors!" she protested before he looked up and she saw the grin that let her know he was teasing her again. "Besides, that's too macabre for the interactive exhibit I'm thinking of. The idea is to try to get more families with toddlers or elementary school groups to come in, not to scare them away."

"I like it," he said, scanning her list. "Especially the part where kids can excavate little toys out of ice by experimenting with droppers of warm water and other stuff. I still have some of those little plastic penguins. We can get more figurines like that, and then the kids can just keep them."

"That's what I was thinking," she said, "except I'm not sure about the choking hazard aspect. We'll have to consider that one more."

He raised his eyebrow at her use of the word "we," and she took a deep breath, telling herself to just go for it. If he said no, no big deal, right? She wouldn't even be able to blame him, after what a production she'd made of turning him down again and again.

"Would you want to work together?" she asked. "I mean, obviously you can still work on your mural idea, and in fact I was thinking that this could use some art to show how cute we could make it for the kids . . . I'd help you with any budgeting parts you needed assistance with, and I have a bunch of other thoughts on changes we could make to cut costs or increase revenue even more, like there's a local peewee hockey team that needs a place to practice, and our rink isn't regulation but we could make it work if they came in for an hour during the slow part of the day—"

"Lauren." Asa cut her off, laughing. "I'd love to work with you on this. Seriously."

"Yeah?"

He leaned over the notebook, angling his body so she couldn't see what he was up to until he was done. When he slid it back to her, there was a doodle of a little bear wearing bell bottoms, shivering little lines around his shocked face as he stood under a palm tree covered in snow. Lauren's surprised giggle came out more like a squawk, and he smiled.

"I might have to research late seventies fashion. Maybe more disco than hippie? I have no idea."

She added a wobbly Afro to the bear, trying to give it more of a late seventies feel.

"Perfect," he said, and when she went to stand up, he pulled her down onto his lap. His arms were wrapped around her waist, his chin on her shoulder when he said, "See? I told you we'd work well together."

"Let's not get ahead of ourselves."

"Why not? It's so much fun." He kissed the sensitive skin at the side of her neck, his lips brushing her earlobe. She felt the flutter of his breath against her cheek as he said, "Am I getting ahead of myself?"

Her own breath was caught in her throat. She was afraid to move, afraid to break whatever spell had wrapped around them at her kitchen table. When she finally spoke, she could only manage a single word.

"No."

She was conscious of his bare thighs under her, the light dusting of hair, the way his muscles flexed as he drew her back against him. And then she was very conscious of the hard length of him against her ass, the layers of clothing between them doing little to disguise just how turned on he was. It made her feel powerful, knowing that she could do that to him with such little provocation.

"How about now?" he asked, his fingertips skimming the bare skin of her waist under her shirt. She shook her head wordlessly, sucking in a breath as his hands slid up farther, his thumbs rolling her nipples through her bra.

"Now?" he rasped into her ear.

She tilted her head back, her neck exposed as she arched against his touch. "I don't—" she started, breaking off with a ragged sigh when he reached to cup her breasts fully under her bra, his hands warm and possessive. "I can't follow what you're asking me."

His hands dropped to her rib cage, and immediately she wanted them back where they were, his palms rubbing the tender tips of her nipples. "I'm asking permission to touch you," he said. "To show you how much I want you. Because, god, Lauren, I want you."

She turned so she was more sideways on his lap, burying one hand in his hair as she looked down into his gray eyes. She loved his hair, how soft it was under her fingers. She loved the way he looked at her with his full attention, his gaze on her face like he was still cataloging every tiny detail, like he hadn't yet run out of new things to notice.

"Only if I can show you, too," she said. "It's only fair."

"Tit for tat," he said solemnly, then immediately closed his eyes.

"Was that a joke? It was terrible."

He cracked one eye open, biting his lip in an adorably self-deprecating expression that would make her forgive ten more equally cringeworthy puns. "Sorry," he said. "I'm a little nervous. I joke when I get nervous."

Nervous was her default state, but weirdly, hearing him admit to feeling the same way made her own nerves fly out the window.

"Maybe I should do something to shut you up."

She'd never been good at dirty talk, and her every instinct wanted to immediately apologize for saying something so rude, but Asa didn't seem to mind.

"Please shut me up," he said. *"Please."*

She leaned down to slant her mouth against his, her tongue darting out to lick the place where he'd just bitten down on his lip. He groaned against her mouth, pulling at her shirt until he'd drawn it over her head, almost taking her glasses with it. He took those off next, setting them on the table before pulling her down for another kiss, his hand wrapped in her hair.

She had his shirt off in an instant, and this time there was no fumbling as he reached around to unclasp her bra, letting it slide down her arms to the floor. He'd seen her before, of course, when she'd unbuttoned her shirt in his room, but this felt different. Bright morning sunlight broke through the gauzy curtains over her living room window, and she was half-naked on his lap at her kitchen table. She felt exposed, suddenly shy.

"They're small," she blurted. "And I've always had this freckle right"—she pointed to the tan smudge near her left nipple—"here."

Asa pressed his thumb into the freckle. "You're perfect. And that is officially my favorite freckle. I'm obsessed with it. It's unseemly how much." He kissed her there, his lips dragging over her nipple in a way that made a shiver run up her spine. "And now you've got me running at the mouth again, when I can think of much more interesting things I want to do with it."

He ran his tongue lightly over her collarbone, a tease, before finding the hollow at the base of her throat.

"I like the way you talk," she said, her own voice coming out a little breathless. She realized she couldn't put into words just how much she liked it, or how he made her feel. It wasn't just the pulse she got between her legs when he touched her, when he told her how much he wanted to. It was the way it brought her back to herself, reminded her what she was doing and who she was doing it with. The fact that it was Asa, looking at her like that, causing this swirl of emotion and desire, made it that much better. And the fact that she was *her* . . . well, it made her feel like she was enough.

Her hand went to the hard ridge of his erection through his boxers, tentative at first, then a firm stroke with the heel of her hand along the length of him after she heard his intake of breath. He captured her mouth with his, taking her lower lip gently between his teeth before kissing her more deeply. "I want to see you," he murmured against her mouth. "All of you."

"Here?" The word came out as a high-pitched squeak.

He lifted her until she was sitting on the table, careful to move the notebook and her glasses over to one of the chairs. "What if I said *please*," he said, his hand wrapped in the waistband of her jeans, the backs of his knuckles brushing against her skin while his thumb ran down the length of the zipper.

She lay back on her elbows, raising her hips in tacit acceptance as he flicked the top button open and pulled her jeans down her legs, laughing a little when they got snagged around one ankle.

"Lauren," he said. "*Jeans?* You don't own a nice pair of sweats for around the house?"

"I had a houseguest," she said primly. "I was dressing up."

Asa pressed a kiss to her calf, sliding his hands up her thighs and giving a squeeze. "What's the situation on the cat pants," he said. "If they're stretch I'll buy you three pair."

"Stop," she said, laughing, swatting at his shoulder, but then he was sliding her underwear down her legs and her breath caught.

She wouldn't have called herself inexperienced, per se. She'd had sex before. But something about this, what she and Asa were doing, felt wholly new. Maybe it was the daytime effect, the fact that she could see him clearly and could feel his gaze on her, drinking in every inch of her body in the same unfiltered light. Maybe it was the sudden urge she had to do all kinds of dirty things with him, things she normally would've been too embarrassed to think about even in the heat of passion. Maybe it was that the passion had never really felt that hot . . . until now.

Still, she was surprised when he hooked her knees over his shoulders, his hands under her as he dragged her down closer to his mouth. She almost protested, but then any thought flew out of her head as he kissed his way along her inner thigh, ending with his mouth pressed against her hot center.

"Ah," she choked out as he licked her like she was an ice cream cone, that one firm swipe of his tongue making her hips buck off the table. And then his tongue was inside her, her legs falling more open as she gripped at his hair, consumed by the sudden need to have him as close as possible as he licked and sucked, as she let out a moan that didn't even sound like her.

"You taste so good," he said, his breath warm against her. That would've been enough to do it for her—his words, that feathery touch, the sight of his blue hair between her pale thighs—but then he sucked her clit so hard she felt everything inside her shatter and break apart into a thousand pieces. She clenched her fingers more tightly in his hair, realizing only after she'd come back down that she'd probably been pulling too hard.

"Sorry," she said, massaging his head where she feared she'd done the most damage.

He kissed the sensitive skin of her lower belly, then up to her breasts. "Pull my hair anytime."

But she had her mind on another part of him as he slid back up her body to take her mouth with his, the taste of her still on his lips. She reached down, urging him to strip off the last of his clothes, barely waiting until he was naked, too, to wrap her fingers around his dick, sliding her hand up and down the hard, silky length of him, her thumb rubbing across the head.

"Fuck me, Lauren," he half growled against her throat, and she stroked him harder.

"I thought that was the whole idea," she said, deliberately taking his exclamation literally. She was feeling completely bold by now, any last trace of shyness shed along with the last of her clothes and her inhibitions. She watched him through heavy-lidded eyes, liking the way the muscles in his throat strained as he fought for control.

"I want you inside me," she whispered. "Please."

She could feel the tremble in his breath as he kissed just behind her ear, could feel him hardening even more in her hand.

"I like the way you talk, too," he said, his voice a low rasp in her ear. "I want to be inside you so bad."

A prickly heat suffused her whole body at his words, and she knew without looking down she'd probably flushed all over. "Condoms are in the bathroom," she said. "Second drawer down."

"Hold on."

She thought he was telling her to wait, but then she realized he meant literally *hold on* as he stood, taking her with him. She wrapped her legs around his waist, kissing his jaw until he backed her against the doorframe to her bedroom, as though he'd already forgotten where he meant to go. His hands were on her ass, his bare chest pressed against her breasts, as he kissed her like she was the only thing keeping him from tumbling backward off a cliff.

He walked them both like that into the bathroom, shifting her weight slightly to free up a hand to open the drawer and rummage around until he retrieved a condom packet from the box. Then he carried her to the bedroom and laid her down on the bed.

"Call me traditional," he said, "but I thought a bed might be nice. Something new for us."

She'd had his body crushed against hers, had stroked her hand along the length of him, but this was her first chance to see him totally naked. She'd always been struck by how comfortable he seemed in his own skin, the easy grace with which he moved, and she was struck again by that now. He had a beautiful body, lean and lightly muscled in all the right places, and he seemed totally unselfconscious about his erection even as she was unable to take her eyes off it.

She watched him as he opened the packet and rolled the condom down over himself, her attention so intent that he gave her a crooked little smile as he came back over her.

"Will there be a quiz later?" he said.

She clutched his upper arms, braced on either side of her head. "Well," she said, "I'll want to know how to do it for next time."

Something flickered over his face, so fierce and tender it almost took her breath away, but then he was kissing her and she felt him nudging her legs apart. He dipped one finger inside her, the sensation so unexpected that she felt her body spasm as he rubbed her swollen clit.

And then his hand was gone and he slid into her for the first time and her breath really did catch in her throat. For a moment all she could do was grasp tighter at his arms, like she needed the support even though she was already on her back.

"You good?" he asked softly, his gaze on her face.

She nodded, feeling her breath come back as she tilted her

hips a little, encouraging him deeper. And then they found their rhythm, her hands coming down to clench his bare ass, her knees bracketing his rib cage as he thrust into her. She wasn't expecting to come, was feeling no particular pressure to after he'd already gotten her off with his mouth, but she could feel it building inside her nonetheless. At this angle, he filled her so completely, his pubic bone grinding against her clit, and she closed her eyes as she felt a wave of pleasure roll through her body. It was softer than her first orgasm but no less potent, turning her limbs to jelly.

"Asa . . ." she breathed, and then he was coming, too, his cheeks flushed as his body shuddered in release. He glanced down at where their bodies were still joined before looking back up at her.

"Holy fuck," he said.

She couldn't lie—it was quite gratifying to hear him say that. She stretched under him, feeling sated and a little smug. He pressed a hard kiss to her mouth that reminded her of the one he'd given her the morning after their night at Cold World—like he was declaring something, or sealing something. Then, she hadn't known what. Now, she dared to hope.

He finally rolled off her, disappearing into the bathroom for a minute to take care of the condom and wash his hands before returning to her. She lay on her stomach now but hadn't bothered to cover up, and for a few minutes he just lay next to her, rubbing small circles on her lower back.

She turned her head on her pillow so she was facing him, trying to judge from his expression what he might be thinking. Kiki's voice intruded then—*Asa is fickle*—but Lauren pushed it out of her head. He'd given no indication that this was a onetime thing for him, had he?

"You didn't flush the condom, right?" she asked. "If anything happens to those pipes they'll take it out of my security deposit."

She could've kicked herself. They just had sex, and *that* was the first thing she thought to say? It was so classic Lauren that all her old insecurities and fears came rushing back.

But Asa only smiled, pressing a kiss to her shoulder.

"I threw it in the trash," he said. "Your security deposit's safe with me."

She wanted her *heart* to be safe with him, but that felt like too much to even think about right now, much less bring up. No matter how much he said he liked her as she was, she didn't want to scare him off.

"What's your plan for the rest of the day?" he asked.

It was with that imperative in mind—*don't scare him off don't scare him off*—that Lauren gave a little shrug. "I need to go grocery shopping," she said. "I have two books to read before they're due back to the library next week. What about you?"

"My sister's baby shower started"—he reached over her to grab her watch off the nightstand, grimacing at whatever number he saw there—"forty minutes ago."

She shifted so she was on her side, facing him fully. His gaze flickered down to her breasts, the way this new position squeezed them together. Desire kicked in her belly just from that warm, focused attention, but she also didn't want to risk any distraction for this conversation that seemed like it could be important. She drew the covers back over them both.

"You should've told me," she said. "I wouldn't have let you oversleep."

"I wasn't planning on going, anyway," he said. "My parents will both be there, and I haven't seen them since . . ."

He didn't finish that sentence, but he didn't have to. She

knew the answer with heartbreaking precision because she could see the numbers tattooed on his chest. Lauren couldn't blame him for not wanting to see them again, but she also thought it curious that he'd brought it up at all, if that were the case.

"What about your sister? When was the last time you saw her?"

He adjusted the pillow under his head, pausing as if he had to think. But something told Lauren that he knew full well what the answer was, and was delaying for another reason— because he didn't like to think about it, maybe, or because he was worried it would reflect badly on him, this lack of contact between him and his family.

"A couple years ago," he said finally. "We'd met up a few times, since I left home . . . the last time was at a coffee shop a few weeks before she was getting married. I thought it was only decent that I tell her in person I wasn't going to come to the ceremony, and she . . . didn't take it well. She said I was selfish, that I was ruining the biggest day of her life. She was probably right. I should've just sucked it up and gone. It would've been half a day of bullshit, but when it was all over I would've come home to my friends and my life, and at least I wouldn't have been the piece of shit who couldn't even muster the courage to go to his own sister's wedding."

His gray eyes searched her face, as if needing to see understanding reflected there. "Now, I don't know if I avoid her because I'm still angry with her for not being there for me over the years, or because I feel guilty for not being there for her. It wasn't fair of me to expect her to take sides, much less my side against them."

"I don't have any siblings," Lauren said, unnecessarily. Of course Asa already knew that. "Maybe it was for the best—I saw a lot of siblings split up in the foster system, one placed with a relative while another was in a group home, that kind of thing. But I also saw a lot of siblings who only had each other, whose resilience came in part from having that one person who knew exactly what they were going through because they were going through it, too. If my parents kicked my little brother out of the house solely because they didn't like that he kissed other boys, I'd take his side so fast it would make their heads spin. I think it's fair for you to expect that kind of support from your sister."

"Well," he said, giving her a crooked smile. "I do consider you the ultimate arbiter of what's fair. So thank you."

He reached for her hand, and she thought he was going to hold it, but instead he circled her wrist with the watch strap, his tongue at the corner of his mouth as he worked to adjust the buckle. Once it was secure, he kissed her palm.

"I've fantasized about you just like this," he said. "Naked except for your watch."

Her eyebrows shot up. "That's what does it for you? You have a real thing for timepieces?"

He laughed. "It's weird, what I suddenly have a 'thing' for. Don't get me started on those tights you wear to work."

She wouldn't have minded getting him started, actually, but she reminded herself *no distraction*. There would be time enough for that. "So what are your plans for the rest of the day?" she asked.

Asa's fingers were in the strands of her hair that had fallen over her shoulder, twisting the ends in a gesture she wasn't even sure he was fully conscious of. "That depends," he said. "Any chance you'd be up for going to a baby shower with me?"

Chapter
TWENTY-TWO

THIS WAS A MISTAKE. THIS WAS A MISTAKE. THIS WAS A MIS-take.

The phrase kept repeating itself in Asa's head as he stood outside his sister's door with Lauren, waiting to ring the doorbell.

He blamed sex with Lauren. Well, *blame* was the wrong word, but being with her had given him such a rush of euphoria, of bravery, that he'd let his guard down. It had scrambled his brain, or maybe it was more accurate to say it had *unscrambled* it. Suddenly it had seemed possible, not that his family would've magically changed, but that he'd be strong enough to withstand it when they hadn't. And at the very least, he wouldn't feel like he was running from it anymore.

But now they were standing there, an hour and a half late, empty-handed. Lauren looked Audrey Hepburn pretty in a black dress with a pale pink cardigan, her hair in a French braid that had blown his mind to watch her do herself. Meanwhile, he was still dressed in his rumpled clothes from the night before, because there hadn't been time to stop at his apartment to change. He'd rolled the sleeves down over his tattoos, and kept messing with the buttons at the cuffs, unused to the feeling of having fabric loosely circling his wrists.

"Do I smell okay?" he asked.

Lauren pressed her nose to his shoulder, taking a deep inhale before letting it out on a little sigh. "You still smell amazing," she said. "It's honestly obscene."

"Maybe it's better if we don't go," he said. "I'll visit her after she has the baby. I'd always planned to do that, anyway."

Her gaze was calm and steady on his face. "Whatever you want."

Before he could talk himself out of it, he reached forward and pushed the doorbell with one finger, depressing it long enough to hear the tones ring out inside the house.

He didn't recognize the woman who opened the door, and for a second he had the bleak, anxious thought, *I haven't seen my sister in so long I've forgotten what she even looks like.* But then he realized that the woman wasn't eight months pregnant, and was looking at him with a polite, if slightly quizzical smile. Of course. She must be a friend of Becca's.

"Sorry we're late," he said. "I'm—"

"Oh my god, *Asa?*" His sister's voice came from behind the woman, and before he could react, she'd enveloped him in a hug, her very convex belly making the embrace more awkward than it already was after the noticeable delay before he returned the gesture. When she finally pulled back, her gaze went immediately to his hair. He could tell she wanted to make a comment, but didn't, so perhaps that was progress of a sort.

"This is Lauren," he said, resting his hand briefly on the small of her back. He didn't quite know how to introduce her—*coworker* laughably inadequate at this point, *friend* closer but still not enough, *girlfriend* a hopeful zap to his heart but not officially sanctioned—so he left it at her name. "Lauren, this is my sister Becca, and my future niece . . ."

He trailed off, realizing he didn't even know what they planned to name the baby, if they had a name picked out at all.

"It's nice to meet you," Lauren said, reaching out to shake Becca's hand but getting treated to a hug instead.

"I can't believe you came," Becca said, ushering them both in and shutting the door behind him. "I mean, obviously I'm glad you did. We just finished eating, but there's lots more in the kitchen, so help yourselves. We were just doing the gifts, so everyone's in the den, if you wanted to . . ."

Asa couldn't keep up with whatever his sister was asking him to do. She'd mentioned food, but was leading them right past it without pausing for them to fix plates, so he supposed they were meant to worry about that later. He hadn't yet eaten and should be starving, but the idea of snacking on little appetizers while surrounded by his family and sister's friends made his stomach twist. He'd forgotten that she'd be the kind of person who had a "den" now, in addition to the more formal living room they'd already stepped through at the front of the house. He couldn't remember what her husband did, but it was something that clearly paid well, because he was willing to bet that most of their furniture had been sourced from actual stores instead of the side of the street.

When they entered the den, there were at least thirty people piled around the sectional and seated on wooden chairs that had been pulled over from the dining room, and every single pair of eyes immediately turned on him. Most people seemed to have an expression similar to the woman who'd answered the door, politely curious but welcoming, but Asa could only focus on the two people seated in the middle of the longest part of the couch.

His mother stood up, a shaky hand going to her mouth, while his dad stayed seated, his arms resting on his knees like he didn't have a care in the world. God, they looked . . . *older*. Of course they did. But it still struck him—the gray in his father's hair, the lines around his mother's mouth. She was thinner than he remembered, but he didn't know if that was the effects of time or memory. Probably both.

"This is my brother Asa," Becca said, introducing him to the room with a bright smile. "The new uncle. And this is . . . I'm sorry, did you say Laura?"

"Lauren," Asa bit out. Already he could feel himself getting defensive, ready to take any oblivious comment as a slight.

"Hi," Lauren said to the group from next to him. "Congratulations on the baby. Madeline is a beautiful name."

How the fuck did *she* know the name, when . . . Asa's gaze caught on the banner hung up across one wall, realized there had been similar banners throughout their short journey through the house. **WELCOME, MADELINE!!!** Okay, so maybe his family didn't have the corner on obliviousness.

"Oh!" an older woman seated on the armrest of the couch said, pointing directly at Lauren. "You can't say that word!"

"They don't have clothespins yet," Becca said. "So that doesn't count." She turned to him, rolling her eyes in that private way she used to do across the dinner table when their dad was off on one of his lectures about *living for God's glory*. It was the first time she looked like *Becca*, the impossibly cool older sister he remembered from childhood, and it socked him right in the gut.

Becca reached into a decorative dish on a side table, retrieving two clothespins, and handed them to Asa. "The idea is that you're not allowed to say the b-word—you know, the kind of shower this is. If you do, someone can take your clothespin. If you catch someone else saying it, you can take theirs. The person with the most at the end gets a gift bag." She gave him a conspiratorial smile. "It's not much. A gift card and some nail polish."

From the couch, his dad made a sound like a grunt. It could mean anything—was probably just him clearing his throat—but from the timing of it, Asa didn't think so. He had an immediate flashback to the one time he'd painted his nails black in middle school, how quickly his mother had handed him the remover and told him to get rid of it. "You'll be bullied," she'd said. "I'm trying to protect you."

And sure, there had been some snickers from kids in his class. But they hadn't really bothered him as much as that look on his mother's face, the way he knew even then that what she really meant was that she was trying to protect him from his dad.

Lauren took the clothespins from him, clipping one to her cardigan before clipping the other to the collar of his shirt. She leaned in, her mouth brushing his ear as she said, "Watch me *clean up* in this game."

He snorted a laugh, the unexpectedness of it burning his nose. "So competitive," he murmured, pulling her close to kiss her hair.

When he looked up, his mother was still standing, watching them with an expression of such raw pain that he had to glance around the room, blinking away the sudden sting at the corners of his eyes. There was a pile of wrapped presents in the corner by an empty wing chair, and he gestured vaguely over to it.

"You've got a lot left," he said. "Go ahead and get back to it. We'll stand over here."

"I can get you chairs . . ." Becca started to say, but Lauren seemed to understand that he needed to be on his feet, needed to feel like he could bolt at any minute even if he had no intention of doing so. She demurred, saying they were fine as they were, and Becca took her seat again.

His sister proceeded to open a series of presents that made no sense to him—a breast pump that looked like a torture device, a long circular piece of fabric that was supposed to somehow wrap the baby against her body, a thing that heated up wipes. He was only half paying attention, trying to remember to smile or make a similar sound to the one other people were making. Most of his focus was on his parents. Even though he hadn't looked directly at them since entering the room, he knew that his mother hadn't stopped looking at him, whereas his father hadn't glanced over once.

Lauren leaned over to address the woman who had opened the door, seated closest to them. "What's that thing do?" she whispered about the last present.

"Oh!" the woman said, brightening. "It's pretty nifty. I had one for my kids. Sometimes the cold can be a real shock to their skin, so when you change your baby's diaper—"

Lauren held out her hand, and the woman flushed when she realized her mistake. She unclipped her clothespin and gave it to Lauren, a sour twist to her lips.

Asa glanced down at where Lauren was clipping the clothespin next to her other one, and when she looked up, she did the most surprising thing. She winked at him.

He couldn't stop the grin that split across his face. God, he wanted so bad to just haul her out of there, go back to bed, forget this stupid impulse that had him surrounded by strangers and baby paraphernalia. But if he had to see this through, at least he had the distraction of watching her work the room.

She was scarily good at the game. One by one she targeted people, making polite small talk until eventually they slipped up and said the forbidden b-word. It wasn't long before she had a conspicuous five clothespins, and people started eyeing her like she was a hustler walking into a pool hall. Who knew, maybe that was what she was.

After the presents had all been opened, the room cleared out a bit, some people leaving early for other engagements. The significance of the date and time only hit Asa then, and he grabbed Becca as she was heading into the kitchen with a stack of paper plates.

"It's Sunday," he said. "And the shower started at ten."

He didn't have to spell out what he meant. Growing up, Sundays had always been untouchable. Not just because they were the Sabbath, but also because it was a day that his dad's schedule was completely spoken for—last-minute preparations for the sermon, the sermon itself, and then a disciplined block of time afterward for reflection and study. When Asa was a kid, he hadn't been allowed to join a Little League team because it had a few Sunday games throughout the season.

Becca gave him a slightly sad smile, and for the first time he noticed that despite the makeup and her bouncy blond hair, her brightly flowered maternity dress, she looked . . . tired. He could only imagine how hard it would be to get any sleep right now, and if the rumors were right she was staring down the barrel of at least a few more years of not getting much sleep.

"Follow me," she said. "I want to show you the nursery."

He made quick eye contact with Lauren, who seemed to understand his wordless message as he followed his sister. *I'll be right back.* But hopefully she also understood the plea under that, somewhere even beyond wordless—*If I'm not, come rescue me.*

The room that Becca showed him into was down a hallway, small but painted a cheerful yellow, early-afternoon sunlight coming in stripes across the hardwood floor. There was a crib, an overstuffed rocking chair in one corner, and a scuffed dresser with bright red drawer pulls. The room looked a bit unfinished, boxes still stacked in one corner, impossibly tiny baby outfits strewn across the chair. But nice.

Asa shoved his hands deep in his pockets, looking around. "I kind of can't believe it," he said, the reality fully hitting him. His sister was having a *baby*, an actual human person who would be part of his family forever. Somehow, it had felt a little theoretical before this moment—his own fault, for not making more of an effort to see her.

He opened his mouth to apologize, but Becca cut him off before he could say anything.

"I planned this shower so they wouldn't come," she said.

He didn't need to ask who she meant, but he was still confused. "You didn't want . . ."

"I wanted *you* to come," she said. "And I knew you probably wouldn't if they were here. So I purposely scheduled the shower for a Sunday morning, figuring they'd say they couldn't make it, and then I could call you up and tell you that it was safe if you didn't want to risk running into them."

"But instead they canceled church."

Becca picked up one of the outfits draped across the back of the rocking chair, using her belly as a shelf as she folded it into a neat square. And then she undid it and laid it the way it had been before, as if she wasn't even conscious of what she was doing.

"Dad got someone to fill in for his sermon," she said. "It's not like he straight canceled."

But he'd canceled church for *himself*. That was almost

bigger than if he'd shut down the entire operation. The service had happened—in that same building Asa remembered from childhood, cream-painted stucco with brick accents at the corners, one end more traditional with a tall spire, the other more utilitarian, added on sometime in the nineties. His dad just hadn't been there.

"Well," he said, because he didn't really know what to say. "Thanks for trying, I guess."

Becca had picked up the pink onesie again, but threw it back on the chair with such force that it slid to the floor. "No," she said, "that's what I need to apologize for. I *didn't* try. I couldn't just call and tell them they weren't invited, because I was inviting you. I took the chickenshit way out instead, and then tried to pressure you to come anyway. Just like I tried to pressure you into coming to my wedding, yelled at you when you wouldn't. It was *hard* not having you there, I'm not going to lie, but I do understand why you stayed away. I just—"

He was surprised when his sister appeared to be wiping away tears. Growing up, she'd always been so tough. She'd pinch him when their parents weren't looking, and then make fun of him if he cried. But she also didn't stand for anyone else bothering him, had once grabbed a kid's bicycle by the handlebars and forcibly turned him around when he rode by to call out insults. Asa didn't know when exactly that had changed, when he'd started to feel like he was on his own.

But he didn't want to be on his own anymore. His relationship with Becca wasn't perfect, but if she said she wanted to try, then he was ready to try, too. The old hurts were still there, but maybe they could move forward through them.

"I needed you on my side, Bec," he said. "I *need* you on my side. It was always us. Don't you remember? I'm not asking you to cut them out, I'm not even asking you to try to change their minds. I just need you to support *me*, to stand up for me the way you did when we were kids, before it ever became about who I was with or how I identified. Do you think you can do that?"

"Yes," she said, so quickly it was like she'd been offered a chance to win a prize on a radio show and she didn't want to lose it. She was definitely crying now, the skin around her eyes blotchy and red. "I can, I will. I'm so sorry I didn't do that before, I can't even—"

He didn't want to talk about the past anymore. "It's okay," he said, reaching out to envelop her in a hug. "It's really okay. I'm glad I came. I'm going to be an uncle, you know."

This time, when Becca picked up a onesie, she blew her nose right into it before tossing it into a hamper in the corner. "What?" she said, catching his look. "It's going to be non-stop laundry around here anyway."

"You excited?"

"Sure, and nervous, scared . . . it's hard to imagine they're going to just let Stephen and me bring a kid home and take care of her all by ourselves."

"I guess now isn't the best time to bring up what happened with the crickets."

She swatted him. "I was eight! And those were destined to be your turtle's food, so I saved them from a worse fate."

"I'd rather take my place in the food chain than death by a child sitting on a baggie filled with me and my friends five seconds after we left the store."

She shot him a dubious look, but at least she seemed back in control. He was already on such a thin edge, he didn't know that he could deal with Becca if she got too warm and fuzzy on him. That was why he didn't know how to respond to her next comment.

"I think they wanted to see you, too," she said. "Mom especially. I think she pressured Dad to skip church so they could come, in hopes that you'd be here."

He made a humming noise in the barest acknowledgment, but he knew it was time he faced his parents. "I should probably head back, check on Lauren. She doesn't know anyone else here, so I don't want to leave her alone too long."

"Right. Of course." Becca rubbed her stomach, her eyes widening a little. "Maddie's really doing somersaults—want to feel?"

Before Asa could answer, Becca grabbed his hand and set it on her stomach. Immediately, there was a distinct rolling sensation, and he couldn't help but think of old cartoons he'd watched as a kid, the roadrunner running into the ground until eventually all you could see was the mound of dirt traveling quickly away from the coyote. It was a little freaky, if he was being honest with himself. But it was awe-inspiring, too, and he was grateful she'd invited him to experience it.

"Does she do that a lot?" he asked once he'd pulled his hand away.

"Oh yeah, especially if I drink something sweet. I had a bunch of orange juice earlier, which is probably what woke her up." Becca tilted her head, as if considering her next question before deciding to just go for it. "What about you and Lauren? Is she . . ."

"God, no. I mean, we've only just—and we used protection, so—" He felt the tips of his ears go red hot when he realized that she hadn't been asking if Lauren was *pregnant*. Maybe he'd been too quick to consider his brain unscrambled. Between all the baby talk and being with Lauren only a few hours ago, he was having trouble thinking straight.

But Becca just laughed, seeming to enjoy his discomfiture in the way only an older sister could.

He scrubbed his hand over his face. "It's very new," he amended. "Whatever *it* is."

Her arched eyebrow seemed to say *And you brought her to this?*, but thankfully she didn't say it aloud. He didn't feel like he could adequately explain himself.

And yet he couldn't seem to stop talking. "We've worked together for a while," he said. "So I've known her for years, technically. But we only recently started . . . well, whatever. Dating."

It wasn't lost on him that he and Lauren had yet to go on an official date. If he and Becca had a closer relationship, if they didn't have the awkwardness of all those lost years between them, this might've been where he would've asked her advice. *I'm crazy about her*, he would've said. *But how do I know if she feels the same way? How do I tell her without freaking her out?*

Maybe *that* had been the true mistake in inviting Lauren to this fraught family event. He'd been so focused on how good it would be to have her support that he hadn't thought about what it might do to their burgeoning relationship, throwing her straight into the deep end of this swimming pool of adolescent trauma.

And he'd just left her in the living room, where his parents had probably cornered her by now. Who knew what they'd say. He'd be lucky if she didn't jump in her car and drive away, tires squealing.

He rubbed at his chest, at the sudden burn of panic. This time, he really *did* need to get back out there.

Instead, as if conjured by his thoughts, his mother appeared in the doorway to the nursery, peering in uncertainly like she was waiting to be invited. Standing behind her was his dad, and once they'd entered the room, Lauren followed close behind.

Sorry, she mouthed, but he only shook his head in confusion. What did she have to be sorry for? Not stalling them longer? He hadn't meant to put her in that position.

"I still don't know why you didn't go with pink," his mother said, a quaver in her voice. She was looking at him, although the observation was clearly directed at Becca.

"I like the yellow," Asa said. "It's a very happy color."

"Are *you* happy?" his mother asked, taking a step forward but not reaching for him. The room was way too small for the five of them. The way she'd phrased her question, it sounded like a genuine expression of interest in his well-being, but at the same time he couldn't help reacting to it like an attack. "Lauren says you're still working at that winter place . . . the one with the ice skating rink. And you're happy?"

Maybe that was what Lauren had been apologizing for—giving up information about him to his parents. But he'd already figured they knew basic stuff like where he worked. Becca would've told them that, and his mother's use of the word *still* seemed to confirm some prior knowledge.

He tugged at the left sleeve of his shirt, his gaze sliding to his dad's.

"Yeah," he said. "I am."

It was the truth, but it also felt like a tiny *fuck you*, a nuance that he knew wasn't lost on his father. Even if, as usual, his dad's expression gave nothing away.

He wanted so badly to break the tension by just saying aloud all the things that had built up over the years, all the pain and anger and misery and hurt. To ask why they hadn't reached out to him before now, to tell them that they didn't deserve to know if he was happy when they'd actively worked against that very happiness. But he also felt trapped by the situation, conscious of it being Becca's event and not wanting to cause a scene, aware that for whatever reason everyone seemed to want to play it like this reunion wasn't that big a deal.

He was still messing with his sleeve when he felt Lauren's hand nudge against his, her fingers sliding over his wrist and resting against his pulse. It only took a slight shift for their palms to press together, and he linked his fingers with hers and gave a squeeze.

"Maybe . . . you could come for dinner sometime?" his mother said. "I'll make that potato soup you always liked. And of course you can bring Lauren."

At his side, he could sense Lauren's attention turn to him, as if caught by something his mother had said. Maybe it was the dinner invitation—he couldn't blame her if she wouldn't want to go. *He* didn't particularly want to go. But he also somehow didn't have it in him to reject his mother right to her face.

Or maybe it was the way his mother kept referring to Lauren as though she weren't standing right there, brandishing her name like some kind of olive branch, or more of a shield.

"We'll see," he said.

His mother's eyes got that sheen that told him she was about to cry, but he couldn't tell whether it was because she was disappointed his answer wasn't a *yes* or because she was relieved it wasn't a *no*. Sometimes it had felt like his childhood had been a never-ending quest to manage her emotions, to try to read her mood and play the jokester when she was sad, to act like he didn't need anything when he could tell she was overwhelmed. He wondered who'd taken up that job in his absence. Somehow he doubted it had been his father.

Who still hadn't said a word. Asa stared directly at him, daring him to say something, *anything*. It could be the most surface, banal statement, and Asa would play along. It could be something harsh, and, well, that would be even better. It would give him the excuse to say everything he'd wanted to say for the last ten years.

His father maintained eye contact without flinching, the tic in his jaw the only sign that he had any reaction at all. Asa knew that tic well. His dad was angry but apparently wasn't going to say anything to disrupt whatever peace his wife was trying to broker.

It was Lauren who eventually broke the tense silence.

"Asa actually makes that soup himself now," she said.

"Oh, really?" His mother turned to him, a tentative smile on her face.

"Well, he's had to, hasn't he?" Lauren said. There was a vibration in her voice he'd never heard before, subtle enough that anyone else in the room might miss it. He'd heard Lauren annoyed, irritated, maybe even as far as fed up. But this was something different—she was angry, too. "He had to learn to do all kinds of stuff for himself after you threw him out. Find a place to live. Get a job. Take care of himself. So yeah, he can make his own potato soup."

The look on his mother's face was a frozen mask of shock and something else, something like . . . shame.

"We didn't—" she started, then swallowed when Becca crossed her arms, giving her a look as if daring her to finish that sentence. By the time she turned to him, she was definitely crying. "You were eighteen. An adult."

There was an aching knot in Asa's throat that prevented him from responding, from pointing out that he'd been a month away from his eighteenth birthday, not that the arbi-

trariness of that date should matter. Lauren had no such issue, however.

"He was still in *high school*," she said. "And you—"

"*You* don't know anything about it," his dad broke in, his
eyes blazing. He still had that deep, commanding voice, one
meant for projecting to the back of the room, and Asa could
feel Lauren flinch next to him even as she stood her ground.
Even his dad seemed to understand that perhaps it wasn't the
time to be raising his voice against a stranger at his daugh-
ter's baby shower, while guests were still in the next room
over. He made a visible effort to get control of himself before
speaking again.

"You seem like a nice enough girl. We're certainly glad to
see that Asa's past his phase—"

"It's who he is," Lauren said. "Not a *phase*. Just because
he's with me, it doesn't make him any less bi."

His dad scoffed at the term. "And that doesn't bother you?"
he asked, a look coming over his face like he didn't have the
energy to be mad at some random girl holding his son's hand
when he was too busy being concerned instead. Asa was familiar with that move, too—a need for control that masquer-
aded as paternalistic care. Deep down, he knew that his father
truly believed he was only looking out for his son's eternal
soul.

"The fact that he has bigoted parents bothers me," Lauren said. "But that's part of who he is, too."

Becca's eyes went wide at that, but more impressed than
shocked. Asa could see his mom clock the reaction. Maybe
she saw that they were outnumbered in that cheerful yellow
room, because she hunched closer to his father, automatically
making herself smaller. He hated seeing her that way, hated
that he couldn't just have the relationship with his parents

that other people he knew had, where they were a source of support and understanding. But Lauren was right. It was part of who he was, but it was also baggage he didn't have to carry around with him every day.

"It really hurt me," he said, grateful when his voice came out clear and strong. "When you rejected me . . . you really hurt me. And it's not going to be enough for you to turn the other cheek now and pretend it didn't happen."

He looked for a reaction from his dad, *anything* that would indicate he'd heard and had an emotional response. But that was the problem, of course. He was never going to get his dad to budge. All those years he'd stayed away, maybe he'd convinced himself it was because he knew that. But the truth was, on some level he'd been resting up, preparing for round two. Assuming that eventually he'd get his life to a point where he'd feel able to face down his dad and have this fight. Now they were face-to-face, and he realized he didn't care about round two. He could close the door on it.

"You hope I'm happy?" he said to his mom before turning back to his dad. "I used to hope you were miserable. I used to hope it kept you up at night, thinking about me, about your *son*, who you threw away like I was a piece of garbage. But I know it doesn't. And that makes me sad for you. It really does."

That caused a flicker in his dad's face, a brief moment when the older man looked away. But Asa knew he wasn't going to get anything more than that, and he genuinely didn't want to turn Becca's baby shower into an ugly scene. He squeezed Lauren's hand, about to say their goodbyes, when his mom spoke up from next to his dad.

"It does keep me up at night," she said, her voice tremulous with tears. "And I *do* want to be part of your life. I—"

She glanced up at his father, looking for approval the way she always had. Asa knew she was just as much a victim of his dad's rigidity as he was, in a way, but he also didn't have it in him to fight her battles as well as his own.

"Well, you know how to get in touch with me if you have anything more you want to say. And I'll be around," he said to Becca, giving her a brief smile. She'd been watching the whole exchange, her eyes shining, her hand resting protectively on her belly. She gave him a watery smile back.

"Maddie is going to need her uncle," she said. "*I'm* going to need you. Of course you'll be around."

Chapter
TWENTY-THREE

BY THE TIME THEY LEFT BECCA'S HOUSE, LAUREN FELT LIKE she'd been wrung out. The most strenuous thing she'd done was clip multiple clothespins to her cardigan—her final tally was six, probably enough to win the nail polish, but it hadn't exactly been on her mind by the end of the shower. It had been a *day*, and it was only two o'clock.

And if *she* was feeling spent from the emotional tension of the last few hours, she could only imagine how Asa must feel. He was quiet as they walked to her car, his hands in his pockets. His sister had let him go with a few laughing reminders to *actually check your phone, dude* as her due date approached. His mother hadn't made any more overtures, whether out of respect for Asa's boundaries or deference to her husband's, it wasn't clear. Lauren suspected whatever fractures existed in that marriage already, today may have cracked them wide open. She hoped for Asa's sake that they had, that things would be different, but she also knew that it would be a long road ahead.

Since they'd arrived late, they'd had to park halfway down the block. Asa was walking on the grass, the sidewalk too narrow for the both of them, and she didn't know if the distance was deliberate on his part. Back in the nursery, she'd held his hand, but now he seemed self-contained and pensive.

"I shouldn't have gone off like that," she said finally. "They're your family. I had no business—"

He shook his head, but whether it was because he was agreeing with her or rejecting her apology, she didn't know. "How did you know about the potato soup?"

"Oh." She curled her fingers into her palms, hoping she didn't sound like too much of a psycho. "Kiki told me. That you make it sometimes, anyway, and then when your mom mentioned it, I figured . . ."

She shrugged, not needing to state the obvious. It hadn't been a stretch to assume it was the recipe from his childhood.

"Did you mean it?" he asked, still not looking at her. "When you said I was with you. Did you mean that?"

Lauren's first instinct was to play it off. It was too soon, after all—they'd been hanging out more, they'd been physical a few times, she was sure that the last thing he'd want to do would be to give it some kind of label or definition.

But that was a disservice to the way she felt about him. And, she was beginning to realize, it was a disservice to *him*. She'd had this impression of Asa for so long as this easygoing, flippant guy, but the more she got to know him, the more she saw how serious he could be, how sincere. How sweet.

"I meant it," she said. "And I'm with you."

It would've been perfect if she could've left it at that, but of course the minute the words were out of her mouth, she started second-guessing herself. Maybe she'd misunderstood the question and was making all kinds of assumptions and bold declarations she shouldn't.

They'd reached her car, and she was grateful for the excuse to dig through her purse for her keys, fumbling with them before locating the right one. It gave her something to do, something to focus on other than Asa's reaction.

"If that's what you want." Why did she have to be the only person on the planet who still had to open her car door with an actual key, instead of a push-button key fob? Manual dexterity was apparently one of the first things to go in moments of stress. "We don't have to—"

She never got the rest of that sentence out. Asa came toward her so fast she had no time, could only let out a surprised squeak as he pressed her against the car door, his hands in her hair and his mouth hard and hungry on hers. Dimly, she was aware of the sound of her car keys hitting the pavement as her arms went around his neck.

"It's what I want," he said against her mouth. "No doubt."

She couldn't help the smile that spread over her face, even though it made it harder for Asa to keep kissing her. "So where do we go from here?"

His body was crowding hers in the most delicious way, the scratch of his stubble abrading her neck as he dipped his head to kiss behind her ear. "As in, my place or yours? Yours is closer, but I'd like to get a change of clothes at least from mine." His hands found the bare skin of her shoulders under her cardigan. "Unless you meant the question in more of an existential sense. In which case, we can go anywhere we want to, baby."

Lauren slid her hands up his chest, dragging her fingertips slowly over his nipples through his shirt, lingering long enough to hear his intake of breath. Then she plucked the clothespin that was still clipped to the collar of his shirt and fastened it below the others on her cardigan.

"Caught you," she said.

He grinned. "I knew you would."

• • •

IN THE WEEK LEADING UP TO CHRISTMAS, LAUREN FOUND A rhythm to being with Asa. She'd worried it would be difficult or awkward, simply because it had been so long since she'd been in a relationship with anyone. She wasn't used to the idea of checking in with someone about their plans, or having someone check in with her. She found herself waiting all day for the time when they were both off work, and they kept making plans to see a movie or have dinner but then never made it out of her apartment.

Even working with him on the Cold World proposal had been great so far. She'd looked up more facts and interactive activities, and she'd write up sample displays or directions while he sat next to her on her small couch, his sketchbook propped on his knees, drawing mock-ups for the final exhibit.

They only had one area of disagreement. Although of course Kiki knew that Lauren and Asa were dating—it would be difficult to hide, given that Asa had slept over at Lauren's apartment more times than he'd been home in the last few days—Lauren thought they should wait to make their relationship public at work. It wasn't against any policy per se, but she didn't feel like answering any questions about it or worrying about the slightest appearance of unprofessionalism.

Asa saw no reason for the secrecy—"People are going to catch on eventually," he pointed out—but grudgingly agreed to keep everything under wraps at least until after the proposals were presented. And if she thought he knew how to make her life impossible at work *before*, that was nothing compared to the games he could play in this new dynamic.

Like the last day of work before she'd be off for the holidays, he came into the break room while she was fixing her usual cup of coffee, doing a double take like he hadn't expected to see her there. Which, of course, was a laugh since she made her first cup of coffee at practically the same time every day, whereas he wasn't even supposed to be on shift for another hour. Sonia had arrived early, too, and was eating her fast-food breakfast while reading one of the romance novels Lauren—Asa, really—had gotten her for Secret Santa.

"Good morning," he said cheerfully to both of them, resting his hand lightly at the small of Lauren's back while he reached around her for one of the K-cups. It was an innocent enough touch, lingering only a half second longer than would've been appropriate between two colleagues. But the problem was the immediate ache it put in Lauren's lower stomach, the way it made her *want* him to linger.

From the side smirk he gave her at the coffee machine, he knew exactly what effect he'd had on her. "You look like *you're* having a particularly good morning," he said. "You're practically glowing."

She wanted to hit him. It had been less than an hour ago that she'd had his fingers inside her, his mouth around her taut, slick nipple as he urged her to come in the shower.

"You really are," Sonia said from the table. "It's a very *I'll have what she's having* type of look, unless you're coming down with something, in which case no thank you."

"I guess I'm just excited about Christmas," Lauren said, and immediately couldn't believe *that* was what she'd gone with. She'd have been better off just copping to a flu like Sonia had suggested.

"Are you doing anything fun?" Sonia asked. "Spending it with family?"

"Oh, um." Lauren's gaze slid to Asa's, but he was just lean-

ing back against the counter, watching her like he was as interested in her answer as Sonia. They hadn't expressly discussed
the upcoming holiday, whether they would spend it together.
But the night before, she'd been sitting up in bed, trying to
read her library book, with Asa lying with his head on her lap
while he teased her about how she called reading a hobby but
was treating it more like homework and tried to get her to skip
ahead to the "salacious bits" and read them aloud.

"This was short-listed for the Booker prize," she had said
primly.

He'd snorted. "I bet it would've won if it had more salacious bits." She'd felt the bed vibrate, and he reached into his
pocket for his phone, pulling it out and frowning at the screen
until she set the book down on her chest.

"What is it?"

"My mom," he'd said.

For a minute he hadn't said anything else, and even though
Lauren had been dying to know more—*What does she want?
What did she say?*— she'd threaded her fingers in his hair,
waiting patiently for him to tell her.

"There's this fancy tea place, and she wants to know if I
want to meet her for Christmas Eve tea?" He'd said it like a
question. "She put in a lot of details about the scones and
mulled wine. There's even a screenshot of the menu."

"Do you want to go?"

"It looks fucking delicious," he'd said.

"Of course it does. It's *scones*. But do you want to see
your mom?"

He'd tapped on the screen, zooming in on what looked
like a pink filigreed invitation straight out of a Jane Austen
novel. She'd expected more commentary on the menu, some
funny observation or rant about the prices, because she was

sure a place like that would be expensive. She knew Asa well enough by now to know that humor was one way he dealt with stress, and sometimes the higher the stakes the more he joked his way through it.

He'd turned his head so he was looking at her, and for a moment there'd been something in his eyes that almost took her breath away. It had felt like . . . but she didn't even want to put words to it, the way you weren't supposed to speak a birthday wish aloud.

"I'm not ready," he'd said finally. "I know it's the time of year when you *should* reunite with family . . . I tear up at the end of *Home Alone* when the old man picks up his granddaughter, just like anyone else. But I'm not ready to do this yet."

"Okay," she'd said. "Then the scones can wait."

From that conversation, Lauren knew that Asa's usual Christmas tradition was to hang out with John and Kiki at home, since neither of them went home for the holidays, either, for reasons Lauren didn't pry into. Elliot seemed to be the only one who had family relatively nearby and who was still on good terms with them, so Asa said that they were usually around before or after but not on the actual day.

He hadn't expressly invited her to join them, and even though Lauren knew she was probably welcome, she hated the idea of being the needy, friendless person who hitched onto someone else's plans. Maybe it would be better if she disinvited herself before the topic even came up.

"I'm actually going out of town," she said finally, grabbing a stirrer for her coffee to avoid having to make eye contact with either Sonia or Asa.

"You are?" Asa's voice was pitched a little higher than mere interest, sounding closer to surprise, and Lauren glanced at Sonia to see if she'd noticed. The woman had set aside her romance novel, her focus completely on the conversation, and Lauren wished she could tell her she needn't bother. The sooner she was out of this situation, the better.

"Where to?" Sonia asked.

Lauren had never been a good liar. And she didn't particularly *want* to lie, so the idea of seeing this through to making up a location and a fake itinerary seemed exhausting. "I don't know yet," she admitted. This time she couldn't help but look over at Asa, whose gray eyes slid over her face, then down to where she was frantically stirring her black coffee, then away.

"Oh, to be young and single and free," Sonia said with a sigh. "My in-laws have been staying with us for the past week, so I get the impulse to split town, for sure. What about you, Asa?"

"Not sure yet," he said. "My plans keep shifting."

This time she willed him to look at her, but he was staring down into his coffee mug like it held some kind of answer, so she muttered her excuses and headed back to her office. She wasn't really surprised when Asa followed her, shutting the door behind him.

"People are going to think—"

"So let them," Asa said. "What was that back there? Was that for Sonia's benefit, or are you really planning to spend Christmas out of town?"

She shrugged, the movement stiff and unconvincing. "I might," she said. "It's a long weekend. Why not?"

She'd meant the question to sound casual, carefree, like December 25 was any other day and it shouldn't matter one way or another what she did. But it came out all wrong, more like *What other reason could I possibly have to stay*, and she only realized how hurtful that implication was when she heard the words echoing in the silence that followed.

Lauren took a deep breath. "I only meant that I'm not really a Christmas person. You know that."

She sat down at her desk, rummaging through a stack of papers until she pulled out the blue folder of yesterday's Z reports. The numbers swam in front of her eyes, but she tried to look like she was studying them carefully, running her pencil down the margin. Jesus, sometimes pretending to work took more energy than actually working.

She heard the click of the lock before Asa knelt on the carpet in front of her, spinning her chair until he was between her knees.

"Lauren," he said, grabbing the armrests so she couldn't move the chair. "Is this the beach all over again?"

"What?" She wasn't being purposely dense—it was legitimately difficult for her to follow the shift this conversation had taken when he was so close, when she could feel his body heat against her inner thighs.

He smiled, an almost private expression of amusement, like he was thinking back to some inside joke. "You told me you couldn't come out because you had to clean your closet."

"Which I *did*—"

"And then you drove all the way out there because Kiki wanted taco backup." He ran his hands up her calves, his palms rasping slightly against the silky layer of her tights.

"Tacos are important."

"Except you didn't even stay," he said, his hands flirting now with the hem of her skirt. She had two equally strong urges—one to clench her thighs together, the other to spread her knees farther apart—but instead she held herself so still she felt her muscles tremble with the effort.

"You've seen my closet," she said, her voice coming out breathless. "You have to admit, it's very neat."

"You are a paragon of organization." He pressed one thumb against the back of her knee, some pressure point she'd never been aware of before, but now she felt in her very core. "I was really disappointed that I didn't get to see you in your green bikini."

"How'd you even know it was a bikini?" She was only half-conscious of what she was saying, already slipping into the fuzzy edges she got when he touched her.

"I could see the lump under your tank top, where it was tied around your back." He was still only touching her with that one thumb, but the pressure was so exquisite that she felt a tingling through her whole body, similar to when you'd sat on your limbs too long and felt them static back to full use. "And also the place where you'd tied it around your neck. I could draw you a diagram of that knot."

"Asa . . ." she said, pushing against his shoulders, but the effort was halfhearted and they both knew it. "You have to get to work."

"I'm early. Don't need to clock in for another hour at least."

"*I* have to get to work."

He grinned, squeezing her knees before rising to lean against her desk. "You're incorruptible, which I respect. Although for the record, I would still respect you if you let yourself be corrupted."

Lauren would've never considered herself the type of person to have sex *at work*. Fooling around with Asa that night they'd been locked in had pushed every boundary, but at least then she had the plausible deniability of it being after hours. But she was surprised at how strongly she wanted to, how tempted she was, how *disappointed* that he didn't push it further even though she knew it wasn't the right thing to do. Especially when she was the one preaching secrecy and discretion.

Which, a closed door to her office probably wouldn't help with. It occurred to her that she *still* didn't know how they'd gotten to talking about the beach in the first place. "What did you mean, *Is this the beach all over again?*"

He blinked, as if rewinding the conversation in his head. "You wanted to hang out," he said. "But you were scared. That's why you almost didn't come, and why you left early."

Scared of what? she almost asked, defensiveness a knee-jerk reaction. But she knew he was right, and it would be pointless to pretend otherwise. She'd spent so long feeling practically invisible that it still shocked her sometimes, moments like this that made her realize how well he'd seen her all along.

He hooked his foot in her desk chair, pulling her closer to him. "We would love to have you over for Christmas," he said, looking suddenly serious. "If that's what this is about. And I'm not just speaking for myself—John specifically asked if you were coming. If you'd truly rather spend it alone at a Holiday Inn, hey, that's your call. Just promise me that you won't make that kind of decision out of some notion that we don't want you there or you don't deserve to be there or whatever other outrageously wrong idea you might have. Okay?"

"Okay," she said quietly.

"So what's my exit strategy here?" he asked, nodding toward the door. "Do you want to go first and make sure the coast is clear, or—"

Her hands fisted in his T-shirt as she pulled him down for one more kiss, nearly toppling them both over in the process. "I hate being wrong."

"Oh, I know," he said, laughing as he regained his balance and exaggeratedly fixed his T-shirt as though she'd ravished him in the office after all. He cracked the door open, glancing out in the hallway before giving her one last grin. "I, on the other hand, am loving every second of it. Just come over Christmas Eve and be wrong at our house."

Only after he'd left did she realize the cheesy pun he'd made with the *Holiday Inn* reference. At various points throughout the rest of the day she found herself randomly thinking about it, which would explain why she kept catching herself smiling for no apparent reason. It was as good an explanation as any.

LAUREN SPENT THE EARLY HALF OF CHRISTMAS EVE HANGING out with Eddie, his caseworker, and his mom, Ms. Ramirez. It was awkward at first, given that Lauren didn't quite know her role—she didn't want to interfere too much with Eddie's opportunity to connect with his mom, but she also didn't want to just be some weird person lurking on the edges.

She'd ended up buying Eddie a set of graphic novels that Asa had suggested, and the present was the perfect icebreaker because it gave them all something to talk about. She genuinely liked Ms. Ramirez and was relieved that the missed visit last time had seemed like a true logistical struggle and not a sign that she didn't want to connect with her kid. Lauren was very conscious of her own history, knew that she couldn't see her work with Eddie as some way to go back in time and fix what had happened with her own mom. But still, it gave her a lot of hope to see their clear bond, to hear from the caseworker how well Ms. Ramirez was doing with the case plan.

Asa had told her that he always worked a crisis line shift on Christmas Eve, because it tended to be a busy night, but she was welcome to come over whenever. She'd worried about showing up too early and having hours to kill hanging out with his housemates, but that turned out not to be a problem at all. For one thing, it took her way longer than she expected just to *pack*. She couldn't remember the last time she'd spent the night at someone else's place, not counting the impromptu night at Cold World where there'd been no opportunity to plan beforehand. Was it weird if she brought pajamas? Was it weird if she *didn't*?

But even those dilemmas aside, it was no hardship to hang out with Kiki and John. Elliot had already left to see their family in Jacksonville, but they'd left gifts for everyone under the tree, and Lauren was touched to see her name on one. It made her feel self-conscious about the succulent she'd brought as a gift for the whole house, but John made a show of finding it a perfect spot near the front window.

"So you're still not telling anyone at work," Kiki said, her mouth full of iced cookie as she surveyed the fridge for something to drink. "How long are you planning to keep that up for?"

Lauren sipped on her own sparkling apple juice. Apparently John had bought it because he didn't drink, but it sounded good to Lauren, so she'd accepted a glass herself. It fizzed on her tongue and made her feel mildly celebratory, a small taste of the promise of the holiday season that had always eluded her.

"I haven't really thought about it," she said. "It just seems easier if people don't know. There will be lots of questions, and teasing, and people will talk if we're standing too close or not standing close enough . . . And especially with the presentations coming up, I don't want to give Dolores any reason to think we've been less than professional."

"Uh-huh." Kiki didn't sound particularly convinced. "There's no rule against it. You're not his direct manager or anything. Is this about Daniel?"

Surprisingly, Lauren hadn't even thought about Daniel since the holiday party. She'd had no chance to interact with him since then, which she was grateful for, since she had no idea how you came back from someone comparing your breasts to snowy hills. She didn't know that she wanted to.

"No," she said honestly. "It has nothing to do with him."

Kiki slammed the fridge door shut, apparently dissatisfied with the choices. "We have *nothing* good here," she said. "I'm going to the gas station to get some red Gatorade or some boxed wine. Text me if you want me to grab anything else while I'm there."

Lauren was still staring at the doorway where Kiki had left when John strolled through the kitchen. "Those are her two pinnacles of quality," he said. "Gatorade and boxed wine. God knows why."

"Is she mad at me or something?" Lauren asked. "Or is it weird, me being with Asa?"

John ran a hand through his black curls, wrinkling his nose. "She and Marj broke up," he said. "So she's a little cranky in general. It's probably not personal."

"Oh." Lauren knew Kiki hadn't been thrilled when Marj bailed on the Cold World party after Kiki had gone to Marj's stuffy law firm party. Still, breakups sucked—especially around this time of year. "I'm really sorry to hear that."

He gave her an assessing look, as if weighing whether to

say anything else. She assumed it would be more about Kiki's breakup, but when he spoke, it was about Asa. "We're all a little protective of him," he said. "Of each other, really. And especially with her own breakup being so raw . . . Kiki wants to make sure Asa's not going to get hurt."

Lauren understood what John meant, about how that wasn't meant to be personal against her. Asa and his housemates looked out for one another, which was one reason she liked hanging around them so much. At the same time, it felt strange to think of Kiki being worried about how Lauren might treat Asa, when *she'd* been the one to warn Lauren away from Asa in the first place.

"She told me Asa was fickle," Lauren blurted. The comment had stayed with her, wriggled somewhere in the back of her head.

John raised his eyebrows. "Fickle. That . . . is not a word I would use."

"So then what word *would* you use?" Normally, she would've been embarrassed by the idea of grilling one of Asa's housemates so hard about him, but right now she had no pride. She wanted information, and she didn't care if John thought she was being needlessly nosy.

And if there was one thing she'd learned about John from their limited time together, it was that he was always thoughtful. If he was going to give her an answer, he was going to consider it carefully first.

"I would've said . . . *searching*." He tilted his head, giving her a small smile. "But when Asa knows what he wants, he commits to it. Look at how long he's been at Cold World— what is it, ten years?"

"True." Sometimes Lauren wondered if that was a good thing, though. Obviously, she was glad for her sake that he'd been there that long—if he'd worked a year, two tops, like most other people would've done in their first minimum-wage job, she never would've met him.

But for his sake, she wondered if it had held him back, stopped him from pursuing other dreams.

She could've mined John for more intel all night, but at that moment Asa's door opened, and he stepped out, his face lighting up when he saw her. "Hey," he said, pulling her against him with one arm, pressing a kiss against her hair. "Merry Christmas Eve. I can see you're already celebrating."

Lauren handed him her flute of sparkling cider for him to try. It had become something of a running joke between them, how many times he'd ended up sharing her drink before they'd gotten together. It had always given her a little thrill, and it still did. Something about the casual intimacy of it.

"Mmm," he said now, taking his sip. "Hitting the hard stuff." He set the glass on the counter, pulling Lauren toward his room. "Come on, I want to give you your present. I can't wait any longer."

She'd come prepared with a present of her own and was trying not to feel insecure about it. The minute Asa shut the door behind them, she pulled the small wrapped package out of her Cold World tote bag, pushing it across the bed toward him.

"Open this first," she said. "It's not much. A step above a fart maker, maybe, but. Not much."

He grinned at her, and she could see how touched he was that she'd gotten him anything at all. She really hoped she'd set his expectations appropriately by referencing the fart maker, but she still felt like she needed to apologize for the Secret Santa debacle.

"I'm not good at presents," she said, knowing she was

rambling but somehow still wanting to delay the moment when he opened the gift. "You said once that I don't like to do things I'm not good at, and—"

"Lauren," he said, cutting her off. "No matter what it is, I know I'll love it. Although you did wrap this like you own stock in Scotch tape."

Okay, she'd gone a *little* crazy with the tape. She'd tried to use the three pieces he'd recommended in his tutorial, but they'd ended up being very long pieces. Wrapped around the entire present, mummy-style.

He finally ripped the paper off to reveal a handheld random number generator device that she'd found online. It looked like a small plastic calculator and had inputs for the bottom and top numbers in your range and then a button to push to generate the random number onto a small screen. The shipping had cost more than the product itself, which didn't give her a lot of faith in its potential longevity, but she hoped he liked it nonetheless.

"In case you ever want to try my method of to-do lists," she said. "Or replay our game, not that I remember what all the numbers stood for."

Asa reached around her to pull open his desk drawer, sliding a few papers aside until he came out with a folded, yellow lined sheet, the top edge torn from a mini legal pad.

"Number one," he read, "ask me anything. Number two, my favorite blank is. Number three, I dare you to . . ."

She grabbed the paper from him to read the rest. "You kept this?"

"Of course," he said, rummaging through the drawer to pull out another sheet of paper. This one had a word bubble on it that said I'm getting a strong "A" vibe . . . Asa? Ass? It took Lauren a minute to register her own handwriting, to remember that she'd left this message on the fridge the first time she'd ever visited the house.

"Oh my god," she said, groaning. "I can't believe I wrote that."

"I *did* get you to call that Rick Astley hotline that one April Fool's," he said. "So I can't blame you for thinking I was an ass."

It had been the April after she'd started at Cold World, and although she'd heard rumors of a few pranks in the past, she figured that she'd be immune from them as a newish member of the office staff. So she'd been totally unsuspecting when Asa came into her office with a Post-it note with a number written on it, saying that Rick "something" had called with a billing question, and could she call him back? She'd thought it was odd that he would've fielded the phone call, and had been annoyed when he stood in her office while she picked up the phone, assuming he somehow didn't trust her to do it.

"I just got hold music," she'd said after hanging up. "What did you say he was calling about?"

"What was the hold music?"

It had struck her as the most asinine question, but she started describing it as the "never gonna give you up" song, until it dawned on her what he'd done. At the time, she'd been more focused on her own embarrassment at having fallen for it, her own mild irritation at the wasted time. It was so funny how getting to know someone could cast all prior interactions in a completely different light, how clearly now she could see it as a very benign prank, done more to make her feel included than to single her out.

"Okay," Asa said now, pulling a large, flat rectangle from his closet. It was wrapped in metallic blue paper with tiny silver snowflakes, *To:* and *From:* filled out in black Sharpie. It looked like a picture frame, just from the ridge around the edge, slightly raised above the flat expanse of the middle. But a picture of what?

She slid her fingernail carefully under the seam of the tape, peeling back the wrapping paper to reveal the framed art underneath. Her first impression was of all the *flowers*—drawn on curlicue vines around the edges, filling in the spaces in between. And even inside the small ovals placed in three perfect circles, nested inside one another. It took her a second to register that the picture frame appeared to have originally been one of those dated ones meant to showcase school pictures—the soft green of the background had been painted with enough transparency that she could still see the script underneath each oval, starting at the top and moving clockwise. Kindergarten. First grade. Second grade.

In the first-grade one, he'd drawn a rose, blooming until half the petals were outside the outline of the oval. In second grade, a lotus. Third grade, a pair of violets, so vibrantly purple she could see where he'd pressed down with a colored pencil to build up the pigment. And in fourth grade, an iris, simple and tall.

"I found the frame with the mat while thrift shopping with Elliot. It made me think about what you'd said, about not having any school pictures, and I thought . . ." He broke off, reaching up to cradle her face and brush away the tears she was only dimly aware were starting to fill up her eyes.

"Hey," he said softly. "Hey, I hope I didn't . . ."

She shook her head. They weren't sad tears, not really, although there was a dull ache in her chest when she thought about her mom. It was enough of a bittersweet edge to prevent them from being completely happy tears, even though she was awed by how much work Asa had obviously put into this, how much thought and time. They were complicated tears, but in a good way. In a grateful way.

"I love it," she said, standing on tiptoes and wrapping her arms around his neck to bring his body close to hers. "I love it," she repeated in between kisses. "I love it. I love *you*—"

She couldn't believe she'd just blurted it out like that. And from the way he stilled under her touch, she couldn't even hope that maybe he hadn't heard. The last thing she wanted was to stop to have a conversation about what she'd said and what it might mean, especially when she'd barely thought through all the ramifications herself. And she really, *really* didn't want to hear him say something gentle about how he liked her a lot but he wasn't quite there yet.

So instead she kissed him harder, and hoped it said everything she wanted to without words.

Chapter TWENTY-FOUR

SHE LOVED HIM? *SHE LOVED HIM.*

Asa knew he hadn't imagined her saying it, but maybe she'd been caught up in the moment, carried away by expressing her feelings about the present. In the seconds after those words still hung in the room, she'd certainly made it clear that she had no intention of elaborating on them further. They'd barely come up for air.

"Take this off," she said, pushing impatiently at the hem of his shirt.

He had it over his head in a single fluid motion. "You telling me what to do?"

There was a mischievous tilt to her mouth, but something shy around her eyes. "Is that a problem?"

"No problem here."

"Good," she said. He was only wearing the gym shorts he wore around the house, and the light brush of her fingertips under the waistband shot straight to his dick. "Now these."

It wasn't long before he was completely naked, even as she was still fully dressed in the casual long-sleeved shirt and leggings she'd worn to come over. He leaned in, partially because he wanted to speak directly into her ear, and partially because he enjoyed the way her self-control cracked the closer he got, the way she trembled at his breath on her cheek.

"You might want to lock the door," he said. "To preserve my modesty."

A brief, embarrassed streak of color shot across her cheeks—whether because she was remembering the last time they'd gotten caught out, or because she felt bad she hadn't considered it happening again, he didn't know. But she turned the lock in the doorknob and switched off the brighter overhead light until the room was lit only by his desk lamp. By the time she was leaning against the door, she seemed to have gotten over that momentary lapse.

He didn't know that *he* was over it yet. He didn't know if he'd be able to explain it to her, the effect she had on him. One of the first things he'd noticed about Lauren was that, despite how guarded she could be, her emotions really played across her face. And even in moments like this one, he found it so appealing, so fucking *hot*, the way he could see her vacillate between vulnerability one minute, taking control and getting off on the power the next. Even in the last week, she'd opened up so much with him, and the sex was mind-blowing but it wasn't even about the sex. It was about the way he sensed her trusting him.

Loving him.

She stepped forward, reaching for him, but he gently encircled her wrists to keep her hands at her sides.

"I love you, too," he said. "I just wanted to clear that up."

Her dark eyes searched his. "Really?"

"Is that so hard to believe?"

"Well, it *is* hard . . ."

Asa felt his eyebrows shoot up into his hairline as she pressed her pelvis into his. "Lauren Fox, was that a *dirty joke*?"

She dropped her forehead to his chest, the exhale of her breath a warm pulse on his bare skin. "I'm nervous," she whispered. "I joke when I get nervous."

He released her wrists to cradle her cheeks, tilting her face up. If he thought about it too much, he could get intimidated, too—about what this meant for them, about where they would go from here—but all that disappeared when he looked into the deep brown of her eyes.

"Don't be nervous," he said, pressing a soft kiss to the corner of her mouth, then catching her lower lip between his teeth. "This is the easy part."

THEY WOKE UP LATE ON CHRISTMAS MORNING. FOR ONCE IN his life, the draw of staying in bed was greater than the promise of presents, but Lauren was adorably excited by the stocking full of candy John gave her. Asa knew it was the dollar store stocking with Lauren's name written on it in Sharpie, identical to the ones John had propped on the couch for the rest of the housemates, and not so much the candy, which he'd probably end up eating most of.

They FaceTimed with Elliot, who grudgingly agreed that Kiki could open their waffle maker if she promised to clean it immediately afterward. "Don't forget the whisk we had to throw away after the alfredo sauce," they said. "Don't just soak it and think that's the same as scrubbing."

It took a few batches for Kiki to get the settings right, but then they had golden brown waffles and more presents to open, mainly useful things for the house or low-cost novelty gifts like a *Betty & Veronica* for Kiki or a set of guitar picks with lewd sayings on them that Asa had custom-ordered for John from an Etsy shop. John was almost as easily embarrassed by that kind of thing as Lauren was, so between the two of them there were a lot of pink cheeks as they passed the guitar picks around.

All told, it was the best Christmas that Asa had ever had. Later that night, when they were alone in his room planning to watch a movie, he tried again to get Lauren to tell him her favorite.

"No guilty pleasures here," he said, "only pleasures. I'll watch whatever. You a Muppet Christmas fan? More of a Hallmark kind of girl? Has there ever been a Muppet Hallmark crossover event?"

He was already pulling up a few streaming sites, starting to search, but Lauren reached over to close the laptop. "What happens after the presentations?" she asked.

There was something about the way the question was framed—the presumption that something *would* happen after—that clenched around his heart like an icy fist. "What do you mean?"

Lauren tucked her hair behind her ear. "If Dolores likes our ideas, then we'll be working together to implement them. But if she doesn't . . . or worse, if she goes with something Daniel comes up with . . ."

"Then everything goes back to the way it was," Asa said. "Only now we have each other. Right?"

Lauren nodded, but she still seemed troubled. He couldn't tell if she was scared that everything would change, or that nothing would.

"Look," he said, sliding the computer off his lap so he could face her on the bed more fully. "Our presentation is in great shape. We have concept art, you've written up really clear descriptions and plans for the educational exhibit and activities, the cost of materials and labor to put it in action won't be prohibitive . . . Honestly, I don't see how Dolores *doesn't* go for it. But even if she doesn't, it won't be the end of the world. Or the end of Cold World."

He'd said that last bit as a joke, to lighten the mood, but the very idea of Cold World ending made *him* anxious. Their plan had to work. And even if it didn't—even if, by some miracle, Daniel came up with something even better—Asa was determined that they'd figure *something* out. Cold World was an institution. It wasn't going anywhere.

Especially now that it had brought him Lauren.

They were silent for a few moments, until Lauren nudged his foot with hers. "There was this animated movie I saw as a kid . . . maybe from the eighties? Or even older, possibly. The shelter where my mom and I were staying had taped it straight off the TV, and it still had the commercials in it and everything. My favorite was this old Rice Krispies one, remember when Snap, Crackle, and Pop were like actual characters?"

Asa smiled, even though he had no idea. He couldn't remember having ever seen a commercial for that cereal before. But he liked the way her face lit up as she talked about it.

"Anyway." She shook her head, giving a little laugh. "The movie was about this clockmaker and his family, and then a family of mice who lived in the house, too. It's silly, but as a kid I liked the way the humans and the mice coexisted like that, so casual. Like when they have a problem they need to solve together, the dad mouse just pops up on the clockmaker's book at bedtime, dressed in a full coat and scarf while he tells the clockmaker about how his son wrecked his apology clock to Santa."

Asa frowned. "Wait, you lost me. Apology clock?"

"The mouse son is a real skeptic. Apparently he wrote a letter to the local newspaper, saying that Santa was a myth, and signing it 'from all of us.' So Santa boycotts the town, and all the kids are pretty down about it, until the clockmaker has the idea to build this giant clock that will play a special song for Santa at the stroke of midnight. But then the skeptic mouse son breaks it trying to figure out how it works, and . . ." She wrinkled her nose self-consciously. "It sounds so ridiculous when I describe it out loud."

"Try narrating the plot of *The Santa Clause*. These movies don't have to make sense, they just have to feature a lot of snow and the spirit of the season. Let me guess—they fix the clock and save the day?"

Lauren beamed as though she had something personally to do with it, like she'd reached into the clock's mechanisms and adjusted them herself. "Even a miracle needs a hand," she said, and then sang the line with a roll of her eyes. "That's a song in the movie."

"Hmm." Asa was surprised he'd never seen this movie before. Not only because he loved Christmas movies and considered himself something of a connoisseur, but because the messaging sounded right up his parents' alley. If they had known about this movie when he was a kid, one hundred percent it would've been shown on repeat as the perfect blend of holiday magic and an allegory for a punitive higher power. He didn't want to harsh on Lauren's childhood, but he had to know if he was understanding this movie correctly.

"So, let me get this straight," he said. "Santa was so mad that this town called him fake—an allegation that *cannot* be new to him—that he just stops bringing presents? And then only starts back up when they grovel with a clock?"

The line between Lauren's eyebrows deepened. "I may not be remembering everything exactly right, but yeah, basically."

Asa made a *yikes* face that had Lauren laughing, but she sobered as she seemed to think more about what he'd said.

"If you think about it, though, there's an inherent flaw in the Santa logic. Because he's not supposed to discriminate, right? He only cares if you're naughty or nice, which is within your control. And yet when you show up to school after winter break, somehow Santa brought the rich kids new electronics while you were left with a used pair of shoes or something."

There was a thread starting to come loose around the edge of Asa's bedspread, and Lauren picked at it, unraveling it a few more inches before seeming to realize what she was doing. She smoothed the thread down against the teal cloth, as though that could weave it back in. "Not that I wasn't grateful for the shoes," she said. "But this was why it was better not to believe in the first place. It was easier to accept that my mom just couldn't afford something than to wonder why I wasn't worthy of it."

Asa rolled over until he was covering Lauren's body with his own, his arms braced on either side of her head so he didn't crush her with his full weight. He had so much he wanted to say, but the minute his eyes locked with hers he realized that his throat was suddenly tight, and it was difficult to push any words out. So instead he kissed the corner of her mouth, threaded his fingers in the silky strands of her hair that were now splayed on the pillow. "You're worthy," he said, but his voice was hoarse. He wasn't sure she'd heard him until she pulled him down for a deeper kiss and tasted the salt on her lips.

Chapter
TWENTY-FIVE

LAUREN COULD TELL THAT ASA WAS NERVOUS THE MORN-
ing of the presentations, which paradoxically made her feel
calmer. Leading up to the big day, he'd been the one who'd
repeated his assurances that they were prepared, that their
ideas were solid and actionable, that it was going to go great.
But now that they were standing in the hallway with Daniel,
about to be called into Dolores' office, he was fiddling with
the long sleeves of the button-up he'd worn in a gesture she
recognized from his sister's baby shower.

"It's going to be fine," she said, reaching over to fasten the
button that had come undone at Asa's right wrist. She realized only after she'd done it that it was way too domestic and
intimate a move for two supposed colleagues with no connection to each other outside of work. When she glanced at Daniel, she saw his eyes were narrowed.

Just then, the door to Dolores' office swung open, and the
woman herself appeared in the doorway. "Oh, my babies!"
she said. "I hope you haven't been waiting long. I was on a
call. Come in, come in, and we will get started. I can't wait to
hear what you've come up with!"

Outwardly, Dolores seemed her usual self—dressed to

the nines in an emerald green dress with flapper-style fringe at the bottom, her long hair curling down her back in a *Real Housewives* eat-your-heart-out kind of way. But there was something slightly off about her. Lauren suddenly had the strongest desire to beg off the presentations, suggest they do them another day. But she was already stepping into Dolores' office, Asa's hand at the small of her back, the barest ghost of a touch and yet it still had her turning to frown at him. *Not now.*

Dolores took her seat behind her desk, but as if by tacit agreement Daniel, Lauren, and Asa all stayed standing. Lauren suspected Asa did it half out of chivalry—he wouldn't sit down until she did—and half out of nerves. Daniel, on the other hand, probably saw standing as some sort of power play. Why Lauren didn't take a seat, she couldn't say. She still couldn't shake the feeling that she needed to be vigilant. She just wished she knew for *what*.

"Daniel," Dolores said, turning to her son. "You've already filled me in a little on your plan for Cold World, so why don't you go first. How can we improve this place in the new year?"

Daniel started laying out his idea for building the slopes where people could go snow-tubing, which didn't seem that much more involved than when she'd first heard his half-assed pitch. He claimed to have a couple more investors interested in putting in up to twenty thousand—although Daniel "knew" he could get them higher—and had also done a poll through Instagram where his meager frat boy friends had agreed it would be "awesome" if you could snowboard in Florida.

Lauren had already filled Asa in on the details of what Daniel would probably present on. He was a nicer person than she was, so he'd at least acknowledged that it was a cool *idea*, although he'd agreed with her that the actual implementation of it was impractical if not impossible, at least given Cold World's current location. Now, he caught her eye as Daniel was dancing around an answer to Dolores' very straightforward question about liability waivers, and Lauren had to struggle not to let a smile crack through.

Then Dolores turned to them, registering a flicker of surprise when she saw they were presenting together, then rewarding Lauren with one of the biggest, most open smiles Lauren had ever seen from her boss. That smile wiped away the last of that low dread feeling in the pit of Lauren's stomach, and her voice was clear and confident when she started describing what she and Asa had come up with. The interactive installations for the kids, the events they had planned, the budget-conscious improvements they could make that would have the biggest impact. Asa jumped in to describe the new aesthetic for Cold World—the mural in the Snow Globe, the merch in the gift shop.

Lauren couldn't help but watch him and think back to the last time they were in this very office together. Then, they'd sat in the chairs in front of Dolores' desk, two little islands with governments hostile to each other. She'd been so *cold* that day—literally, because her hands were still raw and chapped from picking up balls of shaved ice, her sweater and tights dappled with damp spots. And yet she remembered this one sliver of a moment—they'd been talking about whether they could ever get it to actually snow in the Snow Globe, and Asa had looked at her with such a sudden scorch of heat that she'd felt her skin prickle with fever.

She'd discounted it at the time as a weird fluke, like seeing an airplane in the night sky and mistaking it for a shooting star. But looking back, there seemed something almost inevitable about it. Also terrifying—the idea that she might get warmth from someone else, how quickly her body learned to crave it. To need it.

"Lauren?" Asa was saying now, his voice gentle. She realized she'd been staring at his animated face while he was talking without registering most of his actual words. They'd rehearsed their presentation a few times, so she knew basically what he'd said, but still. She cleared her throat.

"These outline estimated expenses, as well as projections for ticket sales adjusting for the discounts and deals we came up with," she said, passing the report she'd prepared to Dolores. Out of the corner of her eye, she saw Daniel make a face, as if she'd literally pulled his work off the printer and tried to hand it off as her own. She gave him a placid smile and was gratified when he broke eye contact first, looking down at his pointy-tipped leather shoes.

"This looks fantastic," Dolores said, scanning down the first page before flipping to the next. "Truly, I'm impressed by the attention to detail here, and the creativity."

Lauren allowed herself a quick glance at Asa, who looked about two seconds away from an actual fist pump. "Thank you—" she started, but Dolores cut her off.

"I've been in touch with a potential buyer for Cold World, and they have such a vision for how they can modernize the place. It's the same group behind that boutique hotel on Orange, the one with the iron gate, what's it called . . . Anyway, this report is going to be so helpful in showing them all the possibility here."

That dip of dread was back, but this time it was a full plummet. Lauren almost didn't know what to say. A potential *buyer*? Had that been the plan all along? To come up with ideas for Cold World only to have them . . . used by someone else?

If she was stunned by this news, she could only imagine how Asa must feel. And yet she couldn't even look at him. She didn't want to see the look on his face. She didn't want to see his heartbreak, knowing that on some level she was responsible for it. Why had she let them dream at all? Why had she thrown herself into this, instead of practicing caution the way she normally did?

Surprisingly, it was Daniel who spoke up first. "You're selling Cold World?" he demanded, his familial relationship with Dolores allowing him to openly say what they were all thinking.

Dolores hesitated, looking genuinely regretful. "I don't know," she said. "I haven't decided yet. But it would make sense to do it now . . ." Finally, she seemed to remember who she was talking to, the circumstances that had brought them all into her office. The meeting *she* had called—and then completely changed the rules for. "Of course, any contract will have clauses about retaining key employees. Lauren, the business will always need someone to handle its accounts, no matter what it turns into . . . there might even be a promotion in it for you. Vice president of finance. Something like that. I don't know how these investment groups handle these sorts of things, but it would be a great opportunity. And Asa—"

Dolores broke off abruptly, dabbing a manicured finger delicately under one eye. "You're the heart and soul of this place," she said. "You have been from the day you first arrived, all bony elbows and that uneven hair, like you'd taken a Weedwacker to it. You walked into the Snow Globe and started singing 'White Christmas' like you were Bing Crosby himself, even though you couldn't carry a tune to save your life—" She reached out, even though she was too far away to put her hand on Asa's arm like she clearly intended. "—I'm sorry, my darling, but you know it's true."

Lauren did risk a glance at Asa then. His jaw was tensed, his Adam's apple working as though he was having difficulty swallowing. "I remember," he said.

"I know you've always said you didn't want to be in management," Dolores continued, "but I could recommend—"

"What if I went to part time," Lauren cut in. She couldn't stand to see that look on Asa's face anymore, couldn't stand the idea that Cold World would be run by some soulless corporate overlord. "I could do the most important parts of my job in twenty hours a week. I know I could. That would save you half of my salary."

Dolores frowned. "But your benefits—"

"You'd save on those, too," Lauren said, taking a deep breath. "I applied to go back to school to get enough credits to sit for the CPA exam. I'll be eligible for cheaper health insurance through that program, anyway. And we can also—"

"Wait, you applied for what?" Asa said, and when Lauren turned to face him, he didn't look any better than he had before. If anything, he looked worse.

"Well, technically I already got in," Lauren said. "It's a master's in accounting, half the program's online, I don't think it's that competitive so it's not like—"

"You *got in?*" Asa's expression was completely inscrutable to Lauren. She could see a flash of something familiar, a hint of pride or joy or another emotion she might've expected. But then that fell away, and she couldn't interpret what was left.

Dolores interrupted before Lauren could say anything more. "That is very generous of you, Lauren, and I do appreciate the thought. But it wouldn't be enough. The truth is that Cold World—"

She broke off as Asa turned and, without saying another word, left through the office door, shutting it quietly after him. She looked up at Lauren, seeming more bemused than upset by his sudden exit.

Lauren just stared at the closed door. She knew how much this place meant to Asa, could only imagine what he must be going through thinking that it might be sold. But couldn't he see that was why they had to keep working, come up with another idea, find some way to convince Dolores not to do it? She couldn't shake the fear that he was upset about more than just Cold World. That it had something to do with *her*.

"Good riddance," Daniel said, breaking into her thoughts. "Like some paint on the wall is going to completely revolutionize this place. But Mom, listen—"

Lauren couldn't stand to hear another word that came out of his mouth. "I don't know how much you're paying him," she said to Dolores, indicating Daniel with a dismissive gesture, "but there's another line item you could cut from the budget. Not to mention untold legal fees and the amount of any future sexual harassment settlement."

"Hey!" Daniel said, but Lauren didn't bother sticking around to see what he could possibly have to say for himself. She had to go after Asa.

Chapter TWENTY-SIX

ASA DIDN'T KNOW WHERE TO GO. HE FOUND HIMSELF TURN-
ing toward Lauren's office as if by habit—she was the person
he most wanted to process this with. But then he remembered that she'd been there, that she was part of what he
needed to process in the first place, and he headed in the opposite direction instead. He kept going until he found himself in the "scary back room," as Lauren had once called it,
sliding down the wall until he was sitting on the floor next to
a pile of broken ice skates.

Cold World was closing. Or being sold—as far as he was
concerned, it was the same thing. This place—the place he'd
considered a second home for the past ten years, the place
where he'd found some measure of security and peace—was
ending.

And Lauren was planning to leave. Just like she'd said she
would, if the presentation didn't go well. She'd gotten into a
master's program—a program she hadn't even told him she'd
applied to—and he knew part time was only a gateway to her
moving on.

He was still sitting on the floor when he heard the door
creak open, and Lauren stood in front of him, her face in

shadow as she looked down, before she folded herself into a sitting position next to him on the floor. It wasn't easy for her to do in her pencil skirt, and she apologized when she knocked her knee against his thigh. The soft "sorry" made Asa close his eyes.

"That could've gone better," she said finally, her voice deceptively light.

He swallowed. "Yeah."

"I actually thought our presentation went great," she said. "Dolores seemed into our ideas. It's just—"

"When were you going to tell me?" he asked. "About the master's program."

"Classes don't start for two weeks," she said. "And like I said, it's mostly online. It's not going to change anything."

Change. If there was one thing Asa didn't handle well, it was change.

"Aren't you . . . happy for me?" she asked tentatively, and he hated the doubt in her voice, hated that he'd had any role in putting it there. At the same time, he didn't know what he felt. It was too complicated to boil it down to *happy*.

He opened his eyes, looking over at her for the first time. He loved her so much it was physically painful, an ache in his chest, his throat, until he realized his eyes were actually starting to sting. He had to glance away, blinking a few times. *Despite what the Cure might lead you to believe, boys* do *cry.* How was it possible that only a few weeks ago he'd been teasing her with little jokes like that, *testing* her on some level, he realized only now, and here he was unable to find a single lighthearted thing to say?

"I am happy for you," he said. "I want the chance to *be* happy for you. But Lauren, why wouldn't you just share that with me?"

She shrugged, the motion stiff. "At first, I guess I didn't tell anyone in case I didn't get in. And then even afterward . . . I don't know. It didn't seem like that big a deal."

I didn't tell anyone. He didn't know if she knew how much that word hurt. Was he just *anyone* to her? He wanted to ask. He was scared to ask. He didn't know if he wanted the answer.

"I know you're upset about Cold World," she said. "I am, too. I wish—well, I wish Dolores hadn't blindsided us with that at the presentation. That we'd known going in that any ideas we'd come up with would be fed straight to an investment group. Maybe we could've gone all-in on Daniel's dumbass idea."

She smiled at him, and he could tell she was joking, trying to make him laugh. He wondered vaguely if that was the first time he'd ever heard anything approaching a swear word from her. She'd written it on that note on his fridge, back at the start of all this. It was such a stupid thing to focus on, but it was better than any of the alternatives.

"At least if Cold World closes down, we can be public with our relationship, right?"

It came out sounding more bitter than he'd intended, which was exactly why he *shouldn't* be trying to joke at that moment. He felt completely depleted of any humor.

Lauren blinked at him, like she was trying to figure out how to respond. "I mean—of course. If we didn't work together, there would be no reason to hide it."

"But as long as we're both still here . . ." he finished for her. "You realize everyone probably knows, right?"

She flushed. "I don't think—"

"Dolores knows."

"She might suspect, but—"

He gave her a look.

"Okay," Lauren said, flustered now. "Okay, so maybe she knows. But that's still different from us being obvious about it at work. It's more professional if we don't *act* like we're together. It doesn't have to change anything about—"

That fucking word again. It made Asa literally tug at his hair, frustrated beyond words at how much she didn't seem to get it. "*Everything* has changed, Lauren," he said. "Everything. We just got out of a meeting where our boss told us she was going to recommend us for vice president of finance and middle management at some new version of Cold World, which you know won't look anything like what it is now, maybe that version will have some dumbfuck HR contract we'd have to sign about not dating colleagues, who knows, but all I know is *I can't do it.* I can't do this anymore."

He meant he couldn't hide, that he couldn't take it if she was going to still shut him out even after all they'd shared and been through. He didn't mean that he didn't want to be in the *relationship* anymore. But he could tell from the stricken look on her face that that was exactly how it had sounded. And before he could say more, fix it, he saw the way the look fell away until her face was a blank mask. No, not fell—was *pushed* away. A return to Robot Lauren.

"That's fine," she said.

"Lauren—"

"No," she said, giving a little laugh that splintered in his heart. "No, that's fine. I get it. It's been a lot to take in. It's probably better if we don't—"

"Lauren, *listen* to me—"

She pushed herself up to standing, brushing her hands on her skirt. She seemed about to leave, then had second thoughts and turned back around. "You say *middle management* like it's the worst thing that could ever happen to you," she said. "And maybe it is, that's fair—but Asa, you have to do *something*. You can't just guard the Snow Globe for the rest of your life."

He got to his feet, too, breathing harder than that simple exertion should've required. This had been what he'd always been afraid of, deep down—and to hear her say it was like a punch to the gut. He'd known she was too good for him. He'd just lived on the prayer that maybe she wouldn't notice.

"I like my job," he said. "What's wrong with guarding the Snow Globe?"

"*Nothing*," she said. "It's not that the job is beneath you. It's that it doesn't *challenge* you, and at some point you're just standing still when you should be moving forward. Do something with your art, go back to school, I don't even know! Just do *something*."

She said all that like it was so easy. "Maybe some of us don't want more school," he said. "Despite what the student loan industrial complex wants you to believe, that's not always the answer, you know."

He'd meant it more about him, but he could see how it was a poorly timed comment, coming on the heels of her revelation about going back to grad school.

"Fine," she snapped. "Don't go back to school. At the end of the day, it's none of my business what you do. I wouldn't have said anything, except that I lo—" She took a deep breath, seemed to catch herself. "I care about you a lot. I want to see *you* happy."

Wow. Downgraded off *love* already. Asa had never wished for anything harder than he wished for a time machine right at that moment, when he could go back to the beginning of this conversation—the beginning of this *day*, even—and do everything all over. He had so much he wanted to say but his throat was too tight to say any of it, which was why maybe he landed on the most asinine and blatantly false thing he could think to say.

"I am happy."

She gave him a brittle smile, her eyes bright. "Well," she said. "Good. If it's not fun, don't do it, right?"

His voice was barely a rasp. "Lauren—"

"We dated for what, a week?" she said. Had it really been that short? Images from their time together flashed through his head—Lauren taking the clothespin off his shirt at his sister's baby shower; snuggled on the couch in her apartment, her feet in his lap while she read aloud from their presentation draft document; the hitch in her breath when he'd entered her the night before, the way she'd clung to his shoulders as he'd started to move. Their time together felt like it had been so much longer. It hadn't been enough.

"We both knew it wasn't going to be forever," she said. "But it was fun while it lasted."

And then she was walking away, her words still ringing through his head. *We both knew it wasn't going to be forever.* Had they both known that? Asa felt like he'd missed the memo.

He wanted to run after her, tell her that *he'd* certainly been ready for forever, he was ready for it still, and if she wanted them to keep their relationship quiet a little longer, that was fine by him. But he also was shaken by how quickly she'd folded, the blink-and-you'll-miss-it transition she'd made from supposedly being in love with him to telling him goodbye. And with their differing reactions to the Cold World news, the different trajectories they apparently wanted their lives to take—who knew. Maybe there wasn't anything left to say.

Chapter

TWENTY-SEVEN

"MISS LAUREN?"

Eddie had been trying to get her attention for the last thirty seconds, Lauren realized, and she'd been busy staring off into space. "Sorry," she said, giving him and Ms. Ramirez an apologetic smile. "What was that?"

Ms. Ramirez had completed her parenting classes and been very dedicated to her visitation schedule after that hiccup with the first visit. She saw him twice a week and even though Lauren knew she didn't have to attend every visit, she genuinely enjoyed spending time with them. That was why Lauren had suggested Eddie and his mom meet her at Cold World to have the day they'd originally planned back when she and Asa had ended up taking Eddie ice skating.

Even thinking about Asa put that pit back in Lauren's stomach. She'd tried to stop thinking about him, tried to stop always searching for him, seeking him out in every room she was in, but it was impossible. Even now, she was hyperaware that he was back on the rink, skating in lazy circles with his hands behind his back, occasionally stopping to reach a hand down to a kid on the ice. She lived in fear that Eddie would ask to go back out there. How would she beg off?

"I wanted to show my mom the Snow Globe now," he said, and she should be relieved, that he didn't seem to have any interest in ice skating. So why did she feel a flutter of disappointment instead?

Lauren looked at her watch. Jolene was supposed to be there in ten minutes to pick Eddie back up, but she was loath to deny this experience if it was what he wanted. "Sure," she said, gathering up the plastic wrappers from the prepackaged muffins she'd bought them at the coffee stand. "We can do that. Ms. Ramirez?"

Eddie ran ahead toward the Snow Globe, and Lauren expected Ms. Ramirez to be right behind him, but she hung back a bit to talk with Lauren instead.

"I really appreciate all you've done for him," Ms. Ramirez said.

"Oh," Lauren said. They were passing closer to the ice rink now, and Asa was skating in their direction, his head turned to one side. If he looked over, just once, he'd see—but something caught his attention, and he shifted direction, until he was skating away. Lauren swallowed. "He's fun to hang out with. He's a great kid. How's the job search going?"

Right now, the main sticking points to Ms. Ramirez's reunification with Eddie were her job situation, and her pending home study, both of which depended on each other to make the other one work out. But Lauren felt gratified that her instincts about Ms. Ramirez had been right—she really cared about her son. And she was doing everything in her power to make a safe home for him to return to, now that she was separated from her abusive ex.

Weirdly, seeing the whole situation from this angle had made Lauren set parts of her own story to rest. Parts she hadn't even known still bothered her—lingering questions about why her mother didn't fight for her harder, why the system hadn't done more to help them. She still felt sad, when she thought about her childhood, but seeing how much flawed, messy humanity was at the heart of all these issues took the edge off the anger she hadn't even realized she'd been carrying around.

Ms. Ramirez was in the middle of telling her about one promising interview she'd had at an auto supply store when Lauren saw Dolores flagging her down.

"I'm so sorry," she said. "That's my boss. I'll be right here, but—"

Ms. Ramirez waved her on, hurrying a little to catch up with Eddie, who was already inside the Snow Globe. Cold World was experiencing its usual post-Christmas lull, so there weren't many people there that day despite school being out. Lauren tried to remind herself that was totally normal and expected, but she still couldn't shake a slight despondency as she thought about the possibility of the entire place shutting down. She kept waiting for some formal statement from Dolores at an all-staff meeting, but it had only been three days since the disastrous presentations.

Three long, excruciating days. Three days where she kept picking up her phone, wanting to text Asa, before remembering that she couldn't. Three days where she'd cried herself to sleep at night and woken up with her eyes almost swollen shut. Three days where she'd splurged on Starbucks she absolutely didn't need just to avoid any chance of running into him in the break room. Three days where she wandered into the break room aimlessly, half hoping he'd be there.

"I know you took the afternoon off," Dolores said now as she approached, "but I had to tell you the news."

Lauren steeled herself for it. The deal had gone through.

The investment group was buying Cold World. There was a promotion in it for her—or there wasn't. She didn't really care.

"I took the plans you and Asa came up with to the city," Dolores said. "They have grants for the arts and educational programs in particular, and they said we'd be a shoo-in for one if we can fill out the paperwork before the January fifteenth deadline. I know you have classes starting up, but I was hoping you and Asa might be available to help?"

Of all the things Dolores might say, Lauren hadn't expected that. She felt a surge of hope before remembering that there was no her and Asa anymore. "Um," she said, not wanting to turn Dolores down but not knowing what else she could say. "That seems like good news at least? That we might get a grant?"

"I did a lot of thinking after you all left my office that day," Dolores said. "There are a lot of adjustments that could be made—including about Daniel. He's my son and I love him, but you're right, he was a drag on the payroll."

Okay, of all the things she could've said, *that* was actually the most shocking. "Really?"

"I want to talk to you more about that comment you made as you left," Dolores said. "But I know this isn't the time or place. Perhaps you would be willing to come to my office tomorrow morning, and we could go over the grant and other concerns or ideas you might have about the way Cold World has been run? Asa, too, of course."

Lauren glanced over at the ice rink, as though she'd be able to see Asa from where they stood, but of course they were too far away now. Maybe this would be good. They could work together, right?

I can't do this anymore. She'd always known, deep down, that one day he would say something like that. It was better that he'd done it sooner rather than later, surely, before her heart was *too* engaged.

At least that was what she told herself. But then why did it feel like every last corner of her heart had been cracked from that one sentence?

"Tomorrow's New Year's Eve," Lauren pointed out. "I'm off—and then the next day is New Year's Day, when Cold World is closed. Maybe Monday?"

Dolores beamed at her. "Perfect. Will you tell Asa?" She gave Lauren's arm an affectionate squeeze. "I love that you're together, by the way. I had an inkling after the incident in the Snow Globe, and then when you got trapped in here overnight. The way that boy lights up when he looks at you!"

"Wait." Lauren reached out to stop Dolores from leaving before she could think about the gesture, about how probably inappropriate it was to manhandle your boss. "You *knew*? About the overnight thing, I mean?"

"Of course," Dolores said. "Daniel told me. I asked him to check in with you, to see if you needed the security code, but he said you told him you were fine. Obviously I would appreciate if you didn't make a *habit* of staying here after hours, but I trust you and Asa. If that's what you felt you needed to do to put together your presentation."

And then Dolores winked at her—*winked*. Like "put together your presentation" was just a euphemism for something else. Lauren didn't know if she was going to burst into flames of embarrassment or start hysterically giggling. The only thing that stopped her from doing both was that at least she *knew* there were no cameras in her office, so Dolores couldn't know just what a euphemism that was. She also realized Asa had been right all along. Of course Dolores *knew*.

And she didn't care. Nobody cared. Except Lauren, and she'd messed everything up.

Lauren's head was still spinning when she turned back to Eddie and his mom, who were kneeling down in the snow, trying to take a selfie next to a lumpy snowman Eddie must've built. Lauren rushed over, reaching for Ms. Ramirez's phone.

"Here," she said. "Let me."

AFTER EDDIE AND HIS MOM LEFT, LAUREN WENT EVERY-where, looking for Asa. He wasn't at the rink where she'd last seen him. He wasn't in the break room, or the gift shop, or the coffee stand. He wasn't even outside, where some of the other employees took their smoke breaks and where he could sometimes be found if he was keeping one of them company. That was the last place she looked, so sure she'd find him there she could picture him—in the middle of laughing at something Marcus said, kicking at the gravel of the parking lot, looking up when he heard the door, his eyes turning to pinpoints of an almost black when he saw her. Would he be welcoming? Or distant, angry? She didn't know. She just knew she needed to talk to him.

Lauren was checking out the break room one more time when Kiki came behind her.

"He went home."

Lauren spun around. "What?"

Kiki reached to open the fridge, taking out a LaCroix she'd labeled with a piece of masking tape and a bold note written in Sharpie—**KIKI'S—TOUCH UNDER PENALTY OF DEATH!** "He left for the day."

"But I thought his shift ended at eight." Not that Lauren

had memorized his schedule, double-checked it on the board earlier.

Kiki shrugged. "Said he wasn't feeling well."

That wasn't like Asa. Lauren tried to remember a time when he'd called out sick to work, and couldn't think of one. There'd been a flu going around—was it possible he'd caught it? Or maybe food poisoning? Personally, she didn't trust the hot dogs at Cold World because she'd seen them get left in a vat of water all day and then reheated the next morning. "Is he okay?" Lauren asked. "I mean, does he need—"

Kiki snorted at the same time she took a sip of her La-Croix, which couldn't have felt great for her nose. "What do you think? No, he's not okay. You broke his heart, Lauren."

"I didn't."

Kiki rolled her eyes so hard it looked like it physically hurt. "Okay."

"He broke up with *me!*" Lauren said. How was it possible for *her* to break *his* heart when it had been the other way around?

"I'm really not looking to get in the middle of it," Kiki said. "I want to be your friend, obviously I'm still his friend, but all I'll say is that your stories don't match."

"He said he couldn't do it anymore!" Lauren said, feeling the corners of her eyes burn even at the memory of those words. She didn't know what Asa was telling his housemates, but she remembered *that* part very clearly.

"Oh my god." Kiki set her drink down on the table, as if she needed full use of her hands to have this discussion. "It would be hilarious, what clowns you both are, if it weren't for the fact that you're both miserable to be around. He meant he didn't want to *hide* with you anymore, Lauren. Think about it. He spent years hiding relationships from his dad. He loved

you, he wanted to be with you, he just wanted you to acknowledge it."

Lauren rewound through the conversation in her head.
She was ashamed that it hadn't even occurred to her, that part
about his dad. He'd never seen any need for them to hide their
relationship at work, but he'd gone along with it, because
she'd said it made her more comfortable. He hadn't said how
uncomfortable it made *him*, but she should've seen it.

"Why didn't he just say that?" Lauren asked, her voice
small.

"Because you were rushing to tell him just how fine it all
was! And how, by the way, his job isn't going anywhere. And
how you only dated for a week, so it should all be fine, right?"

Wow, Asa really *had* told Kiki everything. Thinking back
on that conversation through that lens, she saw how awful it
all sounded. How cold she'd been. How she'd shut down, and
shut him out.

"I thought . . ."

Lauren wanted to finish that sentence, but Kiki was staring at her with such compassion that she had a hard time
forming words around the lump in her throat. Kiki, who'd
questioned her choice to keep the relationship secret in the
first place. Kiki, who had loyalty to Asa before she'd even
met Lauren, and who had every right to hate her now.

"You thought he was rejecting you," Kiki said, giving Lauren's shoulder a squeeze. "And you wanted to make sure he
knew that he couldn't hurt you, that you'd already expected
the rejection."

Lauren let out a very ungraceful hiccup, wiping the back
of her hand across her nose. She didn't even want to think
about what a wreck her face must look like.

"But don't you hear how fucking *asinine* that sounds?"

Kiki said. "People want to show up for you, Lauren Fox. You have to let them."

"I know," Lauren said, even if she wasn't sure she *did* know. "But what if . . ."

What if they don't. What if it's too late now. What if what if what if.

"Then you show up for yourself," Kiki said with a crooked smile. "Bloom where you're planted."

It took Lauren a minute to realize Kiki was referencing that coffee mug she'd given her, back when Lauren had first started at Cold World. She gave a phlegmy laugh that probably sounded disgusting. "Bloom. Okay, I'll try."

"So?" Kiki said. "You coming over?"

Lauren almost said *yes*. She didn't want to waste another minute. But she'd also made such a colossal mess of everything that she worried it wouldn't be enough, just telling him that she wanted him back, that she wanted to be better this time. She had to show him.

"I actually have an idea," she said. "But I'm going to need your help."

Chapter
TWENTY-EIGHT

ASA SLUMPED DOWN IN THE PASSENGER SEAT OF JOHN'S car. He had the worst headache and the last thing he wanted to do was go to a party.

"How long do we have to stay?"

Kiki leaned up from the back seat, sticking her face right next to Asa's. "You know you'll have fun once you get there," she said, and he winced from how loud and close her voice sounded. At least Elliot seemed to take some pity on him, because they pulled Kiki back, muttering something Asa couldn't catch.

John glanced over at him. "We'll leave as soon as you want to," he said.

Asa knew that the minute he got there, he'd probably feel too guilty to actually pull his friends away if they were having a good time. *Someone* deserved to enjoy New Year's Eve, after all. But it meant a lot that John would even offer—and Asa knew his housemate was as good as his word. If John said he'd get him out of there, he would.

"Thanks," he said, leaning his head back against the seat.

He wondered what Lauren was doing at that exact moment. Knowing her, she was probably organizing her closet again. Writing down lists of her resolutions for the year. Reading one last book to get in under the wire on her Goodreads goal. He almost smiled at the thought, before he remembered that he had no right to smile at anything she did anymore. Whatever she was doing, it was without him.

He pulled his phone out, started to click on their last text exchange before putting the phone back in his pocket. He didn't know why he was torturing himself. Maybe he'd text her *Happy New Year* at midnight. That was allowed, right? The same message he sent to a dozen random colleagues and acquaintances.

Maybe he'd get really drunk and call her.

That moderately cheered him up, but then he glanced out the window and sat up straighter in his seat. "Wait," he said. "Where are we going?"

John glanced in the rearview mirror, obviously looking for Kiki to answer, and that was when Asa knew. He went to turn, got caught up in the seat belt, and unbuckled it in frustration so he could completely face Kiki, who had a faux innocent expression that would fool no one.

"Why are we going to Lauren's?"

"Safety first," she said, pointing at his seat belt.

"If you're so concerned with safety, *why* aren't you answering my question?"

"It's Lauren's party," John said.

They were turning into her apartment complex now. The parking lot was more full than usual, the spot Asa would've normally used taken up by an eighties Oldsmobile. He wished he could turn all of this institutional knowledge off, wished he could stop thinking about the tiny little routines they'd built together even in that one perfect week. He thought he must not have heard John correctly, even when they were pulling into a space, the stairs leading to Lauren's apartment visible just around the corner.

"Lauren's throwing a *party*?"

Kiki and Elliot were already climbing out of the car, but John stayed back a second while he turned the car off and pocketed his keys. "Do you want to leave?"

A part of him desperately wanted to. Why was she throwing a party? Was this how quickly she'd moved on? Did she know he was going to be there? Was this Kiki's twisted way of trying to get them back together? He'd told her everything—he hadn't been able to help himself, he needed to get it all out and she'd been there—but he had no idea what Lauren might have said. Did Kiki think that there was any chance they could get back together?

Who was he kidding. Of course he didn't want to leave. Because up those stairs and on the other side of the door—there was Lauren.

"No," he said. "Let's go."

He could hear music coming from behind her door, and Kiki didn't even bother to knock before walking right in. There was a surprising number of people packed into Lauren's tiny living room, and Asa recognized most of them from Cold World. He intercepted a weird bro fist bump from Marcus, Saulo's arm shot up from across the room in greeting, and Sonia smiled tipsily at him while handing him a beer. The one person he didn't see was the person he most wanted to.

The music was "Party in the USA," and it was a little too loud. His head was pounding, and he cracked open the beer and took a sip, hoping that maybe it would take the edge off, do *something*. It was his favorite brand, which made him wonder if Lauren had some extras in the fridge she was trying to get rid of. But no, he'd never brought over a six-pack and left it there—it had to be a coincidence. His brain was concocting the most ridiculous scenarios now.

And then he saw her, and he almost dropped his beer. She was wearing the same red off-the-shoulder dress she'd worn that night in Cold World, her hair loose around her shoulders. She was so beautiful he literally couldn't take his gaze off her, which was why when she finally looked over, their sudden eye contact was a jolt to them both. He held up his beer in a mini salute, then wished he hadn't. Who wanted their ex-boyfriend showing up at their New Year's Eve party, staring moonily at them across the room? This was a mistake.

But she was making her way toward him, weaving her way through the crowd. "You came!" she said when she got closer. She was smiling at him, which was very confusing.

"Was I supposed to?"

"Yes!" she said. "I threw this party for you!"

The music was way too loud. It had switched to another song, this one by the Beastie Boys. What decade was this playlist from? He leaned in, not sure he'd heard her correctly.

"I'm sorry?"

She rested her hand on his forearm, stood on tiptoes to make herself heard better. Her breasts brushed against his bicep, and her breath was warm in his ear when she repeated herself. "It's for you," she said. "The party."

The good news was that his head was no longer pounding. It felt like all the blood had rushed from his head to lower parts of his body, and he felt a little dizzy. "Like a surprise party?" He looked around, but no one had jumped out from behind couches to yell anything when he walked in. They didn't even seem to register his presence, except Kiki, who was watching them but whipped her head around fast when she caught Asa looking at her.

"Well, it's kind of for me," she said. "But for you. Can we talk?"

"Sure." What else could he say? She threaded her fingers through his, leading him through the party, and it occurred to him that if she didn't want people to think there was anything going on between them—not that there was anymore, but whatever—bringing him to her bedroom and shutting the door behind them probably wasn't the best way to accomplish that. But if the thought didn't occur to her, he wasn't going to put it in her head.

She leaned against the closed door now and looked at him. Just when he thought he'd go out of his skin if she didn't say something, she said a single word.

"Hi."

"Uh," he said. "Hi."

"Sorry," she said. "I'd prepared a whole speech."

On the wall over her bed, Asa saw that Lauren had hung up the flower painting he'd made her for Christmas. For the first time, he allowed something like hope to bloom in his chest, but he tried to take a deep breath, settle down. Her speech could be about anything. It could be more about why he was wasting his potential at Cold World or how fun their one week together was. He'd listen to any version of whatever she wanted to say.

"Start with the party," he said. "What did you mean, it was for me?"

"Technically, it's for *me*," she said. "Kiki pointed out that people are willing to show up for me, that I should be willing to let them do it. So what more literal way to put that to the test than a party? I've never had this many people in my apartment before. I didn't even know I *knew* this many people. But when I asked them to come to a New Year's Eve party with twenty-four hours' notice . . . they came. I mean, sure, the free beer and snacks probably helped, but still. And I also did it for you, to show you that I can be more open to this kind of thing."

He still wasn't one hundred percent sure he understood, but he knew what a big deal it was for her to invite so many people to her apartment. He gave her a crooked smile. "Is this a return of Fun Lauren? Because the last time she made an appearance, she encouraged everyone to drink antifreeze."

"I did not!" she said, but she was smiling, too. "Not Fun Lauren. I'm trying to be . . . Brave Lauren. Honest Lauren. The last time we talked . . . I don't think I was either. All I heard was you rejecting me, and it felt so *inevitable* that all I knew how to do was curl back up inside my shell like a little hermit crab, wait for the threat to pass."

Asa swallowed around the lump in his throat. "I never meant to reject you."

She gave an adorably self-deprecating eye roll. "I know that *now*. Kiki called me a clown."

Kiki had called him one of those, too. "I never meant that I didn't want to be with you. It was just hard for me, keeping it a secret. I want to be able to talk about you, to touch you in public, to go out together without worrying someone is going to see us. I want to make you coffee in the break room or say shit like *Let me check with Lauren and see if we have plans* or take a picture with you and make it my lock screen."

"Asa, I —"

"*Not* flavored coffee," he said. "I'm aware, believe me. I'll rinse out the Keurig and everything."

She pressed her finger to his mouth. "I trust you with my coffee," she said. "I was just trying to say that you not being comfortable with a secret relationship makes total sense, especially after what you dealt with from your family. I'm sorry I didn't see that."

"Well," he said. "Yeah. That's part of it. But also—you're important to me, Lauren. I understand your concerns about keeping things professional, but I don't know how long I can hide that."

"I know," she said. "And I'm sorry I said all that stuff about your job. I was way out of line. I just think you're so talented, and—"

He shook his head, not wanting to hear her go too far down that road of beating herself up about something he'd needed to hear. "You weren't wrong," he said. "I felt comfortable at Cold World. I didn't want anything to change. But ultimately, that's not what's best for me. It's time to move on."

"Oh!" she said, biting her lip. "Then maybe this is an awkward time to tell you . . . Dolores actually cornered me yesterday. Apparently there's some grant she thinks could help save Cold World? She wanted our help in putting the application together."

"Lauren," he said, bracing his hands on either side of her head against the door. "I really don't give a fuck about Cold World right now."

"Sorry," she said. "I got off track."

He could tell she was affected by his proximity, the way her chest rose and fell, the way the pulse at the hollow in her throat fluttered. "May I?"

She nodded, even though he didn't know that she knew what she was agreeing to, and he dipped his head to kiss the line of her jaw. "So let's get back on track. You were saying?"

"Just that I want to be with you," she said, sighing as his hand settled at her waist, his mouth next to her ear. "And I don't want to hide it anymore."

"Thank god," he said, giving her earlobe a tug with his teeth. "Because I don't think I can keep my hands to myself in public."

As if prompted, she placed her hand over his at her waist, holding it more firmly there. She pulled back a bit, as much as she could with the door there, and looked him in the eye. "I love you," she said. "I really do love you, Asa Williamson. I don't quite know when I started, but I know I haven't stopped."

"Well, I know right when I started," he said. "It was somewhere around that first Christmas party, when you said you wanted to cancel Secret Santa."

He'd bent his head to kiss her and felt her smile against his mouth. "It was not."

"Don't argue with me about my own experience."

"But you didn't act like you even *liked* me until . . . I don't know, but it was definitely after that."

"What can I say, I'm a clown."

She full-out laughed then, and the sound was so pure and wonderful, Asa had to lean his forehead against hers, just grateful to be holding her again at all. Through the door, he could hear the haunting tones of a slow, sad song, and it took him a second to place it.

"Lauren?"

"Mmm."

"Did you just . . . find a playlist where all the songs had 'party' in the title?"

Her eyelids flew open, and she looked up at him. "That's exactly what I did. Why?"

He pushed away from the door, reaching down to take her hand. "Let's just say 'When the Party's Over' by Billie Eilish is a good song to play only when, you know, the party's over. We better get back out there before it takes a turn."

"Do we have to?"

He pulled her closer until he could press a kiss to her hair. "I love you, Lauren. Which is why I want you to have the best New Year's Eve party possible. And then I love you so much I want every single person out of here five seconds after midnight. Deal?"

She smiled up at him. "Deal."

He opened the door, letting her through first even though she didn't drop his hand. "See?" he said. "I told you we'd work well together."

EPILOGUE

Almost One Year Later

"IF THERE'S A SINGLE SCRATCH ON IT, I SWEAR TO GOD—" John was saying as he retrieved his guitar from the back seat, Elliot standing nearby with their hands in the air, already proclaiming their innocence.

"What good is a case if it can't protect your guitar on a simple car ride?" Elliot pointed out. "You're telling me you used to go on *tour* with this thing? Better invest in some bubble wrap before that concert cruise."

"What concert cruise?" Lauren said, joining the conversation. Even though she'd moved in with Asa and his housemates six months ago—her lease had been up, and fitting right in their little group had been surprisingly easy—she and Asa had driven to the Cold World holiday party separate from the rest of them. She turned to Asa now, giving his hand a squeeze. "Did you know anything about this?"

"What?" he said. "Oh. No."

He'd been acting weird all night. She imagined it must feel a little awkward, returning to this place where he'd worked for so long. For close to a year now, he'd worked at a local LGBTQ services center, and he'd started building an online shop where he sold his art. He'd even been commissioned to paint a few murals for local businesses—including the one for the Snow Globe, which he hadn't let her see yet. He was supposed to show her tonight. Was it possible he was nervous about that?

"You gonna reprise your karaoke performance from last year?" Kiki asked, waggling her eyebrows.

Lauren groaned, but she was smiling. "Please don't even remind me."

"Maybe you could sing 'Let's—'" Kiki started, then made an exaggerated *oof* sound when Asa elbowed her in the side. She pantomimed zipping her mouth and throwing away the key.

"Sorry," she said. "I've been listening to Bleachers a lot."

Asa held out his hand, and Kiki acted like she was removing more keys from her pockets, around her neck, tucked inside her socks, then reluctantly handing them over. Some of their inside jokes Lauren still didn't fully get, but she was happy to see Asa grinning by the end of it.

They entered the party, which was still in the chill early stages before the music had started and the real festivities got going. John immediately split off to set up his equipment with the band, and Kiki and Elliot made a beeline for the drinks counter, leaving Asa and Lauren standing in the middle of the lobby. Lauren had kept her job part time at Cold World, after all, while she went back to school, so she was able to introduce Asa to a few new people he wouldn't know. But he seemed distracted, shaking their hands and saying a perfunctory hello but without the usual easy conversation he was so much better at than her.

"Are you cold?" he asked at one point. "Want me to get your cardigan from your office?"

"I'm good," she said. The weather outside was balmy, as was common for a Florida winter, but she'd worn a long-sleeved shirt on purpose, knowing how cold they kept Cold World.

"I think I'm cold," he said. "I'm going to go grab it, if that's okay."

"Sure," she said. Was it possible he was sick? She tried to remember if he'd felt any warmer than usual, but he always felt warm to her. After a minute, he came out of the office area wearing her cream-colored cardigan, oversized on her but fitting him almost perfectly. His hair—now back to his natural brown, a little longer than it had been before—was tousled like he'd been running his hands through it, and her heart skipped a beat.

When he rejoined her, she pulled him in to kiss his cheek, and he blinked down at her. "What was that for?"

"Do I need a reason?" she said. "You're cute."

He barely seemed to register the compliment, though, because he had his hand on the small of her back, guiding her through the people. "Let's check out the Snow Globe now," he said. "I don't want to wait."

That was fine by Lauren. She was dying to see what he'd come up with for the Snow Globe mural—she'd seen some of his ideas when they put their presentation together, but she knew it had changed since then. And if the mural *was* the cause of his jittery nerves, she'd rather get it out of the way so they could enjoy the rest of the party. She already knew she'd love whatever he created.

They stepped into the enclosed space, snow crunching beneath their feet, and the minute Lauren saw it she felt like her breath had literally been snatched from her body. It covered one entire side of the curved wall, which couldn't have been easy to manage, but it was perfect. Designed like a vintage postcard, **WITH LOVE, FROM COLD WORLD** printed in large block letters, it had so many details and fun Easter eggs included throughout that Lauren felt like she could've spent hours in there just trying to find them all. There was the hot chocolate stand in one corner, people ice skating in another, including a kid who looked a little like Eddie. There was the little penguin with the striped scarf, which made Lauren smile, and tucked away in another part of the mural was an incongruous rosebush with a fox curled up peacefully in front of it, a reference that she somehow knew instantly was for her.

"What do you think?" Asa asked from behind her. He had to know she would love it, but his voice had a slight vibration to it, an edge that told her he didn't take her good opinion for granted.

"I love it," she said. "I—I don't even know what to say. Asa, this is incredible."

She knew he'd been working on it, of course. They'd had to close down the Snow Globe for a few days, and he'd spent that time locked inside, putting on all the finishing touches. He'd come out only to take the occasional break, enjoying a prepackaged sandwich with her in the café area, sitting in her office and building chains out of paper clips that she'd find later next to an added little message with a heart doodled on her to-do list.

But the idea that all that time, he'd been making *this* . . . it awed her.

"I had a dream about this place the other night," he said, and something in his voice made her turn around to face him.

"Really?"

"It involved you."

She raised her eyebrows. *"Oh."*

He laughed, running his hand through his hair. "Not *that* kind of dream. Not here, anyway. It doesn't seem like it would be very . . . comfortable."

"Fair point."

"In this dream, we're just two tourists, enjoying the Snow Globe. Packing snowballs to throw at each other when the kid guarding the place isn't looking, maybe seeing how far we can push the MPAA rating depending on how comfortable the kid is with breaking it up—"

"Hey," Lauren interrupted. "I had it *handled.*"

Asa grinned at her. "I know you did. Anyway, the point is that it was a nice dream. It felt cozy. Routine in the best possible way. Do you know what I mean? Like this was just our life, these random little day dates, moments we got to spend together."

"I do know what you mean," Lauren said, touched by the way he described it.

"Yeah?" He tilted his head, tugging one sleeve of the cardigan down over his hand, then pushing it back up. "There was more to the dream, though. It's weird, right, the realistic details that work their way into your subconscious? I remember you were looking at the mural, and you were excited when you saw a little part I'd added just for you. So you turned around to point it out to me, and then . . . I got down on one knee to propose."

Lauren remembered that he'd specifically mentioned how he envisioned a post-makeover Cold World being a place that was more Instagram-ready, somewhere that inspired people to take pictures or host their most meaningful moments. She also figured that this was Asa's way of feeling her out on whether she'd want to get married, something they'd loosely talked about but never in an immediate, okay-let's-do-it kind of way.

"I don't know how I feel about a public proposal," she said, scrunching her nose and shaking her head with an expression she hoped he knew was more playful than not, even though the sentiment was true. "But other than that, yes, it sounds like a *very* nice dream."

"Ha," he said. "Noted."

She started to reach for him, but he gestured toward the mural. "I did add a little detail just for you, though," he said. "Do you see it?"

"Of course," she said, turning back toward the mural and scanning it until she located the rosebush again. "It's the little fox with the—"

Only then did it fully hit her, what he was doing, and when she turned back to find him on one knee, a ring box open in his hand, she couldn't help it. She burst into tears. And not pretty ones, either—deep, snot-coming-out-of-her-nose hiccuping sobs.

"Oh," he said, immediately getting to his feet and coming to wrap his arms around her. "Hey," he said, rubbing down her back. "Hey, it's okay. I'm sorry. I was trying to warn you."

That made Lauren pull back from him, conscious that she'd already left a wet patch on her cardigan that he was wearing. "*Warn* me?"

He gave her a crooked grin, and she saw that his eyes were shiny, too. "An ominous word for a marriage proposal, huh? I just meant that I know you don't like surprises. But I also really like surprising you, so . . . I was trying to compromise. I promise if you say yes I'll work on it."

Lauren laughed, hugging him tighter. "Of course it's a yes. Sorry if I ruined your moment."

"Not possible," he said. "But technically, I didn't get to ask. Can I run it back from the beginning? Should I get back down on one knee?"

"That won't be necessary," she said. She didn't want him to be that far away, didn't want to lose the warmth of his nearness and the feeling of his arms around her. "But go ahead and ask, if you want to make it official."

He tucked a lock of her hair behind her ear, looking down at her with such tenderness she almost started crying again. "Lauren Fox, will you marry me?"

"Yes," she said. "Yes, *please*."

Asa kissed her then, a deep, aching kiss that she felt tingle down in her toes, although some of that might have been the snow seeping through her flats. When he brought his hands up to cup her cheeks, they seemed to both realize at the same time that he was still holding the ring box, and had never actually presented her with the ring.

"Fuck," he said. "Sorry. This didn't go exactly the way I'd planned it."

Suddenly it all made sense to her, Kiki's little comments earlier, how on edge Asa had seemed all night. She let him slide the ring over her finger, surprised at how strange and yet comforting its weight already felt on her hand.

"It looks good on you," Asa said.

"Not a bad souvenir," she said. "Better than what they have at the Ripley's Believe It or Not!"

He barked out a laugh. She was always gratified by how much a Ripley's joke seemed to land with him. He just ate them up for some reason.

"I went to Cold World and all I got was this lousy T-shirt," he said, pulling her toward him for a kiss. "And the love of my life."

ACKNOWLEDGMENTS

First of all, I would like to acknowledge that I'm bisexual and that climate change is real.

Those aren't related to each other but I live in Florida so sometimes it's nice to get these things off my chest.

I thought it would be easier to write acknowledgments for my second book, because I could basically just copy the ones for my first book, make a few adjustments, and call it a day. Weirdly, it turned out to be even harder. The truth is that by now there are SO MANY people I feel very grateful for, and also I am so tender over this particular book that I get very emo when I think about its journey.

So, here is a list that I hope is exhaustive and complete but, of course, I will remember more people the second I'm holding the final, printed, unchangeable book in my hands:

Laura Bradford for being an absolute rock star but more importantly just a rock; Taryn Fagerness for talking up my books overseas; Kristine Swartz for being a badass editor and efficient emailer and downright lovely person (triple threat!); the hardworking, passionate people at Berkley including but not limited to Mary Baker, Bridget O'Toole, Hannah Engler, Dache' Rogers, Kristin Cipolla, and Alaina Christensen; art director Colleen Reinhart and artist Jenifer Prince for once again giving me the absolute cover of my dreams—I'm just *waiting* for someone to say "then why don't you marry it" because I absolutely would; my family with a special shout-out to my father-in-law Gary for all the childcare help during the pandemic especially; if I only respond to one out of five of your "fast food news" texts, I'm sorry! As your son would say, if you like everything you like nothing!; Brittany, for being the absolute best sister I could ask for and also for not dying; I guess I could thank everyone here for not dying but you, like, had the opportunity and then REALLY didn't die so I think you deserve the extra gold star; Charis S., how the fuck have we been friends for twenty years?! I don't know what I'd do without you; Erin W. for inspiring me with your glow-up (to be clear, I'm not going to run half-marathons, but it's inspiring that you do); Kristin H. for being a beautiful person inside and out; Jessica C. for being as perfect as a Rose Byrne smokey eye and a trustworthy steward of Taylor Swift tickets; Liz K. for putting together a kickass event and giving *great* brunch chat; Chase H. for your vulnerability and friendship and love of Christmas; Brad P. for listening to me talk about this book on the back porch so many times; Kelly H. for painting the kinds of murals that made me want to write a character who would do the same thing (and more importantly, made me want to mastermind my way into being your friend); Carmen A. (tu eres la reina de los libros!) for having like eighteen separate roles in my life and I would add more if I could; Emma A. for being smashing; Ange for all the email correspondence and making me feel like Cold World was a real place; Jay Vera Summer for being so above-and-beyond encouraging; Kim Karalius for reading this chapter-by-chapter at one point just to cheer me on; Amy Lea and Hannah Olsen for being the Pitch Wars lights of my life; Jessica Joyce for making that badly photoshopped picture that makes me snort-laugh every time I think about it and for generally understanding that with writing friends, sometimes you're the baby and sometimes you're the björn; Rachel Lynn Solomon for being a true gift to the book community and an amazing friend; Julie Tieu for lots of stuff but in particular that time we chatted on the phone for two hours while I circled around looking for a parking space lol; Sonia Hartl and Annette Christie for being so supportive; Regina Black for writing the way that you do; Tracey/Tori/Alanna Martin by any name you're a great friend!; Erin Connor and Hailey Harlow for the New Romantics group chat, where there is no limit on how unhinged we can get; Kerry Winfrey for your gift of making everything cozy and heartfelt and good; K.T. Hoffman for reading a draft of this book and sending me the kindest email I've ever received in my life, truly you don't know how many times I've reread it and it's weird that even a comment like "horny ass" can make me tear up but what can I say; the Berklete Discord; writers I very much admire whose good opinions I shamelessly courted prior to publication (aka asked for a blurb) like Kate Clayborn, Alexandria Bellefleur, and Anita Kelly; the writers I very much admire who read *LITTOSK* early and said lovely things like Ali Hazelwood, Sarah Hogle, Chloe Liese, Nicole Tersigni, and others I've already thanked elsewhere here; Yes, I do hear the music playing me off the stage but I have more I want to say so I'll just lean into the microphone and talk louder. I also have to acknowledge the Ask a Manager blog even if it's the reason I realized Lauren would never have sex at work on the clock, sorry everyone; pizza rolls especially when they're too hot to eat; Phoebe Bridgers for putting out "Sidelines"; the part in *While You Were Sleeping* where she's standing on the stairs and says she doesn't have anyone; the 1975 song "Somebody Else" but also the Chvrches cover of that same song; "Snow on the Beach," which has me convinced that Taylor Alison Swift has access to my Google docs; the two friends of my older brother who I had very mild crushes on as a teenager, please don't make a big deal out of it but one gave me Asa's name and the other gave me the detail about someone smelling so good it makes your knees weak because it's never happened before or since, WHAT PRODUCTS WAS THAT GUY USING?; the Tampa Bay Rays for giving me something to tie my mental health to that's not publishing; everyone at Tombolo Books in St. Pete for creating such a perfect book oasis in this community, including the Romance Book Club that is the highlight of my month; Snowcat Ridge and everything else that makes Florida weird; Harry Styles for releasing *Harry's House* in time to help me finish this book; Greg Jehanian for his Instagram lives where he played songs and chatted and generally made me feel less alone at a time when I sometimes felt very alone; and Paramore for the song "Hello Cold World" that started it all.

If you shout about books on your social media, if you subscribe to author newsletters and preorder signed copies and make trope round-ups or memes—THANK YOU! You don't even know how much it means to authors, including me. My phone is filled with screenshots of things that just make my heart so full. And if that's not your vibe, if you prefer to read a book as a quiet commune with yourself, that's also valid but this is me reaching out to *you*. And saying thank you.

Last but not least, I have to thank Ryan, August, and Kara. I couldn't do any of this without your love and support.

Keep reading for an excerpt from

LOVE IN THE TIME OF SERIAL KILLERS

by Alicia Thompson,
available now from Berkley Romance

OBVIOUSLY A TWO-HUNDRED-POUND VICTORIAN WRIT-
ing desk wasn't made to be moved all by yourself. But it also
hadn't come with those incomprehensible IKEA instructions showing a blocky illustrated guy getting help from a
buddy, so. There wasn't anything saying not to try it.

I took a step back, assessing the desk where it was strapped
to the roof of my car. It was the only piece of furniture I'd
brought with me, and it was a monstrosity. My old landlord
in North Carolina had helped me load it onto my car in the
first place, and it had been the reason I'd made the drive to
Florida in one straight shot, stopping only briefly at rest areas
and a Taco Bell in Starke.

If I undid the straps, it was possible the desk would slide
right off the car. I had an image of trying to catch it and ending up flattened into a pancake like a cartoon character under
a piano. But I could brace it against my body, maybe, ease it
to the ground. Then I could penguin-walk it up the driveway
to the house.

I turned to survey my dad's old house, which had been
sitting empty for the last six months, since he'd died back in
January. I guessed it was my and my little brother's house

now, technically. But this house hadn't felt like mine since the day my mother and I had moved out when I was thirteen, maybe not since before then.

My brother, Conner, could still be awake, even though my phone screen showed that it was already two in the morning. He'd always been a big gamer, and would stay up all hours trying a level one more time or trying to beat the last boss. But that had been before he and Shani had moved in together, before he'd gotten his first postcollege job at a call center. And anyway, I wasn't going to text him to come help me with something as stupid as a desk.

Conner and I weren't that close. We'd barely grown up together, for one thing—when our parents divorced, he'd chosen to stay with our dad, while I'd gone with our mom. He was also seven years younger, twenty-three to my thirty, although that fact alone couldn't fully explain his optimistic exuberance in contrast to my jaded cynicism. We'd spent time together during holidays and select weekends, of course, but still when I thought of him I mostly remembered the way he would eat ketchup by the bowlful when he was six years old.

I typed **how to move heavy furniture by yourself** into a search on my phone, and scrolled through the results. Ads for moving companies, an article about how to use moving straps and dollies and other equipment I didn't have, another couple of articles that basically boiled down to *don't*.

"Need a hand?" a voice came from behind me, and I jumped and gave a little scream. My phone flew out of my hand and hit the pavement with a sickening *crack*.

I spun around, coming face-to-face with the random dude who'd spoken. He was standing on the sidewalk, a decent distance away from me, but still. He'd come out of nowhere.

He had dark, shaggy hair and was wearing jeans and a T-shirt that had a huge rip in the collar. When I glanced down, I saw that his feet were bare.

"What the fuck?" I said, as much about the bare feet as about the fact that he'd addressed me at all.

He took a step backward, as if *he* were scared of *me*, and shoved his hands deep into his pockets. "It just seemed . . ."

"Well, it's not," I snapped. I reached down to pick up my phone, which, yup, totally had a cracked screen now. Great. My search results for **how to move heavy furniture by yourself** glowed brightly through the spiderweb of lines, and I had the irrational thought that he'd totally seen them, that they'd called him here like some sort of Bat-Signal to creepy nocturnal dudes looking to accost isolated women in the suburbs.

And now he knew where I lived. I was tempted to get back in the car, to drive to a local gas station and sit in the parking lot for one full podcast episode, then circle the block a few times before pulling into the driveway again. Although, to be fair, it was probably the podcast episodes that were making me so paranoid in the first place. I could rationally recognize that with one part of my brain while the other part of my brain screamed, *This is the exact scenario two post-Evanescence goth podcasters will one day use for their cold open.*

"This isn't my home," I blurted.

He blinked at me, obviously confused. The more he stood there in his stupid bare feet, the more harmless he seemed. He was only a few inches taller than me, I realized. And he probably weighed less, all wiry and lean where I was curvier.

But wasn't that exactly how guys like him broke through your defenses? By appearing helpful, like the Zodiac Killer telling you your wheel was wobbling and offering to "fix" it for you, only to sabotage your car and take you hostage. Or by appearing helpless, like Ted Bundy with his fake casts, needing help carrying something to his car.

Fuck that. I'd rather be seen as a little rude than risk being taken to a second location.

He gestured toward the desk. "That looks heavy," he said.

Driving ten hours straight must've scrambled my brain, because his words made me snort and then break into full-out laughter. It was absurd—this random conversation that barely hit polysyllables, the giant desk strapped to my Camry, the fact that I was here at all, standing in front of a house that I had very few fond memories of. It was two in the morning and I was wearing coffee-stained pajama pants because I'd thought it would be brilliant to dress so I could roll right into bed when I arrived, only I hadn't factored in my stunning inability to drink from the right side of a to-go cup.

"My dude," I said. "If you think this desk looks heavy, you should see my trigger finger on my Mace in about five seconds if you don't back off."

He looked at me for a moment, almost as if he were about to say something else. And maybe it was coming up on time to reread *The Gift of Fear* again, because I realized that the butterflies in my stomach weren't from anxiety but from . . . anticipation. Like there was some quiet watchfulness in his expression that pierced through my armor, and I wanted to know what he saw there.

But instead I turned back toward the desk, making a show of tightening a strap even though that was the opposite of what I was trying to do. When I glanced over my shoulder a minute later, he was gone, as stealthily as he'd arrived.

My forehead dropped to the roof of the car, my grip around

the legs of the desk relaxing. I was so tired. I doubted anyone would be interested in stealing a desk, and it wasn't supposed to rain that night. I should go inside and go to bed and let this be a problem for rested, freshly caffeinated future me to solve in the morning.

I grabbed my backpack out of the passenger side, hauled my bigger duffel out of the back seat, and locked up the car. My dad's neighborhood was older, somehow escaping the homeowners association restrictions that would regulate things like streetlights, so it was dark, too. I gave one last sweeping glance around the street—to the left, where an outside cat looked up from its position laid out on my neighbor's driveway, to the house to the right, where a single light still shone through one window. Satisfied I was alone, I headed up to the front door of my dad's house.

The first thing that hit me was the smell. Musty, like a damp towel that had been left on the bathroom floor too long, with a slight antiseptic undercurrent like that same towel had been sprayed with Windex a couple times. This must've been what Conner meant when he said he'd been coming by once a week to "clean."

The place sure didn't look clean. That wasn't completely Conner's fault, I knew—my dad had been a bit of a pack rat, not so bad they'd put him on a TV show but definitely hoarder-adjacent. Even as I walked in, I stubbed my toe on a plastic tub filled with magazines and mail in the entryway, and then knocked a broom to the floor. The bristles of the broom were covered with cobwebs, lest I think Conner had been using it.

I set my bags down on the first empty expanse of floor I could find in the living room. My dad's room was to the left, but there was no way I could sleep in there. He hadn't died in there or anything—it had been a heart attack at the grocery store, mercifully quick, the doctors had told us—but still. It was my *dad's* room.

I opened the door anyway, just to see inside. More magazines, stacked next to the bed and fanning out from where they'd toppled over. What had it been with him and magazines? I'd never even thought of him as much of a reader. But he'd been such a sucker for those commemorative magazines at the checkout aisle in particular, *100 Greatest Films* or *Remembering D-Day* or *Photographs that Changed the World.*

Next, I checked out the kitchen, not expecting anything edible, but just hoping that there wasn't some open bag of sugar that had fallen over in the pantry and been allowed to attract ants for the last six months. When I opened the fridge, it was surprisingly clean—and with a large bag of Kit Kats and a twenty-four pack of Mountain Dew inside.

There was a Post-it stuck to the Mountain Dew: **WELCOME BACK, PHOEBE!** written in sloppy capital letters. It wasn't signed, but of course, there was only one other person who had keys to this place. And only one person who loved Mountain Dew so much he'd been arrested once trying to steal a six-foot-tall cardboard cutout of a two-liter from a gas station. He'd wanted it for his dorm room, he said.

I smiled to myself, shaking my head as I closed the fridge. It was actually kind of sweet that Conner had thought to leave me something. *Sweet* being the operative word, since I'd be in a sugar spiral in five seconds if I tried to subsist on his gifts alone. I'd have to go shopping in the morning.

But for now, I was exhausted, and all I wanted to do was peel off these coffee-stained pajama pants and fall into bed. I only hoped that my dad had kept the bed in my brother's or my old room. My brother had lived in this house more recently than I had, leaving only three years ago when he'd transferred from community college to a campus a few hours away. But when I checked out his room, I saw that he must've taken his bed with him at some point, or else my dad had gotten rid of it. There were still some signs that he'd lived there, like the huge *Red Dead Redemption* poster he had hanging on one wall, but otherwise it was just an old table pushed to one corner, a couple laundry baskets filled with household items and not a piece of laundry in sight, and the pieces of a computer laid out on the floor like someone had been interrupted in the middle of putting it together.

It did something to me, seeing the computer like that. I could picture my dad working on it, could imagine him trying to explain to Conner how some of the parts went together and then getting impatient when Conner kept asking questions about some aspect of the process my dad hadn't gotten around to explaining yet.

For all I knew, it hadn't happened like that at all. But for a moment, I could see it as clearly as if he were still alive and in this room. My dad, smiling gently as he described what a microprocessing chip did or whatever. My dad, slinging the motherboard across the room and leaving a dent in the drywall as he yelled at Conner to *listen*, just fucking *listen*.

I took a deep breath before opening up the door to my old room. I hadn't stepped foot inside it for fifteen years, not since I was fifteen and said I wouldn't come here for weekend visitation anymore. My dad wasn't the type to want a home gym or even a guest room, since he'd eschewed most physical activity and never welcomed a single guest. I had no idea what to expect.

It was exactly the same. My twin bed with the wrought iron frame, the blue-and-yellow quilt from Walmart, the black painted walls, the collages of eyes I'd cut out from magazines and tacked up everywhere. A desk in the corner where I'd spent most of my time, chatting with friends on my laptop. A vase of dried flowers on my dresser, a stack of my favorite movies on DVD. So that was where my copy of *Heathers* had gone.

I found some more sheets in the linen closet—they had that closed-up scent of mothballs and neglect, but they had to be better than what was on the bed—and changed them out. Then I carried my bags into the room, plopped them on the floor, and made as quick work as I could of brushing my teeth and getting ready for bed.

The last thing I did before clicking off the light was rip every single eye collage off the walls. If I had to deal with old *America's Next Top Model* rejects staring down at me as I slept, I'd have nightmares of Tyra trying to "edge" me out by bleaching my eyebrows.

Well, the second-to-last thing. After I lay in bed for a few minutes, I sat up again, switching on the nightstand lamp and reaching down into my backpack for my bullet journal, where I'd been writing all my dissertation notes.

Encounter w/ strange man June 3, approx. 2 a.m.
White, 5'9", slightly scruffy, shaggy brown hair.
Ripped T-shirt, jeans, no shoes. Origin and destination
unknown, believed to be night wanderer.

I chewed on the end of the pen, wondering if I should include any other details. It had been too dark to tell what color his eyes were. His voice had been deep, with a rasp, almost . . . but I couldn't write that. If my body was found in the woods behind the house, and investigators were competent enough to do a forensic analysis of this notebook, I didn't want editorializing words complicating the narrative. Words like *compelling*, or god forbid, *sexy*. I set the notebook on my nightstand, and switched back off the lamp.

Alicia Thompson is a writer, reader, and Paramore superfan (albeit apparently not a Ticketmaster Verified Fan!). She does not know how to ice skate at all but loves to watch other people ice skate, which could be a metaphor for her entire life. She currently lives in Florida with her husband and two children and a mischievous cat named Luna.

Ready to find
your next great read?

Let us help.

Visit prh.com/nextread

Penguin
Random
House